I, JOHN

I, JOHN

C R Taylor

Newton Grove
Falling Creek Publishing

Falling Creek Publishing
An imprint of Falling Creek Inc
PO Box 779
Newton Grove, North Carolina 28366

www.crtaylorbooks.com
info@crtaylorbooks.com

Publisher's Cataloging-in-Publication

Taylor, C. R. (Christopher Ray)
    I, John / C.R. Taylor. -- First edition.
    pages cm
    LCCN 2014914427
    ISBN 978-0-9906426-9-5
    ISBN 978-0-9906426-1-9 (pbk.)
    ISBN 978-0-9906426-0-2 (e-book)

    1. John, the Apostle, Saint--Fiction. 2. Lazarus, of
Bethany, Saint--Fiction. 3. Faith--Fiction.
4. Christianity--21st century--Fiction. 5. Fantasy
fiction. 6. Christian fiction.   I. Title.

PS3620.A9354I36 2014   813'.6
                              QBI14-600142

ISBN 978-0-9906426-1-9

20 19 18 17 16 15 14   1 2 3 4 5

To Lauren, Malachi, Annette and Ray

*You only remember the past
because you could not bear to remember the future.*
— Adriel

John

The morning that we found Jesus on the beach stays in my mind. I have never understood why. It was not the most impressive day in my memory, but it has become one of the most persistent. Finding him on that beach was miraculous, or so we thought at the time. Now it haunts me.

I see angels, and I see other things that are not angels. At least I see and hear beings who are not like us but who think and act and move, without bodies like ours. A few of them are brilliant and astonishing. Some are dark and fearful. I think that they are different beings, but they might be differing versions of the same kind of thing. And there is Adriel, whom I have heard and seen every day since we found that empty tomb.

Seeing creatures and hearing voices doesn't mean they are real. A great many people see things that do not exist outside their minds. Of course, even if I couldn't see these beings, couldn't hear their voices, it wouldn't mean that they weren't there.

In the beginning was the word. That is how it began, just words and a man who walked down the shore and found us in our father's boat. That's the truth of it. He walked around talking to anyone who would listen, and he found us. Why we got up and followed him, I wonder.

Look where it got us. Look where it got him.

My father's boat—we spent so much of our childhood in it. I can barely remember what he looked like, my father, but I do remember his beard, his hands. And I remember his eyes, looking at me when Jesus called us to follow him—my father was staring at me like he was gauging the strength of a net. He nodded, I thought, at least it seemed to me later that he had nodded, had offered us that small blessing with the quick understanding of a father. He could read water, read the sky, read the fish swimming, and he read my brother and I, though he was looking at me. My brother James was always like a fish jumping for a light, holding back just for me and for our father to decide. James was the oldest, but while he often walked ahead of me, he somehow always seemed to be following me.

So our father, Zebedee, looked at me and nodded, and James and I put down the nets and walked away with Jesus. It was never the same afterward. Maybe that is why I remembered that moment. Something in me knew that it was important, that it marked a change. There are moments in our lives that matter, not that there are moments without value. It is just that some moments are like a point when we are touched by God. We are brought into contact with something greater than ourselves, outside ourselves, that resonates with the spirit within us. We never returned, not really, not to stay. Our father's boats were finally given to the servants, and sometimes I felt regret and doubt for leaving that life. We had not understood when we walked away with Jesus that we would never return. I don't know whether my father knew it, but we did not.

Maybe that is why I agreed to look after Mary in the end. I was an irresponsible son who walked away from my father and our family business, and looking after her offered me a sense of redemption. Not that I had any choice. He had found the strength to speak while hanging on that cross. "Behold your mother!" What was I going to say? No, thank you, I have other obligations? Maybe that was the reason he said it, made that effort as he hung there to place Mary in my care and me in hers. It was a gift, something that would heal the sense of guilt inside me that he knew I carried, though I never spoke of it. Perhaps he had known how much I missed my father just from my voice, or from the way I sometimes spoke to James, or perhaps Jesus simply knew.

I loved her, of course. Who could not love Mary? If James and I were marred by what we saw that day, watching him suffer, watching him die, then she was more so.

And he was certainly dead.

I was left remembering all of it, at least I was left remembering those days. They were in my mind with the vividness of dreams, the ones that somehow seem more real than memory. Not that all of it was the same. Some moments stood out more than others, as with any memories, and not always the moments that I would have thought. One might think that the crucifixion was my most vivid memory, but it was not. Oh, I remembered that day, certainly, but it was not what haunted my dreams or crept into my waking thoughts. I remembered blind men, and Mary. I remembered Peter's great bobbing head as he made his way through the crowds. I remembered the bread that Jesus gave us.

Most of all, I dreamed of that morning at the shore.

Smoke was rising from a small fire on the beach, and I saw him standing next to it. He was looking over the water toward us as we made our way to shore. I thought I knew him, even from that distance, but I couldn't place him.

No one was talking. Peter's boat was creaking, leaking slightly from having seen little use for the last three years. Maybe it was good that we had caught nothing. We probably would have torn the nets and sunk the boat with us in it. A fine bunch of fishermen we were. Perhaps we had forgotten how to fish, forgotten how to live like regular people, make a living.

Peter was mending a hole in the net. He dropped the netting shuttle, and I could hear him muttering and cursing as he felt around in the coils of rope for it. He had a curse for everything, all manner of language rearranged to suit the target. When his muttering died down, the only other sound was made by waves gurgling on the side of the hull.

"Friends, have you got any fish?"

I heard his voice over the water. Friends, he said. Something about the voice was like it was speaking inside me instead of from the beach, a crazy idea.

No, we told him. Nothing. No breakfast here. Go away.

"Throw the net on the right side of the boat, and you will catch some."

All of us stared over the water at him, at the small fire, the smoke. That voice, I thought. We each turned and looked over the side of the boat. Nothing, no ripples, no flash from fish swimming in the morning light. We looked at our nets, piled in the bottom of the boat, wet and empty. Nobody spoke; we just started moving, pulling a net up, throwing it over the side.

The ropes pulled tight right away. We must have snagged something, I thought, and I leaned over the side to see into the water. Fish, schooling, a flashing churning shoal of fish, were filling the net, drawing it down. The others started pulling on the net ropes, straining against the weight. I was holding a mast tie, leaning out the other side of the boat for a counterweight, and I looked back to see him on the beach. He stood perfectly still, watching us, and I thought he smiled. That was when I knew him.

"It is the Lord," I said, leaning out over the water. The boat lurched as Peter grabbed his tunic and jumped into the water, swimming for the shore. The rest of us struggled to get the net into the boat, fish piled gasping at our feet. As we made for shore I again held a mast tie and leaned out over the water, this time at the bow to listen and watch. It seemed to me that their voices murmured across the water, Peter and Jesus, but I could never tell what they said over the sounds of the oars and of the others talking in the boat before letting their words die as they also looked to the shore and to the one sitting with Peter on the beach.

There was a bump and the sound of sand dragging against the hull, and we were ashore. We left the boat and the fish, not bothering to cover them with our net or to wet them as was our wont. We stepped onto the sandy beach still unbelieving but wanting to believe, waiting for our vision to clear or the moment to resolve itself into something other than what we perceived.

Jesus was sitting by a fire, his arms around his knees as though simply sitting there was natural, was what he always did. He is dead, I thought to myself. I watched him die, slowly, crucified. Most of the others had run, not that I blamed them. I stayed. The women were there and somehow I could not leave them, could not leave him.

"Mother, behold your son," he had said. I thought he meant himself. "Son, behold your mother," he had added, and I knew he meant me, though at first I thought he meant to call me his son rather than Mary's. Later I was not so sure he did not.

In years to come it was the sea that I thought of, blue green at the surface that day, black in the depths and shoaling with silver fish unseen from above.

Adriel

Steam is rising from the coffee urn in her hand, but the old man is gazing down the street, not hearing her question.

"Sir, would you like some more?" He lifts his head to see her. His hair is white, or nearly so, and he has a short grey and white beard. At first he is mumbling to himself, as though he were senile or a harmless lunatic, but then he smiles, simple and warm.

"Yes, thank you," he says. "I wasn't paying attention."

I watch the coffee pour into the cup, light and fluid and heat, marveling once again at the shape of the liquid as it comes out of the spout, three-fold, as though a liquid could fold, but it does. The autumn sun shimmers on the surface of the coffee as it slows and settles into the form of the cup it has found. He does not reach for it. He sits still, trying to forget the presence of the other afternoon customers in the cafe, trying to ignore me. The breeze shifts his beard, his hair, and I see it move, though I do not recall when it became so white. I should remember, I have watched him all these years, but always in each moment of my mind it is white. Perhaps it was always so, in my perception, which is all that I have.

A sparrow lands on the next table, its claws three and one against the tabletop. It stands looking at me, brown head tilting from side to side. The old man breaks off a piece of bread from the roll on his plate and places it on the floor. The sparrow hops to the edge of the table and, with a bird glance into the man's eyes, flies down to the meal. I wonder what the bird sees as it looks at me, whether it sees me. I wonder whether it knows anything more than the man is giving it bread.

I have watched him breaking off bits of bread for a very long time, crumbs of memory stretching back, communing in my mind. He does not write anymore, which is a pity. I watch over his shoulder at the words forming at his hand, and I enjoy his words, the way they loop back on themselves, like the bread and the light, a slow whirling in words rather than dance.

The bird finishes the bread, fast work for so small a thing. Another one joins it on the ground, and they both look at him with quick turns of their heads. He gives them a bigger bit of crust. Of course, he does. I look around at the trees, where more of their kind gather, chattering to one another about the feast provided by the white haired man. In a few minutes we will have more attention that will be welcome in a cafe.

The same realization flashes in the old man's mind like something silver swimming across his thoughts. He looks up at the trees and then tosses the remaining pieces of bread over a low wall that runs beside the tables. The birds gather and feast together on the scattered fragments, an unruly communion of their own with no wine, but perhaps a bird has no need of wine.

Another patron joins me at my table. She stands by her chair for a moment watching the sparrows, thinking of whether they will return to the tables when they are done, then sits and pulls a laptop computer out of her shoulder bag and places it on the table. Apple, I think, still troubled by the random associations of names and objects. She sits near me so that I can see my reflection moving on the screen. The woman turns her head as though the light hurts her eyes and shifts her machine so that it mirrors the birds instead. She ends facing the old man, albeit over the divider of her screen. She does not speak to me, nor I to her. In fact, she acts as though she does not know I exist. I am not surprised, since I do not choose to make myself known to her, but I am little disappointed. From time to time I hope that one will be able to see me without my purposing it, as John does. The old man chuckles to himself, and the girl and I both look at him. He glances first at me, then at the girl's eyes.

"Oh, don't mind me," he says to her. "I was just watching the birds and thinking that what amuses one person annoys another."

He is talking to me, of course, but she has no way to know. To her credit, she simply sips her mocha and looks back at her screen without replying. The brown foam on her lip lessens the intended slight, though the old man takes no offense anyway. He is like that, except with me. Still, when two people have been together as long as he and I, the relationship changes. I am perhaps a third arm to him, something that encumbers him and yet he would not have removed. For my part, I am glad not to live in a world where I may only remember John.

And so we sit at a cafe with him feeding sparrows. I could shoo the birds, perhaps take flight with them, but that would be petty. I often enjoy being petty, but I decide to stay. The birds are annoying most of the people, after all, and that serves the purpose.

"Are we going to sit here all day, old man?" I ask.

"Perhaps," he says. He sips his coffee, though I know he does not want any. "Why not?"

The girl raises her eyes over the computer screen and glances at him. She takes another sip of the mocha, which does nothing to help the foam on her upper lip. I suggest that she wipe her mouth, and she does before looking back down at her computer. She decides to ignore John. I am beginning to like her, but John choses that moment to leave.

I follow him, of course. I always do.

A mile or so along the road, John sees the shimmer like sunlight falling through the leaves of a tree, the light brightening the dash near the passenger seat, but he refuses to look at me. He is obstinate, this old man.

"I like Volvos," I say aloud. My voice is beautiful but different from his, as though frequencies have been filtered out or added.

The old man sighs and keeps driving slowly down the street.

I like his street as well, this neighborhood, the small stone wall running along the sidewalk, the modest houses. There is enough room between them for some privacy, not too much grass. Growing grass in one's yard, on purpose, only to work at cutting it still seems odd to me. The grass grows beautifully if they would only leave it to itself. The houses are small, bungalows they call them. The word sounds like something from Australia, some aboriginal musical instrument. I can see it in my mind. A wise old aborigine blows into a tube connected to a bladder of air, an Australian bagpipe. A child asks what it is called, and the native man pauses just long enough to lick his lips and say, Bungalow.

"I do like Volvos. Even the old ones, like this one." I pause. An unkind image forms in the old man's mind. "We never play the radio. Does it work?"

"No," he says. I know it does.

"Now, John," I say. "Why would you lie to me like that, and about a radio?"

"Why don't you ever go deliver messages or something?" asks the old man. "Get a real job, an avocation, a calling. All these years, you just follow me around."

"It may be, you know, that I am not a messenger. Your saying it does not make me so." I fiddle with the radio, turning it on, moving the tuner to different sounds. "Perhaps I am delivering a message. Not all messages are in words. You know that."

John sighs again and purses his lips, bunching the neatly trimmed bristles of his beard.

"Now who is lying?" he asks.

The light shifts, and the radio frequency carries a song by U2, almost as pleasant as the nearby static I had found that sounds like sunlight. Neither of us says anything. Another song starts, Barry Manilow, so I shut it off again.

"U2 to that? What are they thinking?"

John smiles.

"You should get satellite radio."

The old man glances at the light pattern on the dashboard. "Now you want to talk about music," he says.

"Well, it's a good thing to talk about," I say. We ride in silence. Silence seldom bothers John, which I have found to be an unusual trait among humans. Actually, I never experience silence. There is always the sound of birds, or the wind. In the reaches between planets there is the sound of the sunlight passing, the sound of distant stars singing. Here, there is the sound of the small, the unseen. Insects. Plates of the earth shifting, moving across one another. "There are spiders that vibrate in the same manner as the tires of this car," I point out, which is perfectly true.

"You manage to make dimensions of reality a little creepy, you know."

"It is true," I say, though I know he does not doubt my veracity.

"Creepy."

We are nearly at John's driveway. The house next to John's is old, and slightly neglected. The shrubs are grown slightly too large and too irregular, and there is a loose shutter at one window. Our neighbor, a young woman, is taking groceries inside from the car. She has lived in this place before, as a young girl. It is the house of her mother. She looks at John and smiles, her hands full.

"She is sick."

John quickly glances back at me. "The girl?"

I say nothing. We wait for the garage door to move up, neither of us speaking.

"Does she know?"

I think about it for a few of her heartbeats.

"No, not yet."

John looks back over at her. He waves once more and drives into the garage.

"Why do you tell me these things?"

"Just having a conversation. She is there, that's all," I say. The garage door slowly rolls back down, leaving us in darkness though I am light enough. "Why did you feed those birds earlier?"

John looks at the light on the back of his hands.

"They were there," he says.

John

The pool was crowded, but the light reflecting from the water brightened the pillars and the mosaics. So many sick people, waiting for this miraculous cure—jump in the pool when the water moves. It was ridiculous. They must have been idiots as well as invalids, because that water was never going to move on its own. Not that a bath wouldn't do some of them good, but they'd likely drown as soon as they rolled themselves in the pool.

I'm sure that the Romans thought they were idiots. They thought we all were, anyone who wasn't Roman. The sooner we passed through, the better.

Jesus stopped, though, and so did we. He was looking around at the invalids, and some of them were looking back at us. No doubt they were hoping for charity. I felt awkward just standing looking at them. Peter, his hair at all angles, stared at the people lying on their mats as though they were something odd washed up on the shore. I was trying to think of something to say quietly to Jesus to get us moving again. No good could come of a bunch of us standing here looking at these people.

Jesus stepped past a blind fellow, his head bobbing around like a bird as he slept sitting against a pillar, and stood at the feet of a paralyzed man. He was perfectly still, watching Jesus and only glancing at the rest of us. I could see daylight streaming through a portico. I was thinking that if we quietly walked through that opening, perhaps Jesus would follow us.

"Do you want to be made well?" Jesus asked the man. A stupid question, I thought. I was embarrassed.

The man explained that he did not have anyone to help him get to the water when it was stirred by angels. Angels, I thought. Really. I just wanted to walk quietly into the light of the portico, melt into the people going along into the city, but we couldn't leave Jesus standing there.

"Stand up," Jesus said to the invalid. "Take your mat and walk."

The man's legs were shriveled, a waste, and Jesus was telling him to stand up. Peter was over at the other side, jutting his great head forward and staring, first at Jesus then at the man's legs. I felt like everything stopped, just for a moment, the particles of dust in the sunlight stopped without movement, and it seemed that I heard water gurgling, a fountain or splashing.

The man was looking into Jesus' eyes, then the man put his arms out and started pushing himself upright. That's when he moved his knee, drawing his leg up toward him. He stopped again for a moment, alarmed. Around me, the other sick men were moving as well, dragging themselves toward the pool where the water was swirling.

"The angels stirred it," I said, then I put my hand over my mouth, not believing I had said it. We began helping the men into the pool, all of them except the one in front of Jesus. That man stood up on his own, Peter reaching toward him to steady him in case he fell. Peter was staring at the man's legs. They were as straight and as muscular as my own.

I felt someone take my arm, a blind man sitting near me, and I began helping him toward the pool. All of them, all the sick, we put into the pool, and I couldn't tell if the water was moving because of them or on its own. As soon as the blind fellow I was helping stepped into the water he stopped and turned to me. He was looking at me, looking at my face as though I was the most beautiful thing in the world, and I realized he could see.

I looked back at Jesus, but he just walked through the portico into the sunlight, the dust in the air making him vanish as he went.

Adriel

Jesus is talking to the crippled man near the wall, but I cannot focus on his words. The blind man near me is thinking too loudly, and he is difficult to understand. He is blind from birth, and all of his thoughts blend the abstract and the concrete, a place name with a sound, feelings of fear and the touch of leather, memories of home with the smell of bread, and I realize too late that he is dreaming the dreams of the blind. Dreams are dangerous at best, but with his odd sensory associations I am captivated, falling, not seeing the ground but knowing it is there.

I fall into a pool, and the water envelops me. It should not matter. I am not a physical being, but the blind man's dreams make me reach out to touch this world, and suddenly the water knows I am there.

Miraculous. They lay here expecting the water to move, and it does.

I rise from the water to gauge whether anyone has seen, and the man Jesus is looking at me. He says nothing, just turns unsurprised and continues talking with the invalid.

There are more splashes, and some of the people are hurling themselves into the pool, water surging out onto the tile floor. The healthy men and women who had been following Jesus start helping the sick into the pool. It is madness, a bizarre game of Adriel Says, though I have said nothing, just fallen into the water.

I feel the power, though, power that is in the water with me, not from me. The sick ones are changing, leaving the pool with stronger bodies. The dust stirred by the crowd sparkles in the sunlight, and the water splashing from the pool and dripping from their bodies mirrors the light. Jesus is already walking away, and the blind man is staring at one of the followers, both of them wet and dripping.

John

"That was a long time ago," I said, perhaps to myself. I saw that there was no one, no sense of presence, no light. Maybe that is all there ever was, a pattern of light and a conversation in my head.

I stepped to the door and watched the girl carrying the last of the groceries into the house. She was young lady, not a girl, not any more. Her hair was pulled back in a ponytail and her jeans were scuffed, colored on one knee from working on some project in the house. I remembered her as well, from when she was a child living here with her mother.

Why did Adriel tell me that she was sick? Now what?

I couldn't just go over and perform a miraculous healing. People didn't go in for that sort of thing anymore. Be well in the name of Jesus of Nazareth. Not that I ever performed any miracles, not really. I don't know how they were healed, what mechanism did it. We would say some words, and something would happen. Not that I minded looking like a fool, not any more. That's one of the best parts of living a long time, you get to leave a lot of things behind. I simply didn't know if it would work any more, or why it ever worked for that matter. It is worse, sometimes, if it does work—look where that got us. Crowds of excited people, and lines of needy ones, but in the end you couldn't help everyone. We didn't change the world. Well, if you count a new religion as changing the world, maybe we did something. It was all fine, until it wasn't, until the crusades, until nearly everything.

There is a natural order to things, that is all. Except for me, of course. And how was I going to explain me? A genetic freak, some kind of biological oddity? How would anyone prove my assertion? Carbon date my beard? It was still growing.

"I'm going to have a cup of tea," I said. Nobody responded, which I took for a good sign that I was finally having some alone time this day.

Adriel suggested that I invite the girl to dinner. How was I to sit down to a meal with her, knowing what I knew? That was his plan, knowing I could not simply stand by, not when she is that close, not when she needs the help we can offer her. What did I really know, though, except what I heard a pattern of light in my car telling me? I'm finally insane, I thought. I finally made it, thanks be to God.

Bread, so many meals, I thought, then caught myself. I did not want to sink into the lethargy of memory. I sometimes drifted into the past and did not emerge for days, simply sitting, looking off at nothing, and forgetting to notice the shadows and the light of present time passing.

I did not know how angels do it, how Adriel did it, handling the memories of so much time. Angels move through time differently than we, touching it less, touched by it less. There is no past for them, no sense of things passing beyond their touch. Memories for Adriel were present events, not mere recollection. If I asked Adriel about an experience, trying to recall a detail, he would tell me the entire event as it happens, present in his memory, as though it has not already happened. I was not so sure that he was wrong. Perhaps recollection of the past is the substance of the present moment.

I didn't know, and I was losing my ability to separate the times and the days. It did not bother me anymore. Perhaps I was senile, or perhaps I was becoming more like the angels. There may be no difference. No one knows how old the angels are, when they came to exist, except that they remember themselves and the universes around them from time out of reckoning for mortals. It may be that they have all slipped into a pernicious reverie, unable to lift their minds from the weight of time.

I headed to the bathroom for a shower.

Sarah

I don't know what I was thinking.

In the end, all of the things that mattered to me fitted into my car, which was both amazingly handy and amazingly depressing. There had been no furniture in my apartment to speak of, nothing for a moving truck to bring. My precious things were not furniture. I brought back a teakettle, copper and beautiful. There were some photo albums, most of the photos taken here at my mother's house or on some small vacation, a trip to the beach, a visit to the mountains. I had some jewelry, though not much. I had some savings, a little more left from Mom.

And now I had this house, my mother's house. I came back, because everything I ever cared about was here. Either it was here, or it was gone forever.

A two-story cottage and an acre of land, and I was alone in it. I hadn't really thought about the fact that the grass would grow, but surely I could mow it? I knew the old mower was out in the shed with her rakes and her gardening tools, her flowerpots.

I missed her.

I was standing in the living room, which opened to the dining area and the small kitchen, when the doorbell rang. I jumped. The sound of the bell was enormous in this quiet space.

Looking out of the window, I saw an old man standing on the front steps, a box in his hands. He was fairly short, about my height, and his skin was either tanned or more likely was always that color. He was familiar, a neighbor. I remembered him from childhood, though it seemed that in my mind he looked the same as he did now, standing on my mother's porch, my porch.

I peeped at him again through the spy hole of the door. His eyes were blue, but he might otherwise have been Middle Eastern. Did some people from there have blue eyes? I realized that I didn't know.

I opened the door.

"Hello, Sarah," he said to me. "I am your neighbor, next door." He pointed to his right, the house beside mine. The yard was neat. The house was simple. Everything was in place. Truth be told, the neatness of that house was part of what we had always liked about this neighborhood.

"Oh, yes," I said. I had never been particularly good at this sort of thing. "Hi."

"I am John," he said, shifting the box to his left hand and reaching out his right. I took it for a brief handshake. His hand was warm. "It has been a long time. I was very sorry for your loss."

"Thank you," I said, then I remembered his last name. "Mr. Zebedee. It is nice to see you again. I like your house. I think that I have always liked it."

"Oh, well, thank you. Here, this is for you. A small welcome." He placed the box in my hands. It had a substantial heft for a not overly large box. "Cheese. It is cheese. I hope you like cheese, though perhaps I should have asked…"

"Oh, yes. I do like cheese, and thank you very much."
I hesitated, thinking that he might possibly be a cleverly
disguised axe murderer. Such a quiet man, they would say.
Who would have thought?

"Would you like to come in?"

He seemed to hesitate. "Only for a moment," he said.
"You must be busy trying to get moved in."

He stepped inside. We left the door open, the sunlight
streaming in across the nearly empty hallway to land on the
few boxes I had.

"Actually," I said, "the unpacking will not be lengthy. I
don't really have much in the way of things."

He looked at the boxes. "That can be good. Sometimes
our things can weigh us down."

I was not sure what to say. He walked across the room
to look out the patio doors.

"You will have to be careful. The squirrels here are bold
rascals."

I laughed, the first time I had laughed in this house
since returning to it. This may have been the first time I
had laughed in many days, I couldn't remember. I carried
the cheese box to the kitchen, not sure whether it was more
polite to open it or to leave it closed.

"I'm going to have to go shopping for a few things,"
I said. "Most of what is here was my mother's. All of it
reminds me of her."

"Well, take your time," he says. "If you only get the
things you need and love, you will only have things you
need and love. Less to dust."

I smiled, and he walked back to the living room, soft
footsteps bouncing around the room.

"Why don't you come over for dinner?" he asked and smiled. "You must be too tired to cook for yourself. The weather is warm enough that we can sit on the back deck and watch the squirrels. We'll have something simple."

I usually retreat from people, and I hesitated.

"You would be doing me a favor, truly. I seldom have company," he said. "Think of it as a kindness to an old man."

I was surprised to hear myself agreeing, and a few hours later I walked across to his little house.

Dinner was simple, but good. Sandwiches with chips, not what I anticipated from this older gentleman, but delicious and somehow more comforting than a more sophisticated meal would have been. I thought that somehow he knew that would be true.

"You remind me of someone from long ago," he said. "That is a good thing. She was an amazing person."

"Thank you," I said, then, unable to help myself, "What happened to her?"

"Oh, nothing terrible. No," he said. "Just time. She was quite old when she passed away."

"You miss her," I said. Again, I should not have. I did not know this man well enough to press a sensitive subject, but he did not seem to mind.

"I miss my mother," I added.

We watch the squirrels, and I thought that my neighbor might have been right about them. They were bold, smart. Several times they came to the rail of his deck to see whether we had dropped anything for them.

I thanked him for dinner and for his welcome. I was starting to walk across the yard back to my house when I stopped and turned.

"You didn't tell me her name," I said. "The woman you knew long ago."

He looked at me, paused, and I wondered whether I should have asked.

"Mary," he said. "Her name was Mary."

I thought that I saw a flash of light in the edge of my vision, but it passed. It was probably a trick of the mind, maybe something the squirrels had done. I thanked him again, and I walked home. We had not talked much, but somehow I was more encouraged than I had been in a long time.

Adriel

Drifting up from the house I stop to watch the horizon move toward the sun, then a flight of sparrows fly through the space where I linger. I turn and follow, a flicker of wind and feathers, to land on the grass at the burgeoning roots of an oak. The birds are pecking grass seeds, while I gaze at the bark of the tree and move inside to the dark cool center. The sensation of the sunlight on the leaves flows down through the living lines of wood so that even in the darkness I am surrounded by the energy of light.

Best is the water, drawing up cell by cell, flowing slowly but unfailingly up, a fountain from the roots splitting at branches into thousands of tiny jets of leafy water. I let myself flow with the water, breathing out into each leaf shimmering in the sunset, feeling the steady swaying of the limbs. As the sun fades, I gather myself upward to stay in the light, crowning the leaves, still feeling the water flow in the tree and gazing into the sun like that blind man gazing into John's eyes, both of them dripping and alive.

I have not left him since that day. Well, occasionally I leave to take care of other matters or simply to give us each a bit of privacy. No one likes everyone all of the time, even if we love them. It is in our natures to seek both solitude and company, the same dichotomy of everything that lives.

I see Sarah come from her house, her mother's house, and walk across the grass to his house, our house. No doubt she would react badly to seeing me, require a reassurance, a classic 'Fear not!' I suppose.

Better for her not to see me or any like me.

They think that if they could see with their own eyes, then they would believe more, understand more, but they are wrong. I watch it. Their mind denies, explains. They only have more questions and wonder about what they saw, whether they had seen, and what meaning it had, if it had meaning.

They see each other all the time, and they never wonder if that has meaning. Why should seeing a being like me convey something more? As if I have a special wisdom to impart. Perhaps I know things they do not, but knowing more is not always helpful, and it is not always wise. Knowledge is not wisdom.

Looking to the east I see others shimmer in the lingering sunlight, some going about the city. One sits on the rooftop across the street, though I cannot not quite tell whether she is watching me or the sun behind me. Her thoughts are not open to me.

As I settle on the shingles of her rooftop, she keeps gazing toward the sun. I watch her for a while, and then I do the same as she and turn toward the sinking glow. Soon there is nothing but a thin edge of light slicing across the end of the sky. She turns to look at me.

"So, you are the one with him?"

I am surprised by the summary. It has not been so many days. "Yes," I say. "I suppose that I am."

"You suppose," she said. "Oh, I see. You are wondering about the nature of the relationship."

I think about her analysis. "Something like that."

We watch the blade edge of light slip from view. Clouds, pink and rose, shifting mirrors made of water, float above the horizon, a beautiful distortion of the sunlight beyond.

"It seems you have formed some kind of friendship," she says, and turns back to watch the sunlight refracted in the water vapor.

"Perhaps that is what it is. We are friends. I am not sure that he would agree."

She shifts her attention. "I saw you enter the tree. It seemed you enjoyed yourself, flowing with the light and the water."

"It is pleasant, moving with the life of the tree. You should try it."

"Oh, no. It is not for me, I think." She pauses. I wait for her thoughts. "It seems too limiting, like being trapped, held to one form and one time."

"It is alive," I say. "You should try. Flowing up with the water into the light falling within from the leaves is calming."

We watch in silence. There are the sounds of the people, in the houses near us, machines. There are other sounds as well, sounds that the humans cannot hear. We sit and listen to the earth squeezing the rock, stone sliding on stone along the fine cracks like faces of porcelain deep in the ground. As the earth turns to block the static of the nearest star on the far side from us, the distant voices of other energies reach across space. We hear other suns and darkened stars, voices of quasars singing of distant time, voices singing now of what they once were.

The leaves of the oak vibrate, shifting in the breeze but also with the fall of the vibrations from the darkening sky. The sounds of the stars fall like dust on the quivering leaves.

"Soon the leaves will fall," I say.

She turns to look at me.

"Everything falls," she says.

John

Two grey squirrels cantered across the back yard and reached the deck, each of them urging the other along, daring one another to acts of bravery as they approached the bird feeder. The problem was that I was sitting there, drinking my coffee and watching them. I have never harmed them or scolded them. In fact I filled the feeders with food, but they were still slow to trust that I would let them eat in peace.

The morning was cold, but I had a sweater, and the coffee was still warm. It was Sunday morning, and I should have been readying myself to attend a worship service, but I found that I was inclined to share a wary communion with the squirrels. I was a member of a small Baptist church, a whiteboard structure three blocks away. Alternately expanding and deteriorating with the population of this town, the church grew and shambled its way to cover a third of the block. It was a wood and metal rabbit warren, an object lesson in the value of architectural planning.

I have been Baptist, and Anglican, and Roman Catholic, even Methodist for a time. All of them were unsatisfactory, each in its own way. Nevertheless, I long ago ceased to present myself as an authority in the life of the church. I found myself sometimes more disturbed by the artificial banana pudding than by the muddled theology, if only because I realized that for most of the congregants of any church the ingredients of the pudding would be ingested with more gusto and reflected upon with much greater effect.

I thought of the people of my neighborhood, wondering about their Sunday morning routine. Most were sleeping, no doubt. An excellent plan. People underestimate the value of sleep, of the rhythm of the days, the value of communion with the birds and the squirrels.

Perhaps sleep would help Sarah, I thought.

Adriel was a meddler. After all this time, I still didn't know if he did it out of curiosity, spite, or sheer indifference. He sometimes could not sift the relative value of what he saw, placing equal interest in the particular color of a beam of late afternoon sunlight and in the well being of a person, each presenting interesting facets to his mind's eye. Not that he would have allowed harm to come to anyone simply for the spectacle of it, but he would have been fascinated by the intricate detail of a car crash. In his defense, he would have been equally fascinated by the way a snail moves across a leaf or the reflection of light on a raindrop.

When I say fascination, that may not be quite the right word, but there may not be a correct word in our languages to describe the utter attention of which an angel is capable. Adriel could render such complete focus on the detail of an object that his observations extended to the level of subatomic particles, the effects of gravity and of solar radiation, things that I have only learned about by watching Neil deGrasse Tyson on television and by listening to Adriel describe the sounds emitted by a rock in the sunlight. He was astonishing in what he saw and knew, and equally astonishing in what he did not. In that way, he was nearly human.

Of course, he claimed not to be a 'he', rather simply a being, but there are differences among them. Reflections of our expectations, they claim, but I had my doubts.

I had many doubts.

We have seen his glory, that is what it says in a Gospel that bears my name, and still I had doubts. I did not know whether that was a sign of my humanity or of my intelligence, or both at once. Yet I talked to Adriel, remembered what I saw and heard and touched, and still I prayed, to a God whom I was sure I did not know well, perhaps at all.

And the squirrels did not trust me.

I did not blame them.

So Adriel told me that Sarah was not well, a simple and nearly thoughtless observation on his part, and I was trapped in layers of ethical, theological and practical considerations. Healing was not really something that I did. It never has been, even when I was part of it; at least I knew that the power never came from me.

The first time that it happened, at least on purpose, I was walking with Peter to the temple, which was already fraught with difficulty. Walking anywhere in public with Peter was difficult. You never knew what he might say, what he might do, and that was true before the years with Jesus. Peter would see someone who interested him, and he would lurch over to them and begin talking, or worse, simply stand and stare at them. If Peter had been a less imposing figure, there might have been more trouble in those instances. Seeing this tall, ungainly, shaggy man, most people either tried to ignore him or simply found a reason to move away from him.

This particular day Peter became engrossed in a man who was begging at the temple gate. The man was lame, so when Peter stopped and began staring at him, his options were limited. I could tell he was hopeful that we would give him a coin, but looking up at the unruly hair jutting out from Peter's head was enough to unsettle the fellow. I don't know what he thought of me. I don't recall him really even giving me much of a look. It was Peter who held his attention.

I have forgotten who spoke first, Peter or the man, but something was said about money, or perhaps the man simply rattled the few coins he had in his cup. At any rate, Peter looked at me, then back at the lame man, and he said, "In the name of Jesus, the Christ, of the city of Nazareth, rise up and walk."

I remembered the words because of how awkward they were. It occurred to me that there certainly were not enough men named Jesus who were also called anointed or messiah that we had to specify the city of residence as well. Of course, that was Peter. Everything he said and did was awkward, even when it was perfectly right and true.

Peter reached down and took the man by the arm and pulled him to his feet. Even without the power of God, the man would have risen from the place where he sat, for Peter was a powerful man. Pulling one lame man up from the flagstones was nothing compared to pulling in nets full of fish. Up the man came before I even had time to be astonished or to doubt that God would respond to our words, Peter's words, and there the man stood. He was healed. It was just as we had seen happen when Jesus was with us.

I was amazed.

The man began to dance and jump around, a crowd gathered, and there we stood. Peter was perfectly calm. I may have appeared calm, but I felt both empowered and afraid. What was this new thing, that we should call down the power of God with nothing but words?

It was not the last time, of course. Over the years, it became part of our routine, part of what we did as followers of Jesus, the Christ, the one from Nazareth. In years to come, I ceased calling upon the power of God, of course. It was necessary, because immediately those who saw such a thing wondered who I might be. When they began to suspect that I was John, after so many years, inevitably their attention moved from God to me. It could not be so, and one day I realized that I had to cease being John the disciple of this Jesus of Nazareth. I would have to become something else, someone else, and so I did.

I could have moved again, taken up a new name in a new place. That would have removed Sarah from my sphere of influence, but I would simply have remembered her. Adriel would have made sure of it, again whether from empathy with her or from idle spite I could not say. The problem was not geographical. It was human.

I preferred geography.

I decided that I would have to help her, in some manner, and that was the end of it, or the beginning.

"Good." It was Adriel, shimmering behind me.

"Stop doing that," I said. "It's rude."

"Mmm."

He sat in the other deck chair, which settled a bit with his presence. I always found that odd, the weightiness of a spiritual being. Energy being? Anyway.

"Physics is not your strong suit," Adriel said.

"Nor is privacy yours."

"Metaphysics, perhaps," he said, ignoring me. "You are better at metaphysics."

"No one even knows what that is," I said.

We sat watching the squirrels, a two thousand year old man and an angel, unless I was deranged. Of course, I could always be both quite old and quite deranged, plenty of people managed both, I thought. If I was insane, the squirrels were right to be wary.

"You're not deranged," Adriel said.

"I told you to stop that. Besides, if you are the product of my demented mind, who are you to validate me?" The circular logic of my situation was maddening.

Adriel sighed. He seldom did that, given that he did not truly breathe, so I looked over to gauge his mood.

"There is something happening," he said. "Others are watching."

I waited. Then I said, "There are always watchers."

"More, I mean. They are, well, I think the word is indifferent." Adriel seemed concerned. Again I waited, but he sat there, quiet.

"Indifferent? I don't understand."

We were silent long enough that a squirrel made it to the feeder.

"If they were human, I would say they were agnostic. I don't have a word for what they are."

I looked at him again, something between substance and the reflection of light. Agnostic angels, I think.

"Yes," he said, though he was not being rude this time. He simply paid no attention to whether I spoke aloud.

We each sat there thinking until the sky slipped into darkness. Neither of us spoke, and if Adriel was listening to my thoughts he made no indication. When I finally looked around, the squirrels had long been in their nests.

Water

I did not know the family, but we had been invited. We were gathered in the courtyard, a group within the group, although Peter was going around talking and laughing, his great shaggy head easy to spot. I was sitting near Jesus in the shade of a fig bush just tall enough to offer a screen from the sun, and I saw Mary making her way toward him before he saw her, although I was never sure what Jesus knew about his surroundings. He picked people from the crowd when I had not seen them, ignored others who were standing in front of him.

Mary could not be ignored. She waved at people across the courtyard and smiled at them, then came and knelt beside Jesus. She reached up and rubbed his shoulder, and I supposed she was happy to see her son. That's when I noticed two servants had followed her from within the house.

"They are running out of wine," she said.

Jesus sighed.

"What do you want me to do about that?" he said. "It is not my party, and it is not my time. This is their day. Their party."

Mary ignored him and waved the servants over.

"Do what he tells you," she said. Jesus just sighed again, looking around the courtyard. It was only a little theatrical, enough to say, 'See how much I love her, even when she annoys me.' He pointed at some large stone jars standing at the wall of the house.

"Go and fill them with water," he told them. It was not a small task. Each jar would hold a number of buckets of water, and the process would be tiresome in the heat. The servants looked at him, then at Mary. She nodded and shooed them with her hand.

"Go ahead," she said. "Do what he told you."

They did not look happy, but they hurried over to a well and began pulling up buckets of water and carrying them to the stone jars. It was warm enough in the courtyard that the sound of the water was welcome. When they had filled all of the jars, they stood waiting to see what idiotic task they would have next. I knew that if this ended badly, we would be leaving quickly, but things never ended badly around Jesus, at least not until the very end. I sat still and quiet, waiting like the servants.

Jesus appeared to be lost in thought. Mary nudged him in the side, and he turned to look at the stone jars, wet with the water splashed on the sides and along the tiles near them.

"Draw some out, and take it to your steward," he said.

They stood with backs straight, looking first at Jesus then across the courtyard at the head servant who already appeared displeased with all the water carrying. Then, dour and resigned, one of them took a dipper and filled it from a jar. Drops fell dark on the ground. With round eyes he stared at the liquid all the while that he walked across the courtyard. The head servant took it and tasted it, the disgust on his face shifting to surprise.

Quickly he sent the man back and told them both to draw more from the jars and to serve it to the guests. Some of them had been watching as well, and the rest certainly noticed when they began to drink the new wine. We would not be leaving quickly after all, it seemed. Mary was enormously pleased and went off to talk to someone, probably to say that she was the mother of the one who had brought the wine they were now tasting.

As I said, things tended not to end badly with Jesus, not until that very bad ending itself. That was a different sort of event anyway, more something that Jesus endured than something he did. This was like the people at the pool, the blind man who stared at my face in amazement. It was a sign, a sign for us, for Mary, and for as many of the people who realized what had happened. At the same time, it was ordinary, just wine being served at a wedding. What was miraculous about that? It was only a miracle if one saw it as a miracle.

Of course, that was always the case, I thought. Maybe those crippled men who got up and walked out of that pool weren't really crippled, maybe they had been pretending for the sake of being able to beg money from those who worked for a living. It was possible that the blind man was the same, pretending, and when Jesus caught him in his pretense, he had to abandon it. Of course, that would have been a sort of miracle, some would argue, just not one that required the power of God. I think that changing the behavior of men like that would require more power, be the greater miracle. Changing the mind is a greater sign than healing the body.

But I saw that blind man, saw his eyes when he could not see me. And I saw the amazement on his face when he could see me, when I was suddenly the most beautiful thing in his world. I knew things that the people sitting here drinking wine did not know, and even when we told them, some would never believe.

I got up and walked along the row of jars, and I saw my face reflected in the new dark wine.

Adriel

As John sleeps I move up to the roof to watch the night and to think. It makes no difference, the roof, and I do not need any place to settle, but it seems better to rest on the roof than in the air, and so I do it. Perhaps at some point, my kind had bodies, knew the support and the need of the physical world. Maybe that memory is held in my mind somewhere. I do not know, but resting on the roof is better than resting nowhere.

I know the temperature is much cooler, though it has no effect on me. I wonder what would, externally. If I wish, I could touch the face of the sun, but I do not know if it would harm me to be so close to that original flame. In our tongue a star is called a lake-of-fire. There are stories told of those who plunge into the raging heat, never emerging. There is no need to test such ideas: the sun's light comes to us, and no one is there to talk to should I make such a journey.

There are others along the street, some moving above the city, some stationary like buoys. Most of them, like me, have clouded their thoughts so that they are not open to hear. A few are simply singing, most beautifully. Music is an unequal gift, even among my kind. Occasionally, one of the great ones flashes past the night sky like a meteor and is gone. It is said that they come and go from the presence of God, but there are none who can tell me the way.

I have asked.

I feel a gaze and realize that the one I had spoken with on the rooftop is back. She is watching me and watching John. I think of joining her again, and then I am beside her.

"He sleeps," she says. "Dreaming of walking around Galilee, with him, with others like himself."

I am surprised at her interest and wonder about it, but do not let her know my thoughts. She is clouded, so I remain so, though I remember a time when none of us clouded our thoughts, or it seems I remember such a time, and then it is gone. Sometimes it is as though I remember a glimpse into other rooms, like a child who slips from her bed and peeks into the room where the adults sit and talk, their voices and laughter and a brief glimpse of light and faces the only part that stays in her memory in the years to come.

"He often dreams, of Jesus and the other ones who follow him," I say. Across from us an owl leaves a tree and swoops low on wings that make no sound, or rather a sound that only we can hear. I wonder whether even the owl can hear the movement of its own feathers. It moves like thought along the street and into the darkness.

"He wonders whether he is sane," she says, meaning John. I doubt an owl would ever have reason to do so.

"Yes," I say. "He knows we could be part of the same dream."

Again, she looks at me for a very long time.

"I am no dream," she says. Later, as the morning sky begins to lighten and color with the approaching sun, she says, "My name is Adi."

"Adriel. I am Adriel," I say. I don't know why we introduce ourselves. We can find each other's names in our minds, but it seems more friendly, more honest. More human.

"Yes, I have heard," she tells me. "They say that you are the one who watches him."

Not the only one, I think. I look around with new interest at the others lingering within sight, wondering how many are interested in the people or life where they are and how many have simply come to see something of John. It makes me uncomfortable, though I cannot think of a reason. Something of this attention, this passivity is not natural.

"How did you come to be interested in him?" I ask. Don't you have anything better to do, I wonder to myself.

She turns to me with an expression that may be surprise though I cannot read it fully. "It's the light. The light is different around him. You know that."

I do know, I think. There is light around John, always light, but it is not so different from the light of others. Is it?

"That must be why you stay near him," she adds, not looking at me.

There is more light coming from the house as we watch. I can see it flowing around, not in lines but light like glowing smoke moving, a cloud that shimmers and dissipates as it flows from the structure. I know from the way the light flows upward that John is awake, that he is praying. The energy changes.

"There, you see what it does." She is pointing at the light. "The others do not do that, not so much as that. I want to understand it."

What is to understand, I think.

"What makes the light, and where does it go?" she asks.

At first I hesitate, thinking that she is asking me for the answer, but I realize that she is assuming that I do not know any more than she.

And I realize that she is right.

There is a shift in the shadows along the street, like leaves in a breeze, but it is the darkness itself that seems to flutter. Adi notices it as well. It moves like the owl, but more quietly, like secret thoughts in a dark cave.

"The others have come," she says. "They come more often than they did."

I know that she means the dark ones. I feel one near the edge of the light, lurking along the street curb and the shadow of bushes planted along the sidewalk. It is waiting, though I do not know for what. This one is no great power. It is ordinary in strength and mind, I can sense. I wonder whether it has come with the purpose of meeting John, or by chance, or for something else.

If by chance, it will move on, I think. If on purpose, it will wait, and so I wait to see which it would be. Soon, though, another comes shifting across the lawn of the house where Sarah lives. It creeps toward the window, as though needing the glass to see within the structure. This one slips across the grass like a crawling thing, limited by walls and space. I find myself growing angry at the sight, unsure of whether I am angry at its purpose or at the nature of the being.

"No," I shout at it. I feel the nearer one pull together like black wings beating and withdraw as I fly across the street to Sarah's house. The dark one from the window slithers to the shadows beneath an oak in their yard.

"Leave this place, leave these people," I say. It hisses at me and laughs, which is why I lose my temper, I suppose. Suddenly I am aware of standing under the branches of the tree, light filling the yard, my anger illuminating the grass, the branches of the tree, houses along the street. The dark one is caught out in the open spaces, falling back across the grass like smoke in a storm wind, and then it flees, dissipating into darkness.

I feel how quiet the night has become, and I realize that Adi is beside me. She is not illuminated, but I feel her power all the same. Others are watching us from along the street. Somehow their restraint angers me more, and I resent their distance, their lack of engagement. Behind Adi I see the curtains of Sarah's room moving and I cease as light, becoming once again unseen.

Adi looks up at Sarah's window. "She saw, but she does not know what she saw."

I do not say anything. I am motionless, watching Sarah pull her curtains back together against the night and the darkness.

"That was something," Adi says, an echo of human expression.

I look at her but cannot think of a reply. I am empty but somehow full of power, like clear water in a waterfall.

"I didn't realize how much you care for these people as well," she says.

I look back at the window of the human, a child compared to me.

"Neither did I," I say.

John

Mornings were best, especially Saturday or Sunday mornings, when the world had turned its hustle down a notch.

On this morning I was sitting on my deck watching the distrustful squirrels when I heard a car stop near the house, heard the thump of the closing car door.

"It's a car," Adriel said.

"Yes," I said. One would think an angel capable of offering more insight. I could not tell if the car was in front of my house and I had no intention of asking Adriel, so I took my coffee and ambled through to the front door.

It was gray, the car, and parked along the street rather than in my driveway. A man in a suit walked across my yard, a thick black book in his hand. His face was slightly downcast, with a scowling sort of smile as he glared at the grass as though reflecting on what it had done to offend him. I knew that book, and I knew that scowl.

"Oh, dear Lord," I said aloud, though quietly. "Deliver us from missionaries."

The man looked up, seeing me through the glass of the door. His lips smiled while his eyes examined my coffee and me. When did we begin to teach people that religion is a basis for judgment? Oh, yes. Before my time.

"Good morning, friend!" He raised the hand carrying the Bible in way of greeting, or as warning, or as some form of talisman, I could not tell. Adriel may have been able to read his thoughts, but I regretted that I could guess his intentions.

"Good morning to you as well."

I heard a groan behind me, Adriel summing up the visitor.

"I have come to share the good news with you friend!" Again, the Bible was held like a talisman or perhaps a fudge sample. "God loves you, and he wants your life to change."

"I see. You are supposing that my life is in need of change, it seems."

The man frowned, unable or unwilling to examine the thesis. After a moment of reflection, unsatisfactory to judge by the facial expression, he continued.

"May I come in and bring you the good news?" He clasped the book to his chest with both hands, this time more like a present than anything else, though I was sure from the body language that it was his present, his toy, not mine. If I played my cards right, his folded arms were telling me, he might let me look at it.

"As it stands, I have heard the good news," I said. I even wrote down part of it, I thought, and I was willing to bet that a bumper sticker on his car made reference to that fact.

"Indeed!" His eyebrows arched, though his eyes still did not yet joined the rest of his face in smiling. His joy had the peculiar quality of not fully informing his face. "I have come to share that news with you. And with your neighbors, and all people."

I have never in all my years approached anyone this way, certainly not among people who have grown up hearing the stories of the gospel. In centuries past, walking into villages and towns where nobody had heard the story, I would tell it, and it was a story. Something fresh, new, entertaining even as it was mesmerizing. So long as the Romans were the rulers and opposed to us, most of the people resonated with the story, the cruelty, the inversion of power, the unlikely presence of God. Once Rome embraced Christianity, it changed. Constantine subverted it, making our story a tool of his power, and preaching the gospel needed a new path, a new way to separate the story of God from the power of the emperor.

"I believe you will find that the people living along this street have all heard the good news," I said. So get into your car and go away, I thought, somewhat uncharitably.

"Indeed!" It was a watchword for him. "And have they accepted the good news? Have they invited the Savior into their lives? Do their lives tell the gospel? Are they living in the ways of the living God?"

He licked his lips quickly, taking another breath and going on about our living in the Last Days. I was repelled, and puzzled over the reason. I had encountered many hundreds of men like this one, and as for the last days, I had been living in them for two thousand years.

I wanted to slam the door, to hear his voice muffled by the wood and the distance, to shout at him that he knew nothing, could teach me nothing.

"If you do that, he will simply go next door," said Adriel from somewhere behind me, his voice registering in my mind. I knew he was right. The man was chattering on, something about a red heifer.

"I could give him a religious experience right here," he suggested. "No one outside need see."

I could imagine it—the man silenced by the appearance of an angel, here in my hallway. Adriel in all his brilliance, and my house becomes a shrine to religious freaks.

"Well, that is one possibility," said Adriel.

"Stop that," I said irritably, not meaning to say it aloud. The preacher standing at the door paused, his mouth still open. Whether he meant simply to take a breath or was taken aback by my outburst I did not know, but it presented an opening.

"Stop going on about the last days," I said. "People have been going on about the last days since Tiberius was on the throne."

"Who?" he said, looking at me and then down at the Bible in his hands as though the answer was there. I doubted that it was.

"Never mind. The point is that every sign in the book was fulfilled in Jesus lifetime, and everyone ever since has gone on about living in the last days." I paused to look at at him. "And they've all been right."

"Surely, sir, you do not mean the signs and wonders of the Book of Revelations!" He held the book in one hand and raised a finger with the other. "For I have made a special study of the things that are to come in these last days."

"Revelation," I said. "It is called Revelation, not revelations, and perhaps I should have kept it to myself."

Again, he paused in his sales talk. "Kept what to yourself?"

"Nothing." I took a breath and tried to remind myself of the brevity of this man's life. It usually helped to restore my perspective and sense of charity, but it was not working in this case. I found myself looking at the unlikely wrinkles in the polyester suit, the wingtip shoes that had walked in who knew how many houses, and I knew that I was being unkind.

He looked down at his Bible, hesitating, but then his gaze shifted to Sarah's house next door. I would not have it.

"I will tell you what you need to do," I said, stepping out of the door and forcing his retreat. "You need to stop preaching and start listening."

"Listening?"

"If you are going to read these words, pay attention. Listen more than you talk, and you will be closer to God. You might manage to draw someone else along with you."

He was blinking, looking at me.

"Sir, I am called to preach. I cannot be silent when souls around me are in peril. Their blood would be upon my head!"

Finally, I could pity him. He was caught in a maze only partly of his own making. At the least, others had added walls and doors, and he had entered it bewildered. For some it was all they had known from childhood, and for others it was their escape from childhood. They spent the rest of their lives trapped inside walls of theology and soteriology, most of which did not exist in the scripture. He was surrounded by the work of men who had explained, defined, and with great zeal had built a church of ideas that would have been alien to Jesus.

And I had helped lay the foundation of the house that was burning down around him.

He turned around, looking at the other houses in the neighborhood, his attention ending with Sarah's house once again. She had just emerged to refill bird feeders in her yard. Seeing us standing on the front steps of my house, she waved. Sarah appeared curious, though she had seen the man's suit and his book and seemed to lean more to reservation than interest.

"I can vouch for her," I said. "There is no need to preach to her."

He appeared doubtful. I have spoken with many doubtful people over the years. Most of the time I am one of them.

Then I noticed a glimmer on the doorpost and realized that Adriel was adding light effects. I tried to ignore it, but the preacher widened his eyes and stepped back.

"It is the word of the Lord," he said.

I rubbed my forehead, wondering if it were possible to kill Adriel with a shovel. One smooth smack to what would be his head.

"Just go," I said to the preacher, and amazingly he did. I could see the wingtip shaped impressions on the grass marking his retreat, and I watched him take a last look at my doorway as he drove away. Maybe Adriel was good for something after all.

"No, I don't believe so," he said.

"You're not good for anything?"

He appeared to scowl, which he seemed to do quite a lot for an angelic being.

"No, I do not believe that you could kill me with a shovel," he said. "In fact, I'm not sure I can be killed by anything on this planet. I did wonder the other day whether a star might do it."

I turn to look at him, as best as one is able. The bits and pieces making up his appearance still shifted subtly in time and space even while he was presenting corporeality. There was a liquid mosaic effect.

"Having suicidal thoughts?"

He was surprised.

"No, just curiosity. Thinking of following a light beam back to touch the sun, wondering what would happen to one like me inside a star." Adriel sighed, which always seemed an affectation. "Just thoughts."

"Bored are we? Need a vacation somewhere in the galaxy?"

"No," he said. "I am never bored."

"That's a shame," I replied, and I left him wondering.

John

The Temple was magnificent. It was huge to my eyes, with enormous walls and smooth paved courtyards. So many stones, so much space. Then there were the uniforms of the guards, the robes of the priests, the movement of people and of animals. Our synagogue was one thing, but this was a dwelling place of the almighty God, and I had carried a sense of awe about the Temple ever since I was a small child. I was a fisherman's son, and entering the Temple made me feel a little light headed, with that odd sensation of watching one's self from slightly above one's own body. It was unsettling, but we were with Jesus after all. What better way to visit the Temple?

Jesus was too quiet this time. After we walked inside the walls to the first great court, Jesus stopped and stood still for what seemed to be hours. He was looking at the tables for the doves, the stands with the livestock for sacrifices, tables where people exchanged foreign coins for proper ones. I remember as a child hearing my father and others say to one another that there was more money made in the court of the Temple than a fisherman would see in a lifetime. Jesus was standing beside Peter, that great hairy head turning from side to side as though he, too, were taking stock. The difference was that Peter was smiling. He still believed that we were simply here as part of our observance of Passover.

I, on the other hand, had already seen enough of Jesus' face to know that we were in for something different.

Jesus walked nearer the animals and picked up a length of rope that was left near a stall. He began looping it back and forth, making a whip. Peter was walking with him, nodding his enormous head at people and holding up a hand in greeting, as though these people had some interest in talking to any of us. Then Jesus just walked over to the first stall of livestock and threw down the wooden bar closing in the sheep. Seeing it, I couldn't move. Peter looked around at the sound of the wood on the stone floor and took a step toward Jesus.

"Here, master, let me get that," he said. He didn't know Jesus had thrown it down purposefully.

Jesus didn't say a word, just headed to the next stall full of oxen. When the stall keeper tried to stop him, Jesus began beating the man with the cords, driving him out of the way. The man fell back to the stones, astonished, but no more so than we. Jesus again threw the wooden beam aside that held back the animals and began driving them toward the gate.

The next few minutes were filled with shouting, animals bleating and lowing, dust rising up from the paving stones, pandemonium. Then Jesus walked straight to a table where moneychangers sat with their piles and bags of coins. I still had not moved from where I stood, horrified at the disturbance Jesus was causing, unable to believe what he was doing. The disturbing light-headedness was growing stronger, so that I stood still in the middle of the swirl of animals and men, the sounds of language that should not be heard in the temple, Jesus flailing with the rope and beating anyone who approached him. I was sure I would faint, and I may have blacked out for a moment, for suddenly there was the sound of coins striking the stones, a great cacophony of coins, curses shouted by the merchants, priests yelling for calm. I looked across the open way to see the Roman soldiers in a watchtower from which they could look down over the temple walls at the commotion.

Angry priests, angry merchants, Jesus beating people with the rope, and the Romans were watching. It was a scene difficult to improve upon, though the terrified animals dashing through the crowds managed as they found open gateways and made their escape into the streets around the Temple grounds. I could hear people shouting from beyond the Temple walls now. Looking behind us at the gate, I considered leaving quietly, unnoticed, but I could not leave Jesus, my brother, the others. James was standing with his mouth open, as unmoving as I except for the twitching of his hands and his eyes following Jesus' movements.

That's when I heard Jesus yelling about his father's house and thieves. I had never seen him angry before this, and it was impressive. The priests were yielding, some even looked embarrassed, though most of them were angry, outraged. Meanwhile, the merchants were either chasing the livestock down the adjoining streets or on their knees gathering coins, all too busy to enter a dialogue with Jesus about his motives.

I thought they would kill us all. They would arrest us, beat us, and maybe even crucify us for all I knew. What was the punishment for disrupting the temple? I did not know. The last man who had done it had used an army, and men called him insane. We had no army. The Temple had guards, though, and there were the Romans who did not enjoy disturbances. At the least they would throw us into prison. I thought of my father, of word reaching him that his sons were in a Roman prison.

No one tried to arrest us. I kept watching the faces around us, waiting to see who would think of it. Surely the idea would occur to someone very soon.

Finally, Jesus threw the rope back into the empty oxen stall and walked out of the temple grounds. I was glad to follow. As we walked, Jesus a few steps ahead of the rest of us, we kept looking back to see whether we were being chased by the merchants and ahead to see if the Romans were coming to arrest us. Neither happened.

It was a miracle.

Adriel

God doesn't appear to do very much. At least, I have not witnessed anything that appeared to be the definitive action of God either before or since Jesus' death, and that whole scenario is itself baffling. I think many of the men are right, that John is right, that God is about to change everything, remake human society. It does not happen.

Instead, everything goes on as always. Occasionally there may be some energy, some stray person healed, some disciple killed by other men. The number of people who believe that Jesus was God in human form ebbs and grows.

I followed John and Mary to Ephesus, watched them teach among the people there, watched Mary die.

John didn't speak for a month afterward. He buried her quietly, and I helped him with the grave so that few would know where it was. There were always lunatics attaching themselves to the Way, as they called it, and some of them would be sure to dig her up, worship her bones, use them for talismans, for profit. When followers came asking, John simply told them that Mary had been received by God. He would tell them nothing more. Soon we heard stories of how Mary had been lifted into heaven on clouds, angels attending, Jesus guiding her.

I do not understand the human ability to hold onto such lunacy. The world is flat. Heaven is up. Some humans don't die.

Of course, John does not, at least not so far.

That John lives I do suppose may be an act of God, or the result of mutated genetics. While I see nothing particularly excellent about John's genetic composition, the fact is that neither do I see evidence of God's action. Lacking explanation, I fall back to God and the miraculous, just like the religious freaks do. What eludes my method must be magic.

I see Adi standing by the oak in the yard, her energy casting a glow along the side of the tree and under the leaves. I wonder whether my mind had been open, whether she has heard my thoughts.

"You think of the limits of your sight," she says.

So much for wondering, I think.

"No," she says. "Please do not close your thoughts to me." She watches me for a moment and then lowers her gaze.

"Alright," I say, and though I am not sure why, I allow her my thoughts, as she allows me her own.

You are thinking of Mary.

Yes. More, I am thinking of what I do not understand.

Yes, she thinks.

Theotokus, they call her. *God bearer.*

They explain more than they experience.

Perhaps, I think. *Was it true? Did we see God as one of them?*

Images of light, sound, what John would call the throne of God, flash in her mind.

That is where they think we go, she thinks. *They believe we stand in the presence of God.*

Perhaps some do. You have seen the Presence.

Yes, she thought. *Perhaps I did. I think that I did, but long ago, like a memory that I cannot see...*

It is there, in the matter and energy around us, dancing, I think, then regret the 'dancing'.

No, it is good, dancing, a good image. I feel it as well, know that it is God, but it is not the same as being in the Presence. Why are we not summoned there? Were we ever?

Suddenly she stops and rises a bit, gazing at the others resting in the distance. *I should not share such thoughts with you.*

Why? I have them also. I look around as she is doing. *I imagine that all of them do as well. If not, they are not particularly bright.*

I may have heard her laugh, briefly. I cannot tell, though in her mind is laughter.

It is good to laugh. It keeps us from being the statues they think we are.

Wings. Who has wings?

We both laugh.

I think we all put things in pictures we understand, I offer. *We move through space, so they think we move through the air like birds.*

They think we know more than they do.

We do, sometimes. At least we see different things than they experience.

She is quiet for a moment. *And they see things that we miss.*

Many of the same things, but so differently.

She is quiet. I see brief images of a burning presence in her mind, and she wonders whether she is remembering the presence of God.

The memories are true, aren't they?

I have something like them as well, I say. *They are in a place in my mind that I can almost find. Almost. So much time ago, before Jesus, before this world, I think.*

Perhaps God is no more, she thinks.

She glances at me then away at the others down the street. A few look our way, feeling the strength of our thoughts passing but unable to hear them.

No, God is, I think. *I sense this in everything, flowing, vibrating. Perhaps with Jesus' death God changes.*

I stop, but she stares at me, knowing I do not share my fear. She waits, quiet, as only we who do not die can wait.

Perhaps God allowed himself to die. There, I had said it to another being.

How could that be? If God created death, how can God die? I can tell that though she voices the objection, she does not believe it.

Absence, I think. *If God is absent in person, God is in that sense dead. Perhaps God is trying to lead them, draw them forward. If they are to become what they may become, they had to kill God, kill their ideas of God. They killed their expectation of God, their understanding of God. And God let them do it for their own good, for God's own purpose.*

I turn to look at her. *It is just that it is taking them this long to realize it.*

John

"Of course, I have to help her," I told him, the obstinate arrogant obtuse peeping Tom. Angels, all that power, all that time, and what do they do with it? They watch.

"We also watch," Adriel said, just to further antagonize me, no doubt.

"Also. Also." I wanted to throw my glass at him, but it would only have passed through and made a mess. Still, that would have been something. "As though you do anything else."

"You are only angry about your own reluctance to engage."

"What? My what? Reluctance to engage?" Nothing makes one as angry as when someone else is right. I could feel spittle on my lower lip, but I did not stop. "What about you, what have you engaged with, you simpering shadow of..."

"I AM NOT A SHADOW!"

That stopped us both. An angel shouting will stop most anyone, but that wasn't it. We were both shocked, both he and I, by Adriel's reaction. As we stood still in the following silence, I think we were both shocked as well by the depth of feeling to which our argument had led us.

Not that this was our first argument, of course. Like any couple, we had our share of differences, our range of methods for driving the other over the edge, and we were in some odd fashion a couple, so long had we been acquaintances, friends. No, we had often been angry, glad, and remorseful over the many years. I found that I was, indeed, angry at my own withdrawal, my reluctance to engage as he put it. That was sobering. What was new was the depth of Adriel's vehemence, and I realized that he was at least as dismayed as I by his reaction.

"I am sorry, John." He sounded near to tears, if that were possible. "I am sorry."

"No, my friend. I'm sorry," I said. I walked to the chair and sat down. "You were right, I have become withdrawn, somehow reluctant." I stopped, watching him. I could see him turning, looking out from the house at a tree in the yard.

"That is not it," he said. "There was a shadow."

I could tell he meant there, by the same tree, but I did not understand.

"It was there, watching Sarah, creeping toward her."

"A shadow?" Then I realized the meaning, knew why my words had angered him. "You mean a dark angel was here, seeking her?"

Adriel was still, but I felt peace return between us.

"I banished it," he said. "At least, I hope I have done so. It was more power than I have channeled in many, many years, and it fled. I don't know to where."

We waited for our thoughts, he and I, watching through the window.

"Something is happening, gathering. Growing," he said. "And I don't know what it is."

"Is she safe?" I meant Sarah.

"Adi?"

"Who?" I said. "Did you say Adi?"

"You meant Sarah. Yes, she is safe, though I do not know if others will come. I suppose it could be chance, this one passing by and noticing her, but I think not. If one noticed, if one came, others will also."

I waited, thinking. "Who is Adi?"

He was quiet a moment. "She is watching as well, nearby. She is another like me, but she is wrestling with questions. She has not experienced the Presence in so long, she has begun to wonder whether God may be found."

I understood her feeling. It was still strange to encounter the doubt of angels, or the agnosticism. Once I had thought them an extension of God, but then I also pictured God as a being on a throne. Now I realize the differences between the images we make and the reality of God, or at least I have come to appreciate some of the differences. If angels themselves struggle with such things, how was a man to escape it?

We thought we would see God. That, I think, is finally what we thought. Jesus had come, he had even worked miracles, and we thought we were following him to the coming of a new kingdom, God's throne on earth. There is that throne image again.

We were wrong, of course. Horribly wrong, on the day they crucified Jesus. So far as we had expectations of Jesus being the incarnation of God, they were crucifying God. When we found Jesus alive, on that beach, we began to think that we had not understood. Still, we hoped for the same things as before. We wanted to see God, actual God, with light and thunder, making everything right.

He had told us, though. When Philip said to him, "Show us the Father." And Jesus told us that we already had seen the Father. We had seen everything we were going to see, in him. It did not satisfy, that answer. It still did not.

All of these many years, I have wanted to see God, and I never have. Unless I did see God, on that beach by that fire, and God did not meet my expectations.

Adriel seemed to sense it.

"I told Adi that I think the Presence has changed, that it vibrates all around us now."

He made the water in my glass move, which was always interesting.

"John, do you remember the pool, the one who made me fall into the water at the temple?"

I did. Of course, I did. All of those invalids making their way toward the water, something between poetry and Night of the Living Dead. And all of them being healed, Jesus walking away through the portico, looking back at me through the dust and light.

"There was something of that when the shadow came and I let the power flow from me." He was watching, listening to see if I understood. I did not. "When I let the light fill the yard, most of it came through me in the way it always had, but there was something else, something vibrating in the light. I think it was God."

I thought about that and looked out at the oak tree.

"Is that what it is like?," he asked. "When you pray for someone to be healed, is that what you feel?"

I suddenly felt the breath in my lungs, realized that I had been holding it.

"Sometimes, Adriel," I said, "I don't feel anything at all." I looked at him. "That is how I know for sure that it is God."

Dragons

There is something peaceful and settling about an evening routine. Sometimes I was not sure whether I had completed all of the tasks, brushed my teeth. I might have been remembering the previous night, or the one before that, and I repeated the process to be sure. It was restful, relaxing. I suspect that even without centuries of practice, other people have the same problem remembering.

Brushing teeth, a shower, putting on pajamas. Not that these routines were the same as those I followed a hundred years ago, or a thousand, but the rhythm was the same. It is the rhythm that matters, I decided, reflecting on it. Like tapping out a beat that one knows without thinking, but one that takes its time, does not hurry to the end of the measure.

Sleep, when it came, was deep, at once plunging into darkness.

In the darkness I heard the hooves of horses, horsemen riding, and without opening my eyes I knew them for what they were, the harbingers of destruction and of death that I have seen before, my eyes open, in the waking dreams of my exile on Patmos.

I had not seen them in many years. Their return was not welcome, and I tried to raise myself from the dream, knowing that it was a dream and that I was asleep, but I was held there in that world that is a halfway point between wakeful inattention and sleeping awareness. We pass through our waking days thinking that those moments are reality, but I had come to suspect that our wakeful moments are the fake ones, the symbolic representation of a deeper reality that has no particular form, no particular shape, only thought and purpose, like God.

The hoof beats, like heartbeats, would not brook my inattention, and they grew louder, insisting that I acknowledge them. When I kept my dreaming eyes closed against the sound, it morphed, changing as only the things that are eternal can change in the reality of dreams.

Now I heard a shrieking, a scream, like something ancient and terrifyingly large had been chained, and it was screaming in pain and surprise and hatred. It was the dragon, and I could not keep my eyes closed.

In my dream the deep shining scales of the dragon's hide shone in a darkening sky, slipping like red foam at the edge of the oldest sea in the world. Then it turned and flew, chains gone, moving through the clouds and against the stars, plunging through the darkness with fire arcing like a burning scimitar through the air, flames along its sides, fire flowing like water along the impossibly long curving body and tail of the enormous dragon. In the firelight I saw the earth below it, and sitting unseeing was a woman, unmoving, not knowing what was plunging downward, spiraling toward her and fiery destruction. Then she started, moved, like someone awakening from a reverie, and I saw her looking up at the scales and the teeth and the talons and the flames, and I heard her scream.

In my dream I tried to scream as well, but I could not make the sound. It caught in my throat, and I was paralyzed with terror.

At first, she was Babylon and a whore, and she was nothing more than a symbol in my mind, and I knew that she was true and real but also that she was not true and she was not real, and the dragon could not eat her because she and the dragon were one, two sides of one truth. But then she changed, and she was Rome and Egypt and every kingdom that ever came and fell, and that the dragon was as relentless as time. And it did not matter to me, did not matter in the least, because I had seen the kingdoms rise and fall and rise and there was always another, greater or smaller or kinder or more evil, but always the same, and it made no difference to me.

She turned, but her face was now different, and her clothes were different, and I knew her. She was Mary, her blue and white robes dancing with the deep orange red of the dragon's breath, and I was afraid, and when she screamed I was running to her.

Except now I saw that the flames reflected on her brilliant robes were not near her, not pursuing her, but rather they were near me, the heat growing on the back of my neck, sudden and astonishing, and I could not breathe. Gasping, I made a sound, then warm air filled my lungs and I did scream, and it seemed that I heard an angel's voice calling my name.

Adriel was standing beside the bed when I awoke. I was wet with sweat, still terrified by what I had seen.

"You were screaming," he said. "So I woke you."

There was something in his voice that told me he knew why I was screaming, but that he didn't want to say so.

"The dreams are back," I said. He did already know, but it was something to say.

"At least this time they are only dreams."

I thought about this. He was right. All those many years before, the images had come as visions, my waking eyes unable to see what was in the world around me. I had lain stupefied on the ground, my mind full of images that I could not touch, could not control, and could not turn away from.

I didn't know whether the images I saw were real. I thought that whether or not they were real, they were true, which was more frightening. I still did not know whether I should have written them down, whether I did justice to the visions in the way that I recorded them. The images lost something in the telling, became more flat, more linear than they had been in seeing, but parchment is flat and there are only the lines of words to record the sights and sounds of worlds and of wars.

"It has changed," I said, still lying in my bed. Adriel was beside me like a nursemaid to a sick or frightened child.

"I saw," he said to me, and I was relieved, not affronted.

"Mary," I said.

"And the dragon."

"I don't even know what was happening. Who the dragon was."

I am quiet for a time, eyes closed, but not sleeping. My pajamas are damp.

"Why don't you take a warm shower?" Adriel asked. "It may help you to return to sleep."

For once, he may have a good idea, I thought. I got up and slipped into the shower, letting the water run over my head, trying not to think. When I returned there were fresh sheets on my bed, again a first. Adriel had sometimes produced tea, but never anything more domestic.

"Thank you," I said, but he was not there, not to my senses anyway.

I lay down on the clean cotton, smoother and so much softer than the stones of Patmos, and I slept.

John

Jesus was at home, they said. Everyone said, or must have, for the crowds came. It was a simple Jewish home near Capernaum, filled and overflowing with people coming to hear Jesus talk. Normally the air would flow through his house, keeping it pleasant, but there were too many people for that.

Later I would hear that Jesus had no home. People would quote that saying about foxes having holes but the son of man having no home, and preachers would make great points discussing the power of God in this itinerant man with no home. A respectable Jewish man, near thirty years old, trained in his father's profession, and he had no home, they would say. Mark even told them plainly, wrote in his Gospel, telling of Jesus being at home, but that was not plain enough. Had I realized it sooner, I would have added a passage in my Gospel telling of how the wind blew in through the open windows, how the tables and doors were built from wood he found in old boats, weathered and smooth. His chairs never creaked, even with the weight of a man like Peter, but the toys were the best. The children were always peeping around to find new ones. Jesus would stash little wooden puzzles and carved animals, birds with moving wings, tiny boats that would float and sail in the breeze. On any given day the children would quietly sneak around the house and find them all, grab them with a squeal of laughter and run away screaming their thanks.

It was a beautiful home, peaceful, but not on that day, not with so many people. They were respectful, quiet, but the day was already hot enough without them. I was near a window, able to gain a moment's breath when the breeze wound through the people standing outside and brought a moment's coolness from the sea. They were so quiet as he spoke that I was surprised each time I looked out to see them standing there.

Then came those four men, carrying another man on a pallet. They were trotting up the pathway, even with their friend carried between them. He did not appear to weigh much. No one gave way, no path opened for them. When they called for Jesus they were quickly shushed, and looking I saw that Jesus ignored them. It was not like him, and I knew he heard. A word from him and they would have made a path, ushered the men inside, but he continued his talk as though they had not come.

When I looked back to where they had been, they were gone. I supposed that they had gone around to the other side. Andrew was standing near the door. He saw my eyes looking for them, and when I looked his way he simply pointed up. I shook my head, not understanding, but he just pointed and looked toward the ceiling. That was when I understood they had gone up onto the roof of Jesus' house, an odd place to go in the heat of the day, but I supposed they needed to take the man somewhere that the crowd would not trample him when they left.

That's when I saw the dirt falling from the ceiling, only a little at first, then more dust and bits of the straw made into the roof. They were tearing it open, in the center above the great room, and dust was falling on the crowd and on Jesus as he sat. After a few minutes Jesus stopped talking, and the only sound was the noise of the roof being pulled back. The gall, I thought. Peter was livid. From where I was standing I saw his face was the color of pomegranate seeds. He stood, near Jesus, and I knew that if Peter made it to the roof there would be five invalids up there instead of one. What a fine show that would be.

Jesus reached out and touched Peter's arm, stopping him, waving him back down into his place. Then he waved the crowd back, indicating that they leave an opening on the floor beneath the new opening in the roof. He was amazingly calm for a man whose roof was being destroyed. The men performing the damage stopped, realizing that they had become the focus of the entire crowd, but they quickly resumed their work. Once the hole was big enough I thought they would call down to Jesus, perhaps asking him to help their friend, but they continued until the hole was as long as the man's pallet.

That's when they picked him up, pallet and all, and began lowering him into the house. I don't know where they found the ropes, perhaps they already had them or one of them ran down to a boat at the shore. The man was terrified, swinging down in the sunlight and dust. When the pallet was low enough, Peter grabbed it and steadied it, indicating with his hand that they should keep lowering him, as though it was Peter's idea to begin with. Like the rest of the crowd, I was fascinated by the slow, swinging descent of the man on the pallet.

I looked past Peter to see Jesus' reaction, to see whether I could gauge anything of what would happen by the expression on his face. Jesus wasn't watching the man's descent at all. He was not looking at the damage to his roof, the mess on the floor, the faces of the men peering down from the rooftop through the new opening in the ceiling. Jesus was watching some men who were sitting, arms crossed, in the chairs he had made. Their robes were clean, though their fingers were a little stained, and they sat watching Peter as though he were a trained monkey dancing for coins. While they watched Peter, Jesus was watching them, and I could not make out the emotion on his face.

In a few minutes, the crippled man was down, lying on his traveling pallet at Jesus' feet, and the crowd who had been murmuring, talking among themselves about the spectacle unfolding in the house, fell silent. Slowly, with evident embarrassment, the crippled man reached out toward Jesus, stopping short of touching him.

"Jesus," he said. "Please."

That was all. Please. Jesus finally dropped his gaze from the scribes and looked down at the man. The scribes were looking down as well, but askance, as though the man were offensive to them. Jesus stood up, beside the pallet, and looking down at the man began to smile. I had not seen him smile quite that way before. There was something in it of a boy who has thought up a new way to steal figs.

"My son," he said. "Your sins are forgiven."

I was confused, which was nothing in comparison to Peter who was staring at Jesus as though he had spoken a foreign language. Everyone began looking around, Peter at Jesus, I at the crippled man, he at Jesus, but Jesus was staring at the scribes who were looking at one another with eyebrows and lips like overturned bowls.

"Does this offend you?" asked Jesus, looking at them. "Speak up, then. Don't sit there wondering to yourselves who I am to say that this man's sins are forgiven."

The effect was almost comical, their eyebrows and lips only pushing upward to greater curves. No one was moving, suddenly realizing that Jesus had started a new show, attacking these fat scribes. I was worried though. I was a fisherman, sure, but I and everyone in the house knew that the temple was where sins were forgiven. Jesus was going off on some rant, and there we were with a standing room crowd, a hole in the roof and a cripple lying on the floor.

"Which is easier, to say 'Your sins are forgiven' or 'Stand and walk'?" Jesus was staring at the men so hard that two of them turned to see if there was a way clear to the door. There was not.

"So that you may know that the Son of Man has authority to forgive sins," he went on, turning his face back to the crippled man, "I say to you, rise up, take your bed, and walk."

I felt something like a breeze in the room, as though lightning had struck somewhere just outside and the hairs of our beards were jolted. Peter, no stranger now to such things, turned his head to stare at the man's legs, watching to see if he could catch the change, mark the moment when reality shifted. I don't know if he managed it, but the man began slowly to look down himself, like Peter, at his legs. He lifted his blanket and sat up on the pallet. Staring in disbelief himself, the man began to move his legs to the side of the pallet, and he stood.

There were murmurings all through the crowd, the fat scribes looking like they would die any moment from the shock. The man who had been crippled began dismantling his wooden pallet, gathering it under his arm. I looked at Jesus, but he was staring once again at the scribes.

"Go home," Jesus said, and the man thought that Jesus was speaking to him. I knew that he was really talking to the scribes, and they understood it quite clearly. As the healed man began making his way through the opening forming in the crowd, it was the fat scribes who followed him, widening the pathway for those who would in turn come after them.

Jesus sat again as the crowd made their way, following the former cripple and the scribes into the yard and along the path toward town. The show was clearly over. A few of the youth stayed, gathering the materials that had fallen from the ceiling and heading up onto the roof to help repair the damage. The man's friends had already left, yelling and dancing with their friend, though they called out their thanks to Jesus.

Jesus, clearly tired, just sat in a chair of his own making and stared at the floor where the man had lain. He was quiet, unspeaking, not moving. Peter called his name quietly, reached out to touch his arm, but Jesus was perfectly still, withdrawn. I went and drew some wine, brought it to Jesus. He sat motionless for a minute, then looked down at the wine in my hand. He took it, reached up and put his other hand on my shoulder so that I knelt beside his chair.

"Did you see?" he asked me.

"I saw," I said. "He walked!"

He sipped the wine, turned to look at me. "No, not him. The scribes, did you see them, see their faces?"

"Yes, I saw them." I did not know what he meant. "They, well, they are scribes."

"Yes," he said. "And they will write, and what they write will last. In days to come, whose story will people believe?"

In days to come, I would remember this moment with Jesus. He was telling me what to do, but I did not know it at the time. I was a fisherman, or had been. It had never occurred to me that I would be anything else. Now I knew that things were changing, following Jesus, trying to learn what he was trying to tell us, but still I was a fisherman and thought I would remain one.

My father had told us stories, though, and he had seen to it that we learned to read, my brother and I. Fisherman who read. It was enough to get us in trouble with some of the other boys. While they were playing, we had to go to our lessons. And I did love the stories. Most of them were from the scripture, but some were not. There were stories of distant lands, of other peoples, of other gods. Not that my father allowed the possibility of any but the one God being God, but he would let us hear the stories. He liked them as well, the strangeness of them, the power of a story to change how we viewed the world.

Sometimes we made them up when we were fishing. One of my father's servants came from a land beyond Egypt, though I had not thought there was anything beyond Egypt. He would tell us the stories that he had learned as a boy, stories of animals talking and of the earth being made. My father would always say that these were the stories of children who knew little of God, but he would listen to them.

In the end, the boats were gone and the fish did not matter, but all of those words remained.

Adriel

"Well, you beat out the scribes, I'd say."

John is still brooding, pretending that he is watching the squirrels again.

"Are you listening?"

"I can hear you, if that is what you mean."

"John, really. What are you on about? You have your memories of the events, of what he did." I sit in the other chair on the deck, and I also pretend to watch the squirrels, or rather I watch them and pretend to be interested. It is not difficult. Squirrels are entertaining.

"Look what they've done with it," he says at last. "It may have been better that I said nothing at all."

"They would still have had the other three stories. You added clarity, opened a new way of understanding."

"Did I?" he asked. "Because I'm not sure that I understand it. I was there, I wrote it, and I'm not sure that I understand it."

He stands and walks to the deck rail. The squirrels take no notice and keep raiding the feeder for seeds.

"I gave them the story, and I gave them a way of thinking about it, but they've made it a system, a set of rules. I don't recognize what they've made it. They go around preaching things that he never taught, never suggested."

"Of course," I say. "They have made of it what they wanted. Of course they have, it is what they do with stories."

"That's just it, isn't it? They treat it like it was a story, something that happened long ago in a kingdom far way…"

"Well, that part is right."

"You're not helping," he says.

I think for a moment. "No, I don't suppose I am." I too rise and move across the deck. "Still, he asked you to write it. And you did."

From next door I could sense Sarah getting ready for sleep, hear the movements of washing and evening rituals in her house.

"Why don't you do something, John," I say. "Act on something. All of this reflection is driving you around the bend."

"Isn't that what your lot do? Sit and watch and reflect?"

"More watching than reflecting, but yes. See what a great help it is? That's why I'm suggesting that you focus on something other than the past. Go help the girl."

Though I am not visible at the moment, he understands my meaning. He had been thinking of it as well, I believe, though his thoughts are more clouded to me than usual.

"Sarah, you mean."

"Yes," I say. "She could use your help. You can make her life better." He says nothing, and I hear the thoughts. "You doubt that you can."

"I don't know that it will work," he says. "And I have never done any of it anyway. The power is not from me, but I don't know where it comes from any more."

"It always has worked," I say, and it is true. Whenever John has prayed for the benefit of someone, it has always come to pass.

"Well, that may be," he says. "I think the problem for me is that I no longer know why. I don't know why the prayers work. I can't sense anything. I don't even know why it is that I am still alive, except that Jesus wanted it so."

I wait. It is rare, over all this time, to get such an admission from John.

"Are you sure that is why you are still alive?" I ask. He stands there staring over the rail, but I doubt he even notices the squirrels.

"No," he says. "I am not even sure of that anymore."

Sarah

I could see him on the back deck, and he was definitely talking to himself. I swore that I had seen that old man look around like there was someone else there with him, but there wasn't, at least not anybody I could see. Mom told me long ago that she had seen him talking to people who weren't there, but she had just thought he was eccentric.

Maybe he missed someone, a wife. I didn't remember whether he'd ever been married, or had children, or really anything, come to think of it. I never asked. I just talked about my mother. He must have thought I was such a bore.

That was unless the old man had turned into some kind of deviant. Maybe he was over there talking to shadows in his brain about how to kill me in my sleep.

I really had to stop thinking this stuff.

Maybe I should start walking, I thought. I felt so tired. Walking would be good for me, I thought, except of course that I felt so tired.

This house was so empty. Everywhere I looked I saw my mother, remembered her. I thought sometimes that she was just in the other room, or sleeping, or making something in the kitchen. A couple of times I called her.

I supposed that was normal. And eventually I'd have to see about her things, her clothes. Still, for the time being, it was nice to think that she might be in the kitchen, or tending her flowers in the yard.

She must have known more about Mr. Zebedee. He seemed very nice, and my mother always seemed to like him. I didn't even know how old he was. He seemed old the first time I ever saw him, and that was long ago.

Still, he was talking to himself. And I knew what they said about talking to yourself.

What would Mom have thought about what I saw under the oak tree the other night? She either would have thought that I made it up entirely, which would not have reflected well on me, or that some freaks were doing something bizarre underneath the tree in the yard, which would have been just as bad. Worse, really.

What did that mean, when the best case was that I was seeing things?

I saw what I saw. It was still dark, but I saw something glide to the oak, and it was intensely interested in me, I was sure of that much. And I did not want that thing any closer, whatever it was, and I was also sure of that much. I just didn't know what it was, and I didn't know where the light came from that chased it away.

Whatever those things were, they were intelligent. I could feel it. And they both knew me—I could feel that as well. And I was pretty sure there was at least a third one, watching, maybe accompanying the one that brought the light.

Only it wasn't like a flashlight or a flare. It just was light, in itself, energy that lit up the yard and that scared whatever dark thing was creeping along through the yard. Creeping toward me.

I thought I was crazy.

If I had to say what lit up the yard, I would have said it was an angel. Only, I wasn't sure that angels existed, and if they did and if this was one, then they were not like in the movies or in paintings. This thing did not have wings, and it did not look human. It looked like energy moving through the yard, only it seemed intelligent, and I could sense thought, its thoughts, which sounds crazy. And its thoughts created the light, or maybe the light was creating the thoughts. Maybe they were one and the same, the light and the thoughts. Wasn't that what thought was, really, a kind of energy?

And if the light was an angel, then what was the dark thing? And why was it interested in my mother's house? Or was it interested in me?

No, that's just scary. But the light one was interested in me as well. They both were, I just knew it somehow, and the light was strong enough to drive off the darkness.

Maybe that was something to hold onto. And maybe I could find a way to communicate with it, because somehow I could feel that it wasn't gone, that it was still nearby. And I thought I knew where it stayed—Mr. Zebedee's house. Somehow I thought he knew about them, knew what they were. Maybe old man Zebedee had seen them, too. Maybe that was why he was over there talking to himself.

What if he wasn't talking to someone who wasn't there? What if he was talking to somebody who was there? Which gave me a plan. I was going to find a way to ask him what he thought about angels, and then I'd know.

Whether he said anything or not, I'd know.

Adi

It is like a glow from within the homes of some of them. And from some there is darkness, or perhaps the light has left like water, drawing the shadow after it.

Rooftop, I think, and I am there. *Tree,* and I am there, the birds startling and fluttering up, then settling to my presence. Why am I sitting in a tree? Surely there are more interesting things to do. Countless centuries, and I sit in trees and on rooftops and watch. There is a problem with my imagination.

In the distance there are others, sitting, moving, appearing to float, all watching something.

Perhaps there is a problem with all of my kind.

At least Adriel is engaged with something, though I suppose that is only first hand watching, watching without distance, which leads to engagement of some kind, unless one remains unseen.

One could watch monkeys, I suppose. They would entertain, but there is a difference. The humans are different, accomplish more, destroy more, do more, a wider range of thought and action. Soon their devices will find us, define us against the noise of the universe, energy fluctuations that demand their attention and definition.

Then where will we sit and watch?

John

"I'm going out to prune the rose bushes," I said. I didn't really want to prune them, but it seemed like a good way to keep my mind occupied. One does not prune roses inattentively.

"Fine," said Adriel. "Need any help?"

"Sure, you can bring the wheel barrow to put the cuttings in."

"Very funny."

I could hear him turning the page of the newspaper I left on the table, as though he needed to turn the page to read it. "Why don't I just summon fire from the heavens to destroy the things, right in plain view. Lo, the roses were evil in my sight, something like that. Ought to stimulate some old time religion, don't you think?"

"Mmm. Might at that. Full scale revival. Foil hat brigade turning out to prove you are a UFO."

"And they would be right."

"I suppose they would," I agreed, and I headed off to the garage to get the shears and the wheelbarrow. I had been at the rose bush less than five minutes when I heard the rustle of younger feet slipping up behind me.

"Good morning, Mr. Zebedee."

"Sarah!" I said, actually glad to hear her voice. She was far fresher company than Adriel. "How are you doing, young lady?"

"Fine, thanks. What are you doing? There aren't any roses yet, are there?"

"No. Just cutting the bush back. It should make it grow better." I took a look at the unruly rose in front of me. "Hopefully," I added.

Sarah was dutifully staring at the plant, but it was clear that she was barely focusing. I just waited. Some things have their own rhythm, their own time, and often trying to spur people on when they wanted to talk about something only backfired. I often hoped people would keep their problems to themselves, but not in this case.

"My mother," she started. "She was the one who kept the flowers going. I never really paid attention to that. I should have learned more from her."

I kept my attention on the rose. "I suspect you learned plenty of things that mattered. You can get what you need about roses from a book. Or some old man like me."

I clipped a few canes back, taking my time both for the sake of Sarah's thoughts and for the thorns.

"Mr. Zebedee?"

"Yes, Sarah?" I went on slowly examining and clipping the canes of the rose, one by one, waiting.

"Can I ask you something?"

Since it was clearly worrying her, I refrained from correcting her with my usual 'You may' and wondered when I became so pedantic. I didn't think that I had always been. "Of course," I said, hoping I sounded reasonable and kind.

"Well, you know how the Bible talks about angels?" she asked.

I did not tell her that the Bible did not talk about anything. People often talked, books seldom did, except in stories, and people who talked about the Bible most often talked about things that were not there. If the scripture contained everything that people said, I would need to use my wheelbarrow to carry it around. At that point, it probably wouldn't even serve to fertilize a rosebush.

"Sure," I offered. It was more kind and succinct than my thoughts.

"Well, what do you think?"

"About angels?" I said, suspecting that I was beginning to get into more trouble than I had foreseen. That was usually the kind of trouble that found me.

She hesitated, the way people hesitate when they are trying to appear casually interested in a topic but have already gone too far to manage it. "Do you think they're real? Do you think people can see them?" she asked.

"Well," I started, only to be cut off.

"Because I think I saw one. Out my window. Beside this oak tree."

I glanced around at her with interest, hoping not to convey any sense of 'you are crazy' with my expression.

"Right here?" I asked. Perhaps I could have been more helpful, but it seemed a reasonable response.

"Yes."

"Well, tell me about it," I said. I tried to decide whether continuing with the pruning or stopping would be more helpful. Seeing her expression, I put the shears down.

"It was still dark, but suddenly there was light streaming in through my window. So, I went to take a look. And I saw a figure standing here, like a man but at the same time not like a man. It was, well, glowing is the wrong word. It was as though it sent the light out from itself, radiated the light. I could tell that there was a figure of some kind at the center, and again it was like a man but not a man."

It had been Adriel, I was sure. He had told me that he had dispelled some kind of creature, but he did not tell me about the light show. I picked up the shears again and trimmed the rose while she found her way through the memory.

"There was something else," she went on, "something that was also a little like a person, except that it was dark, darker than the other shadows, which was strange. I had the feeling…I thought it was interested in me, that this thing had been watching my window when I looked out and saw it. I know that sounds crazy, but that is what I felt, or thought I sensed. And this bright light filled everything else. It was like sunlight, except it was, well, person shaped, like someone made a person into a light, like the light was coming from it or him or whatever."

We were both quiet for a moment. I knew that Sarah was waiting to see whether I would take her seriously.

"And the dark thing?" I asked. "What became of it?"

"It left, like the light frightened it," she answered. She chewed her lip for a moment and studied me. "Do you think I'm crazy?"

"No, I don't think you are crazy, Sarah." I considered telling her a partial lie, planting doubt so that she would simply start to believe that her imagination had gotten too wired up, but I did not want to be dishonest with her. At the same time, I did not want to be laying the groundwork for my own downfall.

"You know what it was, don't you?" She was staring at me. "What was it, Mr. Zebedee?"

"You may have seen an angel," I said simply. There, no one can argue with that. She was still watching me intently.

"And the other thing, the shadow?" she asked.

"Sarah," I began. "If there are angels, then it would stand to reason either that there were other things as well, or perhaps that not all angelic beings were of the same sort."

She shuffled her feet and then knelt down beside me, studying the rose plant.

"So, you mean angels are real," she said. "And you mean that demons are real, too?"

Well, there was no getting the cork back in this one, I thought. Perhaps it was better not to try, even if it were possible to explain it all away in some other fashion.

"Sarah, what do you know about demons?" I asked. "Or, wait, to put it another way, what ideas about demons have you heard or think that other people think?"

"I don't know. They're evil, right? I mean, there is such a hodgepodge of ideas out there. Devils with horns, possession and exorcisms, things like that?" She was blushing a little.

"Evil, well, that is a difficult subject to define, really. Some would take evil to be the opposite of good, and they would view darkness as the opposite of light."

"So?"

"I don't think it is that simple. I don't think it is black and white, light and dark. And no, I don't think we need to go looking for horns. Or thorns," I added, seeing that I had pricked my finger just enough to draw a drop of blood.

Sarah actually chuckled, just a little. She didn't see that when I wiped the blood away, the thorn prick was already closed.

"I think I may know more about rosebushes than I know about angels and demons," she said. "So, you're saying it's not like Hollywood?"

"Well, they may have their share of demons there, but no, not like in the movies," I said. "Probably not like in the church, either."

"What do you mean?"

"Suppose we say there are other beings, around us, in this same space and time but usually not visible to us. Encountering such a being could be unsettling, hard to describe. Wouldn't you say?"

Sarah had picked up one of the cut rose canes and was holding it, turning it carefully in her fingers.

"Sure," she agreed.

"Once upon a time," I said.

"What?"

"Once upon a time, Sarah. A story. A fable. That is one response we humans have always used to help understand the unknown, the frightening, the powerful things that surround us and make us. Angels and demons are part of that—the popular ideas of such beings come from the stories told to help to explain them, to help to prepare the listeners for such experiences. It doesn't mean that the details of the stories are right, but rather that the meanings of them might be."

She picked up a few of the cuttings and placed them in the wheelbarrow for me.

"Of course, some of the details just come from the late show," I added. "Terrifying, some of those movies. And I've only read one Stephen King novel, but it stays with me."

Sarah laughed a little. It is amazing, but one can accomplish more with humor than with force.

"So no horns?"

"No," I said. "Probably no horns."

"But dangerous?"

I looked at her. "Yes, Sarah. Dangerous. Anything with control of that much energy is dangerous."

"So what I saw, that could that have been real?"

"It could have been natural phenomena. Lightning and shadows," I said. "If you would like to think so. Or it could have been actual beings, what we call angels or demons. Either way, it means that you saw something real. It just leaves the question as to what."

She pushed her hair behind her ears, picked up another cutting.

"But I didn't just see it. I felt it as well," she said.

"Prickles you mean? Hairs standing on end?" I knew the answer, though.

"No," she said. "Not that. Not electricity, at least not till the very end. I felt, well, emotions."

"You felt emotional?" I asked her. I was worried that this was not the answer either.

"No, not emotional. Emotions. Feelings, like, something like hatred and a deep wanting all mixed together. Then there was anger, when the light began, and fear from the dark thing. That was the oddest thing. It was not what I thought when I saw it, but it is what I felt." She turned the rose cutting, touched her finger to a thorn and pressed just enough to push the skin inward. "I think I felt what they were feeling."

I waited till she raised her face to look at me. "Sort of leaves out the lightning explanation, doesn't it?" I said.

Sarah smiled as a few tears found their way down her face. I turned back to snipping off some more of the rose canes, trying to maintain an appearance of normal conversation should anyone be watching. Routine things are almost as effective as humor for handling difficult moments. That is part of the reason that tea is such a successful drink. It's a beverage and a ritual, all in one, but the ritual is simple enough that anyone can perform it. All of the best rituals are. Communion, for example. No need for robes and candles, just wine and bread.

"Yes, Sarah, such things are real. And you are not crazy. But if you tell anyone, either they will think you crazy or they already are."

Sarah thought about that for a moment.

"So," she said. "Does that make you crazy?"

I nodded. "I suppose so. At least there are plenty who would say so, plenty more who have said so."

"Really? People have said that about you?"

I put down the pruning shears. "Ever read the book of Revelation?"

"What?"

"Never mind," I said. "Old joke."

I stood up and tried to stretch the soreness from my back. At my age, pruning roses is not as easy as it looks.

"Let's carry these canes to the brush pile at the back, and we'll think about what to do." I gave her the pruning shears and took the handles of the wheelbarrow. "Come on."

"What do you mean, what to do? Do you think we need to do something?" She thought about it for a few steps, going around the end of the house. "You think those things will come back?"

I kept walking till we reached the brush pile and dumped the barrow onto it. I was really trying to decide how to tell her.

"Come up here to the back deck, Sarah. I'll get us something to drink and we'll talk about it. Just have a seat there."

Sarah looked at the chairs and settled on one that rocked. That was good. The motion would settle her down. When I reached the kitchen Adriel was pouring ginger ale into some glasses.

"I was thinking about tea," I said.

"No, you were thinking about that girl, and about how stupid I was to let her see."

"You're not stupid," I said. Actually, I was worried enough about Sarah that I was telling the truth. I didn't think Adriel was stupid, never had, not in all of these years.

"Thank you," he said. "Here, take this to her. She needs some sugar back in her system, but if you give her caffeine right now her head might explode."

I stood there another moment, staring at the drinks.

"What are we going to do?" he asked.

"I think we better make an introduction, don't you?"

"You mean let her see me?"

"She's already done that. I think you impressed her, to tell the truth. Maybe meeting you will bring it down a notch." I thought about the scene she described. "Was it as she said?"

Adriel shifted, shimmered closer to the window to see her, though he certainly did not need a glass pane to see through. Odd, sometimes, the human behaviors in him.

"It was," he said.

"The other, the shadow, it was watching her?"

"I was not certain, but now I am. If she felt his hatred, then yes, it was directed at her."

I stood there for a moment, feeling the glasses in my hands grow a bit cooler. "Did you impress it enough to keep it away?"

"They never stay away, not more than for a time or a season." He focused on me. "You know that. They always return."

I nodded. I could feel the condensation beginning to form on the glasses.

"We better give her something to hold onto," I said. "Would you mind to bring one out?"

Adriel lingered a moment, then it seemed he was gone. When I looked down I saw I was holding it already, a thin but strong leather necklace as was popular with the young, and at the end was a small piece of wood, smooth, a simple hole formed through which the leather passed. I let it hang from my fingers as I took the drinks back to the deck where Sarah was still rocking.

"Here you go. I hope you like ginger ale," I said.

"Thank you, yes. I love it."

"And this is for you," I said, holding out the necklace. "I'd like you to wear it."

"It's pretty, thank you." She studied the charm for any markings or designs, but there were none. "Simple design, just a piece of wood, but it is beautiful."

I looked at it with her.

"Yes," I said. "A small piece of wood, but it is very old."

She put it around her neck and held the wooden charm in her hand. "It feels warm."

I wondered if she could actually feel it, or if it was simply that wood usually felt warmer than metal.

"Old, you say?"

"I will tell you what it is. You may or may not believe me, but it makes no difference. Soon enough I think that you will, and whether we believe or not has no effect on its power."

"Power?" She looked at me, tilting her head but with eyes open wide.

"This is a piece of the cross." I waited, sipping ginger ale, for the reaction.

"The cross," she repeated. She held it up closer to her face, as though proximity would yield confirmation. "You mean, as in Jesus."

"Yes," I said. "What they call the true cross. This is a small piece." After a moment, I added, "There are not many in the world. Not nearly so many as a tour of the cathedrals of the world might make you think. Keep it safe. Wear it, and they will hesitate to come near you, the dark ones anyway."

She was still staring at it, trying to work out whether it was true, whether I was some sort of religious freak. I supposed that I might be the one true religious freak walking on the earth after all.

"Take a sip of your ginger ale. All of this is a lot to process, and we don't want you sinking on us," I said. "Besides, there is someone I want you to meet."

She sipped her drink, looking at me over the rim of the glass. "There is?"

"Well, actually, you already met, in a manner of speaking. But I feel that an introduction is in order."

"OK," she said, glancing around. I hoped that she would trust me enough not to bolt before she had seen him, or afterward from fright.

"Adriel," I said.

"What?" Sarah asked.

"Adriel," he said. "It is my name, Sarah, and it is very good to meet you." Adriel shimmered into sight near her chair.

To Sarah's great credit, she did not drop her glass. She sat perfectly still, holding her glass in one hand, the wooden charm on the necklace in her other hand, only her eyes widening and shifting to me and back to Adriel.

"You are quite right," Adriel continued, his voice set at angelic conversational, much less imposing than angelic evangelistic. "I was very angry, though I did not mean to become visible to you at the time. I meant only to drive the other away."

"You are real," she said. "A real, well, person."

Adriel seemed to think about the statement for a moment. "Well, yes. I am a real person, as you say."

"Oh, my God."

"Let us hope God is with us," Adriel said, "but I am not God."

"You're…an angel?" she asked. I was sure that I heard her mutter something else as well.

Adriel was gathering himself for a reply, but I was uncertain where he might take her.

"Your first idea may be the best, Sarah," I said. "Think of Adriel as a person, one with very different attributes and energies than you or I. That may be more helpful than picking up all the baggage that goes with the word 'angel'."

"A person," she said. "A person who can be invisible, and who can drive off those, those things,"

"Yes," said Adriel.

"I'm seeing an angel," she said.

"Yes," replied Adriel. "And that is part of the problem we face."

"I don't understand," she said. Adriel was watching her, but I knew he was waiting for me.

"Sarah, if Adriel is real, then so was that other being you saw, the one you felt projecting hatred toward you."

"Oh," she said. Again she muttered something else, but I did not catch it.

"Don't worry," I quickly added. "Two things. First, Adriel is nearby, and he is not the only one of his kind."

Sarah looked around as though expecting to see more angels materializing.

"Second, that charm you are holding is not simply piece of wood, nor is it simply a remembrance or a relic. Well, it is, but something altered it long ago. There is power in it, power coming from it. The dark ones will not be willing to approach you while you wear it, or anyone near you."

I thought about her illness, but that was another problem for another time. Sufficient unto the day.

"Are they after us both?" she asked. "Do they come here as well?" She seemed not to know quite how to react to all of this information.

"Adriel?"

"I only sensed an interest in you, Sarah. They know of us, but they do not seek to approach John or me. I do not know why. What he tells you about the wood is correct. It maintains the form of wood, but it is no longer simply wood. The substance of it has been touched by power, great power. Such power always changes what it touches. It always leaves a mark, a trace. For my kind, such a thing glows with power. It is difficult to conceal."

Sarah looked closely at the brown object, twirling it slowly on the leather necklace.

"How did you get a piece of wood from the cross?" she asked.

I sat for a moment, trying to think of what story to tell. There were several that had worked from time to time, though the one about obtaining a holy relic from a hermit in a cave didn't carry the panache it once had.

"He bought it at a yard sale," said Adriel. I lost my temper at once.

"Dammit, Adriel, you know good and well I did not get it from a yard sale!" I was angry, quite suddenly and without meaning to be. All this time together, he knew exactly what buttons to push.

"Honestly, he makes this stuff up," I said to Sarah. She sat with the piece of the cross in one hand. "Adriel, you'll have the girl thinking it is just a trinket from a caravan at the county fair."

"Caravan?" Adriel said.

"No," said Sarah. I looked at her. "No, I don't think it is a trinket, or from caravan or whatever."

I realized that I was standing up and that some of my ginger ale had sloshed out. Adriel seemed amused. Sarah actually started to snicker and then stopped herself with a hand across her mouth. Then I saw that Adriel had merely lifted the foreboding from her mind by his teasing.

"I think it is what you said it is," she continued.

"Well," I said. And then I added, "Good." I was still trying to work out how I lost my temper. After a moment, I thought to ask, "Why?"

"Because of him, mostly." She pointed at Adriel.

I couldn't say anything to that. I knew I would start cursing again.

"I mean, not what he said, but what he, well, is. You didn't get him at a yard sale, or at the county fair," she said. "He proves a lot. Or if he doesn't prove anything, at least it means the ideas are not crazy. He exists, other beings exist, beings like him. So, thinking this piece of wood could have come from the actual cross is not so crazy anymore."

I stared at her. I was amazed at her, still angry with Adriel. "Maybe I should take him to a yard sale," I said.

"I'm not a vase," Adriel said.

"That still doesn't tell me where you got it, though," said Sarah.

"It's been kept safe," I told her. "A piece of the cross, the beam his hands..." I faltered, stood still, and the memory pressed into my mind. A hot afternoon, dark clouds across the sky, and him breathing, hanging up there forever it seemed. A hand touched my shoulder, and for a moment I thought it was Mary, but it was Sarah.

"John," Adriel said, to bring me back, and I remembered where I was, remembered when I was. I don't know how long I had been lost in the memory.

"It's been kept safe all these years," I said, sitting down again. "I'm sorry. Sometimes I let the thoughts overtake me." I took a sip of my drink.

"Sometimes we use a small piece as a protection, or a reminder, a talisman if you like," said Adriel. "Somehow the power of that event transformed this wood, changed what he touched."

"I don't understand it," I said. "And you and I can't see it, but to Adriel, it glows."

Sarah looked at Adriel for confirmation.

"Glow. That may not be the right word, but it is about as close as we can get, I think. It emits power, like radiation. I can see it, feel it," he said. "So can the others."

Sarah was now cradling it in her hand.

"Radiates," she said. Adriel and I look at one another.

"Yes, come to think of it, that may be a better word. Put it on," Adriel said. "It will help to protect you."

She put the necklace on, again took up the wood in her hand and looked at it.

"Thank you," she said, to us both I think.

"You are welcome," I said. "If you see or feel anything else, let us know. I don't know if there is anyone else you want to tell, but I would recommend keeping these things to yourself. I'll leave that to you to decide."

"And your dreams," said Adriel. "Tell us of your dreams, if there are any, for good or bad, if they touch on these things."

She looked at him for a minute, her eyes moving around to try to focus on the shifting light that made his form. I had no idea what she was thinking, but I knew that Adriel did.

"I will," she said."

Sarah walked to the edge of the deck, took a step down toward the ground and looked back at me. I waited, wondering where her thoughts had gone. Adriel already knew, I could tell.

"You are John Zebedee?" she asked me.

"That is as good a name as any to know me by," I answered.

"Wasn't John one of the disciples? And wasn't his father named Zebedee?"

I was surprised.

"Zebedee. Yes, that was his name," I told her.

Sarah looked off at the trees and the birds for a moment, and then back down at the necklace she was wearing.

"Ok, then, Mr. John Zebedee. Thank you very much." She turned back to Adriel. "And thank you, sir."

"Just 'Adriel' is fine," he said.

She took a few steps toward her home and stopped, turning back to look at us for a moment.

"It's all real then?"

I nodded. "Yes. It's real."

"What else is real?" she asked.

"We'd better keep that question for another time," I said. "Let's go with what we've got for now. You keep that necklace on, even when you're sleeping."

She looked back down at it.

"Alright."

She turned and made her way back home. If I had known what was coming, I would have given her something more than just a trinket on a leather string.

John

I had never seen Peter that still for that long. He sat on the floor by a window, looking out at nothing at all. I was sure that if I pulled the shutters closed, he would not move.

Not that the rest of us were any livelier. I moved around a bit, putting bread out on the table. No one touched it, not for the evening, not during the night. Some of us slept, or at least lay down as though to sleep. In the night I just listened to the breathing of my friends.

At daybreak I heard footsteps. People were running up the stairs to the room where we were hiding. I thought we were done for, that the Romans or the priests had sent for us. All night, when I wasn't remembering him on that cross, I had been sure that we would be next. They were going to kill all of us, make examples of us. See what happens when you listen to these rebels? This is how you will die.

Then they were beating on the door and shouting, but it was not soldiers. We could hear Mary Magdalene yelling at us to open the door. Andrew opened it and was knocked back as the women rushed in. Mary looked around at all of us, then ran to Peter and grabbed him by the shoulders.

"They have taken him!" she said.

Peter thought she was talking about the day before. He just took her arms at the wrists and pulled her hands away from him.

"They have taken him, don't you hear me? And we can't find him, we don't know where they put him!"

I didn't see the change in Peter. I was amazed at what she said, and while I was staring at her, waiting for her to say something else, somehow Peter made it to the door. I never saw him move. When I heard him running down the stairs, I understood where he was going, and I ran after him.

It was like chasing a wild pig. Peter ran straight through the stalls of the merchants who were just stirring in the market, past donkeys, past women carrying the night soil from their houses. He did not stop for anyone, did not vary. At least he left a clear path, running with his arms shoving the air aside and that great hairy head bobbing up and down.

When we reached the edge of town, I managed to pull alongside him, and by the time we reached the cemetery I had pulled ahead. I found the tomb, the great sealing rock rolled aside, and I stopped, leaning against the opening and peering inside, waiting for my heart either to calm down or explode. I heard Peter rush up behind me. He never stopped, just ran straight into the tomb.

There was nothing but fabric, the winding sheet and head cloth we had used to wrap him. I kept staring at them, the neatness making the cloth seem strange, out of place, folded up as though someone had put it there for storage or safekeeping, like folded sheets in a closet. Peter picked them up, smelled them for some reason best known to him, then stared at me and walked wordlessly out into the sunlight.

I took the cloth and brought it out of the tomb. I don't know why. We stood there in the cemetery garden, Peter and I. Neither of us said anything. After a while we saw Mary Magdalene returning, still crying. When she reached us, Peter just put his hand on her shoulder and walked away. We left her standing, staring into the tomb, and we headed back to the room where the others were still waiting.

We were nearly back, walking along the street that led to our rooms, when I saw a crippled man lying on a pallet, beginning his day of begging. I stopped with Peter and we stood there by him. He was looking up at us, wondering if we had anything for him. Peter looked at me and shrugged, his purse still up in our room with his cloak. I had mine, though there were only a few coins in it. I shifted the cloth in my arms, trying to reach a coin for the beggar when the cloth slipped, unfolding itself until it reached the ground, the end of it landing on the crippled man's leg though I had not noticed. I was opening my small leather bag to find a coin when I felt Peter squeeze my arm. He was staring down at the crippled man, and I heard him gasp, a quick breath going in. When I looked at him, the beggar seemed puzzled, surprise and fear on his face. He slowly put his hands on the ground beside him and pushed himself up, finding his legs strong enough to hold him.

"The cloth," Peter said. It was the first thing I had heard him say since that rooster screamed at him, naming him a liar in the courtyard of the high priest. "The cloth touched him."

I gathered it up, back into my arms, and with a glance at the former cripple we headed off to the upper room. On the way I began to wonder what I was holding. It looked like cloth, but it wasn't just a sheet any more. It was a vehicle of power, and I knew I had to keep it safe.

Of course, I didn't think in those terms then. I thought it was miraculous, and it was. Miracle was the only concept with which to work at the time. I knew fishing, how to be a reasonably respectable Jew. Subatomic physics did not enter the frame of my mental world. Still didn't, except that I recognized that there are many ways to explain the workings of God: time, energy, particles, and parallel universes. Somewhere in all of that is the work and energy of God.

I guessed that miracle was still a pretty good word for it. The only problem was that the modern world would embrace energy and back away from the miraculous. They didn't understand that all energy is miraculous, and that the universe requires nothing of them to exist, not even faith.

Adriel

"That went well," I say, watching Sarah walk back to her house. John is still a little angry about the yard sale comment.

"You ass," he says.

"John. All those sermons about love. Love one another, love one another, and you call me an ass."

"It is because you are an ass." He stands at the deck rail looking toward Sarah's house and sipping his ginger ale.

"What a way to talk to an angel." Neither of us speaks. Minutes pass. John finishes his ginger ale, burps absently.

"We're going to need some help," I say. John turns and stares at me.

"What do you mean, help?"

"Well, watching her is going to require more than just me. After all, I also watch you."

"I do not require watching," he says. After he reflects for a while, he asks, "What do you have in mind?"

"I met another who has an interest. Her name is Adi." I wait while he thinks about this information.

"Her name?"

"Adi."

"No, I mean, it is a she?" he asks.

"She is a she," I answer. I am surprised to feel defensive toward her, but it may simply be petulance with John's assumptions. All these years and he still does not quite grasp that we are neither male nor female like humans. Nevertheless, Adi is a she, and I am a he.

I am fairly sure.

"Fine," I say, a bit more forcefully than I mean. In fact, I do not mean to say anything at all.

"What are you talking about?" he asks. "Is there someone else here?"

"No, sorry. Just a thought. Never mind."

John looks at me, but moves on.

"OK, tell me about this Adi," he said.

So I tell him what I know, what I see, how we meet nearby, how she watches and sees much that concerns us. I leave out that I enjoy talking with her, but I see the idea flash in John's mind.

"She is trustworthy?" he asks me.

"She is an angel," I say. It does not seem to satisfy him. "There is no darkness in her, only questions. When the dark one comes, she is not afraid."

He turns and watches a squirrel. It is ignoring us.

"Perhaps you should invite her to visit," John says. "Ask her over for dinner. I can make spaghetti."

I look at him, momentarily irritated. John knows perfectly well that we do not eat, and no one eats his spaghetti. I see him smile.

"I will find her tonight," I say. "She comes to watch in the evenings. I think she enjoys the dreams she finds." This last part is probably more than John wishes to know. He looks like he is going to respond, then thinks better of it. I am trying not to intrude overly in his thoughts as I sense he would resent it at present.

"Would she come to talk with us, do you think? Would she agree to help?"

"I think that she would," I say. "I'm not quite sure what we are asking beyond watching, guarding against the dark ones."

"That may be enough," he says. "It may be more than we should be permitted to ask."

"We should introduce her to Sarah," I say. "In case Adi is needed, so that Sarah would know her."

"Sarah may have been happier had we not intervened, not introduced her to this side of reality." John is looking at his hands. He always examines his hands when he is in doubt. His may be the most well examined hands in history.

"This reality is part of her life, whether she knows of it or not," I say. "If they come, if they destroy her, it would not be better. If it happens and it appears to be a disease or an accident, she would not be happier for not knowing why."

"If we let them reach her and she does know, will she be happier then?"

He looks away then down at his empty glass, and he walks into the house. He stops just in the doorway.

"I'm sorry that I called you an ass," he says, and he walks inside.

The squirrel sounds like it is chuckling behind me.

Adi

In my mind I hear him calling me, but I do not answer. I decide to wait where I am, and I share a thought of where that is, on a museum roof. The copper is pleasing and warm in the early morning sunlight, and the there are different sorts of people who come to museums. Their thoughts are more interesting, especially when they encounter something surprising or new, and they do not shield themselves at all at those moments. Most of them would not know how.

Adriel is suddenly beside me.

A museum? He did not expect this place.

"You might be surprised. The items they keep are pleasing, and the thoughts of the people who view them are interesting."

He thinks about this.

"The bones of a whale are flying over the space. Why do they make a whale fly?"

"It is not flying, and you are simple. They pretend to walk through the ocean, here in the building, and the whale is suspended as though swimming." I move to the balcony, eye level with the great whale. Adriel moves with me. The museum is not yet open; the great space was still quiet. *How else would they approach such a sight?*

He looks at the bones that would not swim again.

"John believes that they will come again for the girl," he says.

I look into Adriel's mind. "You believe the same."

"Yes."

For a time we are alone with the whale. I move out past the balcony to the whale's side, reach out to touch the great pectoral fin. For a moment I am swimming through the green blue seawater, the whale is still alive, her offspring following us with great dark eyes, and the sunlight is streaming down through the water like glowing honey.

"I will help you," I say. The baby whale thinks I speak to him, but the thought shimmers and is gone, and I move back to the balcony to join Adriel. I wonder whether the baby whale remembers me.

"We will need for you to meet her. So that if needed she will know you."

"Alright." The whale child thinks I am beautiful, and I think the same about him. Perhaps I can return to his time, swim with him again. It is a pleasant thought. I allow Adriel to see it. "Today?"

He nods, an odd movement. We are beings of thought. I suppose he has joined with much that is human in the man John, perhaps more than Adriel knows.

"I will call for you when it is time."

Alright, I think.

"Thank you." He pauses, and then adds, "Your company is pleasant."

And he is gone.

Now there is only me and the whale, one swimming and one still, the same whale in the ocean and here in this space, one alive and shining and the other nothing but white bones. There is a sadness that remains in the bones, and once more I see the baby in my mind. I wonder what is happening to him in that time and in that space, wonder if he knows that I have not fulfilled the promise he heard me speak. I wonder whether he realizes that my promise was not made to him, whether I will come to realize the same thing.

I go to him, there in that ocean and that time. What is time to an angel? The ocean is cold with green light, bubbles slipping past us in the flowing stream, time and water. The brine is clean with the taste of tears, and the great eyes of the whales can see me.

Slowly we plunge down away from the light and into the restfulness of dark water with its promise of food. I am hovering near the bones in the air of the museum, but now the sounds are whale sounds, songs of deep voices soaring through the liquid air of a lesser sky. From the deep below us I hear the movement of the blind creatures of the dark. High above are sunfish, casting giant round shadows upon the grey skin of the greatest of creatures. I am swimming with the whales, and this whale child is my brother, eyes undimmed by age that do not need a museum to find the beauty of the sea.

I sense a shadow moving elsewhere in the museum, and I am pulled back from the water. My brother sings to me, and hearing his whale song I return to this time to gaze on the bones, unwilling to leave that time with him. The dark one creeps from the closed doors of a darkened room. I rise, small, and linger on the back of a seabird suspended from the ceiling. From there I see the entrance to a gallery, the signs in the writing of the Hebrews, scrolls from a dry cave. Why had one like this come to this place? What does it seek in a room of scrolls? There is no life there to take, no power to consume.

It creeps through the floors and walls, sinks down below the building and follows the dark pipes beneath the ground as it slides away. The lights of the building flicker as it passes a power junction, momentarily sucking away the energy flowing near it.

Whatever draws it to this place, I know it is not satisfied. It is still distracted by the errand it is on, or surely it would sense me.

I move back to the scroll room, dark as it is in the early hours, darkened as well to preserve the writings. At first I know only that this room has been violated by that dark presence, but soon I sense spots, places, scrolls that held its attention. There are words from a prophet. The fragments of the scroll are shifted by the attention of the other. Here and there I sense an added shadow where the creature had lent its attention, but I do not understand why one of these would puzzle over ancient words of humans.

Sarah

Ok, maybe I am crazy or whatever, but I think the old man next door is John. Well, that is his name, but that is not what I mean. I mean that he is John as in the Gospel of John, the evangelist, the one who wrote the Gospel, and maybe the letters, and maybe even The Apocalypse of Saint John the Divine, which is how it is labeled in my Bible.

It is about the only thing that makes sense. Well, ok, there are several things that might make more sense, like the old man is crazy, and I'm a little bit crazy for buying into it, or maybe there was something in my ginger ale. The thing is, I met an angel. I don't know how he would have faked that. Even in a movie they would have needed a blue screen or green screen or whatever and a whole bunch of computer magic, like Pixar dust, but this was live, and there aren't enough makeup artists and projection screens in the world to fake that. Adriel, an angel.

I looked the name up on the computer, and it means something like "flock of God", and it seems to be a really old name, though that doesn't prove anything, because you can give an old name to something new and that doesn't make it old any more than a new name would make an old thing new again. If we started calling great aunt Barbara, say, BeBopDeLemonDrop, that would be a pretty new name, but she would still sit in the rocking chair and twitch a little every once in a while to remind you that she was alive in there.

I could see Adriel, and I could not. Really, it was as though I could touch him and see through him at the same time, like there was one moment when Mr. Zebedee and I were together with no Adriel, and at the same time there was another moment when Mr. Zebedee and I were together and there was an Adriel, and someone laid one moment on top of the other, like a layer cake in time, only the two layers were pressed back together into one and you couldn't tell which parts came from which layer anymore.

I'm pretty sure he was reading my thoughts some of the time, because it was like some of the answers were inside my mind instead of hearing them. That part is a little freaky, since you don't really know what you are going to think at any particular moment. That could have been embarrassing, though I suppose an angel is used to that sort of thing.

Maybe it was the ginger ale.

Wood from the cross? Sure, maybe. I think that I've seen things like that on TV, maybe the Discovery channel, where people searched for artifacts, and one of those was a part of the cross where Jesus died. Ok, that part is creepy, too, if someone really died nailed to this piece of wood, and it is even more freaky if that person was Jesus. I don't even know how to think about Jesus being God. God died on this piece of wood. Yeah, it was bigger, but still, Jesus was God they say, or part of God, which is weird enough all by itself, and then I'm supposed to understand that the part of God that was Jesus actually died. On this object, or on what this wood was a part of. And I'm wearing it for a necklace, which feels right but seems like a heathen religion kind of thing instead of anything remotely Christian.

The wood does feel good, though, and it is warm. I tried it. I touched part of my bed frame, a chair, and a table. I even went outside and touched a tree, though that didn't work since it all depended on the weather, I supposed. All of those were cool to touch, not cold, but cooler than me. This piece of wood feels just as warm as me. I tried it by holding it out from my body for a while, and it never gets as cool to the touch as, say, the table. It is like it has some kind of radiation in it or coming from it. I only hope I don't start growing another head or changing into a lemur or something.

If it will keep those things away, I'll wear it in the shower.

That thing in the yard, the thing Adriel chased away, it was scary and black. I don't mean just black to look at, though it was really dark like trying to see through a forest at night with no moon or trying to look through a hole in the ground when it had no other end for the light to come in. It was black on the inside, dark and hungry. That's the word, I suppose, though it is not quite right, but I can't come up with a better one. Hungry, and I think it had me in mind. I could feel it out there, and it was not anywhere near warm and fuzzy.

Adriel was not warm and fuzzy either, but it was like when the teacher comes back in the room and you know the bully isn't going to try anything. Even better, because now the teacher knows who the bully is, and she doesn't like it any better than you do, and she can do something about it.

Only Adriel is a he, which is also odd, since I didn't think angels were like that, male or female or whatever, only all the stories from the Bible make it sound like angels are male. If they aren't male or female, I don't know what they are, maybe bi-, like they say the guy at the grocery store is. It doesn't matter to me, I suppose. If Adriel is an angel, whatever angels are, and John is that John, then it is better to be with them than to see that thing slithering in my yard.

I just hope they aren't both crazy. I hope that I am not crazy. And I had better start drinking my own ginger ale.

John

Twenty centuries, and I was just a trinket peddler. I gave away bits of the cross on necklaces. I may as well have gotten one of those trailers at the carnival and sold holy water and prayer shawls, except that there was no demand. They might buy crystals or tattoos or wolf teeth, but there was nearly no market at all for holy relics.

The thing was, I didn't even know quite what I believed anymore. I was there, I remembered, but I didn't know what to believe. Now here we were, twenty centuries along, and I didn't know where God was. I prayed, but I wondered who was listening, besides Adriel who seemed to eavesdrop on everything I did. Of course, that had gone on so long that the creepiness had been replaced by habit.

I gave her, Sarah, the bit of the cross because it did have some kind of power. We, Adriel and I, agreed on that. I knew it, even after all this time and all of this doubt, and he knew it in a different way, because he could actually see it. I thought it would be simpler to be able to see the remnant of some power, to see a confirmation of what I still thought happened. Of course, if Adriel was a figment of my imagination, then his agreement was worthless, and that piece of wood was just a piece of wood.

Sarah saw him, talked to him, as other people did from time to time. And she must have seen him since her reaction to Adriel's statements could not have come from my part of the dialogue. She heard the conversation as I heard it. Of course, I could have been so delusional that I imagined her part of the interaction with Adriel. That was certainly not outside the realm of the possible, and the insane appear to be more taken by their own constructs than by reality.

There was an empty tomb. Of that, I was certain. Where the body went was beyond me. I never found it, and I never moved it, though from time to time after moving Mary's body those many years later I would wonder about the similar effect, the stories of Mary being taken up into heaven. And someone did appear to us, someone talked with us, and we knew him as Jesus, except he did not look the same. The words and the voice were of Jesus, the actions were of Jesus, but why did he not appear the same? Sometimes we did not even recognize him, and we had been with him for years.

It was easier when the others were alive, to hear my own faith echoed in their words, my doubts echoed in their faith. And now they were all gone, all except for Lazarus.

Lazarus gave me the heebie jeebies. Not to have died is one thing. To have died and come back, well that is another thing entirely. How about Jesus? How was Lazarus being raised from the dead different than Jesus walking out of his tomb? I don't know that I could have told you, but I could tell you that it was different. There was never anything creepy about Jesus, not even when we could not recognize him. There was everything creepy about Lazarus.

Maybe it was just that he watched too many family and friends die, or that he knew what they were in for, but I didn't think that was quite it. I had watched people die, centuries of them, and I did not believe that I became anything like Lazarus. There was something he brought back with him, some new fascination with things beyond the grave, like a dark habit fed in secret until the eyes sink and tell you everything you need to know. Except with Lazarus, there were no drugs. Well, there might have been, but if so, they came late to the party.

I almost thought he wanted to die, to go back to the quiet of the grave. Maybe his resurrection was flawed—there were a number of days between death and resurrection after all—but that would have reflected badly on Jesus' power to raise him, and despite every doubt I ever had, I never doubted his power. No, whatever happened to Lazarus, it was his own choice.

"Do you ever see them?" he always asked. As though the dead marched through my backyard, stopped for tea on nice afternoons in the sunlight of the garden. Fine, I did see things, I saw beings, I saw light and shadow, things that made no sense but that I of all people could not ignore precisely because of what else I had seen. I saw, but I did not know what I was looking at. I had words for all of it, but I no longer knew whether the words were right, whether the names were right, whether I knew the meaning. Maybe I had misunderstood all of it.

It was a little like one of those drawings with a second figure hidden in it. You could hang the picture on your wall and walk by it every day of your life without seeing what is hidden in it, until that one day when you noticed. It doesn't matter what it is – a man, an old woman's head, the face of Jesus – once you saw the figure, you could never walk by it again without seeing it. What the eye brings the mind to see, the mind will not let the eye forget.

Certainly, I saw them. I saw Adriel when he wished me to, and sometimes even when he did not. I saw others when they came, to bring a message they thought they had received, though none of them could tell me from where they got these messages any more. Sometimes they came simply to watch, to confirm what they had heard, whatever that might be in the gossip mills of angels. Given what two old women can concoct in an afternoon, you might well imagine what an untold number of angels could produce over the course of centuries.

I saw them, beings that were not human. I respected them. I acknowledged them, but Lazarus reveled in them, the stranger the better. I remembered the last time we spoke, on an overlook of the Blue Ridge Parkway in North Carolina. I was standing with my camera, admiring the view. It was one of those overlooks where the mountains stretched away below and beyond you like slow wrinkles in a smoky blanket. A Subaru came pulling up, a particularly ugly orange one, though I paid it little mind. There were plenty of ugly Subaru's in those mountains. Then Adriel let out a small groan, and I knew we had company.

Even in the summer daylight, Lazarus was pale, as though he was recovering from an illness that had kept him inside for months, untouched by the warmth. He recovered from that malady centuries ago, but he never regained the color of the living. After the death of Martha and Mary, his sisters, he had become worse, withdrawing from the interaction of people, wandering in the darkness of the hills around Judea. The people of the region at first had revered him. Later they came to watch him askance, nervous about his presence as though they sensed he brought something else along with him, something dark.

Finally, I had suggested to Lazarus that it was time for him to die once again, at least in the minds of the people. We held a quiet time of mourning, very private, explaining that Lazarus had been mourned publicly once long ago and that he had no wish to bring such grief to his neighbors again. In truth, they were relieved, relieved that they did not have to attend such mourning for this man and relieved, if the truth was spoken, to think him dead again.

We closed his family tomb, Philip and I, sealing the entrance with the stone. There was nothing inside but a pile of cloth, though we were fairly sure that no one would ever bother to check. Late in the night, Lazarus left with Philip for places in the north. They both had their reasons for leaving. Lazarus was supposed to be dead, of course, and Philip had grown tired of walking the same streets and hillsides as Jesus had done. He was tired of waiting, and we didn't even know what we were waiting for. They left in the darkness, two men with donkeys carrying everything they would need on their journey. Philip traveled toward Syria and Turkey, and Lazarus traveled on, never returning to the region of Jerusalem until all who had known him were dead. All but me, that was.

"I am uneasy with him," Philip had told me before they left. "We know that Jesus brought him back from that tomb, but I do not…" His words failed.

"We don't know why he did it," I finished.

"At the time, I just thought it was, you know, love of Lazarus and of his sisters." Philip looked around to be sure that Lazarus was not near. The man could move almost silently. "Now, though, I don't know. Maybe…"

Again he let the words fall away.

"Maybe he brought him back for some other purpose," I said. "He is supposed to do something, be something."

"Maybe," Philip said. "Maybe. But God only knows what."

"I do not think he will do you any harm," I said to him, not knowing why I said it. Philip seemed to start at the thought.

"That is what bothers me," he said. "I don't know why, but I think that he might do us harm. Do someone harm. God forgive me for saying it."

In the darkness I watched them leave, then listened to the sounds of the donkey's hooves on the street until I could hear nothing but the sounds of the night.

"He does well to watch Lazarus," Adriel said. He had been there the entire time, of course, though I never told Philip. Even among the other followers, I was not sure whether any of them could accept the presence of Adriel, or maybe I simply wanted to keep him to myself. It was another thing of which I had never been sure. "His mind is never far from the tomb that he left."

"Well, we have closed it now," I said. "Perhaps he will start to forget."

"The tomb that is in his mind is not a place," said Adriel. "You do not have a word for what it is, but it stays in the minds of those who have seen it."

I did not know what to say to that. So often, I did not know what to say to the things that Adriel shared. It may be that we can only understand aspects of reality, layers, and some of us have touched more layers than others. Lazarus had touched a place that I had never gone.

And then there he was, getting out of an ugly orange Subaru and walking over, paler than the clouds, smoking a cigarette. I had the sudden urge to throw him over the side of the mountain.

"A good idea," Adriel said just loudly enough to slip past my thoughts.

"John, my friend," said Lazarus, and I wondered whether he knew that his greeting grated on my nerves. We were not, strictly speaking, friends, but we had known each other longer than any humans on record, so I supposed that was something.

"Lazarus." It was as friendly a tone as I could muster. "What brings you here?"

"Seeing the sights," he said. "Still traveling. I happened to see you standing here. Imagine my surprise," he added, as though after this much time on the earth I even entertained the notion of coincidence, particularly where Lazarus was involved.

"Well, it is certainly a view worth seeing." I turned back to the scene, letting the beauty calm me so that my agitation was not evident. I offered nothing more, just gazed at the mountains and waited for him to tell me why he had tracked me down.

"John, since we are well met, let's have dinner this evening and catch up. So much time has passed." He rubbed his hands together as if to show he relished the idea. His hands repulsed me, reminding me of the difference between a caress and a lewd feel.

"What do you want, Lazarus?" I saw no reason to be indirect, but I did not inject anything more than directness in my tone.

"John, John, you wound me," he said. "As if I must want something more than simply enjoying the company of one of my oldest friends in the world."

His voice was perfectly tuned, though his was the only human voice that reminded me of Adriel. Like an angel, Lazarus' voice was beautiful, but it carried the same sense of frequencies that were missing, as though part of what he said was understood in a different layer of time. It was a voice that could have sold almost anything to almost anybody, and over the centuries he had. There was no reason for him to be driving a Subaru instead of a Lamborghini, though it must have served his purpose. I turned to look at him.

"One of? Who else do you know who has rattled around as long as you and I?"

Lazarus raised his eyebrows, pursed his lips and nodded as if to confirm the sagacity of my words. It was one of his most irritating traits.

"Out with it, Lazarus," I continued. "You want something, or you would not have gone through the trouble of finding me. It is not as though I have my name listed in the book."

"Well, I certainly hope you have your name down in that great book in the sky," he said.

"Fundamentalism doesn't fit you," I said.

"Yes, well," he said, "Now that you mention it, there is something that I have been thinking, something I might, as you say, need."

I waited. *Here it comes,* said Adriel in my head. I was startled, having nearly forgotten he was still there. So many years, and I still forgot.

"Do you still have the cross, John?"

I didn't answer, just looked at his eyes and turned back to study the mountains in the distance.

"I hope that you do." He studied my face, sucking on the cigarette as he did. "I was thinking that it would be better to separate what remains, to split it between us or perhaps to move it for safekeeping."

"Safekeeping," I said.

"Yes, I think so. After all, with one piece in one place, something terrible could happen to it." He stood there quietly, looking out over the mountains with me like a pilgrim gazing at the holy land. "We owe it to Jesus."

I felt my mind go blank when Lazarus spoke his name, because the alternative would have been to grab Lazarus and hurl him out into the void in front of us.

"And there are people, people I could reach. If they could see something tangible, touch something that proved the gospel to them, they would believe." He paused, and from the corner of my eye I saw him lick his lips. "It would help so many."

"You wish to help people," I said, as much a repeat of his stated intent as a question. He seemed unsure how to answer, sensing my reaction a moment too late.

"You are right," I told him. "I do have the true cross."

"I knew it!" he said.

"And it is perfectly safe where it is," I told him. "Even with the best intentions, placing it on display would serve no good. It would cheapen the meaning, take away the emphasis on love and replace it with magical thinking. They would not worship because of it, they would begin to worship the cross itself."

He was instantly angry.

"Really, John. Think of the good we could do with it." His lips were still smiling, but it was like watching a snake.

"Lazarus, I am not sure of many things anymore. The cross is in my keeping, though. And no good will come of dragging it out now."

He stood there, the cigarette smoldering in his fingers. I could feel the anger building in him, and I had to resist the urge to step back. I knew that with Adriel nearby, Lazarus could not harm me, but I did not know whether Lazarus could sense his presence. He might not, probably did not.

"The answer is no, Lazarus." I said.

He said nothing. Finally he seemed to remember the cigarette and took a long puff from it, staring at me. Then he turned, still saying nothing, and walked toward the little orange car. As a final display of his contempt, Lazarus flicked the cigarette over the side of the mountain. He started the car and pulled out of the overlook much faster than was wise.

I stepped to the edge and watched to make sure his cigarette did not set the mountain on fire. It had landed among some stones, but amazingly I could see it. There was no danger of it catching flame. I stood watching the smoke rise till the paper and tobacco were ash, and I walked back to my car.

"You did well to refuse," said Adriel. "I could not see what was in his mind."

I thought for a moment.

"I may have lost my friend."

This time it was Adriel who thought for a moment.

"I'm not sure that he ever was your friend," he said, and I realized that he was right. "I could see that he has spoken with others. I saw them, flashing in his mind. They are his friends now."

"What do you mean by others?"

"Dark ones," Adriel said. "Dark angels. And I do not know whether they do his will or he does theirs, but they are not equals. That much I could see."

We sat in our car for a while, watching tourists peer down at the mountains below us. Some of the tourists stepped out to the very edge of the overlook, and I wondered what it was that made them go so far, and then I wondered what it was that made them stop.

Wind

I saw him coming along the street with a lamp in his hand. Even though the sun had gone down and there was little light, I could tell he was well dressed, well made sandals on his feet. He had been at the temple, had been with the Pharisee group who were talking amongst themselves. He had looked up and seen us, and while the others seemed unimpressed with us, this man had met our eyes and acknowledged us with a simple nod of his head.

Nicodemus was his name, and he came asking to speak with Jesus. Actually, he came asking to speak with the Master, an odd approach given Nicodemus' age and his own position of respect. Jesus received him without comment, neither demurring from the title of rabbi nor appearing flattered.

The old man began with a bow, and said to Jesus that he and others like him knew that Jesus was from God, that he acted and spoke from God.

"We know that no one can do these things unless he has been sent by God," said Nicodemus. "These are the signs of a prophet."

This was more like it, we thought. Finally, Jesus was getting the sort of recognition that he deserved, though it was not in the temple. Still, if such a one as this man would come and speak to Jesus this way, then surely the others would follow?

We understood so little, so badly.

Jesus sat staring at the fire, not even acknowledging the old man. Nicodemus began to look at one and then another of us for an indication of what to do. None of us knew. Then Jesus turned his back on the old man and walked to the window. He stood there staring out at the stars.

"Truly, I tell you, Nicodemus, that no one can see the kingdom of God unless he is born into the kingdom of God. If you would see God, you must be born of God."

Nicodemus looked around at us for some idea, but we didn't know what to make of it either. Finally, the old man walked over to Jesus.

"How is it that a man may be born of God?" Nicodemus asked. "I have no mother left to me, and I am old."

I also hoped for some explanation.

"You must be born of water and of the Spirit," Jesus said. "What is born of the flesh is only flesh, and what is born of the water has been made clean, and what is born of the Spirit indeed is spirit. If you would see God, then you must be born of the flesh and of the water and of the Spirit."

Jesus looked at Nicodemus as though he should know these things. I was thinking that nobody knew these things, because they were crazy.

Then came the weirdest part of all.

"If you would know that which is above then you must be born of that which is above. You are born of the flesh, and you see the things of the flesh. The wind blows, and you hear the sound of it, and so there is hope for you. Yet you do not know from where the wind comes or to where it is going."

No one was eating or drinking now. All of us were quiet, trying to find some way to make sense of what we were hearing. This was an audience with one of the leaders of the temple, and Jesus was saying such things as to make himself sound crazy.

"Are you amazed at these things?" Jesus asked. "These things are nothing to what you will see. I tell you things about the flesh and you do not understand. How will you understand if I tell you things about that which is above? If you cannot look at the flesh and see what is within, how shall you look upon the faces of those in heaven and understand what you see there? No one has entered into the heavenly realm except those who are of the heavenly realm, but the son of man is also the son of God."

Jesus paused a moment and looked around at us. Nicodemus was quiet, his brow wrinkled in thought.

"And how will you understand when you see the son of man lifted up, as Moses lifted up a serpent in the wilderness for the children of Israel to see? Just as those who looked upon the serpent and believed were saved, so also shall all those who look upon the son of man, for though he were dead, yet shall they live. Like the serpent in the garden, so also the son of man comes to give knowledge to all who would be the children of God."

No one spoke, least of all Nicodemus. I was clueless, and from his expression so was he. Even we who followed Jesus wondered whether something we had just heard might not offend the teachers of the temple, and we knew nothing compared to this man. He seemed amazed by what he had heard.

Jesus looked around first at one of us then at another, until I thought that he must have gazed into the eyes of all who were there.

"God loves you all. Did you not understand? For God loves you and has given you the son so that you might know that the Father loves you. If you have faith in the son, then you walk in the eternal life. Just as those who looked upon the serpent and believed were saved, so also shall all those who look upon the son and believe be saved. Those who do not seek my voice are already lost, for even as they have not heard and do not listen, so also they shall not enter into life, for they have not heard the words of life. My words that I give to you, these are truth and life, and those who believe them shall never be condemned. For this is the judgment of God, that light has come into the world, and people love darkness rather than the light, for they know their own deeds. Those who come into the light are of the light. Those who come in darkness are yet of the darkness."

Jesus stopped speaking, and suddenly it seemed as though he was pointing at Nicodemus, though he was not. He was not even looking at the old man, but all of us were looking at him and at the lamp that he held in his hand. He had come in the darkness, truly enough, but surely he came to find the truth?

"I will think on your words," said Nicodemus. "I confess that I do not understand them, but I feel that there is truth in them."

"I am truth," said Jesus. "And I am the way that you have come to seek."

Nicodemus seemed as though dazed by this answer. He took a step back and opened his mouth to speak, but he said nothing. He turned and walked slowly away.

After the old man left, I sat by the fire and wondered what it could mean. I could not get the image out of my mind, Moses standing there with a snake on a pole, holding it up for the people to see. I never understood the story, not even when the Rabbis tried to explain it, and I did not understand why Jesus had started talking about it.

Later, most of the others had gone to sleep. Jesus was still standing by the open window, looking up at the stars. I could not sleep and sat staring at the embers burning themselves down. Suddenly I realized that Jesus was standing beside me. He was watching the fire, then looked down at me.

"You are puzzled about the image of the snake," he said. It was not a question. I nodded.

"One day, you will see me lifted up so that all the people can see me. That day, you will understand what I meant," he said. He went walking outside after that. He often would go for walks by himself, sometimes in the night, as a way to have time alone, away from the crowds, away from all of us.

That day came, and I did see him lifted up above the crowd, hanging on a cross. I saw them stick a spear in his side, saw them taunt him, and I saw him die. And he was right that I remembered he had spoken about being lifted up, and he was right that I remembered about Moses and the snake, but he was wrong about my understanding any of it.

The snake was evil. Everyone knew that. There was a snake in the garden. It was the story we learned from childhood. The snake had lied and brought evil into Eden, or else it knew where to look for it once it got near enough. But Moses' staff also turned into a great snake, like the Egyptian magic. And the Lord told Moses to lift up an image—an image of all things—of a snake to save the people from snake bites. Like pagans. And Jesus laid claim to the same image, a snake on a pole, as though it were a good thing.

One day I realized that he might have been right. Maybe the snake wasn't evil. Maybe the snake was simply wise, if there ever had been a snake. Maybe it recognized that a moment of realization had come along for the humans in the garden, if there ever had been a garden. What if the snake in the story whispered that first revelation, the moment when humans embraced their mortality and their self-awareness? And so it helped them to make the next step, to understand the consequences of choice. What if there was no curse? What if there was no sin, no original fault, no first cause of our mortality? What if they simply left the garden of ignorance and walked out to embrace their new knowledge, to embrace the blessings of work and of children, the only two things that live beyond us?

That left me standing, weeping, staring at him on that cross, lifted up for the sake of others. It was a moment of revelation, God dying on a cross, hanging on a tree made by men. The good and wise snake had once again come to pull humans along, to raise us to a new understanding. When Jesus died, it was finished, this work of the old snake, opening the eyes that could bear to see something new—God himself hanging dead on a pole at the hands of humans—and all that I could do was weep.

It was Nicodemus who came to take him down from the cross. He brought burial clothes, brought permission from the Romans to take the body down to wrap it before sundown, brought a donkey to carry him once again along the streets. I held Jesus while the old man wrapped the clean cloth around him, holding Mary back from his body long enough to cover him, to clothe him in death. We brought the body to Nicodemus' tomb, newly carved no doubt for the old man himself, but he had not foreseen this day when he bought it. None of us knew what God had foreseen, had planned, in the carving of this tomb, if anything. We carried the body inside the darkening vault, and we laid him on the stone bed carved into the rock. We stood there for a moment, mindful of the setting sun, mindful that we should seal the tomb and go to our homes. Why we cared about the start of the Sabbath was beyond me. Here in this tomb, it no longer mattered what day came with the setting of the sun. We had buried God.

Sarah

I sit at the base of the oak, the big one near my window, and wait for the squirrels to calm down. There are several in the tree, and I can tell their *chik-chik* sounds from those of the birds. Sure enough, in a few minutes a couple of them come back down the trunk of the tree, pausing every few steps to stare at me with shiny black eyes, waiting to see if I do anything dangerous. They manage to reach the ground by scrabbling down the opposite side of the trunk from me, and they stand with triumphant disdain on the grass. They are brave but prudent.

I like the squirrels, even if they are regular grey squirrels with lighter streaks down their backs. I particularly like fox squirrels, bigger than grey squirrels and with different colors, but there aren't many of those left. The ones that remain are mostly down toward the river.

"Rare to see one so near these houses," Mr. Zebedee had said. "They seem to prefer more solitude than ordinary squirrels."

Adriel had somehow lifted an eyebrow at that. I would not have thought of an angel having such an expression, but there it was.

"Surely you project your own preferences onto these squirrels," he had said.

"I do not believe I projected anything. It is true," Mr. Zebedee had replied. "Do you see any fox squirrels around here?"

They had discussed squirrels for another quarter of an hour. In the end, Adriel's habit, revealed to me in the course of the argument, of joining with trees gave him authority on the motives of squirrels due to his repeated proximity with them. I recalled that when I was a child I would hear such arguments between my grandparents over where a relative previously unknown to me was buried, or who was to blame for leaving the the pantry door open when my mother was a child so that the puppy made off with a bag of marshmallows.

I still can't believe that I know a real angel. An angel, like in books, like in the Bible, except that Adriel is not exactly what I would have expected. I realize that I am thinking robes and wings and sandals, really I am, even though I already guessed that the paintings were wrong. I know these things are symbolic, in my mind, but still I carry the symbols around with me. After the shock, I realized that I still expected wings, wanted there to be wings, and on some level I was still disappointed. An angel appears to me, and I am disappointed.

There are some weird descriptions of angels in the Bible. I know, because after meeting Adriel I looked them up. Just in the book of Ezekiel there are enough different descriptions of differing sorts of angels to give me the shivers. Sometimes there isn't any description, just the idea that something about them would scare people, as in the need for the standard "fear not" greeting. Perhaps there are different kinds of angels, and perhaps some of them do have wings. I cannot bring myself to ask Adriel, though I suspect that he is aware of my interest.

Adriel didn't scare me, though, which I suppose was odd. I was surprised, of course. It took a few minutes to convince myself that he was real and that I wasn't cracking up. Still, even with him standing there, he is sort of hard to see. Seeing an angel is more like having an idea, a very certain idea, that there is another being there. I am not so sure that the shape and appearance aren't simply what the mind produce to match the knowledge of the angel's presence. That doesn't make it any less real. It is just that you see some things as much with your mind as with your eyes.

Maybe, since the brain has to process what the eyes send it anyway, angels kind of short circuit the whole vision thing. It is the same with their voices. I could hear him in my ears, just as I hear other people speak, but I knew I was hearing him in my mind at the same time. It was like there wasn't any difference between my thoughts and his voice.

"How are you, young lady?"

This voice startles me. It has a quality similar to that of Adriel's voice, but reaches only my ears and not my mind. Still, I had not heard the man approaching. I had been lost in thought, I suppose.

He stands there, a thin man dressed in a dark suit and a white shirt almost as pale as his skin. He is leaning on a walking stick. I am pretty sure that he doesn't need it, that he just likes having it, but I don't know how I know since he is standing still. Maybe on some level I know I should have heard the tap of the cane on the sidewalk as he approached.

"Fine, thank you. I was just watching the squirrels," I say, and I think of how lame this must sound. I try to keep my face neutral, but this guy gives me the screaming mimis, and all he is doing is standing there.

"I see. Well, I was simply looking for my friend. I believe that he lives near here..." His voice trails off and he is staring at my chest, which makes me slightly angry. Before I can say anything, the man asks, "Now where did you get that?"

I realize that he is staring at my necklace, the piece of the cross that Mr. Zebedee gave me.

"It was a gift," I say.

"A gift indeed," he says, his eyes slowly rising from my chest to my face. "You need to look after that little trinket, Miss. Some things are more valuable than they appear."

Now I have a full-blown case of the creeps. Something tells me that this guy knows precisely what this piece of wood is, just by looking at it.

"I hope that you find your friend," I say and I quickly rise and begin walking toward the house.

"It was John who gave you that," he says.

I am so surprised that I stop and turn to look back at him.

"Wasn't it, dear?"

He takes a step into the yard, just a step off the cement sidewalk and over the small stone wall, but I know he isn't planning on stopping. I am frightened, but I feel like my feet have turned into bricks. I stand there not believing that this man is just walking into my yard. He takes another couple of steps, his walking stick jabbing the grass like he is mad at it. I find that I cannot move, like in a nightmare when your limbs are so heavy that it feels like you are running through water.

Then it seems that the air vibrates, or as though a doorway opens between the man and me, curtains made of air and light pushing back to either side. Adriel is standing between us, as if he had stepped out of that doorway, and it seems to me that someone else is with him, another angel but there is something different about it. For a moment I forget about the man and Adriel, and I just stare at this new angel.

"Hello, Lazarus," says Adriel.

I am having a hard time keeping up. It seems that things are moving a half second faster than I can process them, but I know that name—Lazarus. From somewhere the image of a cave, carved out smooth from the side of a mountain, comes to mind, and I realize that I am thinking about a painting I have seen of a man walking out of a tomb, like a mummy wrapped in cloth. There are people standing around, freaked, and Jesus is holding out his arms.

"...live next door," Adriel is saying, and I realize that I missed something in the conversation, lost a moment of time. Lazarus, I think. What a name. The only one I have ever heard of is in the Bible.

"Yes," someone says, and somehow I know that it is the other angel. I stare at it, and I see what is different. This angel is a girl. I know well enough that angels are neither male nor female. Still, this angel is a female as surely as Adriel is a male. She seems to be focusing on me instead of on the man named Lazarus, as though she knows Adriel needs no help.

I am Adi, she says to me, and I know that now her voice is only in my mind. *I have come to help you, to watch over you.*

I tried to process that for a moment.

"Do not be afraid," she says. I nearly laugh, having only minutes earlier thought of that very same angelic greeting. I am not afraid, not of these angels, and now not of the man with the cane.

"You mean like a guardian angel?" I ask, somewhat disbelieving. She doesn't answer at first. I can tell that she is listening in part to the conversation between Adriel and Lazarus, and partly to me.

"Not quite as you may picture it," she says. "But I am here to help make sure the dark ones do not come back."

Dark ones. I had not thought about what I had seen under this tree all afternoon. Remembering, I feel the fear begin again.

"I am sorry," I hear her say. "I do not mean to frighten you." It seems to me that she is holding out a hand to me, but part of my mind thinks that she has turned to face Adriel and the man. Perhaps she can do both things as once, I think. "The opposite, in truth. I meant to reassure you, but I have not spoken with humans in many years. Perhaps I am not very good with words."

She seems to drop her shoulders a little. I marvel to see it. Here is an angel, and she is concerned that she is not performing well. It makes me feel closer to her.

"No," I say. "It isn't that. You are doing fine. You have reassured me. I mean, now that you are here, I'm not afraid anymore." I let my voice drop to a whisper at the end of that last part, not wanting the man Lazarus to hear.

"...will have to ask him," Adriel is saying. "But I do not think that you will like the answers."

I look back at Lazarus, partly past Adriel and partly through him. Lazarus is still standing on the grass, his right hand moving the head of the cane around slowly like a long thin spoon.

"I will be back," he says. "And we will have a nice little visit. Tell John that I said that I hoped we could catch up on old times. Very old times."

"I will tell him," Adriel says. "Meanwhile, you should not bother this girl."

"Bother?" Lazarus leans his head nearly all the way over to one side so as to look around Adriel at me. "I hope that I wasn't a bother, young lady,"

I don't say anything.

"You take care," he says, as though we are already close friends. "I'll be coming back soon to visit my friend, John, and I certainly hope to see you again."

I still say nothing at all. The man walks away, his cane clicking between steps on the sidewalk. This time I can hear them, and I know that he had carried the cane quietly when he approached me earlier. Adriel is motionless, watching him walk away. When Lazarus turns the next corner, Adriel turns to me. He just stands there looking at me for a moment..

"Sarah," he says. "This is my friend, Adi."

Adi tilts her head and looks at him as though she is surprised by his words.

Adi

Adriel is speaking to the man John about the conversation with the man Lazarus. I feel John becoming angry, warmth in his face and hands, his voice tensing. Adriel notices as well, I am sure, but it does not affect him. He seems sure the anger is directed elsewhere.

"Damn him!" John says. "There is no reason for his coming, no good reason anyway. And there is no reason whatsoever for him to bother the girl."

His thoughts are a swirl. I can see ancient streets, a home with two women, others, the man Jesus talking, a tomb, a walking mummy. I see wood being carved, buried. Mary. I see ships, more streets, houses, and faces. Finally, I see him thinking of the necklace Sarah wears, the power held in the wood. Then he turns to me.

"Adi," he says. "I apologize."

No man has ever apologized to me. I cannot recall an occasion for it, and I struggle to understand the occasion for this apology.

"You were kind to help, to protect Sarah." He looks at Adriel, who is continuing to watch out the window, though I do not understand his use of windows. "Adriel had told me that you would, that we could rely upon your help."

I am again surprised. "He tells you this?"

"He has a high opinion of you," John says. Adriel shifts but does not offer anything more. "And now so do I.

Lazarus is dangerous, and dark. He bears watching. And he is looking for something."

The wood, I think.

Power, Adriel says but only to me.

"Adriel said that you were, well, I forget the words he used. I took his meaning that you were questioning, wondering about certain things."

Now I stand motionless. Adriel turns to me.

"I told him that I meet others who are seeking, who realize questions have come to mind," he says.

Questions have come to mind, I think. Yes. That is what has happened.

"Questions," I say. "I think that I have questions. But I do not know whether there is a place with answers."

John looks at me for some minutes, then he walks into his kitchen. He flows water into an electric kettle, power flowing through coils of metal, radiating heat.

"Answers don't come from places," he says. "But you didn't mean it literally, I suppose."

He takes a ceramic cup from a cupboard, dips a spoonful of dark crystal into it. He turns and sees me staring at them in his cup.

"Coffee, Adi. It is just instant coffee. Add water and it dissolves. Doesn't quite taste like regular coffee, but it isn't bad." I look at him and his eyebrows raise, small hairs reflecting light above his eyes. "Would you like a cup?" he asks.

I think about it, what I might do with it.

"You wouldn't have to drink it," he says. "You could simply enjoy looking at it, if you liked."

I am again shocked. For a moment I believe that he has read my thoughts, knows that in some way I do want a cup to hold, to watch, but it is absurd. Finally I decline.

"No, it would be ridiculous," I say. "It is kind of you to offer, but perhaps I may simply watch yours as you drink it?" Immediately I wish I have not said it, but Adriel is only watching me. I sense no condemnation or laughter from him.

"I blend with trees, and you think I would condemn your fascination with the color and swirl of a cup of coffee?" he asks.

John turns to Adriel. "Blend with trees, yes. There is a thought."

"It is best to go on to something else," Adriel says.

The water swirling hot, John pours it into his cup and stirs. It is fascinating how the crystals become liquid, brown and black, bits of orange, purple and blue shifting, edges of the spectrum. There is a warm smell of spice burning in moss. I realize that the man John is standing, also watching his coffee, waiting for me to switch my attention back to something else. I do not know how much of his time passed.

"It's alright," he says. "It makes me appreciate the coffee more. Things have a way of becoming commonplace, even the amazing ones."

He sips. I cannot, but I watch it cross his lips and wonder if I might be crossing a boundary by watching so closely. I move away, leaving him more room with the beverage.

Adriel is chuckling.

Stop it.

"So, Adi, what do you wonder about?" John takes a seat at his dining table as though we are simply guests. I see people in homes sitting with one another in such a way. I cast my mind, letting the thoughts come. This man has written much that is read in their religious gatherings. Everywhere the story of Jesus is told, I hear the words this man set down, some centuries ago.

"Eden," I say.

He blinks and glances at Adriel, who is again watching me.

"Eden?" John asks.

"Yes." I try to gather my questions, make something coherent of them for the human. "I hear the story of Eden, in your churches, synagogues, in your stories you tell one another."

"But?"

"I have no memory of it," I say. "I have no memory of Eden, and yet it is told among your kind as true, as the beginning."

He sips his coffee. "What do you remember?"

Again, images come to me, flying through my mind like moth wings or lightning. "The earth cooling and shapes forming. Plants growing, the shape of the land moves. Forests, jungles, deserts. There are animals, changing. Men, some rough like apes, some smoother like you are now."

He sips his coffee again, waiting. I do not say anything else. I am watching a fern grow in a forest while I listen to his mind.

"No Eden. No Adam, no Eve," he says.

"No."

"That is because they never were," he says. "No Eden, no Adam, no Eve."

"But you tell the stories as true," I insist. I hear the stories, hear the thoughts of the people in the churches, the synagogues.

"Yes, many do," he agrees. "But they are stories about truth, Adi, not true stories." He again pauses, sipping the dark brown liquid. "Adam and Eve are a moment in time, not people. They are the moment when humans became aware of themselves, became aware of the power of consequences to choices. They represent the point when humans realized and understood their own mortality."

I watch him, listening for the truth. "And the expulsion, the judgments?"

"The expulsion was the realization, that is all. And the judgments, well, imagine mortality, grappling with the knowledge of one's own impending death. The story speaks of childbearing, and of working the soil. For humanity, the only things that could offset the realization of one's own death were one's work and one's children—those are the only things we can hope will outlive us, a way to reach past death to achieve some degree of immortality."

He drinks again. Adriel is gazing out the window, motionless.

"God wasn't angry. There was no garden. Eden was the bliss of ignorance, and our expulsion nothing more than our realization of mortality. There was no sin. There are only the sins we ourselves make, error and wandering and poor choices."

I look at him, waiting, but he says no more. The fern I watch in my mind is unrolling with leaves like undulating arms opening to the sky.

"I do not think that your churches would agree with you," I say.

"Oh, you are quite right about that, Adi," he says. "Quite right."

Lazarus

That miserable, self-righteous cretin. The Lord himself raised me from the dead, and John has the gall to pass judgment on my intentions.

Jealousy, that is all it is. Envy. He wishes to be the only person so blessed, so chosen, as to live for these many centuries, and it galls him to think of my footsteps echoing back as far as his own.

I will find the true cross, all of it that remains, and I will pour the power of it in the creation of something new, a race of men who will know the freedom of life as I have known it. I will no longer bow, or whimper, or whisper to anything or anyone. Humanity shall rise, and it shall rise because of me, because of the power that I will funnel into the mouth of our species, the door that I will open to a new evolution beyond decay and beyond death.

John is a fool. What is some memory to stand between humanity and a new life? Yet he would protect his stories of Jesus and his memories of Mary and what she possessed against the betterment of all. I know, I saw them, the way he looked at her.

And when has he heard God's voice? John does not hear it any more than I. If God is there, then he is indifferent and his attention is elsewhere. The Church? Not even John can stomach them. And Jesus? He died hanging from that piece of wood, and the power that he contained transferred, in part, to it.

John has it, what is left in one piece of it, what he did not give to the girl. And, of course, what he did not see given to Nicodemus and to Joseph of Arimathea and to who knows who else, bits and pieces decorating tombs and churches scattered all over the world by now. Those parts given to Nicodemus and to Joseph I have. It was not John who saw them last, it was I, and I made certain that they did not leave this world with the cross. Even then I knew it was the key, but I did not understand what might be achieved with it. With John's part, I shall possess most of what may be left of it in the world. With it, I shall begin a new race.

We will not need God any longer, because we will become gods. On that day, perhaps John will write my gospel.

John

"I should never have given her the necklace," I told Adriel. "With Lazarus nearby, things are worse than before."

He just stood there, impassive, looking out the window toward Sarah's house, as if he could see something that I could not. All right, he could see things that I could not, but that doesn't mean that he always did. Most of the time he was just putting on airs, I thought.

"I am not," he said.

"The end of the matter is that we have made things worse, not better," I said.

"I rather think it is the beginning of the matter," he told me, to no great satisfaction on my part. "Unless you intend to abandon the girl and withdraw?"

I glared at him.

"Just putting things in perspective," he said.

"I have perspective aplenty, thank you."

I joined him at the window. Thankfully, it was rather dark inside and nobody could have seen us staring at Sarah's window.

"Whatever Lazarus has in mind, he is not going to stop," I said.

"No."

"And whatever those dark creatures are after, neither will they stop."

"No."

"One likely is in league with the other," I added.

"Yes."

The monosyllabic replies were annoying, but I was trying to ignore them. Indulging this side of Adriel's personality led to days of this kind of behavior.

"We need to know what they are after," I said. "If it is the cross, then let's retrieve Sarah's piece."

Adriel shook his head. "I think that it has great value for her now. To take it back would be wounding to her."

"And not to take it back could be worse," I said, though I knew he was right.

"You know I am right," he said.

"Stop doing that. And fine, you are right, we cannot take it back." I was trying not to get angry. "Then we must be sure it is the cross and not the girl that is of interest to them, and once we are sure then we must dissuade them."

Adriel was silent for a time. We could see a bird flying up to the roof of Sarah's house, near where Adi sat on guard. Adi turned to regard the bird for a moment, perhaps making certain that it was in fact a bird, and then she gazed out across the treetops. I could see her, but I doubted many other humans could. Possibly none.

"I do not think we can dissuade them," he said. "I think the only choice they will give us is to oppose them."

Once again, he was right.

"That is not the path I want to take," I said. "Answering threats with violence and power, it can only lead to more." I turned away and went to sit by the fireplace. In a few minutes, Adriel joined me.

"Why do they not bother you, the dark ones?" he asked. It was a question I had not considered. "They never have."

"Because I speak with power," I answered. I knew that my answer was true, but I had not given it direct thought.

"Yes," he said. "And perhaps we might find a way to equip Sarah to speak with power."

"But I did not find that ability!" I was perplexed at the suggestion. "It was conveyed upon me."

Adriel stared at the fire, though I have never known what his eyes see.

"Was it?"

"Was what?"

"Was this power conveyed upon you?"

"You know full well it was. You were there, you saw us with the Lord in those days. It was he who conveyed this power upon us."

Again he was silent for a few minutes. I could almost hear him thinking.

"Then perhaps the Lord might convey such power upon the girl," he said. "Or, it may be that you are mistaken. Perhaps the Lord did not convey power to you, but rather recognized it, help you to recognize and use it. Perhaps that power is always there, always was, all along the way."

"I don't follow," I said, but I suspected that I did follow. Still, I was feeling irritated, irritated with the situation, with my limitations, with Adriel, most of all irritated with God for appearing to do nothing. We had traipsed around Galilee, wandered the world, and all these centuries I see and hear nothing else. Well, I see these angels who do not live up to the stories in my opinion, and the dark creatures, and plenty of the effects of their interaction with humanity, but nothing of God.

"Nothing at all," I muttered.

Adriel glanced at me and cleared his throat, an affectation that I seldom caught. It seemed so natural.

"You saw a great deal, once," he said. "We both did."

"It was long ago." I walked back to the window. "And I sometimes wonder what we saw."

"No, you don't," he said. "You simply wish to see more of it, more of him."

I just looked out into the darkness at the rectangle of light from Sarah's window. He was right and I knew it.

"For that matter," he said, "so do I."

The Voice

The dream was dark, and it was long. It seemed that there was nothing else, that nothing had come before it, and nothing would follow. I would dream this dream forever.

Then the world changed. There was light and I felt that I had stepped into an open field, sunlight streaming around me, dazzling, so that it was all I saw. Then I heard laughter, as from a child watching from some hidden place, and voices, many voices, speaking to one another. It was as though I had woken from a deep sleep in a room beside a wedding party. I knew that I wanted to join the others, to listen to their stories. Surely there would be good stories, the child had laughed after all.

As I lay contemplating sounds, wondering whether I might rise to join them, I heard it. Something was calling to me, calling only me and nobody else in the world. I could not refrain from listening, even though the voices from the wedding were becoming dimmer. I knew that it was time to rise, that I should get up from the rock hard bed on which I was lying, but it was difficult. Something held me and kept me from moving.

Then there was a sound like stone moving on stone, and I knew that the same voice that was calling me had caused this other sound. The stone was moving for me, like a doorway opening, and a part of me had been journeying, traveling, and now it was back with me. It had come so that we might go out through that doorway together. And still I could hear the voice, if it was a voice, urging me, calling me, ending my sleep.

When I opened my eyes, I panicked, just for a moment. Cloth was draped across my face, covering my eyes like blankets. I shook my head and the cloth fell away. Still, even with my eyes open, there was nothing but darkness. I thought I had gone blind, until slowly I could see a shaft of daylight streaming in from the doorway. I tried to sit up, but sheets were wound around me. I must have turned in my dreams to end wrapped in such a fashion.

The wedding voices were gone. I had not made it, I supposed, or it was a dream after all. I managed to stand up, thinking that the dream in my head would clear quicker that way. Those voices had faded, but still there was the other, the voice that was calling my name. I had forgotten it, but I knew that it was mine.

Again, I heard the sound of stone against stone, and suddenly the daylight poured into the darkness, surrounding me with light. I made my way toward it. Still I heard a voice calling my name, calling me out into the light. I did not know how long I had slept.

I found that I could only shuffle along, making slow steps. The sheets had wound themselves around my legs as well. Still, I was moving, and the light was stronger. I thought I knew where I was going, that I had been to this place long ago, but I could not remember. Perhaps I was still dreaming, I thought. I concentrated on walking, moving toward the sound of the voice, making stepwise progress into the light.

When I felt the warmth of the sun, I stopped. I raised my face to the light and stood still. I realized that I heard crying, the sound of a woman crying, and I looked in the direction of the sound. I did see a woman, her face in her hands. She was familiar. Somehow I knew her. I felt that I had known her all my life. She rushed to me, pulling at the cloth that was wrapped around me. Then I knew her name.

"Mary," I said.

Her crying stopped, replaced by silence. She looked into my eyes, something shining there with her tears.

"Lazarus," she said. "You are alive!"

John

In my sleep I felt the boat rock on the water. I heard the small waves lap against the wood, gurgle their way under the hull, and continue unbroken toward the far shore. I knew that if I opened my eyes, I would see the moonlight shimmering on the sail hanging from the mast, see my father standing in the prow of the boat, impossibly balanced as only a man who has spent most of his life on the water can stand. He would be gazing into the water, watching the moonlight sink beneath the surface, waiting for the glint of light on the backs of a school of fish. From time to time he would glance across at my brother in the other boat, and he would smile proudly.

When I opened my eyes he was not there. The boat had likewise disappeared, and I lay on my bed staring up at the ceiling. Only the moonlight remained of my dream, lighting my room from the window, but without the water shimmering under it the light was still and cold.

I lay there nonetheless, remembering, and then trying to remember again where it was I lay and who I had come to be. Time was like the sea, never ceasing to move and never constant. Sometimes I wish I had sunk beneath the water, drowned somewhere in my past.

Slowly, I realized that I was not alone in the moonlight of my bedroom. Another being was in the room, occupying my rocking chair. Oddly, I did not sense any purpose, any leaning to light or to darkness.

"Who are you?" I asked. Then, becoming somewhat peeved that my privacy counted for nothing with these beings, "Why are you in my home?"

I supposed that were this a burglar, I would be done for, but I knew it was not human. That no longer surprised or frightened me. In fact, I was less inclined to alarm from the presence of one of these others than from the presence of human beings.

"I am the serpent of the garden," it said, and I took it for something like a male creature. His answer annoyed me.

"What serpent, and what garden?" I asked. "You might narrow that down a bit."

"Oh," came the voice, as much in my head as from across the room. "I am sure that you know."

Now I was truly and well annoyed, indeed. Woken from a good sleep to riddles with this odd creature.

"I see. You are supposed to be that serpent from that garden. Eden and all that."

"You do understand."

"Understand. Yes, indeed," I said. "Don't come trying to insert yourself into the stories of my own people. If you are the serpent, and if you are from that garden, then I am carrying on a conversation with a bit of mythological symbolism, and maybe I am finally completely insane."

I could see him looking at me from across the room. The chair rocked back and forth.

"Well, someone woke up in a bad mood."

That statement set me back. Not that it was scathing or brilliant, it was just unexpected.

"You try waking up with Satan sitting in your rocking chair sometime."

"But you don't think I am Satan."

"No," I said. "I would think he has better things to do."

He rocked for a moment. "Better?"

I began to sit up, looking for my housecoat that had slid from the bed to the floor during the night. I retrieved it, stood to put it on, then sat back on the edge of the bed. "More interesting, then."

I rubbed my face and reached up to smooth my hair. I suspected it was still standing out from my head in an odd angle, probably detracting from the dignity of my appearance.

"Where is Adriel, anyway?" I asked. I could have sworn I heard the creature sigh from the rocking chair.

"He went to speak with Adi. I told him I would keep watch while he was gone."

"You, keep watch?"

"I'm not really Satan."

"Really?"

Again, I thought I heard him sigh.

"I am Frederick," he said. I just sat staring at him.

"Frederick," I said. "Now you are joking."

"Yes. Well, it is not the first name I have had, but I grew tired of my first name." The chair seemed to hesitate, just for a moment, in rocking.

"And you picked Frederick?"

"It is a good name. I like it," he said. After a moment, "Do you see something wrong with it?"

It was my turn to hesitate. "Oh, of course not. I was just, well, your name is unusual. For angels."

He was quiet, as was I. I was about to suggest breakfast when Adriel appeared.

"Good morning," he said to me. "And good morning to you, Frederick. Thank you for watching over John."

"You are welcome. We were just getting acquainted."

"I don't need watching over," I said.

"Of course not," Adriel said. He managed to keep the condescension out of his voice. "The night was quiet. Adi saw nothing of interest, only the usual movement in the night. Sarah appeared to sleep well, and safely."

"Well, that is good," I said.

"Yes, it is gratifying," Frederick added.

Gratifying, I thought. "So, where did you two meet?"

After a moment of silence, Adriel spoke up. "It was long ago, before your time. We have seen one another on occasion since."

I was pretty sure that was as much explanation as I was likely to get, and so I headed out toward the kitchen for breakfast.

Later in the day I took my walking stick and headed out the back door, walking across the deck and down the steps to the grass and the woods beyond the edge of the yard. My walking stick was a thin staff, about as long as my arms outstretched. It was smooth in my hands, as it should be. I had carried it for over nineteen hundred years.

The leaves on the ground were still damp, yielding to the shape of my boots rather than crunching beneath them. My steps made a quiet, soft sloughing sound. I was able to get close to the animals of the woods before disturbing them. A little into the forest the ground dropped away then rose again to a ridge, though the trees limited the view at the top. I stopped and looked around, resting from the small climb. Catching movement nearby, I turned to see a deer standing, one of its ears twitching either out of alarm or habit. It watched me, chewed a bit, then with a glance at the forest behind me it turned and ran into the trees. I was amazed at how quickly it vanished, perfectly blending with the undergrowth.

I supposed that it had run from me, though I would not have harmed it. Later I wondered whether it did not see something more than me walking in its forest. We are seldom alone.

I continued down the long, slow slope beyond the ridge, ambling between trees and around patches of briars and shrubs. Eventually I came to a small stream running at the base of the hill, parallel to my home some distance behind me. The stream was not loud and rocky like streams in the mountains. This one was slow and dark, with black water that was deep but only a few feet across. Not far away the water drained into a patch of swamp then into a river.

I found a reasonably dry fallen tree trunk and sat watching the water. Occasionally a leaf or a fragment of one would pass along on the surface, one of the only ways of gauging the speed of the current. Otherwise the black water appeared to be still, like a long thin lake. I supposed there were fish, but there was no sign of them on the surface. Perhaps they were underneath after all, one more thing I couldn't see.

My Lord, I thought and realized that it really was a prayer. So much time, and there are so many things I cannot see.

I cannot see my way any more. Your way, I suppose I mean. So many years of walking on this earth, so many years looking back at those few days when I was in your presence, his presence, if he is you, was you.

And now, I know nothing.

I cannot find comfort in the Church, not what it has become. I suppose that once I could have broken bread with Lazarus, at least taken comfort in the presence of someone else who saw what I had seen, heard the voice that I had heard, but now I hear nothing, and Lazarus is dark and listening only to some voice inside himself.

I walk with angels every day, or my insane projection of them, and yet I am full of nothing but doubt, feel no faith at all, nothing at all.

Where are you? Were you real, even then? Did I see what I wished to see, hear what I wished to see?

I believed that you were God, that he was God. I wanted to believe, wanted to accept the Messiah.

And if it is my will that he remains until I return, what is that to you? That is what you said, what he said, to Peter. I still can see that great head turning to look back at me, wondering at the same words that gave me pause as I followed them on the beach. I confessed it, in the Gospel, but they took it for faith. It was not faith. I did not follow that day for faith. It was for fear, and loneliness, and the shuddering anxiety in my stomach that you would leave again, and here I would be, sitting alone, staring at black water that does nothing but show me my own face, when it is yours I want to see.

I don't believe what they say. There was no original sinner. We each perform our own. There is no guilt with birth, no ransom to pay. Who would God pay? Who is greater than God, that God should pay a ransom for my soul? That is not why you came.

And yet you died, he died, I saw it with my eyes, crying, holding onto Mary. I still feel the warmth of her tears on my own face.

There was no Eden, no magic garden, nothing but the ignorance of people who did not yet know what was wrong or right, who came stumbling into the light, and who could not return to their ignorance, as though an angel with a fiery sword prevented them.

We learned that we die, all except me, and perhaps Lazarus, it seems. What then? There is no curse, no darkness there, but our children and our work. You shall bear children in pain, yes, the pain of losing them, of leaving them in the death we have come to know. You shall work for your food, and our work and our children are that which we leave behind us, the things that make our lives bearable. They are no curses. No child is a curse; no work well done is a curse. You blessed us with them.

Why do I not know you any longer? Why do I not hear you?

You died. I saw you die, and I helped to lay your body in the tomb. And it was no substitution, not for me, not for humanity. We each die for ourselves, all except me it seems, and I cannot die.

At least I have not.

Why did you? Why die? It was not to save us from your judgment, I know that much. How could it be? Are you sacrificed to yourself? No, and if not to you, then to whom or what? What can demand a sacrifice of God?

God is love. That is what I wrote, those many years ago, and still I would say the same, that you are love. And that is why you died, that is why you came and lived and spoke to us on the shore of that great lake, why you made us break our fast on that beach. Love. You died, killing off the wrong ideas of gods and of God.

It is finished, you said.

Go and live, you might have added.

Here I am, still alive. And perhaps more lost than ever I was.

Should I have told them? Should I have written it plainly, kept telling them? No, I wrote what I felt you wanted, and I stopped. And if they knew I lived, if they knew my name, how long I have walked on this earth, they would set me aside and begin to live to suit the idea of me, not to suit them, not to suit God's wish for them, and that is not why you came, not why you died. I understand that much, at least.

I have come, that they may have life.

I remember. Help me with what is left of mine.

"Amen," I said aloud, whether to God or to no one I did not know.

I sat watching the water. There was no sound except the rustle of the woods, the leaves swaying and falling, the water whispering by the banks of the stream bed, the leaves floating on the surface of the water so that one could tell which was the water and which was the sky reflected in it.

Somewhere behind me a bird sang in a tree, high up, then it was gone. I knew the deer was still there, somewhere out of my sight, watching me through the bushes with its great round eyes.

Adriel

"What are you talking about?"

John looks at me, then back down at the staff in his hands. "I've been carrying this thing around for two thousand years."

"More or less," I agree. I see the woods and dark water in his mind, vestiges of a walk through the woods.

"It is just a piece of wood. It doesn't glow, not to my eyes, and it doesn't open doorways to other worlds. It's just a piece of wood."

"Yes."

"Maybe that is all it ever was, this and the other pieces that we saved. Just wood." He turns the staff in his fingers, and the smooth base of it revolves against the floor. "Maybe you're not even here. You are just a projection of my own imagination."

"Of course, I'm here. Don't keep going back to the same thing. You're not insane, at least not for that reason, and I'm really here. Sarah sees me, reacts to me."

"Mmm. A child, reacting as she thought she should. Imagination is a powerful thing in the young."

"Evidently a powerful thing in the old, to judge by you." I watch him for a moment, sitting and staring at the wood grain in his staff. "I'll make you some tea."

A few minutes later I return, putting a tray on the table. There is a teapot, some cookies and one cup.

"There. I suppose the tea trundled itself in here," I add.

John glares at me. "Could have. Or my psychosis is so complete that I only think you put it here. Or maybe there isn't any tea at all. What do I know? I sit around talking to angels."

I watch him until he sips his tea and nibbles a cookie.

"I'm going out. I need some air," I say.

"No, you don't," John says. "Angels needing air. It's ridiculous."

"Perhaps you need the air," I say.

I move outside, or rather I think about movement and it is done. The walls are no more barriers to me than the space they contain. It is true that I do not need the air, but after so much time the space between us is sometimes necessary, for him and for me.

I move across to Sarah's home. Adi sits on the roof, reclining against a portion of the wall of the second floor and watching me. In a moment I convey to her why I have come.

"Perhaps none of us are real," she says. I look at her. "Sorry, I'll stop."

I am sure she is amused. Turning, I let my mind flow out to the space around us, seeking any others who might be near, any humans with doubtful intentions. I sense nothing but animals in the night, some resting, some active and rambling in a search for food. It is as though nothing has in interest in the sleeping girl inside this house, as though we have imagined that as well.

"We did not imagine," Adi says. Then we both sit looking into the night. "I think they are waiting."

"Probably." I rest for a moment. "But for what?"

Neither of us knows.

Lazarus

He came jerking along the walkway like a mannequin on wires, except that his wires were all in his head, pulling him to his goals. He looked up at the house with its well-maintained clapboards, the well-trimmed bushes. It stood as a contrast to the house next door, which appeared to be vacant, though Lazarus knew better. A single leaf lay on the walkway to the door ahead of him, and he was suddenly angry. He swiped at the leaf with his cane, missed, and only caused the leaf to flutter slightly and resettle itself on the smooth concrete of the walkway. The sight of it increased his anger, its presence highlighting the general sense of neatness and well being about the house, but Lazarus was only vaguely aware of the reasons for his feelings.

It would not do to knock on this door distractedly, he thought, and he paused on the steps to breathe and to gather himself. Then the door opened without his knocking, and John stood there, his eyes slightly narrowed.

"Hello, Lazarus," he said, but he did not go on with casual pleasantries. He simply stood there.

"Well, aren't you going to ask me in?"

There was a moment of delay. The wind blew across his back. He thought he could hear the damn leaf blowing along the walkway.

"Fine. Come in." John stepped back and gestured to the open living room beyond him. Lazarus brushed past him and walked down the short entrance hall to the edge of the open space. He stopped, feeling uncomfortable, somehow unwilling to move the next few steps toward a chair or couch.

"I'll make some tea," said John. "Unless you'd rather have coffee?"

"Makes no difference to me," Lazarus said, wondering why he was being so brusque and how he had lost his normal fine sense of control. "Whichever you would rather, John," he added more politely. He made his way to the couch and sat, listening to John heating water and finding cups in the kitchen. The sounds were familiar, and without warning he found himself thinking of Martha. She had always been busy, always rattling through the dishes, washing anything that did not shine. Today, he thought, his sister would have been thought obsessive-compulsive. They would have medicated her. The dishes would have stopped rattling, and the house would not have been so clean.

John was standing beside him, watching. A tray of tea was in his hands.

"Where were you just now?" he asked.

"Never mind that," Lazarus said.

John put the tray down, moved to sit across from him in an oversize chair. He waited, either for Lazarus to collect his tea or to start talking, it was not clear. Lazarus leaned forward and took a cup, spooning some sugar into it with just enough force to spill some of the crystals onto the tray, and sat stirring it, letting the spoon scrape along the bottom of the cup.

"You have something," Lazarus began. He sipped his tea and looked across the rim of the cup at John. John said nothing. "You have no right to it."

John still said nothing, holding his tea and watching his visitor.

Lazarus looked at the unmoving face. He felt his anger rising, knew he needed to control it. He forced his hands to hold the tea steady and raised the cup slowly to his lips to drink.

Why doesn't he react? he thought. Then he decided it was out of spite.

"How are you, Lazarus?" John sat politely watching him.

"You don't care how I am. Don't waste time claiming that you do." Lazarus knew he could not maintain a semblance of polite amiability.

"I do care, Lazarus. You are one of the few with whom I might discuss all that has happened to us."

"One of the few," snapped Lazarus. He looked around the room, angry at the sight of John, angry with himself for being so close to pure rage at the sight of John sitting calmly, politely sipping his tea. He looked like some English gentleman in an overstuffed chair, with a walking stick propped against the arm.

"Where do you keep it?" he asked. "You don't leave it on the mantle, I presume."

John was looking at him through those narrowed eyes, slightly aside. How could he convey such disapproval by simply looking? Lazarus wondered why he let it bother him, this disapproval by the one whom Jesus loved.

"Why have you come here, Lazarus?"

"Don't play the fool with me, John. I want the cross, the true cross, and I know you have it, that you kept it safe. Part of it anyway."

John sipped his tea again. Lazarus had a momentary image of choking the man, but he did not know if it would work. And where would he have hidden the cross?

"I don't know what you think you could accomplish with a piece of the cross," John said. "And I don't know why it is that you carry such hatred around. I have not done anything to harm you, so far as I am aware."

"It's not right that you keep such power to yourself. You have no right to it." Lazarus did not know just when he put the cup down and stood, but he was standing now, looking down at John who had not moved.

"Power," said John. "You think that there is power in a piece of wood, and you believe that I have kept that piece of wood for all these centuries."

"Don't pretend with me. I know there is power in it, and I know that you have kept it. As soon as you give it to me, we will be done with one another." Lazarus was still standing. Though he was angry enough that his hands were trembling, something about John's calm made Lazarus feel ridiculous. That did nothing to help his mood. He realized that he was going to learn nothing, and that this visit had been both a confirmation of what he knew and a waste of time.

He turned and walked out of the house, angry with himself for being angry, angry with John for being so calm, angry that he had no leverage to use against the man.

Lazarus could hear his own footsteps on the walkway. Looking down he saw the same leaf, still there. He swiped at it again with his cane and missed.

Bethany

The Jordan was not deep, not here, perhaps nowhere so far as I knew. Jesus was sitting on a rock in the sun, light reflecting from the water and falling from the sky as he sat there teaching. He answered questions, any questions, and we were busy baptizing people in the water, trying to impose order on the stream of people who came from every direction, alone, in groups, twos or threes. They came and they listened to him, and from time to time one would get up and walk down into the water to where some of us stood. We dipped water in our hands, poured it over their heads. Sometimes we lowered them entirely into the river.

It seemed to mean something to them. We wondered what we were doing, but John had done it as well.

"Wash and be clean," Peter told some of them. The others picked up the saying, or something like it. "Sin no more" was often heard, though even as we stood in that water I wondered whether anyone could manage that one.

I saw him coming, running along a path that led back in the direction of Jerusalem. He was tired. That much we could tell from the way his sandal would catch in the sand sometimes. He stopped, standing bent over at the crest of the riverbank, hands on his knees and his eyes moving across all of us until he found Jesus. He knew him by sight, I could tell, the expression on his face lifting. He jogged the rest of the way down the bank to where Jesus sat. The messenger took a small rolled up piece of papyrus, not much more than a scrap, and he gave it to Jesus.

I had come up from the water's edge, and by the time the messenger had gotten there so had I. It was no proper letter, just a scrap of papyrus like one might use for a shopping list. Jesus read it, sat looking at it, and then he turned and gave it to me.

"You must be tired," he said to the man, who was. "Take some rest, help yourself to the food." Jesus indicated a basket that Philip had placed in the shade of a bush. People kept bringing bread and other things to us, gifts for Jesus and for us. There was no lack of food, even out here in the wilderness.

The man seemed both grateful and anxious for an answer. I looked down at the message. *Lord, one you love is ill.* That was all it said, no introduction, no word of whom had sent it. The messenger must know, I thought, but Jesus had not asked him.

"My Lord," the messenger said. "What word can I take them? They are afraid."

Jesus looked at him again, then away at the water. Peter was waist deep in the river, enthusiastically pouring water over a man's head.

"Tell them I am coming," he said. The man looked relieved. He walked down to the water's edge and stepped into the current, splashing his face with the cool water and cupping water to drink. Peter was watching him to see if he wished to be baptized, but when he had drunk his fill the man turned and walked back up the bank.

I realized he meant to return the way he had come, and immediately. Going to the basket I took a loaf of bread and some dried figs and gave them to him. He made a short bow of his head and thanked me, and then he turned and walked quickly away. That was when I remembered him. It was the way he bowed. No one bowed to fishermen, but he had done it once before when we visited the house of Lazarus in Bethany.

I turned back to see Jesus walking slowly along the river. Catching up I walked beside him.

"Lord, are we leaving?"

He walked farther without saying anything, and I wondered whether he had even heard me. Then, as if he knew what I was wondering, he just said, "Not yet." And he walked away.

Sometimes Jesus would do that, walk away by himself. We came to know his moods, and we could gauge when to let him be alone for a time. I heard steps and turned to see Thomas standing beside me.

"What was that about?" he asked me.

"A message from Lazarus, I think. At least that is where I remember seeing that servant," I said. I handed Thomas the note.

"Who is ill, do you think?" I asked.

"I don't know. Which of them do you suppose Jesus loves?" Neither of us knew enough to guess.

"All of them," I said.

Two days later we were still by the river, sleeping in the open and waiting for more people, more questions, more baptizing. The food was never a problem. Somehow someone always brought enough for us all to share. It was midday, and we had gathered in what shade we could find. Jesus had said little, the crowd had moved away into groups eating their meals and waiting for the midday sun to lower a little.

"We need to go back to Judea," Jesus said. All of us stared at him. Peter shook his head.

"They tried to throw stones at us last time," he said. "They wanted to kill us."

Jesus took a loaf and broke pieces from it, giving them out to each of us. "Yes, but Lazarus is not well."

I thought about the scrap of papyrus. Jesus had not spoke of it since the messenger came. I had wondered whether he had some other news in the meantime.

"Our friend has fallen asleep," he said. Someone, maybe Nathanael, said that it was good, that if Lazarus was sleeping he might heal faster.

"Lazarus is dead," Jesus said. "And I am glad that we were not there."

This was not something we expected Jesus to say, of course. "I am glad we were not there." It was a cold thing to say. Only the tone of his voice kept the words from sounding perverse. Peter turned that great head and stared at me, looking for some explanation, but I did not have any.

"Gather our things," Jesus went on. "We are going to see him." Jesus stood and walked a little distance away, then stopped and looked off toward the horizon, away from us.

"Well," said Thomas, "Looks like we're all going to die with Lazarus." Because we were all Jews, we knew what was going to happen. They had already tried to stir things up, had already made their complaints known. When we returned to Judea, we would be accused of many things, some of them might even be true, and we would be stoned to death in the street, or shoved off a cliff, or turned over to the Romans. The Romans made the cliff sound welcoming.

It was a long walk to Bethany, and we stayed another night in the open along the way. I was beginning to look forward to the house of Lazarus and his sisters. Even if they were in mourning, there would be a chance of sleeping indoors. The village was at the end of a long path, with a cutting into a hillside along the way. The path went through an opening with an earthen wall on one side and a large rock on the other. A boy sat on the rock watching us, a small mob traveling with Jesus. The boy must have seen us before that day, because he stood on the rock and stared, then he climbed down and ran off in the direction of the house.

Soon we could see their roof, but before we reached it Martha, Lazarus' sister, came walking toward us. Several people followed her from the house. I was looking only at Martha, because I had not seen that look on her face before. She was pale, and she stared at Jesus while she walked toward us. We stopped and she walked straight up to him. For a moment I thought she was going to slap him, but she didn't.

"Lord, if you had been here, he would not have died." She stared into Jesus' face for a minute and then dropped her gaze to the ground.

"He will rise," Jesus said. I remember trying to picture what he meant, but I was entirely wrong in my understanding. So was Martha, as it turned out. So were we all.

"As you say," Martha said. "In the last day."

Jesus stood very still, staring at her. It was uncomfortable. Eventually, Martha looked up at him. No one said anything. We could hear people wailing down the path at the house, making a show of grief. It was customary, expected.

"I am the resurrection," Jesus said. "I am the life." Later the words would be famous, and we would think we understood them. This day the words seemed odd, out of place. He asked her, "Do you believe me?"

Martha glanced at me then looked back into Jesus' eyes. "Yes," she said. "I believe you. You are the Messiah."

Messiah. That is who he is, I thought. I had thought many things before that day, but for some reason I had never thought of that word. I wasn't sure that I understood it. I wasn't sure that she did.

She turned and walked away, going quickly back toward their house. Jesus stood still for a few minutes and watched her walking away. The mourners followed her, but they looked back over their shoulders at Jesus. I could tell they were wondering about what they had heard, wondering if they had heard correctly, wondering if we were all crazy.

If they hated us before this, I thought, they are going to try to kill us now.

Jesus began walking again down the path into the village, toward the house of Lazarus. Their parents were dead, and Lazarus had been left with two unwed sisters and the property. They were comfortable enough, had some standing in the community. All in all, they were a few rungs up the ladder from fisherman like most of us. When we reached the center of the village we found everyone gathered at the house to mourn.

Then Mary, Martha's sister, came outside, with a crowd of people who had been gathered in the house. They were all crying, some honestly. Mary came walking straight to Jesus who stood still once more waiting. She walked up to him with the same indictment as her sister and said, "If you had been here, he would not have died."

Once more, I didn't know whether she would slap him or not. Everyone knew how much time had passed since the return of the servant who brought that slip of papyrus. All of them knew we had made no great haste to get there. Nevertheless Mary just fell at Jesus' feet, tears pouring down her face. Martha came back out of the house sobbing. I looked around, and even Peter had tears in his eyes.

Then Jesus started crying himself. There were tears on his cheeks, rolling silently into his beard. It was such a strange sight, Jesus crying. Most of the people were crying, making a general wail throughout the open space. I heard someone say that Jesus could have healed Lazarus if he had come in time.

Jesus took Martha by the arm and raised her up, then he started walking toward the edge of the village where there were tombs cut into the hillside. Martha walked with him, and Mary, and all of us followed along with the mourners from the house. Eventually, Martha pointed at one of the tombs, Lazarus' tomb, and she put her face in her hands and wept.

Jesus was staring at the tomb. I was suddenly afraid, slightly nauseated, as I contemplated what he might be about to try. Surely not, I thought. Surely he will not try this thing.

"Take away the stone," he said. I put my hand to my mouth, horrified. Martha sniffed, her tears slowing with the shock of hearing the words.

"Take away the stone," he said again.

Martha looked around at the stone, back at Jesus. "My Lord, we cannot, not now, it has been four days. The smell…"

People near enough to hear what they were saying began to murmur. I looked around to see if anyone was picking up a rock.

"If you believe, you will see the power of God," Jesus said. "Take away the stone."

It was like one of those dreams where everything gets slowly worse, but you cannot wake up. I wanted to walk away, go anywhere, but my legs would not move. They would stone us, I thought. The Romans would not have to do anything. Our fellow Jews were going to kill us right here in this village. I looked around at Peter, who was holding his stomach with both hands. Peter, I knew, did not care for bodies. The dead unnerved him. It made no difference, I thought, soon we would all be dead.

Martha turned and looked at some men in the crowd and nodded to them. They did not move, but just looked at her as though they did not understand. She pointed at the stone rolled in front of the small cave that formed the tomb. I thought I could already smell the body.

The men looked at one another, but Martha pointed again and they rolled away the stone. Then they backed away, watching Jesus. Martha swayed a little and caught herself. Mary joined her and they stood with their arms around one another.

It was so quiet that all I could hear was an occasional foot shifting on the stones, a bird chirping in the distance.

Jesus began praying, out loud, thanking God for hearing him. Everyone could hear him right then, I thought. Everyone except Lazarus.

Then Jesus stopped praying, and there was silence. I could not even hear the birds anymore. Then he yelled, "Lazarus! Come out!"

I started praying, silently, hoping this was, in fact a dream. I prayed to be somewhere else, that all of this was not happening. There was no way out, the tombs being at the end of a path, and we were surrounded by a crowd who were certainly going to kill us very soon.

Then I heard something moving in the tomb. We all heard it. There was a shuffling sound, like someone's feet sliding against the stone floor of the cave. I glanced around to make sure other people were hearing what I was hearing. Peter was staring into the tomb, his mouth hanging open like a dead man with no head cloth.

There was a sudden gasp, everyone in the crowd breathing in at once, then the murmurs, and finally a woman screaming until she fainted, falling onto the ground. No one had the presence of mind to catch her. We were all watching Lazarus walk out of the tomb.

He was wrapped in the burial shroud, shuffling his way into the light.

"Let him go," Jesus was saying. "Take those things off of him."

Mary ran to her brother and began loosening the same cloths that she had helped to tie around him four days earlier. Martha was crying, hysterical. Two men turned and ran down the pathway, back toward the village and Jerusalem, yelling that Lazarus was alive.

Somehow I knew that none of this was going to turn out well. Lazarus had never been one of my favorite people. Now that he was shuffling his way out of the tomb, he gave me the creeps. He still did.

Nevertheless, I had seen the power of God. Jesus had raised a man from the dead. He couldn't be the Messiah, could he?

Adriel

I am expecting a trick, like something arranged by traders in the caravans who traveled the ancient deserts, one of them dying in each town just to be raised from the dead by another one in the troupe to the applause of the crowd and the collection of gold coins. Not that I catch Jesus in any tricks, not in these things he does, but this is beyond the reach of men.

When they gather at the tomb, I go inside. There are right about the stench. Certainly, something is dead in here. Lazarus is there on a long low stone niche carved into the wall. He is wrapped in cloth, and he stinks of death. I see within him no life, not life of his own, only the small life that consumes the corpses of larger things.

I settle on a shelf on the opposite wall to watch. It is clear that Jesus means to raise the man from the dead, and that is a trick seldom seen even by angels. Here I have a front row seat.

It is quiet outside. I hear steps approaching, then the stone begins rolling to one side, pushed by two men. They back away quickly, and the opening to the cave becomes an uneven doorway of light. Silence. Then I hear the man Jesus praying, thanking God for hearing his words.

In this silence, I think, who could not?

He is yelling, calling the dead man to come out. I turn back to watch.

The first thing I realize is that the smell is gone. It is as though it had never been there. Odd, I think.

The body begins to move. More to say, the body is a man once again, alive, and I am fascinated watching the breath return to the lungs, the hands move to pull the cover from the face. It is the man Lazarus, just as I can see him in a prior visit to this village. He is not only alive, he is restored. It is as though he has never been dead.

But he has been dead. I am sure of that.

I follow him as he shuffles out into the daylight and his sister begins to untie him, releasing him from his burial shroud. The crowd is staring at him. No one can see me, of course, or there would be an even bigger show.

Then I realize that Jesus is looking at me, straight at me, and that he does indeed see me. After a moment, he turns and looks only at Lazarus, just as the rest of them are doing, the ones who are not staring at Jesus as I am.

He raises men from death. More, he reverses the effects of death. Even more, he sees me when I do not wish to be seen.

Who is this man?

Wilderness

I was wrong again.

He raised a man from the dead. Part of me was horrified, and part of me was astounded. At least these people were not going to kill us, I thought, for desecrating a grave.

Lazarus had certainly been dead. His sister was right, there was enough odor when they rolled back the stone to let everyone know that a dead man was lying in there. Making the odor dissipate was almost as much of a miracle as bringing Lazarus back to life. I was amazed and relieved.

Surely, now the word would spread and the people would all come to believe that Jesus was someone sent from God, maybe even the Messiah. I was a little vague on what the word meant, but now I heard it used everywhere. We seldom had a use for it in the fishing trade, and I did not understand much of what I heard whispered in the crowd that day. I did not understand much of what I heard spoken in the many years afterward.

And I was wrong. Some of the people did come to believe that Jesus was of God, whatever that meant. I had not allowed for the possibility that some would be jealous of such a public reaction, or that they would fear it. I did not see that a dead man rising and walking out of his tomb could make people angry. I had not learned yet that fear dresses in the robes of anger when it can.

By nightfall, we had all begun to realize that there was a current flowing through the villagers. Currents were something we understood well. Sometimes you could not see water moving, not on the surface, but underneath it was surging past, and anything caught in that current was lost. Some of the whispering began to sound like a different, darker stream running through the village.

We spent the night with Lazarus, Mary, and Martha. Most of us slept on the floor of their living quarters. There were more people in their garden, more in the streets, and we knew more would come.

Some of the men who came were from Jerusalem. We saw them in the streets the next day, and we knew that they had come to see and to take a report back to people in Jerusalem. They were somber and quiet, staring without saying anything. There were not many of them, but when Jesus walked out of Lazarus' house in the middle of the day, he stopped and stared back at them until they began to shuffle and to move away. We last saw them walking back on the path to Jerusalem.

I left the house that night in order to get some relief from the crowd of people crammed into the space. The house was spacious enough, but not for this large a group. I did not notice where I was walking until I found myself once more in front of Lazarus' tomb. Well, the tomb that had been for Lazarus, I had to correct myself. As I stood there I realized I was not alone, and I saw Andrew smiling at me. He was sitting on a rock beside a fig tree. I guessed that he was here for the same reasons as I.

I walked over to him, and we both sat upon the rock and stared at that tomb. We were each trying to make sense of what we had seen, not only that day but on all the other days.

"I was thinking about John," Andrew said after a while.

I knew he meant the Baptist, not me. "Why John?"

"Do you think he knew what was going to happen, the things we would see, when he sent us following Jesus?"

Before Jesus called us from our boats, before we knew what we were trying to find, Andrew and I had both gone to listen to John the Baptist ranting beside the Jordan. We were never certain whether John was mentally unbalanced, or a prophet, or an unbalanced prophet, but we could not stop listening to him. Then one day Jesus had come walking along the river, and John had stopped midstream and pointed at him. "Look! The Lamb of God," he had said. It was such an odd thing to say about a man that it stuck in my memory. Andrew and I had gotten up and followed Jesus along the river.

I had no idea at the time what John had known. I still had no idea, and I told Andrew so. Then I remembered something.

"It is strange, don't you think, that John came up to this same place from the river?" I said. John had told us about priests from Jerusalem coming to question him. They had found him here in Bethany.

"Maybe it was the Essenes up in the hills," Andrew said. "Everyone knew that John stayed with them sometimes. This is as good a town as any to come down to from there." After a while, he added, "That's an odd bunch."

"No stranger than we," I said. Andrew made a grunt of agreement. We sat staring into the cave for a while.

"He was dead, wasn't he?" Andrew asked, partly of me.

"He was dead," I said. "They buried him." Somewhere in the back of my mind I had also thought that he could have been put into the tomb alive, for show.

After a while, I added, "We smelled him."

Andrew said nothing, but his hand went to his face. We both sat for a while, looking at the entrance to the tomb. The moon had shifted across the sky when Andrew turned to me.

"Do you suppose he will go back to the same tomb one day?" he asked. I had not thought of it, but when I did, it made me more uncomfortable. I did not know what to say. After a while we both walked back to the house for what was left of the night.

In the morning Jesus told us to gather our things, and once again we headed out of town and into the wilderness. This time we walked to Ephraim, not much of a town, some distance north of Jerusalem and across wild hills. Along the path most of the people dropped away, and there were only a dozen or so of us with him. We stayed there quietly, waiting for Jesus to tell us what would come next.

None of us would have believed him. None of us would have wanted to.

Adriel

I sit inside the tomb staring out at the two men. They have been there most of the night, occasionally talking, mostly thinking through the bewilderment of seeing Lazarus walk out into the daylight. I am thinking through the same thing. All of us are sitting in the dark, trying to understand what we have seen.

They think that I already understand. They have never understood my kind. They still do not. I do not hold it against them, and I do not want to disillusion them. Simply having another form of being does not mean that I have greater knowledge; we simply have different insights. Sometimes we interact with other dimensions. Sometimes we interact with the being they call God, or so I think. At least it seems to be so in my memory.

I have not done so since the beginning. At least I think that I did so then. It is difficult to see the beginning, harder to see what is before it.

Once I stop by a stream in some mountains, here on this planet. The water is sluicing past some rocks to a waterfall, and the sunlight shines down into the small valley of the stream, so that the water and the light run together and even I cannot always tell which is water and which is light. I kneel there and watch the water flowing, watch the sun shine and fade, the moonlight and stars likewise, until when I move again lifetimes are gone by and the water is washing the rocks into sand. A few of the humans know of my presence in some way. I hear them speaking of the place in the language of men. They call it Falls of the Angel.

Ironic name.

Some people seem to notice me more, sense my presence in the way that dogs somehow know a cat is walking nearby. The Mayans are like that. It is always difficult to stay hidden around them. I forget myself for a moment, and then one of the women points and says, "There's one. It brings a message."

I have no message. I am simply being. By and large it is far more interesting being on a planet with life as opposed to a giant rock formation or gas ball in space. Those are interesting in their own ways, but there is no spark in them.

Humans, though, have sparks. Animals have sparks. Even plants sense and move and grow. The rocks wash away or crumble into dust.

Fallen. I am not sure that I know what it means, but the humans seem intent upon dividing everything into pairs: light and dark, good and evil. Some things simply are as they are.

The two followers still sit on the rock wall opposite the tomb. They are not Mayan. They do not notice me, though one of them seems more attuned to the possibility. Maybe it is the chocolate that gives the Mayans greater insight. This man has no chocolate, and he cannot see me.

A rule is broken. In all of this universe, things move in certain ways, follow certain paths. The water always follows the pull of gravity. A man's body is broken. It moves toward the next stage of use, so that I see it again in the dust and in the plants and in the eyes of birds hatching millennia from now. Then the movement stops. The system of cells and organisms that was him begins to reorder and then is him once again. I sense them moving like ants, order from seeming disorderly movements. The elements of the world do not reorder themselves without the influence of force. Energy flows from the man Jesus.

It is not entirely so. The man calls for the body to live, and the body lives, but the power flows from everywhere, the space between atoms and the worlds beyond what is seen. I see that power at the beginning of this universe. I do not see it since, not until this man.

One of the men asks the other whether the one who is raised will return to this tomb. Neither of them knows. I do not know what becomes of the man, but I can tell them one thing. The cells and energy I sense in that raised body no longer deteriorate. His body is in a kind of balance that I do not see in animals.

I do not think he will return to this tomb. Unless the stones roll down upon him, I do not think that he will need to return.

Dragons

"What if the dragon is not evil?" Adriel asked.

I looked at him, finding nothing but a collection of shimmering light that appeared to be watching a squirrel. Squirrels are what the universe has devised to distract even the angels.

"It is a dragon, chasing the woman. Of course it is evil," I told Adriel.

"But what if it isn't?"

I sipped the coffee from the mug in my hand and thought about it. In the visions, it certainly felt evil. Just recalling the images made me feel queasy.

"It could be that the dragon is a metaphor for struggles, or challenges," he said. "Dragons are not always evil."

"Have you actually met a dragon?" I asked, truly curious. I had not, but then Adriel and his kind had been around longer than I.

"Well, not precisely," he said. "There were the giant lizards, and many of them lingered, but they were before the humans."

I stared at the shimmering light.

"You saw the dinosaurs." I had been fascinated by them ever since I learned that they existed. As a boy, I heard stories from travelers who told of the skeletons of dragons that had been found. Once a traveling merchant came, her wagon loaded with odd things for sale, silk cloth and dried herbs. She wore a tooth on a leather strand around her neck. The tooth was long and wide and white, and her daughter wore three slightly smaller ones. Our father saw them and told us that they were the teeth of sharks, giant sea creatures. The woman stopped and politely said that it was not so. She told us of lands far away to the east, impossibly far away I thought at the time. There were caves where the bones could be found, she told us, mountain caverns and ravines where the rains washed away the rock to reveal the skeletons of the great beasts. My father asked what manner of beasts they were, to have teeth like these.

"Dragons," the woman said, her accent strange. Strange patterned markings seemed to move on her arms and her neck. We were amazed, but I could tell that our father was doubtful. She waved us over to her wagon and said something in a language we did not know to her daughter. The girl leapt up into the wagon and disappeared behind the cloth cover. In a moment she was back, and in her hands was a wooden box that she placed on the sideboard of the wagon. Her mother nodded to her and she opened it, like a display for a shop window. Inside we saw long curves of bone, sharp at the end and as long as our hands.

"The claws of the dragon," said the woman. Her daughter lifted one from the box and held it out to my father. We each touched it, amazed at the weight, the size, and the terrifying sharpness of the claw end. For a moment, we each could see a dragon, standing by the shore and gazing at us, sharp teeth leering from the open jaws, and claws waiting like stone knives to slice us into the dragon's mouth.

"The teeth and the claws of the great dragon, they are still powerful. If you wear these, no curse can harm you," she said. "The curse will run back to follow the one who sent it against you."

None of us spoke, and my father silently gave the claw back to the merchant. We had no spare money to buy such a thing, and my father would not subscribe to the idea that wearing the teeth or the claw of such a beast would offer protection against magic.

"We will trust in God," my father said. "But never have I seen such things as these. The teeth are much like the great teeth of the shark, but never did a fish have such claws as these."

James and I kept our eyes on the claw while the woman placed it back in the box. The girl closed the lid and disappeared once more into the wagon. While we did not worry much about evil magic and curses, from that day we believed that there must be dragons, if their skeletons were to be found. In museums, centuries later, I saw that there had, indeed, been swimming creatures with claws like these.

I still did not know where that woman found the fossils that she showed us, nor from where she and her daughter had traveled. It was a place only barely imaginable for me at the time. It was still much the same for me, distant mountains and caverns shifting in my imagination. I supposed it may have been anywhere east of Galilee, but with the bones and the tattoos and the silk, I knew it must have been far to the east. Always when I thought of dragons and the monsters of myth, I thought of the woman and her daughter and their necklace talismans of dinosaur bones.

"I saw the great beasts," Adriel said. "None of them spoke, and I never saw one that could belch fire from its mouth, but they were huge and deadly and toward the end of their time many were intelligent. There was a cold brilliance in the eyes of the ones that hunted the others for their food. They would look at us the same way, and we knew that they were measuring whether they might eat one of us."

I pictured an angel standing on a rock and the light glimmering in the eyes of the raptors gathered, watching it.

"Yes, it was much like that," he said. "They were unafraid, even of the light, even in the darkness. Not that there was any way that such a beast could injure one like me. Finally they would realize that we were not flesh, not food, and their interest waned, except for the smartest ones who seemed to begin to wonder about things other than food."

"That was millions of years ago," I said. Sometimes I was again momentarily awed to recall the vast reach of memory that resided in Adriel and the others like him. The centuries he and I had spent together were ephemeral to him.

"We were sorry when that great rock came hurtling from space. Some of us would have spared them, moved the path of it, but we knew that we should not do such a thing. It was like a small planet hurtling with astonishing speed, and when it struck the earth I thought that the earth would explode and be ended in the dust and fire. The earth did not explode, of course, and it did not end, but the clouds of dust covered the planet and the creatures were gone, dead, bodies sinking into the cold earth, buried by time and dust and water."

"The dragons were gone," I said.

The light shifted. I saw Adriel more firmly, more corporeally.

"The dragons will never be gone," he said. "They are creatures of your myths, your stories, the Minotaur waiting in the maze to kill those who wander inside. The dragons wait. When we need to see them, we do."

I sat by the table, images of the dragon swirling through the sky on great red wings and swirling through my mind as well.

"Tell me again, why would we need to see dragons?" I asked, already knowing the answer.

"To bring us back to life," he said. "They are only the image of the thing that we do not yet understand. They are the challenge we set ourselves, or that is set for us. Dragons are the gateway to life."

I grunted at this, not liking the odds of facing a dragon.

"The gateway to life," I said. "They look more like the gateway to death."

"It is hard to tell the difference, and there are worse things," Adriel said. "So many lives are carried in corpses who have not lain down."

I stared at him.

"If we do not face the dragons, then we stop," Adriel said. "And if we stop, what purpose is there?"

John

"Why does Lazarus want the cross?" I asked.

Adriel was by the window. There was no telling what he was seeing. On occasion I made the mistake of asking, and for hours I might hear about the way the water flows through the veins of a leaf he is watching or the way the light refracts in dew. The first few dozen times these discourses had a degree of novelty, but eventually one wants to scream at him to just get on with it.

"I don't know. He has no need of it that I know."

"Need? I'm not sure why anyone would need this particular piece of wood," I said.

"Then why have you carried part of it around for twenty centuries?" he asked.

I walked to a window and gazed out. Why did I carry it? I had no need of a walking stick.

"It helps me to remember," I said. He made no answer. We both knew very well that I had no difficulty remembering. Perhaps I should have been pursuing a method of forgetting, a tonic of lucidity, something to bring me fully into the present so that I did not live so much in the memories.

"You like the memories," he said.

There is nothing so irritating as an angel who thinks he is infallibly right. I knew that anger was lying in wait like a panther in the back of my mind, but I did not want to let it out.

"Yes, I do." I was still staring out of the window, and I wondered whether this was why Adriel so often focused on other things while talking to me.

"No, I simply find them interesting," he said.

He meant no harm in reading my thoughts, though once again I wished he would not. I had learned that most of the time he was not conscious of the difference between what I said and what I thought. Besides, I was distracted, thinking of the walking stick in my hands. I began thinking of a time before I had made it.

When we left Jerusalem, Mary rode in a cart pulled by a donkey. It was a kind animal, grey on grey, never obstinate. I could not remember its name, which bothered me.

We found a home for ourselves near Ephesus, Mary and I. There was a community with other followers of Jesus who knew us. Mary's home was small, an open space for living and cooking, space for sleeping. Her other sons had not wanted to see her leave, but Joseph had died years before. After Jesus' death Mary and I had remained close. It was Jesus' wish.

Mary spent many of her days writing, as did I, though she never shared what she wrote, and she seldom spoke to the people who came each day to her house. She would come out and give them a blessing, smile, and go back into the house. They respected her privacy, but I ordered the leaders of the church there to set a watch around her, just in case.

Adriel was also with us, of course, so there really had been no need of protection. Having the men set a watch around us served the purpose of keeping them at some distance. Besides, one never knew. Not even angels always know.

When I saw finally that she was tiring, I gave some thought to what to do after her death. When we came to this place we had brought the cross piece on which he was crucified. I kept it in my room, near where I slept. So far as I was aware, nobody knew what it was other than a length of wood set up as a shelf, though some had looked at it and wondered about the strange holes and the stains. Few there had seen as many crucifixions as I, and they were unlikely to guess what this piece of wood actually was. Who would keep such a thing?

I had heard that disturbing news of what had become of the bodies of other followers of Jesus. These were my friends who were dying, but some people seemed to want their bodies as relics. I was determined that nothing of the sort would happen to Mary. I would not have them carrying off her heart or her hands to distant places like the pagans. It would not do.

Mary and I spoke about it, privately, eating supper together in her house one evening. There was only the bread and cheese and some wine, but it was good bread that she had made herself. The cheese was from the milk of goats on the hills around us.

"Have you thought of what will happen when we are gone from here?" I asked her.

She nodded and sipped her wine.

"I will be glad, I think," she said. "Do you think we will see him again?"

I knew that she meant after our death, in whatever place one goes.

"I think so," I said, but she may have known that I had doubts. So many years had passed, and I was no longer sure of what I had seen and heard.

"Mary, I would not have anyone disturb your rest, your body, when you have gone," I said. She took a piece of bread and ate it, looking away at the fireplace.

"It will not matter," she said.

"Still, though it may not trouble you, it would trouble me if I were left to see it done." I took another sip of wine, somewhat bothered by saying aloud what I had thought.

Mary turned to look at me.

"Of course you would be," she said. "I had not thought enough about how things will affect you. I'm sorry."

"No," I said. "I'm sorry to mention it. Anyway, perhaps I will go first, or we will go together."

Again she looked at me, and I regretted my polite words.

"We both know that you will be here," she said. "Look at you, nearly unchanged in all these years, and I have grown old."

It was true. I had aged some in appearance, enough to garner the respect of the believers around us, but now many of them appeared older than I. Some had begun to whisper again about Jesus' words to Peter on that beach.

"I should never have given them what I wrote," I said. I meant it.

"No," Mary said. "Your words have helped them. They have helped me. You have taught them to love one another."

"I have not taught them too well," I said. "For that matter, I have not taught myself."

Mary only laughed and turned back to the fire. She often sat quietly thinking, and I always wondered what memories held her. Adriel would not say, though he seemed to have no compunction regarding my own thoughts. Mary would sit at her table, or in good weather she would sit outside. I would often see Adriel standing near her, though I do not recall them conversing, not as he and I converse. Perhaps Mary had conversed enough with angels.

Sometimes she would tend to the flowers that grew outside our home. Occasionally she would have me bring papyrus and her pen, and she would sit in the shade of a tree and write. I thought about the manuscript. It was as long as the story that I had written of Jesus, and I wondered what she had recorded.

"Mary, what about your own words. When will you let them read it?"

She shook her head, thoughtful. "I may never let them. I am not sure that what I have written is helpful."

We let the words settle for a while as we sat quietly watching the fire.

"I will leave it with you, John. You will decide what to do with it." She looked at me. "Another burden for you."

"You are no burden," I told her.

We had carved a tomb into a hillside outside Ephesus, near her home. I had bought the use of it, and others in the church who were skilled with stone had helped me to carve it. They believed that it would be Mary's tomb, and I did not dissuade them. I never told Mary or showed it to her, of course.

Mary fell asleep one evening, and she never woke. It was that simple, that quiet. We had shared supper, talking about fishing of all things. She wanted to know what it was like to float on the sea all night, what it was like to pull in the nets with the fish jumping and flashing around your feet in the boat. Had I known earlier that Mary had wondered such things, I would have taken her fishing myself.

We sat near the fire until we were tired, and Mary asked me to help her to her bedchamber. She lay down on the bed at once, and told me that she would sleep a while before changing from her robe. I let her rest and went back to the fire, where I fell asleep in my chair. It was Adriel who woke me a little later. He was standing very still, even for him.

"She is gone," he said. I went to her door and looked, but she was still there. I thought that she was asleep and wondered what Adriel meant. Then I noticed that she had not moved from where she lay when I left her earlier. When I was standing at the side of her bed I realized what he meant. She was gone.

I wondered then whether she had found Jesus once again, whether she was somewhere that I could not see, with him. I thought that perhaps now Jesus would come, that he would suddenly be in the room with me, but then I realized that Mary had already gone to him. He would not be coming to this room, not now.

We buried her in the tomb I had prepared for her, with spices and a new shroud, as was the custom. There were many who came to weep for her. She had never known anyone who did not love her.

That night, in the dark, I came back to her tomb. We took her body out, Adriel and I, and laid it on a cart, leaving only a new shroud and some flowers where she had been. It seemed to me that something should be there should someone come looking for her body. I did not know who would come, or when they would come, but as I said, the bodies of those close to Jesus had become objects of fascination in some circles. There were macabre grave robbers, though one never could tell for sure whether they acted from devotion or some kind of ghoulish fascination and greed.

They would not find Mary's body, I had decided. They would never rob this grave.

And now I had become a grave robber as well. The little donkey pulled us along the path and away into the hills. The load was not heavy. Mary was small, and there was only a length of wood and a jar besides some flowers and extra spices. In an hour or so we reached another set of tombs carved into a hillside. Three years before this, I had gone to a Greek tomb carver in Ephesus who owned these tombs, and I purchased two from him. I do not know why I purchased two. Later I realized that no one could ever lay me to rest beside Mary. To do so would disclose her real tomb, and it seems I will not require one in any event.

The donkey stopped for me as though it knew where we were. It was a good creature and had often pulled the cart for Mary when she and I had ventured into Ephesus or elsewhere in the countryside.

I had thought from time to time that I would move the stone covering of the tomb with my walking stick or with the help of the donkey, but Adriel simply rolled the stone away. I had been somewhat worried about accomplishing the task alone, and I still had not learned what it meant to walk with angels or how useful they could be. I was relieved when he moved the stone for me.

I lifted Mary's body from the cart and carried it into the tomb myself. She was not heavy, and I do not age, not much. The donkey just turned to watch me, not seeming to take any alarm from the body or any scent of death that it may have been able to perceive. Perhaps Adriel helped to calm the creature, I do not know. I could smell only the spices, sweet and rich. When I had arranged Mary's body on the shelf in the tomb, we took the wooden beam and carried it into the tomb as well. It was the cross bar from the cross of Jesus, or what remained of it. I had sawn it lengthwise to obtain enough wood for my walking stick and for one other, smaller pieces left over as well. This large remnant I laid on the floor of the tomb beside Mary.

I placed the jar at her feet. In it was the manuscript she had written. She had told me, finally, that it described the birth of Jesus and other events from her life and from his. Already I knew that her recollections would not agree with some of the stories told by the church in Jerusalem. It seemed better to let her words sleep with her. If ever I needed to retrieve either her words or the cross, I knew where they would be.

We left Mary's true tomb, the donkey and Adriel and I, and we returned to our home, Mary's home. The sun was rising, and I suspected that some in the church would still come out to what they thought was her tomb and weep. I walked out to the tomb and brushed the ground with an olive branch so that no one could see the cart tracks or my footprints and guess that something had happened in the night. Then I went back into the house, and I slept.

When I awoke, I saw that someone had come and brought fresh bread and a cheese. I washed myself and put on fresh clothes. As I sat at the table and ate, I looked around at our house, and I wondered how to manage my own funeral. Riding with Mary's body during the night I had realized that some day I would have to make the people who knew me believe that I had died as well. I could not very well bury myself. The only solution I could find was that I would need to die in some distant place. Word of my death could be sent back to those who knew me, but only after it appeared that I was already entombed.

It would be a more difficult trick.

The Accuser

Once when the court of heaven was gathered, the accuser, the Satan, came and joined the other members of the court.

The Lord said to the Satan, "Welcome, and where have you been?"

And the Satan answered, "Going to and fro upon the earth, and walking up and down on it."

Just then the Lord looked down upon the circle of the earth and saw the disciple John sitting at the seaside.

"Have you seen my servant John?" the Lord asked the Satan. "There is no one like him upon the earth, a good and faithful man who fears God and turns away from evil."

Then the Satan answered the Lord, "Does John fear God for nothing? Have you not blessed him, and placed a fence around him? Does he not fear God because he fears death and the judgment? He is faithful only because he is fearful of dying and of being judged for his sins."

"Very well," answered the Lord. "He is in your power. Remove the fear of death from him, and we shall see whether he remains faithful."

"Let the Angel of Death be told this day that it cannot touch the man John," said the Satan, and he looked around the court to find the one among the sons of God who was Death. That one stood peaceful and unnoticed in the midst of them. Indeed, such was the odd power of the Angel of

Death that wherever one was, there the Angel was as well. If one stood in the midst of the court, Death stood there also, and if one traveled alone to the distant rim of heaven to gaze upon the stars, upon turning one would see the Angel of Death standing there.

"It will be so," said the Lord. The Angel of Death bowed its head, and all in the court of heaven saw it. Each being in the court saw the Angel standing at its side, beautiful and welcomed.

And the Satan left the court of heaven and went down to the circle of the earth, where he found John by the waters of the Sea of Galilee. Unseen by the man, the Satan walked up behind him and touched him, taking from him all disease and placing a shield around him, so that he was unable to die.

"Now we shall see," said the Satan. "Now it will be made plain, that you are like all of the rest, and that you fear God only because you fear death. When you perceive that you cannot die, you will cast aside your faith."

The Satan called out, and there came slithering from the rocks and the sand two serpents, their sharp fangs dripping with poison. The Satan commanded them, and they crept across the sand to the feet of John, who had not seen them approaching nor had he heard them slithering in the soft sand.

The disciple John leapt to his feet, but the two snakes leapt as well and they bit him, one upon each ankle, their fangs sinking deep into his flesh and their poison flowing into him.

"Oh, I am bitten by serpents," cried the disciple John, and he fell backward upon the sand. The serpents, emptied of their poison, crept away across the sand and the rocks, and the Satan stood unseen upon the rocks to see what John would do, whether he would abandon his faith when he saw that he would not die.

The disciple John lay upon the sand, and the hot sun shone upon him like the face of God. John could feel the poison flowing in his veins, flowing in his blood. And the vultures, having seen the serpents that the Satan called to bite the man, gathered circling in the sky like dark spots upon the sun, and they waited for the man to die.

Time passed and the man still lay upon the sand unharmed. There was no pain in his body, his heart was beating in his chest and the air came and went from his lungs, and even the wounds left by the terrible bites of the serpents were healed and could not be seen. He saw that he would not die.

"Surely," he said, "the Lord has saved me from this affliction and spared my life." And the disciple arose from the sand and stood, his arms raised to the circle of heaven, and he gave thanks to God for his faithful mercies. In all these things, the man John did not sin against God, neither did he renounce his faith.

Again one day the heavenly court gathered at the throne of the Lord, and the Satan came to join the other members of the court. The Lord saw the Satan and called upon him saying, "Where have you been?"

And the Satan answered, "Going to and fro upon the earth, and walking up and down upon it."

The Lord said, "Have you seen my servant John? Even when he saw that serpents do him no harm, he held to his faith in God. He is faithful and turns away from evil. There is no one like him on the earth, and you have accused him without reason."

"That was no test," said the Satan. "The man still believes that he will die, though the serpents cannot harm him, and that is the reason that he remains faithful. He is still fearful of his own death, and he is fearful of the judgment. It is from fear that he is faithful, not from love."

"What do you suggest?" asked the Lord.

"Let him walk in the fire, and remain unharmed. When he sees that even fire cannot harm him, he will cast away his faith."

"Go," said the Lord, "and do as seems best to you. Only do not destroy him or test his mind beyond what he is able to understand."

And the Satan went down upon the circle of the earth and walked until he had found the disciple John. He was in a marketplace, and there were many people and merchants, and in the center of the market was a great metal pot set upon a fire. The cauldron belonged to a giant of a man who served food in the marketplace, and the pot was large enough to cook three sheep at once. The man would fill the cauldron with oil, and when it was bubbling hot, he would place the sheep that he prepared in the oil and let them cook so that the fragrance spread across the marketplace.

The Satan looked at the cauldron and at the fire and at the bubbling oil, and he saw that it would be useful for showing the man John that he could neither die nor be harmed. Going through the crowd, the Satan began to point to the man John, and he began to tell the people that John was a sheep ready to be cooked. The Satan also told the man whose pot this was that the man John was a sheep, cleaned and ready to cook. And so the giant man looked at John and saw only a sheep ready to be cooked. The giant man came and took John, who cried out and asked the man to put him down, but the giant man heard only the crowd saying that this was a good sheep and that its flesh looked good for eating. And John cried out again, for he saw that the giant man was taking him to the boiling cauldron, but the crowd did not hear him, for the Satan told them that they could not hear the man John, and so they did not.

Reaching the cauldron, the giant man lifted John, now screaming, and dropped him into the boiling oil, and John was sure that he would die. He plunged under the surface of the boiling oil and came back up, his face and hair dripping the hot oil. The man John was astonished to see that the oil did not burn him, nor was his skin injured. The hot oil felt no warmer than the water of a bath, and the man John realized that just as the poison of the serpents could not harm him, neither could the fire or the boiling oil harm him.

The disciple John pulled himself out of the cauldron and stepped over the side into the glowing embers of the cooking fire and then to the ground. He looked and saw that his feet were not burned, and his skin was unharmed, glistening with the hot oil that dripped onto the ground at his feet. Then the Satan released the people, and everyone in the marketplace saw that the disciple John was not harmed by the oil or by the fire.

The giant man ran to John and knelt before him, saying "Forgive me! I thought that you were the sheep that was to be placed into the oil!"

And the people of the marketplace likewise said that they had seen him being placed into the oil, and that in their eyes he had appeared as the carcass of a sheep, ready for cooking, and not like a man, and neither did any of them hear him crying out to be saved.

The man John perceived that the sight had been hidden from their eyes and that his voice had been hidden from their ears, and he knew that only one of the sons of God could have done such a thing. And he looked again at his hands and his feet, seeing that the heat of the oil and of the fire could not harm him. Walking back to the fire, he reached into the flames and took one of the glowing embers and he held it in his hand for all of the people to see. And they looked and saw that his skin was not burned and that the heat did not harm him, and they were amazed.

Raising his arms to heaven, the disciple John said to them, "Behold, the fire has not harmed me, and the hot oil has not burned me. Surely such a thing can only have been the deliverance of the Lord!" And he gave thanks to God, and all of the people likewise gave thanks to God. And the Satan saw that his work had failed, and he walked away going to and fro upon the earth to think.

Again the council of heaven met at the throne of the Lord, and all of the sons of God gathered before the throne in the circle of heaven. And the Lord looked and saw the Satan gathered there with all of the court, and the Lord asked him, "Where have you been, and what have you been doing?"

And the Satan answered as always, "Going to and fro upon the earth, and walking up and down upon it."

And the Lord looked out from heaven and saw the circle of the earth, and the Lord saw the disciple John walking upon the earth.

"See," said the Lord God. "There is my servant, the disciple John, and there is none more faithful upon the earth. He is blameless and upright, following the good and turning away from the evil. Twice you have accused him of false faith, and twice he has proven himself before us. You have accused him without cause, and incited me to act against him by preserving his life with no reason."

Then the Satan answered the Lord, "He values only his own skin, and nothing more! Let him see that all around him will perish, but that he will remain, and he will perceive that he does not need the Lord."

The Lord considered the words of the Satan.

"Go," said the Lord, "and do as seems best to you. Only do not bring any to their ends before their times."

And the Satan went out from the court of heaven and the sons of heaven, and he walked to and fro upon the earth, watching all of those whom the man John loved. One by one, they aged and grew old, but the Satan had touched the man John and age did not affect him, nor did he grow old as those around him. One by one each person that John loved died. Each time, the Satan would come and whisper in John's ear, to make certain that he knew that someone else had died while he remained upon the earth, ageless, without harm, out of the reach of the Angel of Death whom John could not even see. After many years, no one whom John had known and loved remained alive.

The other people began to whisper and to say among themselves that this man could not die, and that he was spared from death. John heard their whispers, and he heard the words of the Satan who came and told John that he could not die, and John knew that it was true.

Then John walked away into the desert, away from everyone who knew who he was. And he found a cave and began to live as a hermit, going back among other men only seldom, and making no friends among them. Each day as the sun rose, John would walk out of his cave and stand in the sunlight, raising his hands to heaven, and he would give thanks to God who had sustained him even in the face of this most terrible burden, a life that would not end. Then the Lord looked down from the circle of heaven and saw his disciple John and heard his prayer, and the Lord smiled upon him.

And the Satan saw it, and stomped his feet upon the earth, up and down upon it. He cursed, saying, "How can it be that it is better to this man to die than to live?"

Then he turned and looked, and the Satan saw the Angel of Death standing beside him.

"Why are you here?" asked the Satan.

"As the Lord lives, I am everywhere," said the Angel of Death. "Except that I am not beside the man John, for you asked that it might be so and the Lord granted your request."

"It would be better that you were beside him, and better that you should reach out and touch him to take his soul to the place of death, for look what he has done. Even though he cannot die, he keeps praying his thanks to God," said the Satan. "It would be better for him to be among the dead."

Then the Satan felt a hand upon his shoulder, and turning he saw that the Angel of Death had placed its hand upon him.

"What are you doing?" asked the Satan. "Take your hand off of me, for I am one of the sons of God and a member of the heavenly court, even as you are."

"You were of the heavenly court," said the Angel of Death. "That is true. And where I am taking you there are many who were great before they came to the shores of death."

"Take your hand off of me," said the Satan. "For I cannot die."

"You asked that the man John be unable to die," said the Angel. "You did not ask the same for yourself. Since the man John now cannot die, the Lord has sent me to say that you shall go in his place."

And the Satan walked no more to and fro upon the earth, nor did he go up and down upon it, for the Angel of Death took him, and he was no more.

Adriel

"You keep thinking of her," I say to him. He is lingering in the streets of Ephesus in his mind and so in mine, disturbing my sense of time. For humans the past is always past, but not so for us. Time is more pliable, open to interpretation, open to choice. As John's mind dwells on the past and he thinks of his conversations with Mary, I lose my hold on the present and drift momentarily to that past reality, though for me nothing is past.

"Yes," he says. "And why not? Mary is as good a person to think on as I have known."

True enough, I think.

"I suppose the jar is still there with her?" he asks. I pause, considering the destination, then I am on a hillside in Turkey. It is dusk as I stand near John. Now it is past midnight, a cool evening, dust stirring in a breeze that slips around the hillside. Her tomb is in front of me, marked by nothing.

The tombs here remain undisturbed, hidden in the open within a larger tract of undeveloped land. John had made the investment two centuries ago; it had been his idea. He had needed to ensure that Mary's tomb remained intact, undisturbed, and so far it does. No development, no grave robbers, no archaeologists.

I pause, and I move through the stones covering the entrance: cold darkness, hard crystals forming millennia ago to make this doorway of stone. I illumine the interior of the tomb, not that I need the light, but I enjoy seeing the peaceful space in golden glow. Mary lies undisturbed. Fine dust like snow covers her shroud. The cross piece likewise is covered in the dust of nearly twenty centuries, as is the jar. I look through the wall of the jar, hardened clay and fire and hands of a potter in my mind as I do, to see that Mary's manuscript remains undisturbed within it.

In a moment I am gone and stand in our kitchen near John's chair.

"It is still there." I tell him. "She is still there. Nothing disturbs them."

John sighs and lowers his eyes. I busy myself making tea for him, something I seldom do. I know that he needs something to nourish him, and I know that he does not want to think that I am watching him. After all this time he still grieves for Mary's loss, perhaps more than for her son.

I place the tea in a cup and saucer in front of him, sugar already in it.

"Thank you."

Civility and service are useful things, even after so much time in one another's company. Perhaps they are all the more useful because of the time we have spent together.

"Do you think it is time for her words to come to light?" I ask, knowing he is not ready. He shakes his head.

"I cannot bring myself to do it," he says. "I don't know how the manuscript would be received."

"It is true, is it not?"

"Certainly, but being true and being helpful are not the same. There are a great many things that are true but which are not helpful."

He sips his tea.

"Mary would wish to be both," he says.

I think about that as I watch a squirrel sleeping, high in the oak in Sarah's front yard.

"Perhaps it would be both," I say. "It would make them think, a good thing, and they may come closer to the truth, also a good thing."

John finishes his tea without saying anything else. His thoughts were still of Mary, remembering the way she speaks about everything, about Joseph, and her children, and most of all about Jesus. Her point of view is unparalleled in the world.

He rises and heads up the stairs to sleep, pausing at the door to say goodnight. The memories tire him. They awaken me.

Society

The meeting was usually held at a large hotel with a meeting space, plenty of rooms. There was no advertisement of the meeting, no public announcement. A small sign usually stood at the edge of the lobby or along a corridor, off-white changeable letters announcing "Meeting of the Johannine Society." The group was represented as what they were, people devoted to exploring Christianity from the perspective of the apostle John.

No one on the hotel staff was ever advised that John himself would be attending the meeting. No one at the meeting even called his name out loud, not even in the modern English pronunciation, nor did they ever refer to him by any title, though no passerby would have thought it anything but a coincidence that the main speaker shared the name of the society's founder.

Actually, John had not founded the society, not precisely. They had formed long ago of their own accord. Some time after his supposed death and entombment, a few people had recognized John, and they had approached him with great joy to see that he was alive.

John had been less than pleased to be recognized, even though he was the source of much rejoicing. He had planned too long and worked too hard to have his death negated by accident, and he could not have them surmise that there had been a second resurrection. There had been nothing to do but to take these men and women into his confidence, to explain to them why he had staged his own apparent death, and to pledge them to secrecy. Oddly, though the fact of his being alive was a sworn secret, the society had continued to grow in numbers through the centuries until John realized that he had unwittingly given rise to one of the oldest secret societies on the earth.

Each year the members met. Originally they had sought out locations with some sense of the holy, such as ruined churches and old abbeys. Eventually they found that having their meetings out in the open was far easier and far more secretive. It was the opposite case from an extramarital affair. A group of people gathering at some old holy place tended to draw attention, but at a hotel no one gave them a second glance. If the second coming happened at a Holiday Inn, it is doubtful anyone would take much notice.

John would welcome them and speak to them of his memories of Jesus and of the other disciples. They would all share in a communion service, and the group would disband until the following year. From time to time, John would request some work on the part of some of them, seeing to some errand or work that was needed.

For the most part the group did nearly nothing at all.

The sign outside the Bellarmine Meeting Room was small and brown, held up on a chrome stand that was slightly worse for wear so that the sign was slightly tilted like a model of the earth. At least "Johannine" was spelled correctly. A few people walking through the corridor glanced at the sign. Otherwise, it was unnoticed.

Occasionally, people would walk to the door of the room and go inside, usually alone, never more than two people at the time. Most of them were at least in sixty years old, some were older, with graying hair and more than one walking stick among them. The people entering the room were serene and peaceful for the most part, and almost all of them went completely unnoticed by the other patrons of the hotel.

One man was not like the rest. He was not nearly so old as the others. Like many of them, he was also using a cane, though it did not appear to bear much of his weight. His step was firm and quick. His eyes searched the lobby, the people, the spaces around him. While his face and his manner were calm, his eyes did not stop gazing around the room, examining each person they found before moving to the next. In the corridor he glanced at the name of the room as though to make sure he was in the right place. With a small shake of his head, he made his way through the double doors of the meeting room and began to take stock of the people already there.

As the meeting was scheduled to start, John came walking through the lobby. He carried a walking stick, and his hair was gray enough. While he too gazed around like the smaller man before him had done, John's gaze was calm, never darting from face to face. If someone met his gaze, John offered a warm smile, just friendly enough to put the other person at ease without inviting conversation.

He walked to the doors of the meeting room. As the other man had done before him, John read the name on the meeting room plaque and also shook his head. He peered through the small glass pane in the door to see the people gathered and waiting for him, and he sighed.

"May as well get started," he said, as though to himself.

"Wait a moment," came Adriel's quiet voice in reply, apparently from nowhere. John looked over at the point where Adriel would have stood had he been visible. For a moment he was concerned that Adriel planned to enhance his entrance.

Adriel had done that, once, more than seven hundred years prior. As John had entered the hall where the society had gathered, Adriel had caused the sunlight entering the hall to shimmer and to appear to linger on John's shoulders like a nimbus or halo. There had been some gasps from the people in the room. By the time John had realized what Adriel had done, he had been so angry he had to stand silently for a time before being able to speak, sure that yelling at an unseen angel would be no improvement on the situation. The people in the room had revered John, certain that they had witnessed something like the transfiguration of Jesus on the mountain.

John had refused to speak to Adriel for nearly a month afterward, and Adriel had agreed never to repeat the performance.

"There is something," Adriel said. "Thoughts, partially hidden."

John suspected that the thoughts of some of the people in the room remained hidden even from themselves, but he realized that Adriel was concerned and did not say so.

"The one named Simon," Adriel said. "His thoughts were of the cross relic just now, thinking of how to learn the whereabouts."

John looked through the window again. He saw the man sitting calmly near the aisle, two thirds of the way back. He had taken a cup of coffee from the service along the wall and was sipping it, not engaging with the people nearest him.

"Why would he think that there is a relic?" John asked. He had never spoken of keeping it safe, never mentioned Mary's tomb to anyone but Adriel. It was not a secret shared even with the members of this society.

"I do not know," Adriel said. "But he thinks also of Lazarus. The two have met, and recently. Be careful, my friend."

"Lazarus," said John. He looked down for a moment, unconsciously placing both hands on his walking stick. "Well, we must get on with it."

Saying so, John looked up and opened the door. He walked calmly down the center aisle to the front of the room, grasping hands and embracing each person as he went, including Simon.

John

The streets were crowded with people and animals. A donkey's hoof brushed my foot, and I was still holding to the animal for balance when I heard a man calling to Jesus. The fellow pushed his way through the crowd, and he somehow managed to kneel in front of Jesus. The people nearby pulled back a bit, seeing such a spectacle as this man kneeling in the street.

They knew him, this man. I had seen him in the synagogue myself, and here he was kneeling in the street and begging Jesus to come and to touch his daughter.

"She is sick, master," he was saying. "You must come, you can save her. You have the healing touch."

Jesus was looking at him. For a moment I wondered whether Jesus even heard what the man was saying. Then Jesus reached out, touched him on the shoulder and leaned forward to tell him something. I never learned what he said, but the man smiled and stood and began to beckon for Jesus to come after him.

The crowd parted somewhat, curiosity driving the ones who knew nothing about Jesus. This man they knew from the synagogue ran in front of Jesus, urging him along. The noise from the crowd was mixed with the dust from the street. It was difficult to see any distance ahead or to know where we were headed, except that we were following a man whose daughter was unwell.

Suddenly, Jesus stopped. A woman lay in the street, blood dripping down her cheek.

"Woman," said Jesus. "How long have you lain there bleeding?"

She looked around, dust on her face along with the blood.

"I do not know, my lord," she said. "The crowd has walked around me."

"Who has touched this woman?" Jesus asked. I realized that there was no knowing who had touched anyone in this great crowd.

"How can she tell, there are so many?" I asked. Jesus turned and looked into my eyes for a moment, then turned away again. I felt like I had missed something obvious, that I should pay better attention.

"Then I will touch you," he said to the woman, and he bent down and reached a hand to her face. He pulled her up from the ground, and she fell against him, holding him. I could see her face over his shoulder. The blood was gone.

"Come, my Lord," said the man. "There is little time. My daughter may die if we do not reach her." He was pulling at the arm of Jesus' robe, wanting the woman out of the way. Peter was looking harshly at the man, though I knew that Peter understood about the sick child and the urgency. He just never wanted anyone shoving or pulling at Jesus, as though he could not take care of himself.

I heard raised voices and some curses from further down the street. Since we were on a small hill I could see over the heads of the people between to see that another man came pushing his way up the street, garnering the resentment of the crowds as he came. When he reached us he knelt in the street, his head down, and said, "My Lord."

The man pulling Jesus's arm stopped for a moment, then began to turn toward the kneeling servant. I could see that the man knew the voice, and I realized what the meaning of it must be. At least I was not so dense as to miss that.

"Your daughter, my lord." He stopped. "She is dead."

The man was still standing and holding to Jesus. The woman in Jesus' arms looked at the messenger and understood as well. She pulled back, her hand on Jesus' other arm. The servant looked up at his master and around at the rest of us, saying nothing. Then, a moment later he added, "I am sorry."

The street seemed quieter, people realizing that something was happening, some of them recognizing Jesus, some recognizing the man himself or this woman. There were tears now on the man's face, though he said nothing, his eyes sharing the sorrow before his mind had grasped it.

Jesus touched the woman's head, a sort of caress or blessing, and then he in turn took the man by the arm.

"Come," he said, as much to us as to this man. "Let us go up to your house together."

The servant rose, and turning back led us in a procession through the crowd. Somewhere we heard the wailing of women who had already heard the whispers of grief. We walked as in a funeral line.

I have always hated funerals.

After some time we reached the house, a large one at some distance from the crowded marketplace. Family and neighbors were gathered around it, the women weeping.

They surged forward when they saw the girl's father, crying and saying that she was gone.

Jesus paused then, before entering the house. He took hold of the man's arm the same way that the man had held him in the market.

"Why are you crying?" he asked them. We all stopped and looked at him. I stole a glance at the crowd who were trying to work out whether he was an idiot. Finally, the old women seemed to assume it was simply that Jesus did not know.

"The girl, his daughter, is dead," they began to tell him. Jesus set his face, and I looked around to find Peter.

"She is only sleeping," Jesus said. The words froze me in place, for I knew that they were not true. The crowd paused for a moment, and the father began to stare at Jesus. Then the crowd turned and began to jeer and to insult him, asking whether he were blind or simple. The father himself said nothing, only watched Jesus' face.

Jesus pushed those in front of the doorway aside, which surprised them. It surprised me. I looked back down the street, wondering where we might run when they found some loose paving stones to throw at us. Peter stood staring, his mouth open, his expression lending no credence to Jesus.

"Out of the house, all of you, mourners and trespassers," Jesus was saying. "Out."

Shocked, the visitors looked to the father who, still staring at Jesus, slowly nodded to them. They began to leave, though I could not tell whether it was by Jesus' authority or by the respect they had for this leader of the synagogue. Taking the man by the shoulder, Jesus looked around at

Peter, my brother James, and myself, and indicated that we were to follow them.

We entered the house, suddenly far too quiet except for the sound of a couple of a women crying, genuinely, upstairs.

"Take us to her," Jesus told the father. He nodded once more and began walking up the stairs to the sleeping rooms. It was a spacious house, and cool, and these upper rooms could be opened to receive what breezes came blowing across the roofline of the town.

The girl lay on her bed, and it did appear as though she were sleeping. Beside the girl her mother sat crying, tears covering her face. Genuine grief does not care about appearances. Perhaps nothing genuine does. Another woman stood weeping in the room, though I never knew whether she was a servant or family. The mother looked at us, then at her husband who took her by the hand and lifted her from the chair. Jesus stood at the girl's feet. Suddenly I realized that he, too, was crying, the quiet tears falling across his cheeks.

I thought that Jesus must have been wrong, and that he now saw as we did that the girl was dead. I was mistaken once again.

"Little girl," he said. "Wake up."

For a moment, all of us stopped breathing. I heard it, the quick catch of breath in our throats, all of us for a moment wondering what would happen and whether the girl was, indeed, only sleeping. Then, in the next moment, all of us realized that she was not, that she was dead, that this was perhaps the worst and most shameful moment of our lives. I started to feel the enormity of our imposition on their grief.

Peter's eyes widened as he watched the girl. I turned back to see.

The girl caught her breath, much as we had, and we could hear the sound of air surging through her lungs and from her mouth. Jesus reached across and held her hand.

"Little girl, get up now," he said. "Time to wake."

She held his hand and sat up on the edge of her bed, looking around the room at her parents and the woman, whom she knew, and the four of us, whom she did not. Her mother was the first to recover, leaving her husband's arms and jumping into the bed with the girl.

"You are alive," the mother was saying over and over, and the father began to say the same thing. Peter began muttering a curse, though only I heard him, and then he caught himself.

"Lord, you have done it," he said.

Jesus was only watching the girl. "She is hungry," he said. "Get her something to eat."

"Yes. You must eat," said the father, as though it were obvious that the child would be hungry. Then he turned and began thanking Jesus, who simply pushed the man along with his daughter and wife toward the stairs. They went on ahead of us, shouting and calling for food, then for a feast. At the bottom of the stairs Jesus watched them a moment, then he turned away from the front of the house and went out into their garden. A gate led us out into the street, where the others were waiting for us. Without a word, Jesus turned and started walking away, as though the woman had never lain in the street and the girl had never risen from her bed. He did not speak of it.

I never saw any of them again, except that at the end, when Jesus was dying. That day I saw at a distance a man standing with a woman and a girl. I wondered whether it was this family, come to show their respect, or thanks, or pity. I have never known for sure.

Adriel

There are four of them and they are climbing a mountain. It has nothing at the top but a view of the bottom, so I think that what they are doing is odd. Perhaps they are more like us, doing unlikely things for the pleasure it brings.

The one named Peter is the strongest, but he gives little thought to his path. Along the way he has to stop, baffled by rock, and turn back to the path behind Jesus. I sit on an outcropping watching them pass. Jesus is the only one who seems to know I am there. When he glances over at me, the one named John follows his eyes and pauses, staring at my rock perch though I do not believe he can sense me. James only wipes at the sweat on his forehead. Peter mumbles curses.

A cloud is moving across the peaks, hiding the long fall to the valley. Their group has scuffled their way to the top. Peter collapses, his back on the mountain, and stretches out as to sleep. I move past them when I feel the change. It is like waking from a dream when you did not know you were sleeping. Sunlight strengthens, but the shadows are cast away from the figure of Jesus, light coming from him and now from the others who are with him. They are not the three who made the climb, now lying face down on the hard rock. These are two more, men I think, though even I am not sure.

Jesus turns and tells the three to rise.

"These you know," he says. "Here are Elijah and Moses. Do you not recognize them?"

I do not understand how this has come to pass. Neither, it seems, do these three men. James and John are standing. Peter drops back to his knees.

"Good! It is good, Lord!" Peter's eyes move from one to the other, his arms stretched out wide. The other men say nothing at all. "We shall make a camp for you!"

He is babbling.

Jesus continues to talk with the other beings for a while, not remarking on Peter's plan. The light begins to increase and the wind makes the men's robes ripple and slap against them. There are voices and more beings, a wall sliding away. I hear a great voice speaking, and I know I hear it also long ago in my memory, but I do not know the words. I cannot tell whether the sound begins from above us or comes from inside us, and I am lost. The three men are flat on the rock of the mountain, none of them looking up. I see many figures streaming through the light, then one light as though somehow the sun is within the cloud, and the energy of it sounds like static, so loud, it hums every frequency at once, and then everything stops.

The clouds are gone, as is the light. Now there is ordinary sunlight, no longer appearing so bright on the top of the mountain. Jesus is gazing down into the valley, and it seems to me that he has been standing there the whole time, only looking, that nothing has happened.

Gravel shifts and I realize the three men are still there, Peter beginning to stand, John and James helping one another to move. They are looking around them as though just now waking.

None of us speak. None of us moves.

Jesus turns and looks at the three. Saying nothing, he starts back down the mountain just as they had come. They follow, as do I.

Part of the way down is a rock shelf, high and wide enough for all of them to stand together. Jesus is again watching the valley. When the others catch up to him and stand there waiting, he turns to them.

"Tell nobody what you have seen." He watches them for a moment. "One day you may understand it, and then you may speak of it. Until then, keep it within you."

He does not turn to leave but waits, looking at them. Peter is staring, mouth open. James is little better, looking from his brother and Peter back to Jesus. It is John who manages to speak.

"Lord." A pause. "That was Moses? And Elijah?"

Jesus's face softens.

"Yes, in a way." He turns to look back down into the valley. "Such things are hard to explain to you now, but one day you will understand. Elijah was here. Moses was here."

No one speaks. Jesus keeps watching the valley, the small figures gathering at the bottom of the mountain. There is a village in the valley, and the other followers of Jesus are there waiting.

Jesus turns, and they begin the slow climb down.

John

I barely saw the rocks. I only remember the feel of them under my feet and in my hands, hard and flinting away into flakes and sand, as we made our way down that mountain. What had we seen?

Maybe there was no air, our minds taking leave of us at the top, but we had all seen it. Peter had talked about making a camp. The light had been so bright that everything else still seemed to be in shadow, even in the afternoon sunlight.

I did not know what voice I had heard, and the more that I thought about it, the more I have thought about it over the years, the more I seem to have heard. That voice was saying things that I would not hear until time had passed. I still hear them. The right time comes and the meaning becomes as clear as though Jesus had simply turned and spoken himself. There was nobody on that mountain but us, and there was a complete world without sky and without form. Perhaps it was God speaking, I do not know. It was not a voice like anything else that I have ever heard. It spoke that day, but it spoke outside of time, and the meaning cannot be heard until its purpose has come.

Perhaps God says everything at once, and it is the hearing of the words that require time. The meaning is already there, carried within us, and suddenly we understand it when the time comes. That it why we cannot make out what the voice is saying. It is all the words we will ever hear but spoken at once, and it is time that translates them to our being.

I stumbled on a stone at the bottom of the mountain. James caught my arm, and then when I had recovered he nodded for me to look ahead. Jesus was walking toward the other disciples, all of them standing together with a crowd circling, voices raised. Some of the crowd saw Jesus approaching and turned to run toward him. Their faces were a strange mix, some glad and some with the look of men watching the spectacle of a circus.

Jesus kept walking toward the center, the crowd falling back to let him pass. A boy was lying on the ground, his body stiff and thrashing on the ground. I had never seen such a thing, yet I was sure Jesus would touch him and stop whatever was wrong.

He did not touch the boy, though, but stood a few feet from him and watched. The boy's father came and took hold of Jesus's sleeve, then knelt in front of him.

"How long has he been like that?" asked Jesus. The boy was thrashing on the ground, clearly about to hurt himself, and Jesus was asking questions as though this was a tourist attraction.

"Since he was a child," said the father. "We do not know what to do to help him, but we keep him from rolling into the fire or hurting himself."

The father paused and looked back at his son. He was ignoring the crowd.

"Can you help him? Your followers have been able to do nothing. Are you able to help him?"

Jesus looked across at the other disciples. All of them looked down at the ground or away.

"All things are possible," he said. "Do you believe this?"

I was not sure whether he was speaking to us or to the boy's father. It was the father who answered.

"I believe, yet I do not believe. That is the truth of it, and I would not lie to you." The man looked at his son, then back at Jesus once more. "Still, can you help him?"

Jesus reached out and put his hand on the father's shoulder. More people were hurrying up the path from the village, all of them holding their heads up to see over the crowd already gathered there.

He spoke to the boy, or to something. I could not remember his words. The father turned to see, and the boy stopped moving and lay still. The father crawled across the dust to him and lifted him.

"He is dead." It was someone in the crowd saying so. Peter looked across the faces, and I knew that it was good he could not tell which of them had said such a thing out loud.

"No," the father said. "He is not dead."

We heard the boy gasp for air, and his father turned to look up at Jesus.

"He is alive, my boy is alive."

In his father's arms the boy was limp, breathing as though he had run a race, but he was not thrashing anymore.

"You had faith enough," Jesus said. "If you had told me you had no doubt, then you would have failed me."

He turned and walked away from the boy and his father as though the crowd were not even there.

John

The squirrel was pretending not to see me. It simply stood on the tree stump with an acorn in its paws and occasionally bit at the shell.

I was sure that the creature did, in fact, know that I was sitting there watching it, and I was sure that sooner or later it would have to acknowledge my presence. At least, if I were to stand or to move from the deck toward the tree stump, the squirrel would undoubtedly react.

Little sneaks.

I was happy to sit and drink my tea, leaving my legs propped on the deck railing. Whether the squirrel ignored me or not did not affect my reality. I was sure that I could exist, or cease to exist, whether or not the squirrel concurred. Still, it is nice to have some connection with other life forms.

There, I thought, other life forms. Alien squirrels from outer space. For all I knew, squirrels were alien life forms, highly intelligent beings that had infiltrated our world. One day we would discover that when viewed from space the pattern of oak tree plantings on earth formed a message encoded in tree top symbolism.

"What?"

I looked at Adriel, or at least at the space where he should be. Eavesdropping again.

"Sorry."

I sighed.

"It is not as though I am not used to it by now," I said. "Though from time to time it would be nice to have some privacy." For a moment I had a brief image in my mind of all of the other ones of his kind, spread around the globe, watching and listening to the thoughts of humans, and of squirrels for all I knew. Then I wondered whether I had just somehow glanced into Adriel's mind. It was disconcerting.

"I do not know either," he said, also disconcerted. "Though I can tell you that I have seldom gleaned anything approaching brilliance in a squirrel."

I stared in his direction.

"Well, you were wondering. About the squirrels," he said.

"Closer to say that I was pondering the possibilities."

A pause.

"Of what then?"

Again, I sighed.

"If you are going to talk to me, at least appear. Otherwise it is easier to talk to the squirrel."

A slight shimmer appeared in the other deck chair, like the reflections of a mirror ball mixed with the appearance of heat rising from the desert. We sat for a while, both of us being ignored by the alien rodent.

"It isn't the squirrels," I said. We sat a while longer. Adriel had the good sense to say nothing in the silence, which was not easy even for a being who had been around as long as he, however long that was. "I'm just not sure. Of any of it. Not any more."

We were both quiet after that. The squirrel sat watching us for a time, then gave us up and hopped back to its oak.

Simon

I have spent my life in universities and museums, reading manuscripts, following legends and whispers. I have sat in worship circles, even dark ones, trying to find some indication of what is possible, what is real. Most of the time I found nothing but other men and women sitting in circles, standing in what they supposed were holy places. Incense and chants and prayers and whispers were all that I found, and nothing to show for the time wasted, not until I heard whispers of a man who remembered Jesus. Discounting the writings of lunatics and cults, there were still rumors that the apostle John was alive. Ludicrous, I thought, nothing more than the inventions of people who had read the ending of that Gospel as literally as they read everything else. Even the ending was itself doubtful, certainly a later insertion at best. Then I was invited to one more circle, one more gathering, and I met him. John, the Apostle, son of Zebedee, was still alive.

A charlatan, I thought, a ruse.

Listening to John and to the others who claimed to have known him for decades, though they aged while he did not, I began to wonder. Then I realized that when John came, another came with him. There was always glimmer of light that I found in the edge of my vision, a place where other objects were muted or changed in appearance by having something, or someone, interposed. No one else in the gatherings seemed to notice, but I realized that this man John noticed. He looked in the same places that caught my eye. There was something there. It was an angel.

After all, if I were going to buy into this man being John the Apostle, why not accept the presence of angelic beings as well?

A fine show, I had thought, and I looked for the lights, the wires, the trick, to see what made this angel appear to be present. There were no wires. There was no trick. And the light came from the creature itself. The angel was real, and so I came to accept that John was real. And I was finally part of a genuine secret society, one that had a genuine secret.

Then one day I heard a knock on my door. It was Lazarus. This man was nothing like John, and there was no secret society of admirers and believers around him. And this man had sought me out—me, of all the scholars around the world—and I was amazed. I learned of more secrets, more relics, first hand accounts of first century events and sites. My academic career was rising. No one could find archaeological sites as well as I could with the help of this man. With his recounted recollections, I could also interpret those sites better than anyone.

I was brilliant.

A PhD. All those years of graduate work, smiling and sniveling, laughing at old jokes by old men who held the purse strings. It was life filled with meetings and research, not the kind I wished to be doing but the kind that was required for the program, to satisfy the expectations of smaller minds. Teaching undergraduates was like purgatory, and grading the research papers of undergraduates was worst of all.

Vapidity has no end.

I earned the credentials, though, and doors began to open. I trolled through the vaults of the Vatican itself, searched for lost secrets hidden in drawers of the British Museum. All that I found was what others had found before me. One day an ancient priest approached me as I walked within the Vatican walls, and he introduced me to a quiet network of old minds. Their thoughts were like parchments sliding across one another, dry and difficult to understand. Nevertheless, I had found the door that led to the cult of John.

That is what it is, a cult, built around that fossil of a man. It couldn't be true, he couldn't really be alive, but there he was, or at least there someone was. Finally, I had realized that he was, in fact, John the Apostle.

Then I heard whispers of another man, someone else from those days who also survived to this time. He crept through the world like a dry wind. Lazarus.

Surely, I had thought, this one must be more interesting than John and his old sheep. He was.

When I learned of John, I was amazed. As I was initiated into the society, I was humbled to stand in the presence of one who had stood in the presence of our Lord.

When I stood near Lazarus, he was like a tornado in my path.

John was quiet. He was a man of love, and no doubt of great and deep faith, but he did nothing but talk, and he solemnly forbade anyone to speak of his long life and of his presence among the present day believers. Such a miracle, and he hid it under a bushel. It was as though he could not see what such a thing would mean. A man had lived upon the earth for two thousand years, and what if this man gave testimony to the life of Christ? The world would turn to the true faith by the thousands.

Lazarus, though, Lazarus understood.

To think that there were two men who had walked upon this earth for so many centuries, with so many secrets, watching the church grow and expand across the entire world. Yet today, we were split, in factions, Catholic and Eastern and Protestant, and a thousand other tiny groups that cannot be counted, each with differing beliefs, differing practices.

Absurd.

There is one God, I reasoned. There must be one Church.

It would take a sign to unite them, a sign to bring them under the true banner of Christ. John was himself such a sign, but he would not lead them. Instead he pointed to the gospels and the letters, as though mere words have any power in them. No, it would take a sign, something that could be seen and touched and known as proof of what the gospels merely tell.

Lazarus told me that he himself could not be such a sign. He was simply a man who was brought back from the dead, he said. Who would believe that claim or believe that Lazarus was more than he appeared, simply another man in middle age? How would we prove it? But he knew of something that could unite the people under the banner of Christ. He knew that the true cross still existed, that it had been hidden and preserved all of these centuries, and that the power of the blood of Christ remained in the wood.

It had the power to heal anyone who touched it, Lazarus said. The true light of God shone from it, he said. Scientists would be able to measure something of the energy that radiated from it. It would be the proof that the faithful have needed. It would remove all doubt that Christ was the Lord, and all of those false religions would be put away.

It was the key.

And John was the only one who knew where it was hidden.

John

"We have to help her." As soon as I said it, I knew it was obvious, and I knew that Adriel was staring at me as though something were stuck to my face.

"Of course we do."

I puttered around the counter with a dishcloth. "She doesn't need to know that we intervened."

"Sarah will know."

He was right, I knew. I wiped the teapot, polishing away the dust and the small spots of water and oil that seemed always to find their way onto things near a stove.

"It doesn't matter," I said. "She already knows about you and me. One more thing will make no difference." I knew that I was justifying it to myself, not to Adriel. "Perhaps her knowing will help her in the long run, give her something tangible."

Adriel was on the other side of me. Sudden movements like that were unsettling. There was something of the predator in such speed, it seemed to me. Those moments always reminded me of how different humans and angels are, and of how limited we each are in different ways.

"Building the faith again? And I am not a cat from the jungle."

"What?" He had read my thoughts once again, angels as predators. "No, of course you are not a cat. You are far less quiet and far less lovable."

"Now I'm hurt."

"No, you aren't." I looked out the window, wondering whether Sarah might be in the yard. She was not. "We will invite her over for dinner."

"You should reassure her that I will not pounce on her and devour her."

"Well, at least it will be good not to have to pretend you do not exist. Are you considering making any announcements, offering any light shows?"

"I should leave here and go to Vegas, make my fortune."

"Yes, that is what you need to do."

Adriel made something approaching a 'humph' and was quiet.

That evening Sarah sat at our table. There were three places set. It always seemed rude to exclude Adriel from the table simply because he did not eat, and Adi had chosen to remain outside and watchful. Sarah would occasionally look around to locate Adriel. He would shimmer, and Sarah would be gleeful. It was like trying to dine with children.

"You are certainly in a good mood," I told her.

"What? Oh, yes. Yes, I like being here. Adriel is fascinating. You are both fascinating, I mean." She blushed.

"Don't worry, I understand. It is difficult for an old man to compete with a walking light show." I took a sip of wine and looked at her, smiling across the table. "I hope, we hope, that you return often."

"Yes," said Adriel. "We do."

Sarah looked around the room. "What about Adi?"

"She is watching, outside. Perhaps she will join us later," Adriel answered.

"That would be nice."

"Yes," I said. "She is an interesting person."

"Person?" Sarah said. "Oh, well, of course." Again she was embarrassed.

"Don't worry," said Adriel. "We are accustomed to being thought of as different, as not-human. It is no offense."

"Still, I'm sorry. I mean, I just realized that I had still been thinking of you as, well, angels, these amazing beings. I just hadn't quite managed to think of you as simply people. You know, like us, but different." She trailed off.

"It is a normal thing to have trouble placing us in your understanding," Adriel said.

"Yes," I added. "I still find myself slipping once in a while."

"Indeed," said Adriel.

We sat for a moment in silence. *Go ahead,* came Adriel's voice.

It was always annoying when he did that. Inevitably, he would place his thoughts in my mind when it was most inappropriate to respond. Still, he was right. We must go ahead.

"Sarah," I began. She smiled at me. "There is something else that we need to tell you."

"Ok," she said. I paused, not sure how best to phrase it. She saw my hesitation. "It's all right, you won't hurt my feelings."

She looked at me and around to find Adriel's shimmer. Still, I hesitated.

"It's not like I'm dying, or anything," she said lightly. When she saw my face, she put down her wineglass. Perhaps she would have done better to lift it.

"Well, Sarah, you see, Adriel can, well, see things, sense things…"

"Oh, my God," Sarah said quietly.

"You have cancer," Adriel said. "You do not know yet because it has not grown too far."

"Cancer," she said. I thought about hitting him, but he was right to go ahead with telling her, and I doubted I could land a blow anyway.

"Am I going to die?" she asked quietly. I could see the tears forming.

"No," I told her. "At least not now, and not from this."

I stood and walked around the table to stand behind her chair. I hesitated, but I refrained from looking toward Adriel for support. It had been so long, so many years since I had performed this ritual, this act, and I did not want to appear completely faithless. I touched her shoulders.

"In the name of Jesus the Christ, of Nazareth, be well," I said. So many years had passed since I had said the words.

I felt the power flow into her, though I could not say how the power had flowed into me. It was simply there, had been there these many centuries since he had wished it so. Sarah's face took on a puzzled expression for a moment.

"Your hands are warm." She stopped and closed her eyes. "Something has happened to me. I feel, I don't know, I feel warm myself."

And she began to cry.

That was not what I had planned or foreseen. Seeing the tears on her face now, I knew that it had been inevitable.

You forget these things, Adriel said in my mind.

Yes, I thought to myself. I forget.

Lazarus

Lazarus was unaware that his legs were jerking up a little too fast and that his feet were striking the pavement a little too hard. He was angry.

All this time wasted, he thought. Centuries, when the power to build something has been hidden. The arrogance of the man to think that he was arbiter of what the world could know and see of God. And now it was lost. John hid the cross from the world, hid it from himself, a waste of power and opportunity. It was buried and forgotten.

Buried.

Lazarus stopped. He stood still for a long time, and then he began to smile. He knew where John had put the cross. He had buried it, of course. It was safe and sound in a tomb, waiting to be found.

Now, he thought, all I have to do is figure out which tomb.

Lazarus began to walk again, thinking back through the centuries to remember the graves that would have meaning for John. There were many of them, a great many.

Maybe there were too many.

His smile faded. His footsteps sounded harsh and loud as he passed out of the light of a streetlamp and into the darkness once again.

John

"So, now what?" Sarah asked. The cheesecake was gone, and Adriel's glow was far more reasonable. I was sitting with my head in my hands.

"Now you are well," Adriel said. "Perhaps that is why you have come here."

"John?" Sarah was looking at me. I guessed she wanted a second opinion. I raised my head and looked at Adriel.

"Adriel can sense these things. Which he likely should keep to himself." Sarah was staring at me. "He told me about your illness. I did nothing. Whatever happened was not of my power." After a moment, I added, "I think that God has done something."

She sat a moment.

"God," she said. "Then there truly is one."

I was not sure whether she was making a statement or asking. Sarah kept watching me with widened eyes.

After a minute of silence, she said, "There's an angel right here in the room. Of course, God exists."

"Actually," Adriel began, but I was not going to let that train leave the station.

"Actually, yes," I said. Again there was silence in the room.

"And Adriel has seen him," Sarah added.

"Well," Adriel began again. This time it was Sarah herself who cut him off in her enthusiasm.

"And John has seen Jesus."

Now the room was even quieter, and I was staring into Sarah's eyes. The light glistened in them, and though my body was still, I felt myself falling back into time, seeing other eyes, dark and sparkling with the firelight, Jesus talking with us, a house in Capernaum.

No, I thought. I must not fall into memory. This present is where I am.

Sarah was still looking at me.

"Yes. I have seen him." I was trying to think of what to tell her when she went on.

"That which we have heard, which we have seen with our eyes, which we have looked upon, and our hands have touched. That's right, isn't it?"

"What?" I said.

Sarah's cheeks reddened a bit. "I may have gotten it a little wrong, but I've been reading all of John, all of your writing—in the New Testament, that is. The beginning of 1 John? The letter? You wrote that, didn't you?"

I looked at her for a moment, silent.

"After a fashion," I said. "There were others, a community." I looked around the room. Adriel was moving the rocking chair back and forth like a glittery poltergeist.

"He wrote much of it," Adriel said.

"I wrote some of it. You heard the 'we' in there. That was the community speaking, adding to what I had told them, what others had told them, what they had seen for themselves."

They were quiet. I could tell that Sarah was impressed, which started to annoy me.

"Look, we were there. We were just there. We heard him, we saw him, and finally we saw him die."

"But he rose from the dead." Sarah was looking at me.

I turned to the fireplace, but I saw the beach, that fire, smoke rising slowly in the cool morning. I heard his voice over the water.

"We saw him again. And he had been dead, that was certain."

The room was quiet. We all stared at the fire, at least the two of us who were human. I had no idea what Adriel was seeing.

Sarah spoke again. "Do you still talk to him?"

"To Jesus? I still talk, yes, but no, I do not see him or hear him any more. Not since those first days."

We were all quiet for a while, even Adriel. It was Sarah who spoke next.

"Is that why you hide yourself?" She looked around, back at me. "That is what you are doing, isn't it? Keeping out of sight?"

I sighed. Adriel's chair started rocking again.

"It couldn't be about me. Do you see? As the years went by and I was still alive, people began to wonder. They started paying attention to me. I wasn't why they were there, why the movement began." I stopped and looked at my hands. "I had to let the church grow without me. At least I think that is why I stopped, why I withdrew.

"We thought he was coming back. He had said as much, or so we thought." I watched the fire for a while. "Then years went by, and the others were gone. I was the only one remaining." I started to say, except for Lazarus, but thought better of it.

It had been so long since hearing Jesus speak, since seeing him, touching him. And many years had passed since I had done so much as touched a sick person and prayed for them. Until tonight. Until Sarah came to us.

"Maybe you should tell people who you are," she said.

"It would be a circus," said Adriel. "Or they would simply throw him into an asylum."

"Adriel is right," I said. "John the Apostle cannot be alive, not really. Think of all the ways that it would challenge accepted thought. And think of all the people who would just want to figure out why I am still alive. The only reason I can give them is because Jesus wished it so, and I can't even explain that to anyone."

Again we sat in silence, but we were not separated by it. We were sitting together quietly.

"And now I am well," Sarah finally said. "I am well, and I didn't even know that I was unwell."

My God, I thought. She even has to accept that on faith. She was only healed if she believed that she was sick, and we have only Adriel's word for that. Maybe I will get my asylum one day after all.

Sarah stayed for a while, talking. She left with the understanding that what we had heard and seen and touched, we would have to keep to ourselves. After all, what would she say? That she had met an angel and the Apostle John, and that the proof of all of this was the absence of a disease that no one but the angel had ever diagnosed?

It was insane.

Lazarus

Lazarus stood in front of the black door and rapped the silver knocker. There was a doorbell as well, round and lit, shining in the darkness, but Lazarus preferred the sound of the metal on the wood.

Simon pulled the door open, a little at first, then wide when he saw Lazarus standing on his doorstep.

"Come in, please, come in," Simon said, then nearly added "Lord".

Lazarus strode into the house, making his way to the living room and the fireplace, paying no more real attention to Simon than to a porter at a hotel.

Simon briefly peered out into the dark street and closed the door.

"We must go to the old lands," Lazarus said.

Simon stopped in the doorway to the room. "The Holy Land?"

"John has hidden the cross. It is in a tomb, buried for safe keeping, or so the jackass thinks. We must go to find it."

Simon stood quietly for a moment, staring at Lazarus, then at the floor.

"Where is the tomb?" he asked.

Lazarus hesitated. "I do not know. But it must have been nearly at the beginning, long ago. It could be Palestine perhaps. Israel." Then he decided to share what he truly thought. "But I think it is near Ephesus. Somewhere near where John and Mary lingered all those years ago. He carried it there, hid it there." Then he added, mostly to himself, "Yes, somewhere near Mary."

Lazarus stood leaning on the mantel, his head on his arm. Simon thought about how many tombs there were in Turkey.

"He had time to plan it," Lazarus went on. "Years to think, to decide what to do with it."

"Did you ever see it? The cross?"

Lazarus had certainly seen it, though he had not recognized it. It had been there in the house where John lived, a beam of wood standing against a wall like a shelf, cloth draped from it. Lazarus had given it little thought at the time. Later, realizing the power of it, he had remembered what he had seen, but by then Mary was gone and so was John. The house had been given over to others, and though Lazarus had returned to it, there had been no wooden beam there, no holy relic.

"Yes, I have seen it." He heard Simon's intake of breath behind him. He believes it will save mankind, Lazarus thought. Well, it will certainly change things.

"We leave soon," he told Simon. "In three days."

Now he heard Simon's breathing change again, silent for a moment.

"Three days?"

"That should give you time to tidy up your affairs here and to prepare. Book us passage to Constantinople."

Simon was quiet behind him. Lazarus turned.

"What is it? You will be well compensated."

"Istanbul, sir. The city is called Istanbul."

Lazarus turned to stare at him.

"I remember when it was called Byzantium. For that matter, I remember Constantine. Do not presume to teach history to me."

The sweat on Simon's forehead was glistening in the firelight.

"No, certainly not, sir." Again, he almost said Lord instead of sir. "It is just, well, I will make the reservations."

"Good." Lazarus turned back to the fire. "Meanwhile, what do you have to eat? I have been walking to and fro and thinking, and now I am hungry."

John

"Perhaps she was right," said Adriel.

I turned to look at him, though I do not know why I still bother.

"Who was right?"

"Sarah, when she said that you should tell people."

"Nonsense." I forced the air from my nose, knowing that it made me sound petulant. After all these years, one would think I could learn to control my unflattering mannerisms. "You told her yourself, people would think me insane and put me in a loony bin."

"Certainly, so long as they believed that you believed what you were saying."

"What? What are you talking about?"

"Suppose you made it up." He paused, no doubt for dramatic effect. Angels love drama, every single one I ever met. "What if you give them what they believe is a fictional account?"

After a moment I said, "I did exactly that. They call it a Gospel, if they believe it. They call it something else if they don't."

I made myself a cup of coffee. It still seemed rude, after all these years, not to offer one to Adriel. He was saying nothing, waiting for me to make a more constructive comment.

"A fiction, you say."

"Yes. Like a play," he said.

"Or a novel," I added.

"Yes, that is more of what I was thinking. A novel. Something that tells your story but appears to be nothing more than fiction."

I sipped and thought about it.

"Stories are more true than anything else. I think that is why he used them."

Adriel paused, searching in my mind, I knew, to clarify my meaning. I thought of Jesus teaching, telling stories to the people gathered on a shoreline. I knew that Adriel would see the image in my mind, perhaps remember the day. Perhaps he had been there, I did not know.

"Not that day," he said. "Others like it, later."

I watched the bubbles swirl on my coffee. Somewhere on the deck a squirrel was scampering around with a scratching sound. It likely understood more than we about our conversation.

"Yes, you may be right," Adriel said, a rare statement when addressed to me. "He told them stories, and the truth would slip along with them. If he had simply stated the truths, most would have been forgotten. Or rejected."

The squirrel had run down to the grass and buried something. Now he was contemplating it, no doubt a prelude to digging it back up.

"Then you would have me become a writer once again."

"It is what you do best." He waited. "I have always enjoyed your words, and it would be good for you to put words to paper once again."

I sipped the coffee and thought about it. He might be right, I thought.

"Of course, I am," he said. "I am an angel."

Simon

"These people were using the same donkeys the last time I was here," Lazarus said. "Nineteen centuries, and all that changes are the shoes and cellular phones."

I looked around at him, and I wondered whether the boys from the village understood. If so, they made no indication. They just kept walking beside the donkeys that carried our camp equipment.

When we broke into the first tombs, I was excited, thinking that we would see holy relics hidden by John. All we found were bones and dust. We had to keep finding new helpers as we travelled, and not just because we moved to different regions. After a few days they all seemed to realize that we were not archaeologists. We were breaking into tombs, staring at the bones of the occupants, and shoving stones back into place. At least sometimes we shoved the stones back. Other times we left the daylight streaming onto the old bones, and our assistants would begin to mumble and to look strangely at Lazarus. Not that it mattered to him.

He had spread enough money among the right officials that I knew they did not care what we did, short of leading an insurrection. I did not know where the money came from, and I did not ask. I supposed that if one were around for two thousand years, one would find interesting investment opportunities. I thought about the gold and silver coins in our bags, found in some of the tombs. Lazarus had the boys pick them up and, looking at the dried bodies, sometimes told the boys to push the stones back against the entrance. Coins and pieces of gold, that is all we had found.

We were grave robbers.

Lazarus was angrier each day. Someone so old should have more patience, I thought, but it may not have been a matter of patience. He talked to himself sometimes, quietly, when no one else was nearby. I saw his lips move and sometimes heard a few words, some in English, some in something that must be Greek or Aramaic, but I did not understand them. I could read those languages, but I could not speak them, not like this.

Sometimes it seemed that he was having a conversation with someone, either in his mind or, worse, with someone whom I cannot see. In the night I looked through the flaps of my tent to see Lazarus standing at the edge of the firelight. I could hear his voice like the murmuring of the fire, but I could not catch any of the words. He would talk and wait, talk again, until I realized it was the rhythm of conversation. I just did not know with whom, or with what.

If this man, like John, could still be walking around on the earth after so many years, what else was possible?

I thought of stories of angels, and worse.

I lay in my darkened tent and wondered. If John travelled with an angel, what other than me travelled with Lazarus?

Regardless, I knew that the cross still existed. That was something. And if we found it, imagine the power it would have to instill faith, to prove the truth of Christ. It could save the world, but John would keep it hidden in a tomb like dry bones.

More, Lazarus spoke of it having power. Imagine, the power to heal or to work miracles, the power of God in this piece of wood. We would have the power to bring the world to the one true faith, a faith with something that no other faith can offer—proof.

Lazarus worried me, though. He had said little about how he wanted to use the power of the cross, and I wondered about his faith.

More than that, I wondered who was talking to him in the firelight.

Adi

The trees move in the wind, releasing birds into the sky like leaves that fly instead of fall. I follow them, move with them. Sometimes the ones at the edge of the flock brush against me, and all of them suddenly turn in the sky to move away. I have to speak to them so that they are not afraid, and they turn and reel back toward me, flying beside me, twittering and chirping.

Then I see the shadow move beyond the wood, near an old house, and I am there in a moment. The shadow shifts again, not following the path of the light, and I know it for what it is, trying to hide in the darkness out of the sight of the sun and living creatures.

"You are not welcome," I tell it. The shadow shifts again.

"We are not welcome," it says, an echo, taunting. Something like laughter shuffles behind the wall of the house.

"Go away. We guard this place."

"We," it says, and I hear something dry like leaves.

"We watch the child," I say. "And we watch the old one, John. You have no place here. Go back to your deserts, your dark worlds."

"No place here." The sound is like hissing.

"I have warned you," I say. Silence, then there is a sound like a snake crawling through a pile of fallen leaves. I move to the ground, near the house but in the sunlight, and I raise my arms to let more light shine against the structure. It is abandoned. There is no one to see. The boards whiten and the old windows reflect my light until it seems there is no shadow at all, nothing but the white light flat against the structure.

Something moves, shattering glass and boards from the corner of the house, and I am surrounded by the sound of someone breathing, then darkness, my light still bright but as if in a room so large the light cannot find the walls, or so small there is nothing to light up, and I fall backwards. It is pressing against me, pushing, something like hard hands grasping me and pulling me down, and down, and down into the earth until there is no sunlight, nothing but rock and soil and the distant sound of water, and I scream, and I scream, and I scream.

John

"There already is a story," I said finally. The coffee in my cup had long been cold, and I did not know how long I had been sitting here thinking of her. There were Adriel's words, then the sound of the squirrel, and my mind drifted to see Mary sitting at the table with a lamp and the parchment in front of her.

Sometimes when she wrote she would pause to ask me something, what I remembered, or how to spell a word. Neither of us were the best at spelling, though I had some training. My father believed that it was good for us to learn to read, and he had sent my brother and me to learn at the synagogue. We learned Hebrew, for the scripture, and Greek for business. The children of the other fishermen would tease us. They would bring a fish and ask whether we might read to them what was written on it. James hated the lessons, but I did not hate them so much.

"I believed that Jesus wanted me to write it down," I said. "And of course, I did." Adriel seemed to be listening, though I could not tell whether I had his attention as much or more than the birds in the trees. "And so did Mary."

"Mary," he said. "Yes."

"I may not have ever written what I did without her. Even knowing what I was to do, I would say that he would come back and tell them himself. One day she looked at me, and she said that everyone was dying, everyone who remembered. She told me that I had to write it down for the ones who would come after us."

I moved to the kitchen, pouring the cold coffee into the sink.

"No one has, of course. No one has come after me, I mean. But she was right."

I found a chair. Adriel was still quiet.

"It was she who finally began to write first, though she would not let me read it. You write what you remember, she would say, and then we will see.

"Many evenings there was nothing but the light of our lamp and the sound of us scribbling the words. We should have written more in the day, when we could see, but there seemed always some work to do, something to tend, someone visiting."

"It was good," Adriel said. I looked at him. I could see the form of him, though he seemed still to be watching the birds outside, or something beyond the trees in the yard. One never knew with his kind. And here I was telling Adriel about Mary, when he was there himself.

"So there is the story," I said. He turned.

"What do you mean?" He seemed not to understand, which was unusual for him given his habit of roaming through my thoughts.

"Mary's story," I said and watched him. "Her words. Perhaps it is time to share them."

Adriel said nothing for a time.

"They are doing no good where they are," he said.

"Sometimes we regret the words we share more than the ones we keep to ourselves," I told him. I thought about the manuscript, resting with Mary. "You may be right, but we need to be sure."

"We?"

"You are as much a part of this as I."

He was quiet. I could not tell from the appearance whether he was looking at me.

"I was there, but…" he began, and then stopped. I could sense his alarm, like a wave pulsing through the sea.

"Adi," he said, and he was gone.

Adriel

I see the birds take flight from the trees, but I cannot see why they flew. Sometimes there is no reason, no alarm. They fly because they can fly. Adi is there, I know. I feel her take flight with the birds, and I see them change direction as they fly near her.

All of them fly out of sight, and John is talking, thinking about the words that Mary wrote. I know them, remember them, sensing them as they appeared on the parchment, in her mind, in my mind.

A small bird is lost, on the lawn, in the tree, looking for the others who are flying with Adi. They will be back, I think, and it calms the creature.

"Mary's story. The words." John is thinking of the tomb, the manuscript. I can see it in my mind, as it was just days ago when I went to check it for safekeeping. "Perhaps it is time to share them."

"They are doing no good where they are," I say. Share them. Let people form their own thoughts.

"Sometimes we regret the words we share more than the ones we keep to ourselves. You may be right. We need to be sure."

"We?" I am surprised. All these days together, yet all of the memories of Mary he holds as his, though not in his conscious mind. He has never noticed, assuming that only he is responsible for the keeping of her words.

"You are as much a part of this as I," he says, surprising me.

Screaming enters my mind, pain and darkness exploding, and I hear Adi's voice in the scream and the pain. Thinking it I am there, following where the scream begins, and I see the old house and the ground and darkness like a writhing tail pressing into the earth and it is gone. I follow the screams into the earth, past the loose soil and the rocks, where there is no light or space but the space between the atoms like worlds ignored. A dark one is flowing, gnawing and hiding all of the energy of the molecular bonds that release and flow like magma, and still Adi screams. She does not like to enter the small spaces, does not like the small worlds, and the dark one is tearing at her, ripping her.

"Adi," I say, my voice itself a scream. The earth is shaking and vibrating. I feel the light and power flowing through me, lighting the interspace, the interstitial gaps, opening the rock, burning the darkness, and I find the edge of the dark thing's being and touch it, scorching it with light where it thinks there is only darkness.

Darkness hurls against me, darkness that is sharp and long and swift, but it cannot pass the light and so it flails against the rock beyond me. Anger surges in me, and the rock is melting when I sense the fear of the dark thing. Adi is not screaming now, she is quiet, but moving and pushing. I feel the light of her touch me and I pull her, pull the dark thing, both of them, up and into the light beyond the rocks. I see the house is falling, trees crashing near us, the birds flying again.

""With her," I say to the birds. "With them," I tell her and she pauses, resting, the birds raising their wings in a flock below her as they take her skyward.

I pull the dark thing, wrestling and writhing against me, slippery with nothingness, into the brilliant light of open space. There is no air, only light from the sun and the singing of stars. It is pulling and ripping with darkness like talons but the light flowing from me is as bright as the star toward which we hurtle. A moment and I think of the shining surface of starlight, and the dark one knows my purpose as I pull it to this lake of fire. I do not stop, do not stop, and it shrieks and hurls thoughts of terror and of pain toward me. Blood flows through my mind, but it is not my blood, I have no blood, it is the image of fear from this creature and I am appalled, that such a one would think blood a horror to me.

We streak across time and the star fire is like touching the face of God. With all of the momentum of my anger I hurl the dark thing toward the sun, hurl it with speed beyond light, and it shrieks once more in my mind and is gone. Starlight explodes out, energy in waves unseen and seen, like the explosion of light at the beginning of this time, and I know in this moment that the sun will not entirely destroy me or one like me, but that in it we burn until time unfolds or the star collapses and turns us into nothing but ash and dust to wait for the making of a new world, and there we might breathe light once more, crawling and wriggling in a pool of new life without memory or shape from this one.

The starlight exploding outward reaches to me, nearly to touch me. Waves pass through me then sink back, the energy dissipating into galaxies beyond reckoning and finally subsiding into the gravity of a billion stars. I think of John and of Adi. I remember Adi screaming, and with a jolt I turn my mind back to find them.

I see a blue green orb moving slowly, seas surging. Adi, I think. There, I sink back through clouds and air, the light mutes with atmosphere, birds, but not hers, then I see her floating, her flock holding her on their back and spiraling to the earth with her. The old house is shambles, flattened, with the trees around it, the earth rent with rocks raised and exposed as though shoved up by the hands of giants.

Then I am with her. I thank the birds and take her from their wings. We are back in John's house, and John is leaning against a wall, coffee on the floor, broken glass at his feet. He is calling my name, telling me it was an earthquake.

"Do not be afraid," I say. He is quiet, and I hold Adi, waiting for her to wake. I do not know that it is the first time I have ever spoken the words of angels.

Lazarus

"Where did he put the body?" I realized that Simon didn't know, of course, but it was useful sometimes to talk aloud. Helped to gather the thoughts.

"I'm sorry? Did you say 'the body'?"

These rocks hadn't changed in two thousand years: same lakes, same wells, same rocks, same villages, and the same idiots. There were some new signs, new cell phones, new watches, and new shoes. The dust was the same as it ever was.

"Yes, Simon, the body." He was dusty as well, I saw. "We've been opening tombs everywhere that John lived in those days, and nothing but dust and the wrong bones to show for it. He put the body somewhere."

Simon looked around at me, uncertainty in his blinking eyes. This was supposed to be an intelligent man, a brilliant academic. Of course, that was partly due to the secrets I have whispered in his ears. His usefulness was waning.

"We have not found the right tomb," Simon said. "If he…"

Whatever the new thought was, he let it drop. I stared at him.

"You're right, Simon, absolutely right. We have not found the right tomb." I saw that he was apprehensive, unsure whether I was sincere or mocking him. I was sincere, surprising even myself.

"I had thought of obscurity, some place that John would remember but that he would believe everyone else had forgotten. Except perhaps me." I turned to scan the mountains. "What if it was not an obscure grave? What if it was a very important one?"

"They have opened the important ones," Simon said.

"Yes," I agreed. "They have opened all of the important graves. At least, they have opened all of the graves that they knew about."

"There are others?"

"Think, Simon. What Christian tombs are the most famous, and which would date back to the first generation of the church?"

"I am not sure. The tomb of Mary, perhaps, but it is empty. And it is in Jerusalem."

"Yes," I said. "It is empty, Simon. And do you know why?"

He paused, thinking. Good.

"Because she was taken into heaven?" he asked.

No kewpie doll for him.

"No, Simon." Taken into heaven, I thought. Really. "It is because that is not where her body is."

I let him think about this while we walked back toward the town.

"There was also the story that Mary was buried in Ephesus," he said, his breathing heavy from the walk. "But there is no body there, either."

"No, there isn't." We walked. I remembered the house. I remembered Mary sitting there under the trees, fanning herself in the heat and eating dates or figs. John would bring her cool water, then go back to his scribbling.

When Mary died, they were still dwelling there. John did not take her body far. He could not have done so. She was laid to rest nearby, and that is where he put it.

Simon had stopped walking. I turned to look at him and saw the realization in his eyes. "You are looking for the tomb of Mary. The real one."

I stared at him for a moment longer.

"Now I know what I'm looking for," I said. "We need to find the tomb of Mary, the real one. Wherever Mary lies, that is where we'll find the cross."

John

Adriel vanished, which he never does, at least not without some parting word. I stood there wondering whether I could have said anything to offend him. Perhaps he felt differently about being part of Mary's story? Then the house began to shake, an earthquake.

I heard dishes fall and break in the kitchen, and I started to walk in that direction, but the shaking threw me off balance. I dropped the cup I was holding and sank against the wall, watching the coffee pot vibrate off the edge of the counter and wondering whether I should crawl to a more protected spot or perhaps get out of the house. The shaking stopped as quickly as it had begun. I called out for Adriel, wondering where he could be, whether he knew what was happening, but he did not reply. All these years, he had never failed to answer my call.

I managed to stand, to walk through the house assessing the damage. It was not too bad, some broken dishes and a cracked window. I looked across at Sarah's house but I could not make out much damage there. Thankfully, the quake was short.

Still, I was unnerved. I had experienced earthquakes before, in different parts of the world, but it was impossible to get used to them. It would be like getting used to an angry bull in your bathroom. No reason to.

I saw the light shimmer and grow stronger. Turning, I saw the figure of Adriel, and he was holding something, or someone.

"Adriel?"

"It is Adi," he said. "She was screaming. That is why I left."

"Screaming? Was it because of the earthquake?" Really I had thought that an earthquake would have been of no great importance to an angel.

"No, not an earthquake." He paused. "That was me, us. A dark creature had attacked her, pulled her down into the earth, into the rock."

"Into the rock."

"There are small spaces, even within elements in the earth. We are able to pass within objects, using the interspaces, shifting among the atoms. Adi does not like it, she told me once. She does not like the sense of confinement, of being within a matter form. And the dark one was hurting her. She was screaming, John."

I walked closer to them. I could make out Adi's form, but I could not touch her. It was like trying to touch the light from a fire.

"She is not awake. I do not know what else to do but to wait."

"Let her rest," I said. "Place her on the couch, if she can rest there."

"Yes, that will be fine."

I could see the shimmering form of Adi on the sofa, an odd sight, and Adriel kneeling beside her.

"Adriel, you said that a dark creature attacked her?"

"Yes. It…attached itself to Adi, and pulled her down into the earth with it. It was old, powerful. I have never seen this one before, but I have seen others like it."

"What did you do?" When he didn't answer right away, I realized the connection. "The earthquake," I said. "That was you."

"Yes, it was. I delved into the earth and found them. I took hold of them both and pulled them back out of the rock and to the surface. Near that low place, the old house east of here. The force of our movements caused the earth to shift." He paused, seeming to become aware of the house, the dishes on the floor. "Were you hurt?"

"No. No, I am fine. It was frightening though. I have never cared for earthquakes."

Neither of us spoke for a moment as we watched Adi.

"I did not know that I have a friend who can cause them," I said. Adriel said nothing, so I asked, "What did you do with the dark thing?"

Again, Adriel did not answer. I said nothing else, but gave him time. After a few minutes, he began to speak.

"When I had pulled them both from the ground, I gave Adi to the birds to watch."

I said nothing again, though I was surprised at such a statement. I had known that angels can communicate with any living creature, but I had never known birds to respond in such a manner.

"Then I took the dark one with me into space. I was angry. It had harmed Adi, known her fear somehow and used it to harm her. So I wanted to destroy it."

Again I waited.

"I pulled it out beyond the earth, toward the sun, the star fire lake at the center of this system. And I threw it in. I heard it shriek as it hurdled into the fire, and I left it to burn until these worlds are nothing but ash."

I was speechless for a moment.

"You traveled to the sun and back?" I thought about it. "And you threw one of those things into the sun?" Adriel said nothing. "Is it destroyed?"

"It will never emerge from that fire, if that is what you mean by destroyed. At least, when the star turns to dust, the thing that was him will be no more than a gasp of energy, particles floating out into space to be made into some other form, some other life."

"You went to the sun. And back. And threw that creature in."

"Yes."

We were silent. After a few minutes, I told Adriel that I would go next door to be sure that Sarah was all right.

"Tell her that I am sorry about the quake."

I paused. "I think it may be better just to let her think it was a regular earthquake."

He said nothing, which I took as assent. When I left, Adriel was still kneeling beside Adi, watching her.

Simon

We were standing in front of a small stone building. We had to drive up a long winding road to get here from Selcuk, the modern city near the site of ancient Ephesus, and I was glad to be out of the car. Lazarus drove. I don't know which was worse, his driving or his complaints about my driving.

Lazarus stood looking at the small building made entirely of stone. I had read that it was only three rooms, a simple home with a fireplace and water from a spring. The Orthodox Church had known the site for many years. In the early 1800's a nun, Anne Catherine Emmerick, shared what she said were visions of Mary's life in the house. By the end of the century, explorers had located and identified this structure near ancient Ephesus with Emmerick's visions. The house became a shrine. Three popes had visited the spot.

"You remember this place?" I asked Lazarus.

Lazarus didn't move or answer for several minutes. Just as I was about to walk away to give him space to think, or whatever he was doing, he turned slightly toward me.

"I remember Mary," he said. "We sometimes sat and ate there." He pointed to an area within the stone wall beside the house.

"Mary would make food for us, and I would join her and John, and whoever else happened to be visiting.

Someone always seemed to be visiting. There was a table under some trees."

The area was now a parking lot. Tourist buses were parked at the far side, drivers sleeping while the passengers walked around the grounds, prayed, lit candles.

"Was she living here when she died?"

He nodded. "It did not look the same. I think the building is in the same place, maybe on the same footing, but the stones of the wall were laid differently. The roof was not the same."

He turned and began to look around us. Hills rose nearby, running along the entrance road, stretching into the distance.

"Somewhere near here," he said. "But I do not know where."

"How will we find it then?"

He shook his head. "It cannot be far from this spot. When Mary died, John placed her body in a tomb that was not far from here, a tomb that was known to others. Then he moved it, secretly, in the night to another tomb."

"He was protecting her body," I ventured.

"Yes." Lazarus started walking toward the entrance to the home. "That is what I believe. He has never said so, and he will not divulge the information now. But I think that her body was laid to rest in what appeared to be an ordinary tomb, one that must have been in the midst of other ordinary tombs, and that the cross is there with her."

I walked along, slightly behind him.

"What about the Assumption?" I asked. Catholic doctrine taught that Mary was taken bodily into heaven.

"Don't believe everything you hear," he said.

John

Adi began to make some sounds, something like a moan or partial words. I don't know whether Adriel could communicate with her prior to my hearing the sound, but he did not seem to. When Adi began moving, Adriel was as happy as I and began to say her name.

"Here," she said, or something like it, which was not quite an intelligible response.

"You are safe," I said, then realized that I did not really know whether she was or not. I had not known of the presence of the thing that attacked her, did not hear her scream, did not save her, perhaps could not have saved her though I believe that this spirit or being could not have been any different from the countless ones over the centuries that I have sent away. And here I stood telling her that she was safe.

I did not know whether any of us were safe any more.

"Yes, you are safe." At least Adriel agreed with me. He seemed to be lifting her upright. "We are here, and you are safe."

After a few moments he added, "And it is gone."

She seemed to stiffen at that statement.

"Gone," she said.

"Yes."

I had the impression that she was slowly looking around her, but what her senses took in of our home was still a mystery to me, even after all these centuries with Adriel.

"You are in our home," I said.

"Your home," she repeated. Seeming to think about it, she added, "Thank you."

"You are welcome, Adi. And you may stay here for as long as you would like." I don't know what made me offer such a thing, but it seemed right.

She was quiet again.

"I was so afraid," she said. I supposed that she was voicing her thoughts out of consideration of me.

"It pulled me into the rock, into the spaces within. I do not like…I do not wish to enter the small spaces."

"It is fine now," Adriel said. "I heard you, and I pulled you back into the light."

Adi was quiet for another moment. "I was screaming, wasn't I?"

"It is no shame to scream. You were attacked." He paused. "It is good that you did scream so that I knew you were in danger."

Adi rose and moved to the window. I thought she was listening for something.

"I do not sense it anywhere nearby. What did you do with it?"

Now Adriel paused, quiet. "I sent it away."

"Adriel?"

He was reticent to tell her, I realized. Perhaps there was some taboo among them, I thought, or perhaps there is simply the regret of destroying even that life.

"I cast it into the sun," he said. "Into the lake of fire. It is no more."

Something akin to the sound of breath being taken in came from Adi. I had never truly known them to breathe, have never know how much was mimicry to make us feel at home in their presence and how much was real. Adi was too engrossed in what Adriel had told us for her to be dissimilating. So they do breathe, after a fashion, I realized.

"You destroyed him," she said. "You have touched the face of the sun, and you destroyed him."

He agreed, but not at once.

"I threw it into the star fire, and it is no more." Adriel moved to the other window. A matched set of angels gazing from my windows, I thought, and it isn't even Christmas. Then I wondered whether they, in their mutual distraction, might accidentally let themselves be seen. Truly, that would bring the grocery store tabloids on the run. Angels seen in man's house, photos inside.

"It was powerful. It was no wonder that you were overcome."

I realized before Adriel did that his remark did not reassure so much as anger Adi.

"Because I am weak, you mean."

Adriel immediately saw his mistake, and he tried to extricate himself from this new danger.

"You were taken by surprise," he said.

"I did not tell you."

Adriel only paused a moment. "He must have done so. I am sure you would have managed things differently had you known of his presence."

I could see the hole that Adriel was digging, getting deeper with every statement.

"You simply did not sense the presence of that thing, or you would have been on your guard. Perhaps you were distracted."

Adi said nothing. I knew she was getting angry again. Adriel was clearly aware of this as well, but he seemed unable to realize that he himself was the cause of her anger, or rather that the things that he said reached to her private thoughts and fears. I was only a human, but I understood this much.

"Can I offer you any tea?" I said. In my mind I held firmly to the image of a teapot and three cups, some sugar cubes. Once they turned their attention to me, tea was all that they were going to read in my mind. Let them make something of that. *Perhaps John has begun to loose his faculties, offering tea to angels.*

"What?" Adriel said.

"Tea. I think that this would be a good time for tea." I did not wish to throw the question out there again, so I turned and shuffled toward the kitchen and kept the teapot in my mind.

"No, not that." Adriel said. "What do you mean, John is losing his faculties. I do not understand."

"No, I see that," I said. "Adi, do you like milk with your tea?"

I flipped the switch on the electric kettle and began clattering dishes from the cabinet onto a serving tray. The coffee maker was still a mess on the floor, but it could wait. At least we still had electricity.

"Ah…," I heard her begin. I kept my mind on getting the milk from the refrigerator. It was becoming like a Zen exercise.

"I think that…I would like the milk, yes."

Just lovely white milk, pouring through the air into a small milk pitcher, I thought.

"You would?" Adriel said.

"Yes," she said more firmly. "I would."

"And you, Adriel, take your tea black, I believe, unless you would like to change your mind."

Biscuits, cookies, snacks, I thought. *Rake the pebbles.*

"Pebbles?" It was Adriel.

"Only a stray thought. Zen, you know. Rock gardens and all." The kettle was beginning to boil. "And stop that. It's rude."

I could have sworn that Adi laughed.

"I'll bring the tray in there," I said. "Just a moment longer."

I poured the water over the tea leaves. I had found the teapot in a shop in Ireland, two hundred years prior, and it was a wonder the thing had survived all this time. Only one chip was missing from the lid. I have more than a chip missing.

"Yes."

"I told you to stop that."

Something like a giggle came from the other room. I was sure it was as much from exhaustion as from humor, but I had never encountered an exhausted angel before this night. First time for everything, as they say.

"We'll have our tea, and then you two need to get some rest, or sleep, or whatever you call it when you are not floating around watching people and reading minds."

I could tell they were both staring at me while I brought in the tray. It is odd to be stared at by creatures without permanent form. When they are surprised, they forget to maintain the illusion of humanoid bodies, leaving something like a translucent store mannequin that changes shape and gives off light.

They were still beautiful, but odd. I should know.

Ashes

Even when we crossed the sea in Galilee, they found us. I should say that they found him, because crowds never followed any of us, not like they followed him, and for good reason. For one thing, he healed them. He healed any of them, of anything. It made no difference what the illness, or who the patient was, once they had reached him they would be healed. He never refused anyone. Well, there was that one woman he nearly sent away, telling her that to help would be like giving the children's food to a dog, but in the end he healed her daughter as well. I still wonder whether I understood what he was trying to teach us. I am certain that we were the audience, and not that woman or her daughter.

"You should be more careful, Lord." It was Peter, at the end of a long day. Even now in the dusk I saw someone walking with a leper, the two of them making their way over the uneven ground and rocks to our campfire on the hillside. "You have all kinds of people coming. You are not paying attention to what kind of people they are before you heal them."

"Peter is right, Lord," I added quietly, standing closer to Jesus. "It may be that some of them do not deserve to be healed."

Even today I am ashamed that I said it. It is strange, the things we forgive ourselves and the things that we do not.

Jesus was sitting by the fire, knees drawn toward his chin. He picked up a small stick and looked at it for a moment while we spoke, then tossed it into the fire.

"And what did either of you do to deserve to be here?"

He asked it like asking whether we would like another piece of bread.

I looked at Peter, and both of us started watching the fire. None of the others said anything. They had been thinking as Peter and I had been, and now we were all caught as though cold water had splashed into our faces. At least they had the good sense or the timidity to keep their mouths shut.

After a while the two people came closer. The others who were gathered near Jesus parted and made a path for them to approach the firelight. I saw that it was a woman helping a man, the leper, to make his way to Jesus. When they saw him, they stopped, the woman squeezing the man's arm then helping him to kneel. He did not look up.

Jesus seemed to take no notice. He sat there staring into the fire, his arms wrapped around his knees. No one spoke for a long while.

"My Lord," I said. Jesus did not move. "They have come to be healed."

Having just minutes earlier whispered against them, I thought I should speak for them.

The man and woman said nothing. A leper was kneeling in the midst of our camp, and nobody was saying anything.

"I see them, son of Zebedee." His voice was quiet, and kind, and I was embarrassed, still wishing I could take back my earlier words.

Jesus rose from the campfire and stepped over to the couple. He looked down into their eyes, the woman's face like a question, the man raising his head more slowly. Jesus put his hands on the man's shoulders.

"Be well," he said, then with one hand he also touched the woman's shoulder, like greeting old friends.

Without another word, Jesus turned and walked away from the fire into the evening. I watched until I could no longer see him clearly, and then I found bread for the couple to eat. The man was holding his arms out toward the fire so that he and the woman could see them more clearly. The skin was healthy, as clear as my own.

She began to unwrap his face, and I realized that she was his wife. All of this, and she had not left him. I wondered whether anyone would ever love me that much, whether I would ever love anyone that much.

When I turned again, I could not see Jesus at all. Peter was staring at the couple as though he had never seen human beings, then he let his gaze drop to the glow of the embers in the fire.

The man and woman were so engaged with his healing that they just held the bread, moving it hand to hand as though it were not food but simply a stone or a ball of cloth. The firelight glinted against his teeth as he smiled, sparkled across her eyes as she watched him, and soon they too had moved out of the firelight, walking back the way that they had come.

Before leaving, the man looked around at us and turned to me. He took my hand in his, and I was taken aback by the touch of a leper, or one who had been a leper. I don't know whether he noticed. I do not think that he did, he was so overjoyed. Thanking us, telling us to thank Jesus for him, they turned and walked away. I never saw them again, or if I saw them by day in one of the villages I did not recognize them.

Every time I saw a leper, I remembered him. Every time I saw a person in need, I remembered my words.

And what did either of you do to deserve to be here?

Sometime in the night Jesus returned. When I awoke early the next morning he was lying asleep, near the coals of the fire. Peter was sitting and watching him. I have no idea what was going on in Peter's mind, never did. The man was unpredictable. He could be loud, and brash, and I have never met anyone with such faith who knew so many curses.

He had simple curse words, 'damns' and the like that everyone knows. It was more than that, though. Peter had raised the comparison curse to an art form. Plenty of men and some women learned that they were related to livestock, and usually unchaste and closely bred livestock. His favorite targets were idiots and Romans, though to Peter the two words meant the same thing. There was nothing worse than a man who could not fish, unless it was a woman who would prevent a man from fishing. An idiotic Roman woman preventing a man from fishing would have unleashed the apotheosis of curses. I am sorry that we never encountered one. It would have been worth remembering.

Peter was a little dangerous where Jesus was concerned. In crowds Peter was like a bodyguard, always watching to see that the crowd did not press too hard, that hands reaching out to Jesus were safe.

The crowds came the next day. I don't know from where, but they came by hundreds, gathering around us, voices like a hum or like waves on the sea, blending with each other and with the wind until we could not tell where the sounds began or ended. Jesus had been sitting by the fire talking with two small boys who were chattering away, delighted, no idea with whom they were speaking.

Finally, Jesus rubbed them on their heads and stood up. He turned, pulling at his robes to make them comfortable while he surveyed the crowds. We were at the beginning of an upward range on the mountain, and we could look out and down at most of them. They grew quiet, watching him. He motioned to the crowd, waving them forward, and I felt something like panic inside as they all stood and began to surge forward, a wall of people pushing toward us. When Jesus turned and began to climb higher, I was relieved, glad to follow him. Peter looked around with wide eyes and wild hair. More than once someone had mistaken him for some lunatic whom Jesus had cured. We all climbed up with Jesus, finding higher ground. At a rock protruding from the mountainside Jesus stopped, sitting and waiting for the people to gather near.

The slope formed an amphitheater. The rock was a natural stage. When they had gathered near us, Jesus raised his hands. The sudden quiet was astounding. I had not realized how much noise the people were making, and I could not believe how quickly they obeyed him. He looked across their faces and began.

"My friends, are you poor?" Silence, their faces waiting. "Then you are blessed by God."

There were murmurs in the crowd. Many of them were poor, I could see, though none thought themselves blessed.

"Are your hearts mournful and weary?" They fell silent again. "Then you shall have comfort and rest. And if you are hungry and thirsty, take great joy, for you shall be filled."

He kept talking, and we took it in like soft rain on dry ground.

John

Adi made an attempt to drink her tea. They can, of course, eat and drink, or at least they can do something with the material that appears to be eating and drinking. It may be an illusion, but I feel that even pretending to drink a cup of tea can be helpful.

We were still in the living room, the light of late afternoon shining through the windows. Soon it would be dark, not that any of us had any fear of the dark. We did understand something of the things that prefer to move when the light is not shining on them. Some of the stories men tell are true, or nearly so. There are things in the night that do not bear being seen in the daylight.

"Why should one of them attack Adi?" I was bothered by it, not just the violence of it, but the motive, the causality. Normally such active interaction between angels and dark ones is over a third party, saving or taking a human life, but here there appeared to be no motive other than hatred and opportunity.

Adi and Adriel were both quiet, considering the question.

"Perhaps it thought I was pursuing it, when I went to see what was disturbing the birds," Adi said, but her voice did not sound confident.

It could be, I thought, and her voice might sound that way simply out of tiredness. It could be, but I did not think so.

"It could have withdrawn," Adriel said. "It wanted to hold the ground, stay where it was, but why? Particularly knowing that we are here."

I usually gave little thought to such things. For years we had lived in a monastery, Adriel and I, though most of the brothers knew only of my presence. I would live for many years among them, move to another monastery, move again. Only a few ever had any idea of my existence, of who I had been, who I am, though it does not matter. My life is only of value because of whom I have known. Perhaps that is true of everyone.

"Could they have wondered what you are doing?"

Both of them seemed to regard me at once.

"John, they know what we are doing," Adriel said.

"We watch," Adi added.

"Yes. We watch. Occasionally we intervene, usually small things. A child stepping in front of a wagon."

"A car," Adi said, after a moment. "Few wagons now. And it is no small thing to the child."

Time catches even them in habits of thought. I once thought them immune from time, different from us. That was centuries ago. Over many years of watching, or being watched as they said, I had learned otherwise. They could move differently through space, their bodies were not held to this dimension as was mine, but they were flowing through the same time as we so long as they lingered with us. That would hold for the dark ones as well, I thought.

How any of them perceived that reality or that time, I had never known.

"They are here because of what you are doing," Adriel said.

"But I am not doing anything," I said, with some degree of guilt. Just living, just remaining, I thought. Was that not what he asked of me, to remain? And yet I carry the guilt of thinking I am to do something else, though I don't know what it is.

I looked after Mary. I kept her safe, kept her as though she were my mother, as he said, though my own mother had long passed away. I shared Mary's meals and found her a home. I gave her the means to live quietly, or perhaps that is part of what she gave me.

"Perhaps they think you are going to do something."

I wondered, thinking of what I had seen of dark ones. Sometimes I have seen them take a person apart like torturing a bug. The people sometimes seem powerful, like that man from the tombs, but they are broken from the inside.

I could not imagine the torture of having one of them inside you, whispering in your brain, snatching at your muscles. It would be like Adriel and the trees or the rocks, but instead of merging there would be such intimate destruction.

Not that any of them would think of attempting such a thing with me. There is that power yet, God within me, quieter than Adriel flowing in the water of a tree.

"They cannot think such a thing, surely." I could not see it. They watched, and they waited. They acted on opportunities for such enjoyment as suited them. "No, if they are watching me, someone has sent them to do it."

We were quiet. Adi's tea was still warm, steam rising from her cup while what little remained of mine was cold. I realized that her own thoughts were keeping the tea warmed in her cup, an unintentional application of energy. All of that power and she could sit quietly sipping tea.

Mary would sit near the fire, sipping her wine. Sometimes the evenings were cold in the mountains around Ephesus, and the warmth of the fire was welcome. In the winter evenings I would move her table nearer the hearth, and the firelight helped her to see her words if she wrote in the evenings before sleep. Most of the time she preferred the daylight near the window, letting the sun warm her and her table, but we were often distracted in the day.

I laid her body in that tomb with as much sorrow as I have ever known. Perhaps that is what I have been doing all these centuries, in my remainder, I realized. I have been mourning. I have mourned Mary, and Peter, and the others, all of them gone to wherever it is that we go when our bodies are worn, or tired, or torn. I have been in mourning for nearly two thousand years, alone except for my friend Adriel.

And Lazarus, I thought suddenly.

Lazarus is still alive, I thought. Like me, he still remains, though there has always been something disturbing about him, something unsettled. When he walked back out of that tomb we were amazed, and Lazarus was himself again. We took joy in seeing him alive, and we were awed by the power that Jesus held to bring him back. Lazarus and his sisters were our friends, Jesus' friends. Then his sisters died, and Lazarus was left alone in his house in Bethany.

I wondered that he did not take a wife. Then I heard the whispers, years later as I paused in the village to buy cheese to bring as I visited. The shopkeeper asked me where I was from, and my parents, then where I was going, pleasant and polite chatter from a man who often must wonder what happened in the world beyond his stall and beyond the families of farmers and shepherds who supplied his milk.

"To see an old friend," I told him. "Lazarus, the brother of Mary and Martha." And I asked whether he had known Lazarus' sisters. He paused, and the shop was quieter, though it took me a moment to grasp the change as I looked for coins in my purse. Then I heard the whispers, his own daughters peeping from behind a cloth divider in his stall. The one from the grave, I heard clearly before the shopkeeper spoke his daughter's name and cut off the whispered gossip.

When I reached the house of Lazarus, he greeted me with the old familiarity and wrapped his arms around me as warmly as ever. Holding me at arms length he smiled and gave me welcome to enter his house. He was the same Lazarus, our friend, except for the eyes. In his eyes I saw that something had changed, something was darker and more distant, and I knew why he had taken no wife. The women were afraid of him. And somewhere deep within I also was afraid, not of Lazarus, but of whatever had changed within him. It was as though he had gone back into the tomb and found something that he brought into the light, into his house, and it was not good.

"Lazarus," I said.

"What?" asked Adriel.

"Look at that day," I said, and I knew Adriel was reading the memories I had just found, however it was that they were able to do such things.

"Lazarus," he said. "But why?"

I thought of Mary's body, peaceful, slumbering in the tomb, the wood of the cross resting there with her, the manuscript that slept with her.

"The cross," I said finally. "He seeks the cross, and he thinks that I will show them where it is."

"What purpose can he have for the wood?" Adi wondered aloud.

"He thinks that there is power in the wood of the cross," I said. "And there is, though perhaps not the kind of power that he wants."

I looked over at my staff, leaning near the door. One day it had helped to hold the arms of Jesus up above the ground, lifted in agony. This staff was carved from a length of wood sawn from the cross before I placed the remainder with Mary. All that remained to me outside her tomb were but a few more small pieces, pieces I had kept for reasons that I did not understand at the time. I used them to make objects of faith, amulets, for those who seemed to need them over the years. There was nearly none of the wood remaining to me, beyond the staff and the main crosspiece left with Mary.

"He thinks that you will lead him there," Adriel said.

"What?"

"To Mary's tomb. He may believe that you will one day visit her, or that you will reveal where you placed her."

"Mary's tomb," I repeated. "You mean that you believe he already knows that I placed the cross there?"

It may be that Adriel had stated his thought before understanding it. We all stood, the steam still rising softly from Adi's cup.

"He knows," Adi said. We turned to look at her. "Where else would you place it, John, son of Zebedee, if not with the one whom you loved?"

She called me by the name that I was known then, in that first century. And the memories were pouring, flooding my mind. My father, the sea of Galilee by day and by moonlight, that beach, Mary laughing under the trees, campfires. Jesus staring at James and me and saying, "You do not know what you are asking…."

"They were precious to you," she said. "If they are no longer with you, then you have placed them together for safekeeping."

"How would he know that I placed it with her?"

"You would not leave her alone," she said. "And it was of her son, after all. It belongs with Mary."

"All the world knows that Mary's body was not in her tomb," Adriel said. Whether the story had come from the tomb in Ephesus or the tomb in Jerusalem, both traditions had merged to say that Mary, too, had risen. There was no body in her tomb.

It was because they never found where I placed her. That was a secret we had kept, Adriel and I.

Lazarus, though, I thought. Lazarus was not deceived. He knew that I had placed her somewhere else, somewhere to keep her safe.

"I told him," I said. My hand jerked away and nearly knocked over the teacup on the table near me. "When next I saw him, after Mary had died. I told him that I moved her, put her somewhere safe.

"Good, he said to me," I told them. "Good. Then they will leave her tomb in peace, he said. And I had known then that he wished he still slept in his own tomb."

Adi dropped her gaze back to her tea.

"He knows," I repeated.

"And he may have set these others to watch you, to see whether you would betray where you placed her," said Adriel.

I was suddenly cold, realizing the truth of it, and that I may have somehow betrayed her. "Can they read what I think, like you do?"

"No, not unless you engaged them in conversation. They cannot eavesdrop, if that is what is worrying you. Stray thoughts from other humans, perhaps. They may even invade the minds of some. But they cannot enter your mind, John, son of Zebedee. The power that keeps you alive also keeps them at bay."

I sat back in my chair from the relief. It had been hard enough to guard against letting the secret slip out for twenty centuries, but to guard even one's thoughts from them would be impossible.

"He is looking for her." It was Adi, more recovered. The cup swirled in her hands, and she was gazing at the pattern in the tea. "Mary. He is looking for her, where you placed her."

She was right, I knew.

"Then we must stop him," I said. I thought about the tomb, how near it was to so many that Lazarus would have known if he remembered them. And I was sure that Lazarus forgot nothing. "We must get to the tomb first, before he can find it."

"If he has not already," Adriel said.

I stared. "You checked it, though. It was fine."

"Yes, it was then, but we do not know how quickly he may find it."

A terrible thought shot through my mind. "Could they have followed you, Adriel? When you went to check the tomb, if they were watching then, could they have followed you?"

Adriel thought for a minute.

"No," he said. "I do not believe that they could have followed me without my knowledge. We feel their presence, their proximity. I do not believe they could have been close enough to know where I went. Not without alerting me of their presence. At the speed I was moving they could not have held back without losing me, and they could not have kept up without alerting me."

"And it was fine, when you were there? The cross was fine, and the manuscript?"

"Yes," he said.

I thought of Mary lying there in the tomb, wrapped in her shroud as I had left her, as we had left her. Somehow I often forgot that Adriel was with me. In my memory I was with Mary, standing in the tomb and saying goodbye to her. In my grief I was alone.

Sometimes, I realized, I am still standing in her tomb. I am still saying goodbye, and I am still alone.

Simon

I was dreaming as I lay in my tent. I struggled back toward wakefulness. There was a sound of wind and a feeling of groundlessness around me, falling in a void without hope of solid ground, and darkness lit only by fire that spun around me in a whirl of flaming hatred. There were eyes in the flames, and teeth, and a hand with claw like talons that reached out and was about to rake across my eyes when I awoke.

My clothes were damp with sweat, and I thought that I had screamed, but I wasn't sure. I realized that it had been a dream, a nightmare, and I was trying to force myself toward calm. Then the sounds crept into the tent, past my breathing and the noise of the blood in my ears and my mind. There were voices in the camp, and firelight against the cloth of the tent.

One voice I knew. It was Lazarus. As I listened, I thought that I knew the other voice from my dream, but it must have been that I only heard it while sleeping and my mind incorporated the real sounds into the unreal dreaming.

I slipped out of my sleeping bag and onto my knees, and I crept silently to the tent flap. It was only partially zippered. Pulling back the cloth I could see Lazarus standing by the fire, and near him I saw someone's shadow. The shadow was in the wrong place, though, and I could not find the person from whom the firelight cast it. Then I saw Lazarus speaking to the shadow, and something like eyes shining back toward him from the darkness.

Lazarus pointed up into the hills, up toward the tombs we have found that day. There were many of them, too many, and we did not know where to start. He was certain that Mary was entombed in one of them, buried with the cross.

"Here she is," he had said, to himself. "This is where he hid her. This is where it is."

The hillside was made of holes, with stones piled against the face in haphazard fashion, though after a while one could make out something like a pattern of openings spaced across the face of the mountainside. They were tombs, ancient tombs, and many of them.

"Which one?"

Lazarus said nothing for a long while. Then he said, "Yes. Which one."

He started walking toward the base of the mountain.

"We'll camp here." He pointed, then he kept walking toward the mountain. "I think we will need some help."

He walked away, and I tended to the tents and to setting up camp. The attendants we had hired were no longer with us, having developed excuses to leave as we visited tomb after tomb. Lazarus disquieted them, and the way he stared into each tomb began to disturb them. The prospect of treasure had left them, and they slowly seemed to realize that we were searching for something else, something that they did not want to find.

"It is better," he said when I told him the last ones were gone. "All we need are the donkeys."

And now here we were, Lazarus and I and three braying donkeys. The animals were clearly as disconcerted as I by whatever it was I saw in the firelight.

The thing slipped away, a darker patch in the night, and as it went I felt my heartbeat lessen, calmer. I decided that it was foolish to remain in the tent. With the talking and the braying of the donkeys only a dead man would remain asleep, so I unzipped the flap and stepped out into the firelight. Lazarus turned to look at me.

"You had fine dreams, I hope?"

The question made me feel uneasy. I must have made some sound in the tent, I realized.

"No. Not fine at all." I glanced over at the animals. They were beginning to quiet down, but I could still see their eyes wide in the firelight. "I am sorry if I made some noise. Strange dreams."

Lazarus laughed, quietly and low. It was as though he could laugh without smiling.

"We needed help to find the tomb," he said. "And now we have it. Our friends will examine the tombs to find the one that we need."

I looked around.

"I thought I saw someone talking to you, but I could not see him clearly."

"That is probably just as well," he said, and he laughed again, and this time I was sure that he was not smiling. "Our friends are not like us."

I thought at once of the dream, the nightmare, and I thought of demons pulling at me like Saint Anthony in the desert. It was said that Anthony would walk across the dry places, demons clinging to his feet and to his robes, but he would ignore them. He would lie down upon the tombs he found in the desert and sleep, untroubled. When the demons came and made noises to frighten him, old Anthony would just beat on the tomb with his staff and tell them to be quiet. And they would obey him.

I was no Anthony. They would not listen to me, nor could I ignore them. I was staring off into the darkness when Lazarus began to laugh once more, low and dry, like the voice of the demons in my nightmare.

On the hillside I could hear rocks tumbling from time to time, pebbles sliding down the mountainside. Something was moving among the tombs, and I was glad that I could not see it. I sat down by the fire, exhausted from little sleep and the exertion of dreaming. Lazarus stood at the edge of the firelight, his face turned upward to the tombs as though he could see what sent the rocks tumbling down the slope.

I realized that the sound had stopped. The rocks were quiet, but the donkeys began to make anxious grunts like the beginning of braying. They shifted on their small hooves.

"It is found," he said, and I knew that he was not talking to me but to himself. In a moment the dread I had felt in the tent returned. I did not understand since I was not asleep this time but awake, still watching and waiting to see what Lazarus would do. Nevertheless, I felt myself begin to perspire, and I had to fight the urge to run or to hide within my tent.

"Well?" Lazarus was staring into the darkness. I could hear something like fire crackling and the hiss of a rabid animal.

"Good, good," Lazarus said. "Soon I will have it. And we will show them their mistake."

The thing in the darkness made another hissing sound and began to move away. For a moment I felt it staring at me, and I wanted to run. I sank down onto the ground, my hand clutching at a St. Christopher medallion around my neck like some fool in a horror movie.

The thing turned and moved off into the darkness. The donkeys began to quiet down, and it felt like I could breathe again after being trapped under black water.

"When the sun rises," said Lazarus, "we will go up the mountainside and look upon the face of Mary."

I was amazed and afraid, and I knew that I would never rise above that black water again.

Adi

"Tomorrow," John says to Adriel. "Tomorrow, you must go. Take Adi with you if she is able and if you are both willing. You must go to Mary's tomb, and you must bring the cross and the manuscript back here."

He stops, and I know he is aware of making the request sound like a command.

"Please, my old friend. There is little time."

Adriel agrees.

"Perhaps you are right, John. They may be nearer to finding her than we had believed. We will go to the tomb."

He pauses to ask in my mind, his voice flowing like cool water into my thoughts. Of course, I will go with him. Of course.

"John, though," I say aloud so that he could follow the conversation. "He may be unsafe here alone."

John looks at me, and he seems to smile.

"I will be safe, Adi. No need to worry about me. I am protected by a greater power than you and Adriel possess. They will do me no harm while you are gone." He pauses. "God help me, I think I actually believe it once again."

There is something in his thoughts, but I do not know this feeling.

"In truth," he says, "I am more afraid for you and for what may await you if Lazarus is as close to the tomb as we believe he might be."

I am curious for his thoughts.

"You believe that God protects you," I say.

"Yes," John says after time passes. "Strange, isn't it? So many doubts, so many questions. I have heard nearly nothing of the Lord in all these centuries. And yet, I am sure that the Spirit of God is with me. Perhaps I am the more certain for having no more proof to offer."

It makes no sense, but I hear Adriel's voice in my mind telling me to leave it be.

Simon

As the sunlight began to ease into our camp, I felt the sense of dread return. Lazarus stood a dozen yards from our tents, a cup of coffee in his hands from the camp stove pot. The donkeys started to shift and to pull at their leads, stamping at the ground, eyes widened.

Lazarus glanced at them, then he turned back toward the mountainside. Someone was approaching or was there. I knew it moved, but I could not track the movement with my eyes. It was more of a shadow than a figure, but the light was not right to place that shadow. It shimmered and moved, and I kept watching it.

"The jackasses are afraid," said Lazarus, but not to me.

I heard someone laughing. The laughter was disconnected, like a radio station partially tuned, part of the transmission lost somewhere in the air. Then the same voice, more clear, spoke words I did not know, and the donkeys grew quiet.

"That one, as well, though he does not bray so loudly," said Lazarus. More laughter, from both of them this time, low and dry. "Perhaps I should introduce you. But then you already know Simon, don't you?"

I was staring at them both. The shadow seemed to shimmer within, glitter in a darkened globe.

"You don't actually recall meeting any angels, do you, Simon?" Lazarus turned back to see me. He sipped his coffee.

"Angels," I managed. Somehow in my mind I saw a painting, Fra Angelico's *Annunciation*, an angel in robes with wings covered in layers of feathers.

"The real thing," said Lazarus. "Though you probably expected light and wings, didn't you?"

More laughter, from Lazarus and from somewhere near the other figure. It began to brighten, light starting to stream from it. I watched it take form like a person, with wings and robes, exactly the angel from the painting in my mind, the light streaming from its clothes and its face. It was beautiful, but I was still afraid.

"Fear not," said the voice, and then more laughter. Lazarus bent over with a hand on his knee, holding out the coffee so as not to spill it with the motion of laughing.

"Fear not," he said. "Yes, that is what they say, isn't it?"

"An angel," I said, but I knew it was not true. I was staring at the creature. The light was nearly white, like sunlight, but somewhere around the edges there were colors, and wisps of what seemed smoke.

"It would have taken us days to search all of these tombs," said Lazarus. "Our friends can manage such things much more quickly." He turned and pointed up the hillside. "They have found the tomb."

I stood still, looking from one of them to the other. Then I turned and looked up toward the mountain.

"Yes, well," said Lazarus. "It is a bit much to take in. Today, Simon, you will see the face of Mary, the mother of Jesus. Theotokos. Imagine that."

He took another sip of his coffee, made a face at the mug.

"Angels and Mary, all in one day." He turned back to the creature beside him. "Leave it. We will retrieve the cross, and then we will see what the world has to say. Is there anything else in the tomb?"

"The wood of that cross, the body of Mary. Nothing else of value." The voice was musical, like hearing a choir speaking, with some of the members slightly out of time.

"Thank you, my friend."

Something moved through the camp like a cold wind, and the creature was gone. The donkeys were braying again.

Lazarus looked at me, and he poured the rest of his coffee onto the ground.

Mary

As I sit writing I can see John through the open window of my house. He goes about the daily chores, firewood, pulling water. He sweeps the stones outside my door. If I would let him he would wash clean the inside of my home as well.

This man needs something to occupy him. Still, it is good that he is busy. Too much time to reflect and we both sink to darker thoughts, like leaves that have gotten too wet and sink to the bottom of the pool. There they are, all of these leaves lining the bottom, yet one almost never sees it happen, the leaf sinking. We are like that, all of us, unless someone takes great care to lift us out of our thoughts.

I should think of him raised up, alive. That is what they said happened, Magdalene and the others. They found the tomb empty, and he appeared to them alive. John also saw him.

I remember him as he looked when we laid him in that tomb, the darkness that moved across his body as they pushed the stone across the doorway. I can see him on the cross, see his blood, his pain.

I dream of it. John knows, though I have never told him. I suspect that he dreams the same dreams. He stood in the same place, saw the same thing, and I know that he loved my son almost as much as I loved him.

Often on the Sabbath or on the so-called day of the sun, others will come here who believe that my son was of God. I am not always comfortable around them, but I try to make them feel welcome. I know that they sense in me some connection to him. I wish that I could sense one.

My son is gone, and before him Joseph. My other sons have their lives, their families. Now John is my son, and I am his mother.

And Jesus is nowhere to be found.

John

"Your family is outside," a man was telling Jesus. He was sitting in his house with people crowding in around him and out into the courtyard. I looked through the people, tried to see through to the doorway or the window, but it was too crowded. "It is your mother, and your brothers are with her," he said.

Jesus stood and pointed at Peter, me, the others of us who followed him.

"Here are my mother and my brothers!" he said. "Whoever follows God is my brother, and my sister, and my mother."

Then he turned and went out of the house, the people making way for him and following him back outside. I was glad to follow him out. The house had become too full, and the air too crowded.

Mary stood there, a stone's throw from the house because of the people. With her were two men, her sons as well, one on each side of her. They were quiet, with hands folded in front of them and simple robes. I could tell that they waited for their mother to speak. She was clearly in charge of them, though they were men of age.

Mary herself was also quiet, her hands also clasped in front of her robes of blue and white. Her head was covered with a blue cloth. She was unadorned, no jewelry to be seen, surprisingly young.

"We came to see if you were well," she said. "It is said that crowds come and go from your house." She looked beyond us at the people.

"It sounded crazy, my son," she added.

All of us but Jesus turned to look at the house. People we did not know were peering from the window openings. A child was standing on the sill of a window and eating something, probably something he found in the house.

"Mother," Jesus said.

"They are walking through your house like it was a market." It was Judas, one of the brothers who were twins. Those two were so similar in appearance that it was disconcerting.

"Yes, brother," said Jesus. "Let them be. One day I will not be living here for them to visit me."

"Don't start that talk again," said the other twin. He was holding a rope halter lead, the donkey behind them biting off mouthfuls of grass. Mary turned to look at the brother who fell silent under her gaze. She turned back to Jesus, glanced over the rest of us.

"Well, then, you may as well invite us in. All the world comes to your house, and we are not even invited to eat," she said. "Are you ashamed of your mother?"

Jesus sighed and turned to Peter.

"Ask the people to go home. Tell them I have other visitors," he said.

"Yes, Lord," said Peter, and he turned his great head to look at the people.

"Gently," said Jesus. "You are not dumping out a net. Take John and the others with you to help."

We turned, each of us nodding to Mary. It was hard to know what to say to the brothers since they were so much alike. Oddly, we did not know whether it was necessary to speak to one of them or both.

It took some time to get the people to move. It was like herding sheep that are ready for sleep. Slowly some of them began to walk out and toward Capernaum, and the rest followed. As evening came the number of people were reduced to Jesus, his family, and those of us, men and women, who would be disciples. The other Mary was cooking, and two women were helping her. Soon we were reclining in the house, eating from tables and bowls, listening to Mary the mother of Jesus tell stories of what was happening near their home, what rumors she had heard.

"You must be careful, brother," said one of the twins, either Judas or Simon though no one seemed to know which. "As the crowds like you more, the Romans care for you less and less."

Jesus was looking into the fireplace, watching the flames while he ate.

"The love of the people," he said. "It will only last so long. You will see."

The other twin was holding one of the toy boats that Jesus had made.

"You can always come home, brother. Build the furniture, even the toys that people want." He looked up. "You can teach the people when they come to the workshop. What about that?"

Jesus looked at the toy boat and nodded.

"It sounds wonderful, my brother. But I must be doing other business now."

This twin started to say something else, looked at their mother and stopped. Then they went on with quiet conversation into the night, as did small groups of us. I sat near Jesus, listening to the family talk. Mary already made me feel as though I were one of her own.

John

I went out to the deck. I thought that I needed some time with the squirrels. Adriel and Adi had gone to bring back the cross and the manuscript until I could decide what to do. Thinking about their journey, I wanted to go as well, if only to see Mary once more, but I knew it would be a double mistake.

It would take too long with me traveling with them. I cannot move as angels can. And I would not see Mary—I would see her bones. That would not be the image that I wanted in my mind.

I do not know whether such things have the same effect on Adriel and Adi, but I do not believe so. So many things that carry connotations for me carry none for Adriel. If something goes bad in the refrigerator, for me it is a chore and the smell can be wretched. For Adriel, the smell is merely interesting, never good or bad in itself. For centuries I thought his lack of aversion to the smell of death came from his immortality, or from some theological immunity. Finally, I have come to understand that since such things cannot affect his biology, if one can call it biology, he has no adverse reaction to them.

That is the upshot of living so long. One learns a multitude of ways that one was wrong.

I took a sip of the wine that I had brought out with me, sure that when Adriel and Adi returned I would need chemical reinforcement. There was a blue glimmer on the edge of my glass, puzzling me. The early evening should not have such a light in the sky, I thought.

"John," the voice said. I knew that voice, and I realized that I must have fallen asleep. Raising my eyes I saw her.

"John," she said again, and I did not think I was dreaming.

"Mary," I said, and I dropped my glass. She smiled, a warm glow lighting in the deck. "But you cannot be here."

"Why not, John? Because you placed me in that tomb?"

I did not say anything, and it seemed to me that she was laughing softly. Of course, I had placed her in the tomb.

"I think you had better sit down," she said. Instead I took three steps toward her before she stopped me with an upraised hand. "John, you cannot touch me, any more than you can touch the light."

I stopped, staring at her face, her robes.

"My body is in that tomb where you placed it," she said. "But it is too late. You will find my bones, but not the cross. It is gone."

I must have made some sort of sound, because she shushed me.

"The cross is gone. What does it matter? It was only wood."

"It was the cross," I managed.

"Yes, but the true cross was not the wood, it was the one they placed onto it." She tilted her head, or what appeared to be her head, to see whether I had heard. "Come, let us walk."

I came to myself enough to look around to see whether anyone was watching.

"They cannot see me unless I will it," she said. "That much is given to me. And more."

She turned and stepped, appeared to step, down from the deck and across the yard toward the trees. After a moment I followed her, catching up in a few strides.

"Others have claimed to have seen you," I said. "From time to time."

"Yes," she said. "They have."

"Then you did appear to them?"

"To some of them," she said. We walked, hearing crickets in the dusk. "But never to you, you are thinking."

I was startled for a moment. Why was it that everyone around me could read my thoughts?

A smile, and I knew that she had, in fact, done exactly that.

"John. You and I are old friends. You have known me longer and better than almost anyone. If I appeared for a few minutes to some people, what is that to you?"

I suddenly felt much younger than my two thousand years, both better and slightly embarrassed at once. We walked along quietly for a few moments. For once, I ignored the squirrels in the trees.

"They will find my manuscript," she said. "The bones are dust, and the wood was only wood, but my words remain."

I thought about her sitting by the window, the sound of her pen tracing the letters onto the parchment.

"Who took the cross?"

She turned to look at me, though I was sure that in this form she did not need to do so.

"Lazarus has taken it." She walked on among the tree trunks. "He believes that it will give him power."

"It will give him power," I said. "Perhaps not as he believes, but power nonetheless." And I realized that I was already used to Mary's presence, as used to her as when we lived together centuries ago.

"Power is in the words," she said. "You know that, John. You wrote that, something like it, all those many years ago."

We walked. When we paused, I touched the bark on the trees for no reason other than the comfort of the touch, and Mary reached out to them as well. Somehow it comforted me. I did not know why Mary would reach out to the trees. Perhaps it was only for the comfort that touching something brought to me.

"You will find the manuscript," she said. "Publish it, John. Let the world read it, those who are willing."

I rubbed the oak tree bark, rough under my hand.

"Are you certain, Mary? Will it help them?"

She nodded.

"And it will help you, my friend." She smiled. "It comes soon. Do not be disheartened. Concentrate on the word. And though you do not see, you are seen, and loved."

She smiled once again, then she turned and was gone.

John

The workshop was more of an escape than an avocation, though I finally learned to make things. Once upon a time I was a fisherman, then I became an apostle, an elder in the faith. That is the story. Most people have heard it, or parts of it.

I was also Mary's protector, and her friend, and finally I was her mourner.

I created the story of my death and built my own tomb so that I could escape the interminable waiting, the questions, the look of adoration in their eyes. I found that I needed work. I could have gone back to fishing, but that life was done for me. My family was gone, my father's boats were gone, and I was no longer supposed to be John the Apostle. I was somebody else. Anybody else.

Then I thought of the toys that Jesus built for the children, and I started to copy them. I began with little boats, little animals, pieces of furniture. I made them all, not as well as Jesus had made them, and I sold them to people for their children. Sometimes I sold them, that is. More often I gave them away. Sometimes I made a little money, and sometimes I gave it away as well.

It is amazing how quickly wealth will amass when you do not need it. I made nearly nothing, but I spent even less. Imagine what adding to a nest egg for a really, really long time can do.

After a century or so, a few different names in different regions of the world, it occurred to me that I remembered more about where things used to be than anyone left alive in the world, with the possible exception of Lazarus. I would read accounts of the first century after Christ's death, and I would correct the details in my mind. Then it also occurred to me that I knew where the bodies were buried, so to speak. I knew where the finest houses had been, where the most elaborate buildings had stood. The more time that passed, the more the old things were sought after. Even the late Romans wanted objects from the earlier empire. So I very naturally and easily began to dabble in antiquities, and I added that to my investment portfolio.

After a while, and once there were sufficient banks scattered around, I stopped having to worry about money.

I was not sure what Jesus would say about investments. Surely I could have earned a small living with the toys. And just as surely I could have given more wealth to the poor— they are always with us. Nevertheless, it seemed good to hold onto enough money to make life less precarious.

I still made the toys. And I did other things as well. As surprising as my brother would have found it, I became a passing good silversmith. Some of my work has been found on altars throughout Europe, though no one knew that I was the artist. I myself was surprised at times to read the inscriptions and to find out who made the items and when. Occasionally I remembered the name. More often my work was attributed to someone else.

I also sat in homes and drank tea, and I watched the squirrels. They bear watching.

Adriel has helped me all these many years. I have not managed on my own. Angels appear to need nothing. They do not eat as we eat, and they do not sleep as we sleep, though they do appear to drift into dreams from time to time. The nearest thing to a need that I have found in them is their unquenchable curiosity, especially regarding human beings.

I could not tell you how to see an angel. If they did not wish it, you would not, at least most of the time. I could tell you how to be sure that an angel is watching you. Just do something interesting, and repeat, like the instructions on bottles of shampoo. Sooner or later one of them notices. They cannot help themselves, and they gather just to watch, like children at a bakery. (Sorry, Adriel and Adi.)

I simply sat and made wooden toys and silver crosses. Yet they watched.

Sometimes I have sensed other creatures. How much was real and how much in my imagination I did not know. Over the years I gained an awareness of death, though I cannot say I recognized it as the coming of a being who gathers souls. I did come to recognize the signs in someone about to move on.

I was not sure that we do move on. I saw Mary, though. She was real enough, on the other side of death, unless I imagined her.

In my darkest moments, I doubted, and more than doubted. I doubted the reality of the afterlife and the durability of the soul. It would be far simpler to accept the idea that at death a human being ceases to be. Once the body ceases, so does that which it contained, chemistry and energy. More often, I entertained doubt regarding the idea of moving to a different state in a new space. I came to think that we merely achieve a different state in the same space, or a similar one: angels on a pin, surely, but more like spirits in worlds upon worlds. Heaven is folded into the space that touches ours, and when the dead appear to us, it is simply that they have wandered back around a corner where we cannot turn, not yet. When they disappear, they have stepped past the threshold of a house built all around us that we cannot see.

Sometimes they are watching us. Perhaps there is little entertainment in that world. Such visions as some have shared of that existence are strange indeed. I myself have seen things that I could scarcely comprehend, scenes that I did not know were real but that impressed me more than the seeming reality around me.

That is how we wound up with Revelation. I should never have shared those visions. I did not think that I understood them myself, and I was more certain that no one else ever understood my attempts to describe what I saw. The Gospel was enough, the few letters someone found and that I could not manage to collect again. What they call the Revelation of Saint John the Divine is dismaying.

I had to try to put it all down on papyrus, just to get it out of my head. That may be how God works to get such things written, I did not know. But how does one describe a world that swirls in time like sand in a whirlpool in the sea, merging and changing, all the layers at once? The image of Jesus, alive, not in human form but human-like, voices that begin inside the ones listening rather than reaching out in waves of decent sound—how does one write such things down and make it understood?

It is like the mental anguish of an epileptic seizure. There you are, sitting quietly, when your mind is terrified by the rhythmic ticking of a clock or the dripping of water, some sound or some light that ticks at the right or wrong moments, over and over, until your mind keels over into darkness. The last shapes your eyes have seen, the lines of ordinary objects of this world, begin to snake and to move, shifting and gathering into new unspeakable shapes of things that you cannot recognize and cannot forget, until finally you sink into a darkness of shapes, a deep sonorous slurring of sounds playing in your head out of time. Voices are like stretched and deepened echoes as twisted as the moving lines that you see even with your eyes shut tight against the world. That was what it was like to slip and fall into heaven, trying to navigate the liquidity of that existence with the clumsy body of this one.

Spiritual visions are the epileptic fits of the soul.

I saw power, and movement. I sensed the intent and the intelligence of God flowing like liquid clouds of gold, and all that I could offer people was words, images of thrones and dragons and terrible angels, appearing in that reality not like and not unlike Adriel, beings of such power that they cannot be seen properly by minds unequipped for the journey.

All that is to say nothing of trying to describe a vision of God.

I was happy to have no more visions, no moments of ecstatic insight into the tumultuous orderliness of that world. Quietness and rest are good, and tea. Occasional there are squirrels to watch, dogs to walk. It is enough, until I reach the point that I, too, may die and learn of death's final joke. We are where we will be, but we cannot know that other life in this one and survive, not often.

I did not know what the angels saw. If you tried to ask Adriel about it, you would receive the nearest thing to an evasion that he was capable of offering you. He did not know a way to convey their experiences to us, not in ways that would mesh with our sensory perception. There are overlaps of course, areas where they see as we see and hear as we hear, but then beyond the borders of our senses there are dangerous places that fall off our mental maps. The ancients were not marking the geography of the earth when they drew their maps flat, edges of the maps marked with warnings that one could sail off the edge of the earth. They were mapping the world as they could still perceive it, the ragged edges showing what they, in their ancient ignorance and clearer perception, knew were the limits of our understanding. Beyond here there be dragons, they wrote: darkness and light and the deep, inescapable epilepsy of the soul.

The reaches of space are nothing compared to the reaches of the spirit.

The angels come, in their visitations, through an opening to everything that is forever, our minds gasping as the air and ether of our world escape. Fear not, they say, fear not, but it is only the voice of a parent lying to a child who knows that there really are monsters in the dark.

It is not angels we fear. It is the doors that they open.

Adi

I do not know they are there, those people. It may be the only time they have come.

I am on a rock, watching the water sparkle in a stream, sunlight flowing like water from the sky, and I let my mind merge with the water, the coolness, the liquid movement, the sparkling light, until without knowing I am also like the water, and cool, moving within my own form, sparkling with light.

When I realize they are present, I simply turn to see them, knowing they cannot harm me. They fall flat upon the grassy slope, hands stretched out toward me in supplication or in worship, I cannot say and they do not know. I realize that they are as curious as they are afraid, and I realize that I am still shimmering with the water like a liquid diamond sitting on the stone.

They do not know what I am, and they wonder. They wonder so much at my appearance that they creep closer, ignoring their fear, quietly, until they are only steps away. The light shimmers in their faces, illuminating their hair with sparkling edges like white fire.

What are you? they think.

"I am Adi," I tell them. They begin to lift their heads to look at me again, and I know that they are still held by their fear. "Do not be afraid."

They come no closer.

"Adi," they say, and repeat my name like a whispered chant.

"I mean you no harm," I say, and make them understand my meaning in their minds. I point to the stream. "I am seeing the light upon the water."

Now they look puzzled, looking from me to the water. I know that our conversation needs to end, but is so long since I have conversed with anyone that even their limited comprehension is a relief. Alone too long in the songs of space, one begins to doubt that there is any differentiation between oneself and the universe. All is one. Then comes someone who can comprehend, and the comprehension, the very need and ability of it, confirms that one is separate and distinct from everything else. One is oneself. Our existence is confirmed in the comprehension of others.

"Adi," they say. I step down from the stone and walk with them to their camp. There, in the firelight, they tell me their stories, the ones handed down among their people, generations of them. I hear of their ancestor, who comes from far away, traveling with his herds and his family. His clothes are like their own, for they have made him so in their minds, each generation, and his words are like their own, for they have changed them generation by generation in the telling of them.

Still, I glimpse the truth. Some wanderer comes, seeking a better place or a different one, with wives, herds, safety. These people, long ago, come from such wandering ones.

In the night, as fires burn lower and their children sleep, I leave them. I am still glimmering and shining, though I allow the light to lower as the darkness grows.

Many years later I return to their children, to hear how the stories change. One of them comes with a bright stone, tied onto a leather necklace. She is beautiful and brave to walk toward me despite her fear. She holds out the stone, letting the sunlight glimmer in it.

"Adi," she says. She means the stone, but I know that she understands that their word for this crystal is the same as my name. Sometime in the generations between that first day at the stream and this one, their people find such glittering stones, and they remember their grandfathers' grandfathers telling about meeting the shining one at the stream, though they do not know what I am. My name is part of their language, part of their stories now.

And I know that I am real. No, I know that I am separate, that I am not cloud or light or any elemental thing. I am Adi.

There are others like me. Scattered through space, sometimes we find another and sometimes we share our thoughts, travel for a time together. Some shield themselves, some do not; some do not seem to know that they may. In all of them there is power, as in me. Some of them are older than I seem, some I perceive are more powerful, and some are less so.

I am born in a moment near the spiraling stars the humans call Andromeda. In a moment I am gazing at the stars swirling in the dust of time, at the edge of the horizon of a collapsed star. Somehow I know that I emerge into this space, but I do not recall the space from which I come. There is nothing for me, in my memory, and then there is the shining expanse of stars swirling from the center like diamonds on strings.

I reach out and touch a door in space, and there is another space and another door, countless time, oceans of space. I gaze along them like mirrors, worlds stretching away into the same differentness and different sameness. Here I exist.

I do not see God. I never see God.

Sitting by the campfires of the humans, I hear them tell stories of gods and demons, monsters and heroes. Yet when they ask me whether I am a god, or to tell them about God, I can only tell them that I never see it. All of them tell me of the gods, and I could not doubt them.

I can see things and touch things that the humans cannot find or see or know. How then shall I doubt that they can find and see and touch the God that I cannot?

John

Peter had gone out for a walk, which was just as well. There were too many people in too small a space. They kept coming, joining, professing their faith and bringing their wealth, such as it was. Few had coins in their bags, even after selling everything they had to join the Way.

That was Andrew's contribution: the Way.

"We have found the way to God, do you not see? That is what we can call ourselves, followers of the Way," he said, holding his hands wide as though he had brought something new into the room.

Peter had stared at him. "Why shall we not just say that we are followers of Jesus?"

There was a small silence. Most of us knew the answer, but nobody wanted to explain it, or give voice to it.

"Well," began Thomas. "There are some who have formed a different opinion of Jesus than we have. And for those people..."

Peter waited for the rest of the answer, which Andrew did not want to give.

"And for them?"

"It gives them a different way to think about it. Keeps the walls down, you might say, so that they can give ear to what we are telling them about God." Andrew stopped, looking Peter in the eye. I could sense the effort it took not to look around at the rest of us for support.

"Plus if we say we follow Jesus, they want to kill us." It was the voice of an old man who had been sitting quietly on the floor by the wall where his family had placed him. It was the first thing I had heard him say, and I had actually wondered whether he was senile. His family had come to join us the day before. Jesus had healed a little girl in the group of some fever that had threatened to take her.

"This way we can stay alive," the old man said. "That's good, right? Stay alive, wait for the Lord to return."

Peter looked at him. Andrew turned and looked at me. Relief and embarrassment were mingled on his face.

"The Way," said Peter, watching the old man. "Well, I suppose it does no harm to let the old and the women have shelter from the Romans."

Just then there was some small commotion, a family entering the hall where we were gathered, someone calling for Peter. He turned and went off to greet them, and Andrew turned away as well, happy to be done with the conversation.

I looked across the room toward the open window set into the end of the hall. Afternoon light was streaming in, lighting a space on the stone floor and illuminating the dust swirling in the air. Just beyond that corridor of light, I saw another glimmering patch of air, more irregular in form and moving as though reflected from something curved and mobile. It moved in the space of the room, closer to the window but still visible. Glancing around I realized that nobody else had noticed it.

Something passing in the street, I thought, and I stepped to the window to see what it might be. Standing there I saw nothing that could be the source of the reflection. I decided that I had missed whatever it was, a wagonload of something passing in the street perhaps, and looked back beside me to where the reflection had been. It was still there, within arm's reach, and I realized that the angle from the street was wrong. Even had a cohort of Romans stood in the street with polished shields, there was nothing in the air beside me to catch the reflection.

And the light was moving.

I reached out, carefully, and touched it. My fingers felt as thought they had touched soft fur, fire and ice all at once. I made a startled sound, and I heard another sound coming from the light itself.

It was Adriel, but I did not know it then.

From time to time, in the markets, in the temple, out in the wilderness, I had seen or thought I had seen some movement, some glimmer of light. Sometimes I would think I saw Jesus looking at the same thing, though he never mentioned it or pointed it out. I had always been sure that Jesus saw things I did not, whether in the world or beyond it.

"Say nothing," came a voice. It sounded like a man, but different, as a man would sound who was made of marble, smooth and crisp.

I was so astonished that I stood mute, staring at the shimmering space in front of me. I realized that this must be some sort of supernatural visitation, but I did not know what kind. The voice was not that of Jesus, but who could guess what his voice would sound like in a bodiless form.

I wasn't afraid. Dumbfounded would be closer. The experience was so odd that I felt as though I was tilted off balance, a light headed feeling like I might faint or simply fall over. I was sure that everyone in the room would share my feelings.

Some measure of control returned with each slow breath that I forced myself to make. I turned and looked around the room. Peter was at the far end of the hall talking with the group of newcomers. Philip and Andrew were moving tables, though I had no idea why. Most of the others were standing or sitting around the room in small groups, mothers playing with children. Some of the people were praying, some were quietly chanting Jewish prayers. No one was noticing the light. No one was staring with incredulity at the source of this disembodied voice.

I wondered how we came to be such a ragged bunch of people. How did we come to be gathered one on top of another in this space? Was this what we had gone through the past years to achieve, a commune of self-dispossessed nomads?

"I thought the same things, to be frank," Adriel said to me, though I still did not know it was Adriel. I realized that I did not know whether he had spoken aloud or spoken in my mind. I turned once more from the glimmering cloud that it seemed only I could see and scanned the room. Again, no one among them seemed to pay any attention to the voice.

"No, they wouldn't hear," the voice said. "I am actually speaking only to you."

I was just about to reply and to ask the voice what manner of being it was, when he spoke again.

"No need to speak aloud," he said. "If you permit, I can glean your thoughts. There is no need to alarm the others."

Or to appear to be insane, I thought.

"There is that," he said.

And this being is in my mind, I thought, beginning to feel the approach of panic, as though I were closed into a box from which I could not escape and within which I could not hide.

An angel.

"Yes, that is what I am."

Jesus saw you, I thought, though I did not know why that particular observation occurred to me just then.

"Yes, I believe that he did, though I do not know how. I do not really understand why you can see me."

I can't see you. Not really. And I pictured what I was actually seeing in my mind, holding the image of the slightly shimmering air in my thought for a moment.

"Oh! I never quite realized I looked like that."

The air changed, like a door had swung closed in a small room, and the shimmer changed. It was now a bare glimmer that I could only just make out. I gave up on trying to see him, and I took another glance around the room.

Why are you here?

"Hmmm. Good question. I have been wondering myself." A pause. "Perhaps we might go somewhere that you could converse more openly? Might you take a walk?"

I had to admit that getting out of that hall for a while struck me as a good idea. I suddenly wanted to be on one of my father's boats, out in the middle of the Sea of Galilee. Alone.

I picked up my cloak, for the afternoon was far gone, and I told James that I would be back later, not to worry, that I needed to take a walk to clear my mind.

"A good idea, brother," he said, and for a moment I feared that he would wish to come with me, and for another moment I wished that he would. I was about to walk away from these my family and friends to walk with some creature that claimed to be an angel. Then someone called to James from across the room, and we parted.

I walked out into the afternoon sunlight of the street, among people moving slower with the fatigue of the day wearing on them. I knew that the angel, if it was an angel, was moving beside me as we passed through the streets heading toward the city walls. I wanted solitude, or as near as I could get to it with an angel for company.

We had reached the city gates and had walked a little way toward Bethany, when I heard him speak again.

"This way, John. There are trees and rocks enough that we will not be seen or bothered."

That might not be my safest route, I thought, before recalling that the creature could read such thoughts. I was beginning to have misgivings about following the advice of this thing.

"I certainly understand. I must be an enigma to you, an angel that only partially appears and then draws you out into the wilderness away from your friends."

There was nothing to say to such clear reasoning.

"Come, let me at least put your mind to rest as to what I am."

A little way from the road there were trees in a grove, with the ground first rising to a rocky slope then falling away so that the area beyond the ridge was hidden from view. We walked, or I walked while he did whatever he did—glided, flew, slid, down into the trees.

We stood still, me wondering where he was. The glimmer was faded and invisible to me now.

"I am Adriel, angel, fellow traveler in this world and many more," came the now familiar voice. This time it was definitely a sound in my ears and not merely in my head.

Slowly the light changed, brightening, shadows falling away like quicksilver poured on the ground. Adriel stood before me, glowing with more light it seemed to my eyes than the sun itself, if only in this small glade.

I knew that at this moment I should be afraid, but I was not, just as back in the large hall where the others were no doubt beginning to prepare the supper I should not have seen him, but I could. I saw in part, anyway.

"Adriel," I said, trying the word.

"Follower of God," he said. "That is the meaning."

"Flocks," I said, and stopped.

"What?" The angel lowered his arms and looked at me quizzically. "Did you say, flocks?"

"Yes," I said. "At least that is the way I remember hearing the name explained. Flock of God, or Flocks of God."

We stood awkwardly silent for a moment. The angel's head was still tilted, looking at me. There were no wings.

"Ah," I said, meaning to go on but failing.

"What?"

"Nothing, nothing really. It is just that I expected, well, that there would be wings. You know. For flying and such." Neither of us said anything for a bit. "Ezekiel does go on talking about wings."

Now he looked up into the trees, as though there might be someone more intelligent to be found.

"With two they covered their faces, with two they covered their feet, and with two they flew, is that it?" The glow had subsided a bit, and he had his hands on his hips, or where I supposed hips would have been.

"Well, that is one of the passages that people talk about," I said. "It always did sound a bit strange, though."

I heard him sigh. I had not ever known that angels could sigh, but then with Jesus there had been little that met my expectations either.

"They are a metaphor," he said, finally. "A way of portraying the qualities of movement and speed and mystery in angels."

I stood there for a while, thinking.

"Metaphor," I said.

"Yes."

"They didn't sound particularly metaphorical in Ezekiel. It sounded as though he was describing physical attributes."

Adriel looked at me oddly. "Just wait until you try to describe something you've seen in a vision. Wait and see how that turns out for you, and you'll understand."

I thought about the way his voice sounded, like a man but with more sound in places and less in others. There was something about it that reminded me of instruments with strings. Like harps. I considered that, and decided not to say it out loud.

"Thank you," said Adriel. He had been listening to my thoughts, which made me angry.

"Stop that," I said. "It is rude."

He stood very still, staring at me. I was still staring at him. I was thinking that here I stood talking to an angel, an angel, and I was getting angry at it. Him. Whatever it was. And yet, I was talking to an angel.

I had no idea what it was thinking.

"You are right," it said.

I was surprised. It was a simple statement, with no rancor or emotion attached to it.

"It was rude, and I had not considered that it was. I am sorry," he continued.

"Well, it is alright." I stood there looking at it, then around at the trees. "I suppose it is just part of what angels usually do, isn't it? You watch, test people, and bring messages. Observing their thoughts is just part of what you do."

I thought I was on fairly solid ground, but Adriel was staring at me again.

"We what? Test people? Carry messages?" He looked a little angry now, and I was honest enough to admit that anger on him was more impressive.

"Yes, well, I mean, that is right, isn't it?"

"Carry messages. For whom?"

"What?"

"You said we carry messages, but for whom?"

"Well, God, of course," I answered. It seemed obvious to me, but I did not think that Adriel was pretending not to understand.

"We carry messages for God?" he asked.

"That is my understanding, anyway," I said. "It is what the word means, isn't it? Angel? Messenger?"

"That is the meaning of the word," he agreed. His anger was somewhat lessened, which gave me some comfort. "I have heard us called by these words, angel or malachi, but I have never understood it. No one has sent me, and I carry no messages."

We both stood for a few moments, thinking over our conversation to this point. I sat on the log of a tree that had fallen. Adriel came and sat beside me.

"I do not see God," he said. I turned to look at him.

"You are speaking metaphorically."

He sat still for a while.

"No, it is the simple truth," he said. "I think that there are some who come and go in the presence of God. I am not one of those. Many of us simply are. We live. We find our own purpose."

I thought about all of the stories that I had ever heard about angels. After a while I came to a frightening possibility.

"There are fallen angels," I ventured.

"I am not one of those. Do not worry," he said. "We see them as well, the fallen ones, the dark ones."

I waited, part of me hoping that he would go on and part hoping that there would be no elaboration.

"The dark ones may have begun as we, but they have gathered a different kind of energy around themselves. Or maybe they have lost something. At any rate, instead of engaging with the universe around them, they have chosen to be at odds with it."

We sat still for a while. A small breeze moved through the trees above us, sending an occasional leaf dancing down through the air.

"They are like the dark places in the universe," he went on. "There are places where one cannot go, where nothing that goes in ever returns, at least not in this world and not in the form it held when it entered. There are dark wells where even the light is lost and cannot return. Can you imagine this?"

I shook my head. "What kind of place could hold firelight captive?"

"I do not understand them," Adriel said. "Perhaps God understands the dark places, but we fear them. Even an angel falling into one of those pits would be lost forever. It is whispered that only power ever emerges, in new worlds that we cannot yet find."

After a while, he added, "There is no darkness in God. So I understand."

Though I was not sure that I even understood anything I had heard, that last statement did reassure me. I have never forgotten it. In God there is no darkness.

We sat for a while in silence. Somehow his presence was comforting to me, and I began to suspect that he felt the same way.

"Why are you here?" I asked him. "Why are we both here?"

"I am not sure," he said. "I started to see the things that your Jesus did, and I listened to the things that he was saying. Like you, I began to follow him."

Somehow I felt that I had understood more about the dark wells in our world than I did about what he had just told me. And I realized that I was, in fact, thinking of him as a he, though part of my mind held onto the notion that angels were not males or females. I made a mental note to raise that subject another time.

"You followed Jesus?"

"You do. Does it seem strange that I would?"

"You have been near us all this time?"

"Most of it. Sometimes I would be elsewhere, but not often," he said. "I was at the temple that day, when the water moved and the people were placed in the pool to be healed."

"You are the angel who moved the water?"

He nodded. "Not that I meant to. It was the blind man near me. I had been concentrating on what Jesus was doing, then I picked up the thoughts of the blind man, and…I lost my balance."

"You lost your balance."

"Yes. It can happen. The senses of the blind are different. There are images in their minds, but not like the ones you hold. I became lost for a moment in his thoughts, fell back, and the water knew that I was there. My thoughts were of the feeling of the water, like the man's thoughts had been."

"So when the water in the pool moved…"

"It was because I fell into it," he said. "Ironic."

"Then you were the one healing those people that day?"

"What? Oh, no. That was not me. I moved the water, but it was another power that I felt moving through the water and modifying those bodies. It was your Jesus, I believe."

We sat for a while. *And he is gone,* I thought.

"He knew that I was there. Jesus. He saw me, even when I did not wish to be seen," said Adriel. "I do not know how he could do that. No one can do that."

"I saw you today," I said.

"Yes," he agreed. "You did. And I did not really intend for that to happen either. For whatever reason, as you stood there thinking, I was drawn to reveal myself at least to you."

"Perhaps God has sent you after all," I said.

Adriel was silent for a long time. We occasionally heard someone passing up on the nearby road. That is one thing the Romans had improved, the roads.

"Perhaps," he said. "Perhaps."

Simon

I was a grave robber.

No need to dress it up. This was not archaeology, not research. It was robbing the graves of the ancient dead for treasure.

And I was robbing the grave of Mary, Theotokos, mother of Jesus. My academic colleagues would be so proud of me. Not that they would believe that this was, in fact, the grave of Mary. *Work from the data, support your thesis on a foundation of facts and solid reasoning.* Their facts never included demons running across the hills at the bidding of a man who cannot die. At least, he had not for twenty centuries.

There must be another explanation. Surely you see how ludicrous the proposition is? This man claims to be Lazarus of the New Testament, and you give him credence?

No. These demons gave him credence. His knowledge of the ancient world gave him credence. Nothing that would serve as a creditable academic source, I was afraid.

And I was robbing tombs.

One large stone and an accumulation of sand and dust covered the opening of this tomb. It was held in place by smaller stones at the base. The face of the mountainside was studded with these plugged holes, a madman's dike. This mountain face formed one side of a valley, out of the way of casual trekkers, protected from time by a combination of geography and the monotonous serenity of a cemetery. The heat was already rising from the rocky terrain, the distance marked by wavy lines of energy rising back toward the sky in a disinterested shimmer.

"Let's get going," said Lazarus. "I don't want to stand in this heat all day."

I took a short shovel and a pick from the back of one of our donkeys. The animal glanced around at me, not so much to acknowledge the lessened weight as to communicate its disinterest.

I took a few swings with the pick. The stones barely shifted, having become accustomed to their resting places.

"You're going to have to do better than that," he said.

I looked around at Lazarus. He was sitting on a large rock a few feet away, sipping tea from a thermos cup.

"You could help," I said.

"Yes," he agreed, "I could." He took another sip and leaned back on his elbow.

After an hour it seemed to me that most of the bracing rock and other material were out of the way or loosened to the point that we would be able to shift the stone. I stood leaning on the pick, wondering whether Lazarus would leave me in this tomb were I to have a heart attack. I supposed that once I was dead, I would not mind where he left my body. There was worse company than Mary.

I realized that Lazarus was standing beside me, a bottle of water in his hand for me.

"You look like you could use this," he said.

I drank half the bottle in one go. This was not the kind of research I had dreamed of doing. No, that was not true. In fact, this was precisely the kind of research I had dreamed of doing. I simply had imagined someone else handling the pick and shovel, me standing by as the lid to the treasure was lifted. And I imagined that all of it would be written up for publication in a journal to astonish my academic colleagues. None of what we had done here would be published. At least, I hoped it never would be.

"Better finish that water," Lazarus told me. "Wouldn't really want to have to leave your body in the tomb. It's not as fun as it sounds."

The small valley was quiet. I didn't even hear any birds in the small grove of trees just below us.

He put his hand on my shoulder.

"Don't worry. I still need you to help get the cross loaded onto the damned donkey."

He turned and walked back to one of the animals. They had been standing calmly the whole time, only an occasional ear or tail twitch or a shift of the tail to prove they were not statues. Lazarus pulled a long pry bar from a pack and climbed back up to the mouth of the tomb. Putting one end behind the edge of the stone, he pushed, groaning loudly. He looked at me.

"Well?"

I climbed up beside him and we both pushed, both of us groaning. I started to believe that God himself had sealed the tomb, and then I felt the steel bar move. More sand and something like dried clay or plaster shifted from around the stone. Another push and it moved, stopped, moved again. The air from inside the tomb was dry but not offensive, like the air in the spare room of an old house on a hot day, finally opened to find something lost. Another shove, and there was enough space for a man to pass inside.

"Get the torches," said Lazarus. His voice was low, like a growl.

I hesitated for a moment, thinking of real torches with flames on the end. I was fairly certain that this was what Lazarus was thinking as well, his mind diverted by the prospect of placing his hands on the object he had sought for so long.

I found the flashlights in a donkey's pack and stumbled back up to him. He snatched one from my hand, flicked it on, and shined the beam of light on the inside of the tomb. He stepped inside without saying another word. After a moment I followed.

The light revealed a small room, as wide as a desk, nearly as tall as a man, reaching back into the cliff wall for several feet. On one side was a shelf carved into the stone, and there the body lay.

Mary.

She was wrapped loosely in cloth, her face and body covered by ancient fabric and the dust of centuries that had slowly fallen inside the room. Lying parallel to her body on the stone floor was a beam of wood, as long as she. I could not believe what I was seeing.

Here, in front of me, where I could touch her, was Mary the mother of Jesus. This was the body of Mary of the gospel stories, Mary of the statues and paintings in churches stretching back two thousand years. And here at my feet was the beam of the true cross. Christ himself had been crucified on this piece of wood. At each end of the beam I could see holes left by Roman spikes, and I thought I could make out darker stains near the holes.

"My God," I whispered.

Lazarus knelt and slowly ran his hand along the length of the wood. When he reached the end near Mary's feet, he stopped and slipped his hand behind the beam. Pulling it, he rolled the cross beam over toward us.

"The fool," he said. "That fool sawed off part of it. He sawed off a piece of the cross."

I looked down at my feet. Someone had sawn off a slab, as long as the beam and about three inches thick. I wondered why anyone would do that.

"John," Lazarus said. "He kept a piece of the cross with him. Put it somewhere else."

I did not say a word. I could feel the anger seeping from him, and I did not want to stay forever in this tomb after all.

"Fine," he said. "Let him keep his fragments. We have the biggest piece."

He stood and stared down at Mary, then turned to me.

"Let's get it loaded," he said. "I don't want to be here when someone comes to check on it."

"Someone else is coming?" I asked.

"John will come, you fool, or else he'll send someone. Or something. Do you really think he just sealed this tomb and walked away? And I do not doubt that somehow he will know that we have come here. He may already know. Pick up your end of the cross. Let's get going."

We put our lights on top of the beam. Despite myself, I felt it was sacrilege. Each of us taking an end of the crossbeam in our hands, we made our way down to the animals who once again turned in disdainful inspection of our doings.

By transferring our items, we strapped the beam to one side of a donkey and balanced the load with pack items on the other side. Surprisingly, the beam was not very heavy. The donkey looked odd, a little of the cross extending in front of it and behind it.

I started walking back up toward the tomb.

"Where are you going?" Lazarus asked.

I pointed at the opening. "To see what else there might be."

"We have what we came for," he said. "Let's get going."

Lazarus glanced around, even up in the direction of the sky. I did not know what he was looking for, but after seeing the being with whom he had conversed at the campfire, I did not want to find out what might be worrying him now.

"What about…" I began. "What about her body? We need to roll the stone back in place, at least."

He glanced around again.

"Leave it," he said. "She will not be exposed for long, and the one who comes will do a better job than we of sealing it back."

I walked back down to take the bridle of the donkey with the cross.

"Take the other one," he said. "This one comes with me."

He glanced at me with a look that made me think of an old man behind the counter of a pawnshop.

"Fine," I said. The sooner we got back to some form of civilization, the better.

John

We were on a mountain, the Sea of Galilee in the distance like a puddle sparkling in the sunlight. There were only the four of us, Jesus standing nearer the edge. James and Peter nearer me. Peter was smiling like a man who might be slightly unhinged. In my dream I new it was the same mountain, the same view, as on that first day. When I turned again Jesus was not talking to Moses or Elijah, but to Peter and to James, though they were dead.

Both of them turned to me, Peter and my brother, and they looked at me as though from a great distance and as though we were still there, still standing on that mountain, had never left.

Then the cloud started to form, moving across and around us, and I was afraid because in my dream I didn't want to hear the voice, didn't want to know what it would say now, after all of this time. Part of me was more afraid that it would not say anything at all but would simply blow across the rocks and my face like water vapor and nothing else.

Since there was nothing I could do to stop it, the voice began to speak, though at first I thought it was the ground moving, an earthquake beginning at the top of a mountain.

Remember what you heard, it said, and there was all of the power of the first time, the *listen to him* spoken on that first day on the mountain. I was face down, feeling the rocks against my knees and my chest. I felt a hand on my shoulder and knew that it was Jesus coming to tell me not to be afraid, but when I looked up it was James, my brother, saying, "We are here."

I awoke, startled, looking around in the partial darkness of my own bedroom. Dreaming, that was all. I was dreaming. I was getting old, I realized, not even recalling the journey to the bed, or whether what I remembered about getting ready for sleep had been from the previous night, or another night before, or another night even older stretching back in my mind for two thousand years.

Repetitive things had become the hardest. Making tea, I often no longer knew where I was in the process without watching my hands. All of the thousands of times that I had made tea blended in memory until I could no longer separate the present or find it among so many yesterdays. Forgetting is not a failure of the mind. Forgetting is necessary for the maintenance of sanity. It is built into the brain in ways that only the very old can appreciate, and I was surely one of the oldest.

This dream, though, was different and troubling. I had never dreamed of that day. I remembered it often, thought of the light, the metamorphosis that we had seen, but never had it been the stuff of my dreams in all these centuries. Now the dream sat so real in my mind that I thought I could still feel my brother's hand.

"Are you alright?"

It was Adriel, who no doubt had sensed my dread.

"I think so." I sat up in bed. "Did you see it?" I asked.

"You were back on the mountain, the voice of God speaking to you."

"It was my brother this time." I felt my arm. "He touched me."

"I touched you," he said. "To wake you."

I thought about the touch of my brother's hand. Which had it been, I wondered. Did I feel James' hand in my dream because of Adriel's touch, or did the two have nothing to do with one another? I had no idea.

"You were uneasy in your sleep. I saw that you were dreaming of the mountaintop, and the view of Galilee, the sea. When you were troubled, I woke you, though I hesitated."

"Why?"

"Being troubled is not always bad," Adriel said. He paused for a moment. "Being untroubled is not always good."

Doubt

There was little that I believed and much that I doubted. Two thousand years of life and reflection on what I saw with my own eyes and touched with these hands, and I still had more doubts than sureties.

Some of it was like the Garden of Eden. On the one hand, there never was a garden. Adriel had no recollection of one, nor did any of his angelic acquaintances. None of them could recall an Adam or any fruit mongering Eve. Adriel recalled looking one day to see creatures like me scurrying around, making their lives one after another and emerging from the simplicity of animal awareness to the reflective awareness of humanity. He heard their first words, saw their fires, listened to the stories told in the mouths of caves. They told tales of the animals, of brave humans, of ice and of water and of fire.

They told one another tales of God, or of gods, bits of kaleidoscope glass they found in their minds and shared with one another, holding the stories up to the firelight and the daylight for a glimmer of the gods. These gods were giving and kind, angry and cruel, like the world around the people who told their stories. Often the gods failed to meet expectations, as did the people whose stories created them.

Jesus was real enough, though. I had seen him, heard him, and touched him. We ate bread that he broke for us. And finally I watched him die.

I remember Mary Magdalene, running to us with terror and joy, ecstatic. It was a good word that Mark used to end his Gospel, ecstatic—to stand outside oneself, beside oneself. It was hard to imagine a better word, anything more fitted to the purpose.

I remembered fish cooking on a beach, and the hands that prepared that early morning breakfast were the same ones that were nailed to a cross. I knew it that day, and I had known it every day for two thousand years. Yet where did they go?

All that time, and I never again saw those hands or heard that voice. And all of the others who did were gone, except Lazarus. Perhaps that is what happened to Lazarus' mind, the emptiness left by the absence of the one who called him back to life.

I long ago gave up trying to understand.

Adi

I know where the tomb is. Even before I see it, Adriel shows me in my mind, or his, not that there is any way of separating us at the moment of sharing the knowledge. And so I move through the night, not so fast as I might move, not as I might be there by thinking it so. Traveling more slowly across the great sea, I have time to sense whether any others are following me. Adriel lets me travel to the tomb alone, in part to linger unknown to watch over John, in part to allow me this journey. I want to see the ocean below me as I pass, to watch for the wakefulness of the whales in the sea.

A pod is below me now, dark and solemn, moving with unnoticed speed and, like me, without apparent effort. They know my presence at once, though how I cannot say and have never known. The whales know more than the humans about their world, but they affect it less.

The oldest mother breaches and blows her breath into the air, filling the night around her with the steam of her lungs. I pause, near them, matching their speed. Her skin is firm, wet, with strong muscle flowing underneath. She rolls to one side, her great eye leaving the water to gaze at me. I let water flow across me as it flows across her enormous back.

A greeting to you, I hear from her, in that strange song that is their speech.

You are beautiful, mother, I tell her.

You are beautiful as well. But you are not one of the great ones swimming in the sea, as we are.

No, I like the sky and the light.

She swims steadily. The younger whales swim nearer, also gazing at me, listening to our conversation.

You are sky and light, she says, and she slips slowly under the rolling water. The younger ones roll once more to gaze at me, and then they too slip down into the water. They are like the sea itself.

I rise and move more quickly, arriving at the valley I have seen. The tomb is there, but the rocks are changed, and I know that they have been here. I can see the rocks were disturbed, see the places where their feet had been, feel the lingering energy of their presence. I stand in the valley and watch, waiting for the others, waiting to see if any are waiting for me.

There is nothing. Silence. Rocks. The tiny avalanches caused by the feet of mice.

I move toward the tomb, willing the stone to roll fully aside as I approach. I am silent, but the stones yield with the complaint of sand grating against the faces of rock. The tomb stands open, the darkness solemn, silent. I listen again to the valley, search to see whether there are any humans who would see, any of the angelic ones who would interfere. There is nothing but the mice, and an owl that hunts them. To me her silent wings are like the surf beating upon a shoreline, the air on her feathers like the wind of a storm, but to the mice she is as quiet as this tomb.

Nothing else.

I will the light to form around me, ahead of me, filling the tomb, and there she lies. Mary, the second mother I have seen this night, and by far the older of the two. Like the whales, Mary is lying peaceful in her dark sea, softly held. In my mind I know her voice, the memories of her body still speak to my mind. Though these things happen in my mind, I cannot explain them. I have never met an angel who explains them. We have no science, only understanding, like the whale understands that the water will hold her up and let her fly across the ocean beds.

The jar seems to me a glowing light, perhaps because of what it holds, perhaps because I simply know what it holds. I stand beside Mary's body and gaze at her, seeing what her face was in life.

"Hello, mother," I say, though I have no mother. There is nothing but the silence and the sand. "I will take the jar to John. He is waiting."

She makes no reply, even in my mind. I take the jar, lifting it from the sand that holds it upright, and walk from the tomb. At the opening I pause, listening again with my mind to the valley. Still nothing.

I think it and the stone returns, guarding her body from the days, and I seal it with sand and stones. I leave her sleeping as she has been, with the owls to guard her rest.

John

I knew the jar when I saw it. I had bought it, long ago, from a potter in Ephesus. I did not want to use a jar that had held oil or wine, or even simple water. Not for Mary's words. For this task I wanted a new pot, one that would seal well against the sand and the dampness of what years may lay ahead.

This one was finished, standing by the door of the potter's shop when I found it. The design was Greek, though with a flat bottom, and the ornament was painted black, fired into the clay. It was simple, patterns of diamond and circles drawn in black, patient work for a man with large hands covered in clay. I had paid him what he asked, not even bargaining, and he had understood that it was praise of his work.

It was still beautiful, even now, when his hands were long past shaping clay and the centuries had rained dust onto his work. Adi held the pot, and I do not know how long I stood there looking at it before the memories sank and my conscious mind returned.

"Thank you, Adi. You have made quite a journey this night." We all looked down at the jar. "Let's place it here."

The doorbell rang, puzzling me. I seldom had visitors, and I was not going to brook the Jehovah's Witnesses tonight.

"It is the girl," said Adriel. "Sarah."

I struggled with the dual reaction. I liked Sarah very much, but this was not the best time for a visit.

"Perhaps it is the perfect time," said Adi. I ignored the fact that she had just been reading my thoughts, and I wondered again just how open I am to her kind.

"How do you mean?"

"She will love seeing what you are about to recover from the jar," she said. Adriel was uncharacteristically quiet, allowing Adi to speak. He seemed in agreement.

I looked down at the jar.

"How many secrets can we expect this girl to keep?" I asked them both, but neither of them answered me. The doorbell rang again.

I left the jar in plain sight and walked over to open the door. I did not bother to check whether Adi and Adriel were visible. It was their own business now as to when and how they appeared to the girl.

"Sarah," I said. "Good to see you. Please come in."

"Hi, Mr. Zebedee." Sarah smiled and looked with lifted eyebrows into the room, as only a young woman can. Mary had looked at us that way, seeing what manner of men her son had collected at the seashore. Sarah waved past me. "Hi Adi, Adriel."

She partly stepped and partly bounced into the room, then paused to look at the large earthenware jar on the floor. It stood like the stones of the valley from which Adi had brought it, silent, the dust lying quietly on it.

"What is this?" Sarah asked. She pushed her hair back behind her ears in the way it seems young women have done for centuries, and she knelt beside the jar. "It looks old."

Looking from the doorway into the room, I saw a strange grouping: two angels standing in a room with a young woman, and the girl so accustomed to the presence of angels that she walked past them to examine an old pot.

Adi and Adriel seemed to take no offense, as none was meant. All of us, to tell the truth, were interested in what the pottery held. Adriel and I were the only ones who knew the entirety of what had gone inside. I wondered how it had fared over the years. The angels were waiting for me to answer.

"It is old, Sarah. Almost as old as I am."

"Wow," she said, then, thinking about it, added a lower and softer, "Wow."

"I bought this pot nearly two thousand years ago. You see, in those days, in that environment, one could save many things in jars. Think of it as the safety deposit box of the ancient world."

Sarah blinked at me.

"I saved a manuscript in there," I added, for clarity. "The pots preserved them in dry places."

"Oh. You mean like the dead sea scrolls?"

Now I was the one blinking. "Ah, yes. Yes. Like that."

"So what kind of manuscript is in here?"

Again, the angels remained silent, turning to me for the answer.

"Long ago someone wrote down a story, a gospel, really." I stopped.

"Like the one you wrote?" she asked.

I thought about it. "Like that, yes. This gospel, however, was written from a unique point of view."

Sarah looked at Adi and Adriel. She seemed to be thinking through the possibilities.

"You don't mean that Jesus wrote a gospel? Would that be an autobiography?"

"I suppose it would." For a moment I thought of Jesus writing in the sand, a crowd of people watching, waiting to see whether a woman was going to be stoned. It was good that we went back and added that story, I thought. People did well to wonder what Jesus wrote that day, though I did not tell them.

"Mr. Zebedee? John?"

I looked over at Sarah, unsure just how long I had sojourned in that memory.

"I'm sorry, Sarah. Sometimes I tend to drift off." I walked over and knelt with her by the pot. "Memories are the mind's way of telling us things, I suppose. I seldom know what, but something."

Adriel stirred, making what sounded for the all world like he was clearing his throat.

"Are you going to open it tonight?" he asked.

I rubbed my hand across the lid.

"Why not," I said. "Why not."

Then, thinking about the condition of the manuscript, I added, "Would you mind to fetch some cotton gloves?"

"So," Sarah said, "Who did write what is in here?"

"Oh," I said. "I forgot that I had not answered your question."

Adriel returned with a pair of white cotton gloves for me. I don't know where he found them, whether we even had any in the house. I put on the gloves and once again rubbed the top of the jar. I was removing the dust, but it almost looked even to me as though I were conjuring a genie.

"Mary," I said. "Mary wrote a gospel, long ago. And this jar holds the only copy, here with us."

Sarah was staring at me, wrinkles between her eyes.

"Mary Magdalene?" she asked.

"No," I said. "Not Magdalene, not this manuscript. This is the work of Mary, the mother of Jesus."

Sarah's eyebrows found a new height.

"Jesus," she said, and I did not know whether it was a confirmation or an expression of surprise.

"Yes, well, I did say that it was unique. And Sarah, this is a secret that you must keep, at least until we determine that the time has come to make it known."

"OK," she said. "I understand."

I glanced at Adriel, and he helped me to take the jar nearer the table. We turned off most of the lights in the room so as to do as little injury to the parchments as possible. I glanced around at the three of them once more, then I slowly slipped my fingers past the edge of the lid and lifted it free from the jar.

There was the smell of dry earth, and of something else more difficult to place, the slight acrid odor of the aging parchment. I put the lid on the corner of the table and reached back inside for the roll of parchments that I knew should be there.

My hand found the parchment, and I pulled it out of the jar. It was nearly perfect, only losing a small fragment as we laid it on the table and began slowly to unroll it. There, for the first time in twenty centuries, I saw the thin neat letters of Mary. In my mind I saw her writing them, finishing the work one night and turning to me with a smile in the firelight.

Adi and Adriel were close to us, all four of us gazing at the words on the parchment as though it was a well and we had travelled across dry deserts to reach it. The letters ran across in neat rows, solid rows of Greek letters.

"It is beautiful," said Sarah.

I looked over at Adriel. He was staring at Sarah in a peculiar way, as though something troubled him. He glanced up at me when he sensed my puzzlement.

Her clothes, he said, in my mind. It was unusual for him, after all of these years to address me silently. In more dangerous times, it had usually signaled that he perceived trouble and that it would be wise not to make anyone aware of his presence.

I looked at the girl, but I saw nothing unusual. Neatly dressed, if modern. She wore a blue skirt with a white blouse, the cross charm on the leather necklace.

What? I thought. I looked at her again, her face leaning down to make out the odd letters on the parchment. For a moment it seemed that I saw Mary once again, looking at her own work.

Exactly, thought Adriel. *See the colors.*

White top. Blue. The colors of Mary, I realized, though really I had seldom thought of them as her colors while she lived. It was only later that people came to see visions of her in white and blue, painted their statues to match.

There is something of Mary in her, Adriel said to me. *I had not seen it before.*

I watched the girl again as she studied the parchment. She was the age Mary had been when I first saw her, or close to it, I thought.

It is true, Adi said. *There is something of Mary in her.*

Sarah was scratching her nose absently, pushing back the hair that fell forward as she leaned over the text. Mary had done the same thing, centuries before her.

Are you here? I thought. *Is it possible, after these many years?*

"An angel of the Lord appeared to me," said Sarah. "It spoke to me, saying Do not be afraid. And the angel told me that I would have a child."

I was astonished. Those were, indeed, the opening words of Mary's gospel, but nobody knew them except myself and Adriel. Now it was as though Mary herself were reading the words back to me, once more giving me the opportunity to be the audience in hearing of the story of Jesus' birth.

Her voice was like Mary's, the same laughter running through it. The words, of course, were written in Koine Greek, the everyday language of the ancient world, but not the language of choice for a young lady in the twenty first century.

"Sarah," I began, "How is it that you know Greek?"

She turned to me, puzzled.

"I don't know Greek," she answered.

I turned to Adriel. *Did either of you put the words in her mind?*

Both of them denied doing any such thing. I turned back to Sarah and smiled.

"Of course, not, dear. It's all right. Just go ahead with what you were reading there, sounds like you've made out the letters."

Sarah squinted down at the parchment again.

"I was amazed, and afraid of what would be, for I was not yet married. And the angel told me that the child would be son of God, and blessed among men. And I spoke to the angel and said, the will of God be done."

She looked up at me. "This is amazing! This is the story of Mary, told by Mary herself!" She looked at all three of us. None of us were moving or saying anything.

It was the first time in all these years that Adriel was speechless, and here I was too astonished to take any joy in it.

"What is it?" Sarah asked. "What's wrong?"

Then Adi spoke up and said, "Do not be afraid." Both Adriel and I turned to look at her, wondering what on earth she was thinking.

"Well," the angel said, "It seemed appropriate."

There was an odd sound in the room, and I realized that Adriel was laughing. In a moment, so was I. Slowly, Sarah joined us, and finally Adi began to think it funny as well, though both of them were more doubtful in appearance.

"Sarah," I said, the laughter trailing off. "There is nothing wrong. She surprised us, that is all."

"Oh, you mean Adi?"

"No, not Adi, but her as well with that fear not." I stepped over beside Sarah and together we looked back down at the parchment. The words were just as Sarah had read aloud. "I meant Mary, or maybe Mary."

"I don't understand," she said.

"Well, Sarah, you did a fine job reading those lines from the parchment. The thing is that everything you read was written in Greek."

"But I don't…" she began, trailing off.

"Exactly," I said. I put an arm around her shoulder. "It seems that now you do, at least where this parchment is concerned."

She looked at the words again. "So that is not English?"

"Not in the slightest. Does it seem so to you?"

"Well, at first, I couldn't read it, but it just seemed like all of a sudden I could make out the letters. I thought maybe it was a weird font."

"It is Greek," said Adriel. "Many of the old writings were in Greek. John wrote in Greek."

"Font," I repeated. "Yes, hmmm. Mary did have a distinctive calligraphic style, certainly. Thin lines, narrow letters. What you call fonts came a bit later, you know." I had a thought and walked to a bookshelf. I picked up a copy of the Greek New Testament and brought it over to the table. I flipped over to a passage in the text I knew best.

"Here, Sarah, take a look at this book. See if you can make out these letters as well."

She stared at the words and absently pulled at her lips. I remembered Mary doing something very much the same as she sat thinking of what to write next.

"It is odd," she began. "On the day the third a wedding happened in Kana of Galilaias and was the mother of Jesus there." She paused. "Oh, I see. The mother of Jesus was there."

She looked up. "Mary, it means."

I nodded. "Mary, yes."

"This is the part where Jesus turned water into wine," she went on, not knowing that she was shoving me into a pool of memories. For a moment I was holding a pen, and I was writing these words to tell of the wedding in Cana. Then I was there, feeling awkward, not knowing the family who had invited all of us to tag along with Jesus to the wedding. They were not rich, I had seen, and I knew that they did not need a bunch of men coming to eat their food and drink their wine. I saw Mary sitting by a tree, waiting and waving to us when we arrived, and the wine, later the wine, dripping from the ladle in the hands of a servant, drops of water falling red to the ground.

Adriel touched me.

"Come back," he said softly. I looked around, and I was still standing by the table. Sarah was sitting down in a chair, watching me with a worried look. Adi was standing behind her.

"Memories," Adriel said to Sarah. "Sometimes they come unexpectedly and hold him for a time in the past."

"I'm sorry," I said to Sarah. I sat down at the end of the table. "Yes, Adriel is right. Memories. Perhaps I am getting old after all."

Adriel started making tea, making something anyway, rattling dishes in the kitchen like a glittery poltergeist. I looked at Sarah.

"You are so much like Mary," I told her. "I had not realized it until you started reading."

"So, this is Greek?" she asked.

"Oh, yes. It is indeed. And you are right about the word order, things get shifted around differently in Greek than in English."

"I've never read anything in Greek before," she said and stared at the words.

"Greek students everywhere will hate you," I said a little absently. Sarah looked up alarmed.

"John," said Adriel from the kitchen.

"Just a little joke," I said. "I taught Greek, from time to time. It always seemed like I was cheating somehow, teaching what I knew from childhood as though it was a special skill."

Sarah was still looking at me, wanting some better explanation.

"Well, it seems that somehow, you have been given the gift of knowing Greek. And not just in the case of Mary's writing, but in general. You've made out the meaning both in this printed font and in Mary's handwriting. I have never seen this before."

Then I realized that it was not true. I had seen such a thing before, but it was long ago.

"No," I said. "I am wrong. We have seen something like this before, haven't we?"

Adriel put tea on the table for me and for Sarah.

"Only the once," said Adriel. "Both of you had better eat something."

Sarah reached for a cookie. "The once?"

"A strange day," Adriel told her. "You know it as Pentecost."

She munched on the cookie thoughtfully and sipped the tea. "Pentecost. Tongues of fire? That really happened?" She stopped. "You were there."

"I wasn't," said Adi. "I was watching the whales swim."

Everyone looked at Adi.

"Well, they are beautiful, and I enjoy talking to them."

Sarah held half a cookie out toward her like a pointer. "You talk to whales."

Adi seemed to draw herself up a little taller. "They are very nice, for the most part."

None of us quite knew what to say. After we had all considered our images of Adi carrying on a conversation with whales, the idea of Sarah reading Greek seemed less odd. Even Pentecost took on a more normal tone.

"It was a strange day, what you know as Pentecost," I said, with one more glance toward Adi. "Even now, I am not quite sure what happened."

"There were some people who claimed to know a new language," added Adriel.

"The speaking in tongues thing?" Sarah reached for another cookie, oddly nonplussed.

"Probably not the best way to describe it," I offered. "But it stuck. There you go, put a catchy phrase out there and the truth doesn't matter any more."

Adi appeared slightly distracted, and I imagined she was thinking about the whales. Nobody could make this stuff up, I decided.

"Well, there was a crowd of us, in that hall. I forget who arranged the use of it, but there were people coming and going, joining the movement."

"You make it sound like a commune."

"Mmmm. Commune. Well, without the hippy thing, I suppose, or the drugs, or the free love…"

"OK, not quite a 60's hippy commune," said Sarah.

"Right. There were all these people, and the market was nearby, all sorts of people coming through there.

Something like a storm came through, wind and… I don't know how to describe it. We believed that it was a God event, something happening among the followers of the Way."

"The Way?"

"Andrew came up with that. Peter never liked it. The Way. It stuck for a while, before they came up with Christianity. Anyway, people claimed to see fire coming down, not like Pompeii, but something like snow, except it flamed at the edges.

"People became manic, energized. It was like they had been waiting for this to happen. They stopped huddling together, waiting, and they headed out into the streets, babbling to people in the marketplace about the fire from heaven. Not that the phrase was well understood—James and Peter and I walked out into the marketplace and stood watching most of that afternoon. You go tell first century Jews about fire from heaven, and they think you are talking about the end of the world, not a new beginning for a religious movement.

"Of course, we didn't know we were a religious movement. We were, of course, still are, but it didn't seem like it.

"That's when we began to notice something odd. Some of the people in that marketplace were from far away, and they did not handle either Greek or Aramaic well. You'd usually get this dumb show going on, one man holding up whatever he was selling and fingers for the price, the other holding up fewer fingers for a lesser price. That sort of thing, you know.

"Then some of our people started talking with the foreigners, in their native languages. One was near us, I remember, at a cart selling cloth. Trying to. We had stopped there because of the shade from the cloth hanging on poles on the cart. The man spoke nothing but Arabic, enough words in common with Aramaic to make his way but not well.

"A woman from our group, we knew her, came to the stall and started talking to him, asking him whether he knew what had happened. He didn't seem to know much of anything. She started talking, and we realized that she was chattering away in Arabic. It was very strange. She and her family were from the north, and we had not known that she spoke Arabic as well.

"There were more like her, people who found that they spoke Greek, or who chatted with foreigners from all over the empire. There were plenty to pick from in those days. Jerusalem was a swarm of people traveling from what you call Europe to Africa and back. Oddest thing."

"It was the only time I have ever seen such an event," said Adriel. "Spontaneous learning."

Sarah turned to Adi. "So, is that how you are able to talk to whales?"

Adi tilted her head.

"No," she said. "I have always talked to whales."

Sarah

Ok, so this is strange. I admit it.

I'm sitting in a room with a man who is two thousand years old, two angels—I don't even know how old they are—and a gospel written by Mary, as in Mary, the Mother of Jesus. That one.

And I can read it. In Greek.

And I am eating cookies and drinking tea as though everything is normal, as if there were such a thing as normal.

Oh, and I have a piece of the true cross around my neck as a talisman against evil, or dark angels, or whatever else may be out there. And there is Lazarus, who turns out to be a creep. If I hear another sermon about Lazarus being Jesus' friend, knowing what I know, it will be too weird.

And Adi talks to whales.

Somehow that part just seems to amaze me more than the rest of it. I mean, the whole John the Apostle being around, and talking to angels, and even a new gospel with Mary herself writing about Jesus, all of that sort of jives. There is a place in my head where all of that can live and not mess too much with the ideas of Christianity that I already had. Looking after people is the sort of thing that angels do, I think. Isn't that the idea of a guardian angel? And all of it has something to do with Jesus, except for the part where nobody has seen him in a very long time. I can make it all work.

Whales do not fit in my whole Christian mythos thing, unless you count Jonah. I've heard people saying that it was a giant fish, not a whale, as if they hadn't missed the whole point of the story. Anyway, angels skimming along over the ocean and talking to whales is definitely not part of my thought world, at least not until tonight.

But it is pretty cool.

The whole thing could be crazy. I could chalk it up to John's delusional perception of the world, except for three things. One, I can read this parchment, and it definitely appears to be in Greek. Two, I can see Adriel and Adi, and they are definitely not like me. It is not just the costumes. They actually, well, dematerialize. It's the science fiction kind of dematerialize, with sparkles and shimmers, but not any sound, at least not that I've noticed. Three, I saw that other thing, outside my house. It was not like Adi or Adriel. It was more like a black hole creeping up to my window, and it scared me.

So I have three reasons to believe that all of this is real and that I'm not crazy.

On the other hand, it may be that I have experienced some kind of complete mental break with reality. John isn't crazy, but I am. I'm really in a hospital, spit on my face, tied down in a bed, unable to distinguish the world in my head from the real world outside it, as if the world outside my head is more real than the world inside my head.

I figure that if I am that far gone, I may as well enjoy this world, because it is a hell of a lot better than the freak ward. And here I have cookies and tea.

And Adi can tell me about the whales.

John

Sarah was looking at me. Her eyes were tired. Even as young as she was, I could see lines under her eyes.

"Are you alright?" I asked. "You seem tired today."

"Oh. I was up pretty late." She sipped her tea. "I read your Gospel again. The whole thing. And then I couldn't sleep for a while."

"I see," I said. "Sometimes it keeps me awake as well."

"Can I ask you something?"

It worried me that she would hesitate to ask me something about those times, that story.

"Of course you can."

"The walk on the beach, at the end of the Gospel. So when Jesus tells Peter that you would remain, that's it, right? I mean, that is why you are still alive?"

A squirrel was hanging upside down on the bird feeder outside. Peter, I thought. I suddenly missed Peter very much.

"I don't know why I am still alive," I told her. "At least, I think it is because he willed it so, but I don't know why he would have. All the rest... They are all gone."

"All except you and Lazarus," she said, quietly.

"Yes. And Lazarus." I thought about it. "We should add Adriel to that list. Not that angels die like we do, but Adriel was also there for most of our time together."

We were quiet for a bit. There was a small fire whispering in the fireplace.

"What made you write it, the Gospel? Was it, I don't know, something God told you to do?"

I looked at her.

"It is more rare than you might think for God to tell us to do anything. Maybe Moses. Maybe some of the prophets, I don't know. Mostly, it seems to me, God leaves us to choose our own doings.

"I have to make a confession. I did not write the Gospel of John, not quite like it sounds. I did write it, of course I did, but I did not write all of what is there, nor did I write it as you read it last night. Other hands took over, other minds added words, edited it.

"I stopped when Thomas made his confession. Blessed are those who have not seen and yet believe. That was me writing, more or less.

"I never wrote the final chapter, the story of Peter taking us fishing once again, the walk on the beach. It is true, again more or less. And it is my doing that this part was added to the Gospel. I told the story, told some people in the congregations. They would come, we would gather together, and they would ask for more stories about Jesus.

"Maybe that is really how I came to write it down to begin with. They wanted more, wanted the story. There were things handed around, passing from group to group like…"

"Like terrorist cells?" she asked. I was surprised.

"Something like that, yes." I thought about it. "Certainly, there were times when we were not looked well upon by the Romans, or by the synagogues. It was dangerous, at times. Now people ride around with Bibles in their cars. Then, we hid what writings we had. There were letters passed around. Paul kept writing letters to anyone who would read them. Mark had written the story, such as Peter told him. What you call Matthew and Luke began to be known. All of them were carried from congregation to congregation, following the Way."

"The Way." Sarah was standing at my bookshelves, running her hands over the spines of the books.

"They began to call it that. The Way. It was a name for us, the followers of Jesus. Then it meant something a little different. It meant several things. Andrew said that it meant the way to God, the way of Jesus. The way to other find other followers—one had to walk to get from one group to another. One cell to another, if you like. There was a way that stretched from Jerusalem to Rome, eventually, a road of followers who knew one another by signs and by words. We sent messages back and forth to Jerusalem, to those who stayed there. Letters traveled, gospels. Stories.

"We never met openly in some places, in some times, under some Emperors. Some governors. Rumors reached them of the Eucharist, of strange gatherings and talk of a God who was not Roman. It should have affected Jewish worship as well, and sometimes it did, but they had managed to distinguish us as a cult separate from them. So yes, we went underground for a time, as you say."

"And you didn't write the last chapter," she said.

"No." I went to put more water in the kettle, to give my hands something to do. "I told the story of finding Jesus on the beach. And I told a few the story of what Jesus said to Peter. Some stories stick. Later, when I seemed to linger, that story began to circulate more, and some began adding it to the copies of the gospel they carried."

"They just added a piece?"

"More or less. I didn't have a copyright, after all. You can hear it in the words, the shift of tense, the shift of the narrative from the voice of one to the voice of the community—from I to we."

"I noticed that."

"Doesn't affect whether it was true," I said. "Sometimes it takes more than one voice to tell a story."

Sarah

I turn to the parchment and try not to get crumbs on it or spill my tea.

Many years later I would wonder about all of the things that I had seen, and I would wonder whether I had understood them, and I would know that I did not.

"Mary wrote this," I say, munching on a chessman cookie.

"Yes," John says. "Mary wrote this. She would sit by the fire, or by the window. I had brought a table for her. She would sit and write, sometimes for hours, sometimes not at all. Some days she would just go outside and walk."

"You stayed with her?"

"I stayed in a room attached. We were neighbors. Like we are neighbors." He looks puzzled as he says it.

"What was she like?" I ask. I mean really, this man knew Mary, mother of Jesus, Our Lady of Everything. This was so much better than whatever was going on in the freak ward.

"She was Mary," he says. "She was kind, and thoughtful. Terribly smart. Very funny. And she brooked no nonsense from anyone."

"What?"

"Well, you know the story of the wedding at Cana. You started reading it a bit ago from that New Testament."

"Sure."

"Why do you think those servants did as Mary told them? They weren't her servants, after all. For that matter, why do you think he did what she told him? I mean, he was a grown man, even if he had not happened to be God as well. He could have stopped with telling her that it was not time for such things to happen, but he didn't. He went ahead with making the wine. It was a sign of what was to come, of who he was, and Mary was the reason that it happened."

"You liked her?"

He laughs a bit. A short laugh, as though he has seen a cartoon taped to someone's door.

"Yes, I liked her. It was hard not to like her, unless there was a reason that you yourself should not be liked. Then she could be tough company. But yes, I liked Mary very much. I still miss her. Sometimes I think I miss her more than I miss him."

He is looking at the manuscript.

"So, why hide it all these years? I mean, why not let people read it, like they read your Gospel?"

"My Gospel," he says. "Parts of it are mine. Parts of it were added, changed, lost. Oh, it is not all bad, some of the changes were good. I even made a few myself. Take that bit about the woman about to be stoned to death."

I had heard the story. A woman is caught sleeping with someone who is not her husband, they drag her out in the street, ask Jesus about stoning her. Nobody drags the man out into the street. Jesus does the writing in the dust bit, tells them that the one without sin should get with it first. They all leave. I have always wondered whether she had any clothes on, and what happened to the man.

"You made that up?" I ask.

"I didn't make it up," he says. "It happened. I just had not put it in the story the first time through. Later, it seemed like a good thing to add, and I put it in there with the passages about the festivals and the light. People were getting rigid, judgmental, in some of the congregations. I thought this story would give them something to think about."

I think about some of the people in the last church service I had attended. "Maybe you need to go back and add some more stuff."

"Mmm. Do you remember the story of Lazarus? Not the one you met, the other Lazarus, the one in Luke's parable."

"I think so. The poor man who was in heaven, and the rich man who wasn't."

"Yes, that's the one. When he asks for Lazarus to be sent back to warn his brothers, Abraham says that if they do not believe what they have already heard, they would not believe even if someone rose from the dead."

I sit quietly for a moment. Sometimes it is as though Adriel and Adi aren't there. Maybe there are moments when they are not. I don't know for sure. I already realized that time passes differently for them.

"So even if you walked into Saint John's cathedral in New York, and announced that you were, in fact, Saint John…"

"Oh, please…"

"…and somehow managed to prove it to them, they still wouldn't listen."

John looks down at his hands for a moment. "Yes, that about sums it up."

I look at the manuscript on the table in front of me. It is a new gospel. It is Mary's gospel.

"What about this?" I ask.

John looks over at the parchment. Not taking his eyes from it, he says, "I don't know what will happen. Not when they read what it says."

"Will happen?" asks Adriel. I had not noticed the verb change, but Adriel did.

John looks up at him and around at the rest of us. "Yes, will happen. It is time, after all. This must be published. It is time that Mary's words are known, and let the truth fall where it may."

I feel uneasy when he said 'truth', like he was talking about a different one than what I knew. I may not be the most devoted Christian in the world, but I am one.

"John, what do you mean by 'truth'? What exactly is in this story?"

"It is always a challenge, hearing something from a different point of view." Again, he looks at the manuscript rather than at any of us. "You will see for yourself. The story that you know is true. You may not appreciate how much doubt is also part of the truth."

"Doubt?"

"We all doubted, Sarah. All of us." His tea is cold in his cup. It must be. This whole time he has held the cup but not tasted it. "Even Mary. Who wouldn't doubt what we were told, what we saw ourselves? Mary, who gave him birth, wondered whether her own story was true, after a while.

"Even after the resurrection. Even after that strange Pentecost. We were left in this world with nothing but our faith and a few signs, and the signs grew fewer as the years went on. Finally, we doubted whether we had seen them, doubted whether we understood them correctly."

"It is only human," I say. "Why should that do any harm?"

"Only human. Yes, that is almost perfectly true. It was indeed only human. The trouble is that the entire story is more than human. It is a God story, and we are just human beings who thought we saw God, and thought we saw God in an unlikely place and manner."

"That is no crazier than what other religions have taught," I say, surprising myself. "In India, there are traditions that would see a god in almost any form, at any time."

"Yes, that is true," he says. "But while there are things in common, our faith sees the particular expression of God in one place, in one person. Never mind that God is everywhere, in everything. A wonderful thought, but it has little to do with the incarnation in the Jesus we knew. In fact, such a view stands in some tension with our own.

"In the end," says John, "how are people supposed to believe something if they think that Mary herself had doubts? How would they understand my gospel if they knew that I have doubts?"

I decide to have another cookie. I reach for my tea and feel the cup warm in my hand when Adriel makes a small movement. That's useful, I think, angelic cup warmers. Or maybe John is crazy, and now I am too. They have probably just put something in my IV line. That's what feels warm.

"Adriel," I say.

"You do not have an IV."

I look at him. "You understand that it's a little freaky when you do that."

He may be a little embarrassed, though I can't tell. Adi turns and looks at him, which I take as supportive.

"Would you do something?" I ask Adriel. "Something random?"

John looks at us as though we have started a game of musical chairs without telling him.

"Just give it a minute," I say to John. Adriel moves across the room, in itself a beautiful thing to watch, picks up a book from a bookshelf, and places it on the mantle.

"Thank you. Now, nobody say anything for a moment." I took a piece of paper that is on the table, not the manuscript, and write down what Adriel has just done. I turn to John.

"OK, we're going to move forward with some itsy bit of empirical truth. Adriel just did something that Adriel himself chose to do. Neither of us told him what to do. We both saw it, and I wrote it down. Now, what did you see Adriel do?"

John looks at me with a sad smile, like he is watching a child try to fix a broken dish with a piece of tape. "He moved the book. From the shelf to the mantle."

I turn with some triumph, now undermined by my suspicion that I am walking a road that John knows well, and pick up the piece of paper. I hold it for him to read. *Adriel took a book from the bookshelf and put in on the fireplace mantle.*

"There," I say. "We both saw the same thing, and so it happened. It can't be in our heads."

John just sighs and smiles. "And how do you know that I am not part of your delusion? Or, for that matter, how do I know that I am not completely insane, locked away somewhere or sleeping naked under a hedge, and you are part of mine? If we are both aspects of the same mind, then of course we each can independently corroborate what goes on in here."

"Right," I say. "OK. I didn't think of that. Thanks. Really helpful bit of imagery, too."

"I know the logic, because I've had a little while longer to think about it than you."

"It doesn't matter," says Adi. We all turn to look at her.

"If any one of us is insane, and the others a product of that insanity, then it doesn't matter. One who has broken with reality to that degree cannot find the way back, and the others do not in that case exist anyway. Whichever one of us it is may as well continue with the dream. Whether it is real for others, or not, it is real for that one of us."

I stare at the whale talker for a moment. "Then I could just be something in your head," I say to her.

"Possibly," she says. "I do not think so."

"Can angels go insane?" I ask, a little more quietly than I intend.

"It would explain some things," says Adriel. John looks at him, either warningly or resignedly, I can't tell which. "The dark ones. Their minds are usually closed, but when we meet their thoughts, they are disordered and disturbing. I have wondered before now whether they may not have turned down a wrong path in their minds."

"All of this is circular," says John. "And maddening." He stands and walks to the window, a rewarmed mug of tea in his hand. "Adi is right, of course. We go forward with the life we each perceive as true. That in itself is an act of faith."

Simon

It was extraordinary news: a called meeting of the Johannine Society.

There had been regular meetings for centuries, but I had never heard of one specifically called by John himself. Not that anyone would have believed it, if the word got out.

This one was in the country home of a member, not a hotel. The estate was secluded in the hills of Virginia. I had glimpses of pastures, horses, four-wheel drive SUV's in the gravel driveways of well-tended homes.

This was very different from scrabbling through tombs in Turkey.

We arrived from different parts of the world. Rental cars littered the circular drive in front of the house.

These people have no idea what I have touched, I thought. What they would give to see the true cross, to touch what Jesus had touched. Nothing could compare to that.

As I walked into the home, I wondered how much it had cost to build. We gathered in the library, an overly large collection for any individual. The room rose to include the upper story, walls of books with a catwalk all around. When I arrived, John was already present. He was standing in the far end, beside a table that was roped off as though we were museum visitors. Ridiculous.

I had stood in the tomb of Mary, and I had carried the cross of Christ, and now I was to stay behind a rope like these other academics. If they only knew, I thought, what I had seen, the things I had touched, the beings I had encountered.

"Friends," John began. Everyone fell silent, sat in the chairs that had been arranged for an impromptu lecture hall. "Thank you for coming. I know that many of you have travelled great distances, at short notice, to be here."

I thought of all of those tombs, wandering through the hills with Lazarus. I had come a great distance indeed. A shimmer of light distracted me from my memories, probably sunlight from one of the cars parked outside.

"Some of you know part of what I am going to tell you. None of you know all of it. I have kept a secret, at least one secret, from all of you for all of these years."

I know, old man, I thought. And we have it.

"As you do know, I stayed with Mary for many years, near Ephesus. We lived beside one another until she died."

John paused and looked at the manuscript. He must have written something else about Mary, kept it all these years. Not that it would make much difference in the world today.

"What you may not know is that Mary also wrote a gospel," he said.

There were gasps from somewhere in the room. The pottery, I thought, the damned pottery. Lazarus would not let me look. He was in too much of a hurry to leave with the cross. Look what we had lost!

"It has been kept safe all these years," John continued. "Until now. Recently, an adversary located the tomb of

Mary. He desecrated it and took a relic that I had placed in safekeeping there. This manuscript, however, remains safe.

"In reflecting on these things, it seems to me that the time has come to release this gospel to the world. I have brought it here for that purpose, and to keep it safe. We as a society will use your positions, your academic standing, to document the discovery of this manuscript. It will be found in the tomb of Mary. I will show a team of you how to find it, give you sufficient cause to lead you logically to the discovery. And in that tomb you will rediscover this manuscript, which in fact was kept there from the world until very recently." He paused, a little too long. "And in that tomb," he continued, "you will also find the body of Mary, the mother of Jesus."

No one said anything. I certainly did not say that I had already found her body, had already gazed upon the body of the God-bearer.

"You may think that you can imagine the effect of either of these things, the revelation of a gospel written by Mary herself and the discovery of a body that can with some credibility be surmised to be that of Mary. Certain doctrines will come into question, simply from the body and tomb alone. The revelation will not be welcome in many circles."

There were murmurs among the faithful.

"Nevertheless, I believe that this is what Mary herself wishes," John continued. He glanced upward at the light from the windows and was silent.

"May we ask, did Mary herself tell you her wishes?" It was the quavering voice of a classicist from Duke University.

John lifted his eyes and looked at the old woman, but he did not answer her question.

"You may view the manuscript today," he said. "No copies will be handed out. The documentation of a copy pre-existing the archaeological discovery of the manuscript would be unfortunate. Most of you, like the rest of the world, will have to wait for the discovery to take its course."

The room was silent once again. They were all looking at the table where the manuscript was lying.

"I think that is all that I have, or can tell you today. As always, you have my thanks, and my confidence that you will continue to keep the secrets you have carried so well."

The Gospel of Mary, I thought. It was nothing but words on a handful of parchment, but think of it. It had been within hand's reach, and I left it there because of that overbearing ass, Lazarus.

I sat staring at the table while my colleagues moved forward to see it like a line of parishioners at the communion rail. Again there was a flash of light in the corner of my eye. I looked around, but saw nothing. Just sunlight, I thought. It was only the light.

Adriel

I am watching. It is what we do, is it not?

I am here with John, of course, to watch him, but John wants me to guard the manuscript, to scan the room, to listen to the thoughts of these gathered together. I am to make sure whom we may trust, or more to the point, whom we may not.

I know the smell of books, the colors of memories, time trailing back from them to the hands and minds that have held them. Libraries are alive for us, holding thoughts like layered ghosts left by those who read the texts. Some of them we can see, concentrating on a volume to find the minds that have held it. Some are blank, no memories, unread, forests where no one has walked. A few glow with the thoughts that have fallen into them.

The manuscript glows, of course, not of the minds of many but of each that has touched it. Mary. John. Sarah. Adi. Me.

Only five minds in all of these centuries, and it is on fire with thought.

The minds gathered in this room are interesting. Most of them are amazed at what they have been told. This is a gathering of the faithful, yet almost all of them are thinking of ways that this manuscript will advance their careers.

Here, though, there is Simon. I consider lifting him from the room, taking him somewhere apart for a truly religious experience.

He and Lazarus were in the tomb. I see the memories and thoughts pouring from his mind, see him in the tomb, see the image of Mary's body through his eyes, know the fear he has of Lazarus, the fear he has of the dark ones, the fear he has of nearly everything around him.

He has no fear of me. Not yet.

Did John not pick each of you, and one of you is a traitor? Lazarus indeed has the cross, and you have helped him. Who, indeed, will help you?

A sparkle of light, John glances toward the windows, questions me. I know that my anger has allowed a glimmer of me to enter the room.

Simon, I tell him as he pauses. *Simon has betrayed you.*

Not me, he thinks. *Simon has not betrayed me. He has betrayed Mary, and he has betrayed her son.*

The anger drops from me, the glimmering light fades.

John is speaking again. They ask whether Mary has spoken to him. They do not know the price he pays to tell them, the love he still feels for her. I watch his tears when he thinks that he is alone.

We will keep the manuscript with us. Adi and I will guard it. When the moment comes, we will replace the jar and the manuscript together, so that it may be discovered by the right hands, seen by the right eyes.

And the world will have to grapple once again with what is true rather than what they believe to be so. That is faith. A closed mind doubts nothing, has faith in nothing, and believes what it tells itself to be true. An open mind walks where it has not been, but brings with it all that it has seen.

There is no such thing as blind faith. Faith belongs to those with eyes to see, ears to hear, and minds to question what mere religion tells them.

Fish

Everyone wanted to know about the fish and the loaves, or they would have if they had known who I was. Even some of the Johannine Society asked.

I didn't really understand the fascination. We saw him walking on the water, but nobody asked about that, not often anyway. The other miracles - healing people, raising the dead - none of them carried as much panache as the feeding of the five thousand. Not that it was five thousand. That was a good round number, and it lets you know that there were a lot of people, but nobody counted them. I doubted Peter would have been able to count that high, not without help, and the rest of us were content to see that there were a lot of people.

It started with Andrew, of all people. We were near Jesus, which on that day was very much like being close to a rock star. There were the devoted fans, the vaguely interested, everything in between. It had been a long morning, and Andrew leaned over and whispered to me, "I'm hungry."

Jesus heard him, of course. For all we knew, he may well have heard people having conversations in Jerusalem, or on the other side of the world.

"What was that?" he asked. "Did you say that the people were hungry?"

Jesus knew full well that Andrew did not. Andrew, to his great credit, came up with a clever response.

"They are hungry, Lord."

I had to admire the beauty of a statement like that. It seemed like a response to the question, but of course it wasn't. Jesus knew the difference.

"What do you have to give them?" he asked.

We all began to look around, to feel in our clothes for an extra piece of bread that might be living there. It was ludicrous. None of us had brought much of anything. Jesus turned to Philip.

"Where can you buy some bread to give to the people?" Jesus asked Philip. "Andrew pointed out that they are hungry."

Andrew was silent. I was also silent, sensing that there may be no right answers at the moment.

Philip looked across the sea of faces. "We don't have anywhere near enough money to feed them. Look how many there are!"

Andrew had been mulling the situation over in his mind.

"There is a boy over there who brought some fish and a few small loaves of bread, but that won't go very far," he told Jesus. I have never known whether Andrew was dimwitted or determined to goad Jesus with the information.

"Bring them," Jesus replied. I have likewise never known whether Jesus was toying with Andrew.

Andrew made his way toward the boy who had the little basket of food. Just negotiating the crowd was not simple, and getting that boy to relinquish his food was not going to be easy. Andrew managed to kneel down beside him. Their voices were too low to make out, though I was pretty sure that Jesus heard the whole thing.

In a few minutes Andrew had, to my amazement, gained the boy's trust enough to get hold of the fish and the bread. He came back clasping the little lunch basket to his chest with one hand and holding onto the boy with the other hand. Neither Andrew nor the boy appeared at ease in the great crowd of people.

He knelt down beside Jesus and gave him the basket. I managed to peek inside. Andrew had slightly overestimated the lunch, or perhaps the young man had already enjoyed a snack. At any rate, I only saw a couple of fish along with a few small loaves of bread, not large and hurriedly made. I could have eaten all of them myself.

Jesus took the basket and lifted it up. The crowd fell quiet, pockets of conversation dying as people realized Jesus was doing something. He gave thanks, looking up into the sky, which I have come to believe was for our benefit. We believed that God was in heaven, and that heaven was in the sky.

Jesus told us to ask the people for baskets, or cloths, anything in which we might share food.

There are only two fish, I remember thinking. If we go asking for baskets, what are we going to put in them?

Our doubts aside, the people began passing baskets forward. At the same time, more people began to bring out food that they had stashed, food that Andrew had not seen. When they saw Jesus sharing his food, or sharing the boy's food, they began to share what they had. Some of the modern theologians had managed to figure out that much.

There still was not going to be enough to go around, no matter how well the people shared with one another. That is when the weird moment began, the thing that I never tell people.

Jesus kept breaking up the same two fish and the same loaves of bread, over and over. He kept putting pieces into baskets, into makeshift cloth sacks. Anything the people sent him, he filled with fish and bread.

In retrospect, I don't really know what Jesus did, or how that much food appeared. I suspect that whatever he was doing, there was a limit to what my mind could process, and I could only see him breaking up the two fish because that was what my mind had learned to expect.

Whatever really happened was something that my mind could not understand. How could I explain watching a piece of bread being broken from a loaf, only to see and in some odd way understand that the bread was still whole, still waiting for the same piece of crust to be broken off? I was seeing something that I could not comprehend, and so I chose to see what my mind could comprehend.

There was more food until no more was needed, and then it stopped.

When it was over, there was more bread and more fish than the crowd could eat. Jesus stepped up onto a boulder so that he could look out over the people more easily. He looked down at Andrew.

"Gather up the bread that is left, so that it will not go to waste."

We went around and gathered up the extra bread, each of us filling whatever basket we found. When the baskets were completely full, it all stopped. No more leftovers. The people were content.

Andrew was quiet for the rest of the day. He was not alone.

Sarah

There is snow on the ground when I see the first news article about the discovery.

It says that archaeologists found a manuscript preserved in a jar in a tomb, one of many in a valley not far from Ephesus. The manuscript was a complete gospel written from the perspective of Mary, the mother of Jesus. The team also found the body of a woman. They would be conducting tests to determine the age of the body and the manuscript, but the appearance was consistent with the first or second century CE. A few other news outlets began carrying similar stories.

Mary had been found. No news report went so far, of course, and there were not many reports. Not yet.

Just wait till they read her gospel, I think. But then again, they have had four Gospels for a long time, not to mention all of the weird ones that people wrote a century or more later. Will one more really be any different?

And no one will ever be able to prove that Mary wrote this one. At best, it is a manuscript found in a tomb, with the skeletal remains of a woman from the first century. All of the rest is simply conjecture, food for the imagination. There is no proof. It will remain a matter of faith.

That is unless John were to break his silence, or Lazarus does something insane.

The Beach

I walked along the beach, stopping from time to time to stand and let the waves roll in toward me. The sand was still damp from the retreating water, firm beneath my feet.

I thought it strange that the beach was so deserted, though it was early in the morning. I had asked Adriel to give me a little time alone. A walk would do me good, I thought, and I didn't want to wonder who was listening. I wouldn't put it past my old friend to have taken the request further, managing somehow to keep people away this morning. Maybe all the people who lived along this beach were having a nice sleep, courtesy of the angels.

I managed a smile, thinking of it, but soon my smile slipped away as I thought of Mary and what I had done. After all these years, was I a failure? Had I done what Mary and her son would have wanted?

I did not know any longer. I had no guide, no map, and time slipped past me like the water in the sand, there but unseen. I wondered whether my footing might get softer and softer until I sank.

"Good morning, friend."

The voice was surprised me, coming to me across the sand. Looking in that direction, I saw someone sitting on the ground beside a small fire, well back from the water where the dunes began to grow. The man was shielded from the rest of the world by the small grassy mountains of sand and could only be seen from the waterside, where I was walking. I stared at him, thinking there was something familiar about him but unable to place him.

"Come and have some breakfast," he said. Something was cooking on the coals.

That voice, I thought. I know this man. Still I could not place him.

I began walking toward the small campfire. The sand became dryer and softer as I approached the dunes. It was like walking into a grotto of sand, open to the sky.

The man was kneeling, turning some fish on the coals. His face was turned away, his hair hanging down shoulder length.

I remembered standing on another beach, another time. I still had not managed to speak.

Finally I asked, "Do I know you?"

The man stood and turned to face me.

"John," he said, and I knew why my memory had pulled at that long ago beach, that voice coming across the water, knowing who it was who spoke.

It is the Lord, I told them. *And Peter leaped into the sea.*

Without thinking I turned to try to see the boat, to see Peter swimming through the surf, but there were only the waves of the Atlantic. I remembered when and where I was, and I turned back to see the face of the man standing with me on this beach.

"It is I, John," he said. And I knew that it was true.

"My Lord and my God," I said, and sank to my knees in the soft sand. He took me by the shoulders and lifted me up, brought me to sit beside the fire.

"I didn't think that I would ever see you again," I said. I felt the shame of admitting my doubt.

"Do not be afraid," he said. "You have been waiting for a long time."

I looked up at him.

"It is over, then. You have returned."

He just turned and took a fish from the fire, a slender stick running through it, and gave it to me.

"Here. Take and eat."

I took the fish. It was real, had some weight in my hands. The taste was clean, seasoned by the smoke.

"I am here to see you, John."

I did not quite have any thoughts. I sat eating, taking in the sight of this face that I had thought I would never see again.

"Then it is not finished?" I asked.

He smiled. "It was finished long ago. Did I not tell you so?"

I remembered him, hanging, bleeding. *It is finished.*

"You died," I said. "Didn't you?"

He said nothing. He turned a fish on the coals and sat with his arms wrapped around his knees, gazing out onto the ocean. We sat together for a while in silence.

"I looked after her until she was gone," I said.

He nodded. "She loved you," he said.

"She died," I said. "And I was left without her."

"Her time was finished," he said. "Yours remained."

We sat together as the sun rose into the sky, and I realized that I had never been alone, not really.

"It goes on," I said.

"Yes," he said. "It goes on."

The Gospel of Mary

An angel of the Lord appeared to me, and it spoke to me, saying, "Do not be afraid." And the angel told me that I would have a child. I was amazed, and afraid of what would be, for I was not yet married. And the angel told me that the child would be called son of God and blessed among men. And I spoke to the angel and said, "The will of God be done."

Immediately I arose and went to the house of my cousin Elizabeth, who was also to have a child. I went with wonder in my heart, not knowing whether the same thing may have happened to her, for she was old and full of years, and it was not likely that she would still be in the way of women. And so I thought that she may also have seen the angel and known of the word of the Lord, that she should have a child at the will of God.

When I entered the house, immediately she stood and put her hand upon her stomach and my stomach, and she told me that the child within her leapt at the sound of my voice. And I wondered whether it might be that a child coming into the world by the will of God might not know more of what passes in the world than a child that has come of man.

But Elizabeth told me that the child in her womb had come to her in the way of women and children, and that her husband Zechariah was the father, but that an angel had indeed come and had spoken the word of the Lord, saying that a child would come. More than this, ever since the angel of the Lord had appeared to her husband Zechariah, he had been unable to speak and could not utter a word. I told Elizabeth and Zechariah, for he was a priest of the house of the Lord, all that had happened, and that the angel had told me that I would conceive and bear a child, and that this child would be called the child of the most high God, for I had never been with my betrothed husband, Joseph. And I stayed with Elizabeth and with Zechariah for three months, and I returned to my home.

In time word reached me that Elizabeth had given birth, and that she and Zechariah had a son, and that his name was John. In days to come he would grow to be a great man like a wild beast, and he would walk around beside the Jordan River and preach to the people who passed and who came to hear the word that the day of the Lord was coming. The same angel that had appeared to me had appeared also to his father Zechariah, and gave Zechariah the name of the child who was to be named John. His father and I had seen the same angel, and heard him, and so we had that bond between us.

Many years later I would wonder about all of the things that I had seen, and I would wonder whether I understood them, and I would know that I did not. And I would remember Zechariah, father of John the baptizer, and I would know in my heart that he also had seen and known things that he did not understand.

The birth of Jesus happened this way. Joseph, my betrothed husband, and I were to travel to Bethlehem. I was already great with child, but Joseph also had seen an angel in a dream, and so he was at peace with the child that grew within me and did not refuse me, as I had feared that he would do. Instead he found a donkey so that I could ride upon the beast on the road to Bethlehem.

Many people had traveled to Bethlehem, and the people of the city had found places for the ones traveling there, for there was not room enough in the houses for all of the people who traveled there at the command of the Romans. The brother of Joseph's father lived in Bethlehem, but his house was small and already filled with relatives who had come. He had a good barn for his animals, and he had prepared a place for us in the barn, so that we would have a place to stay and would not have to dwell in tents in the wild places beyond the city as some were dwelling.

On a night soon after we arrived, the time came for my child to be born. And so in Bethlehem the child that was within me was born, and I named him Jesus, as the vision had told me. Many of those who knew Joseph and the family of his uncle where we were staying heard the cries and came to see the child. Joseph welcomed them with joy and told them that an angel had announced the coming of this child, though some did not believe. Some shepherds and others came who said that they also had seen visions, and dreamed dreams, all about a child being born in this place. And I pondered these things, and I wondered what it might mean that so many different people had dreamed dreams about my son.

The family of Joseph being from the town of Bethlehem, many of them were still living there. Since the child was born and young, Joseph found work among them and a small house where we could live, and for a time we made our home in Bethlehem.

One day there were visitors who came to find us, men who had traveled a great distance. They had rich robes and rode strange animals, and a large group of people traveled with them and set their tents at the edge of Bethlehem. Word reached us that the men were searching for us, and we wondered what it could mean, whether they meant us good or harm, and we did not know what to do. Joseph said that he would go and find the men, to see whether they searched for us with good intent or evil. When he returned, the men followed him and came into the home where we were staying, and they brought us gifts for my child. They said that they had received visions and seen great signs concerning the birth of a child, and they brought gold and spices from their lands far in the east, the land from which Abraham our father had come, and we were amazed. And we saved these treasures, not knowing what to do with them, for they had been given to our son.

Often as Jesus grew, we would meet someone in the great city of Jerusalem, in the temple, or in our home, who would tell us that they had dreamed of this boy and of the meaning of his birth. Then Joseph became troubled in his heart that too many would hear of the child and seek him, and he feared that some would mean harm to the child. We left Bethlehem, and we traveled to Egypt. Joseph worked as a carpenter in the land of the pharaohs, though the pharaohs were no more. In time we grew tired of the land of Egypt and of being far from our families, and Joseph led us back to the land of Israel, to the Sea of Galilee and the city of Nazareth, where we both had relatives and where we might make a home away from those who remembered the birth of Jesus in Bethlehem.

Jesus was a good son, and he grew and was a good brother to the other children who were born to Joseph, but always we knew that Jesus was not like them, nor was he like anyone we knew. We would teach him about the things that a child must learn, but he would teach us about God and the things that we did not know a child might know or say, and all who heard him were amazed, until they came to expect such things from him.

Jesus learned from Joseph how to be a carpenter and how to build things with his hands. From time to time Joseph would come and sit, and he would say to me that Jesus was a mystery, and that he already seemed to know how to work with anything that his hand reached out to touch. Our other children were amazed by him, and often Jesus would help them to learn, teaching them their letters and their work.

When Jesus was grown to be a man, Joseph was already old and he died. We buried him, and Jesus mourned with us all, though we knew that Joseph was not his father. Soon afterward, Jesus told me that he was going away, and he took some of the gold that remained from the gifts of the men of the east and he bought a house in Capernaum, nearer to the Sea of Galilee. And he went to his house as a man, but I heard much of his doings and of his teachings, and often I went to visit with him.

He began to teach openly, as we had always known him to do in private. He walked and taught among the markets and in the synagogues and along the waterfront where the fisherman tended their boats and where the people gathered to buy their fish. Word began to reach us, the brothers and sisters of Jesus and myself, that he had followers and even disciples, and we saw that many would come to hear his words. Then also we would hear that he had done miracles, and we knew that it was so, for often if a certain one in our family or among our friends had fallen ill, Jesus would come and touch them or speak to them, and the illness would leave them.

Soon after he had gone to his own home and had begun to gather his followers around him, there was a wedding in Cana. A cousin of the brothers of Jesus was to be married, and we were to go to the wedding. I urged Jesus to come and to bring his followers, not supposing that there would be a great many. At the wedding we saw him approaching, him and a group of men and women walking with him who were listening to him talk as they came. The groom was alarmed to see so many approaching, for he was not a wealthy man and had not the means to entertain so many, but I told him to rest and not to worry, that these would be my guests, and that we would provide for them.

When Jesus came, he greeted me and kissed me, and we sat together in the shade of a tree to enjoy the gathering. The brothers and sisters of Jesus had come with me to the wedding, and he was glad to see them, and he embraced them. Soon it was told to us that there was no more wine, for those who had come with Jesus had drunk all of it. I spoke to Jesus and said to him that we must bring more wine, for this burden was ours, as we had brought so many.

Jesus sighed. He was much given to sighing whenever he thought that he knew better than those around him knew, and now he sighed and looked around him. I supposed that he was looking for the one who had carried the gifts, more wine or perhaps money with which to buy more food and wine. Somewhere among his followers I was sure that he had brought wine and gifts for the family.

Jesus turned to me, and he said, "It is a small thing, woman. Why should a lack of wine concern you?"

And I called over two servants and told them to do what he told them, supposing in my heart that Jesus had already made provision, for he knew that many had come with him and that his host was not rich. Jesus pointed to the water jars standing under the roof of the house. They had been moved to make room for the many guests, and they now stood where many could see them.

"Fill them with water," he said. The servants stood and stared at him. As the mother of Jesus, I had seen him begin to do many strange things, and all of them came to be a thing of wonder. He took small pieces of wood from the workshop and made toys for the children. He made tiny boats with sails, and told the children to put them on the water. The sails would fill with wind and the boats would travel out onto the water, but the boats always returned to the children.

"Do as he tells you," I told the servants, and they began to fill the jars with water until they were running over. I wondered in my heart what would happen.

"Now draw out some of the water and take it to the steward," Jesus told them. The men stood staring at Jesus, then at the water in the jars.

"Go and do what he told you," I said to them. One of them took up a cup and dipped some of the water from one of the jars, and he carried it to the steward as Jesus had told him. I saw drops of the water falling from his hand as he went, and the drops of water were dark against the paving stones. The steward drank the water from the cup, and he was amazed. They found the bridegroom and brought him to see the jars of water, and his steward told him that it was the finest wine he had tasted.

"How is it that you have saved this wine till now, and so much?" he asked. The servants and those who watched were astonished. I wondered to see such a thing, and I did love my son.

When the wedding was over, Jesus called to us to go with him to his home in Capernaum for a time. We walked along the road, but Jesus found a donkey for me to ride. We were a large group, for the disciples of Jesus walked with us.

At the house of Jesus we saw a man sitting on the ground, and he was blind. He heard our footsteps as we walked in the path, for we were not few in number, and he began to cry out and to call for Jesus. Jesus walked to the man, and he knelt down beside him.

"What do you want, old man?" Jesus asked, for the man had white hair and a wrinkled face. His eyes were white as stones.

"Are you the one called Jesus?" he asked.

Jesus said, "I am."

And the old man said that he had heard that Jesus could heal the sick and the blind, and he had asked his family to bring him here and to leave him, and that he had been waiting for Jesus to return to his home.

"I have sat here alone," said the old man. "For a night and a day, I have waited for your return. I am a burden to my family, and they have no use for me. Perhaps you will heal me, I thought, and I will be a burden no longer, or perhaps you will let me die here."

Jesus turned and looked on a hillside nearby and he saw there a young man who was watching. It was the old man's grandson, but the old man did not know that he was there.

"You are already blessed and do not know," said Jesus to the old man. "And would you still ask God for more?"

"It is a small thing to God, but it would be life to me," said the old man.

"May it be as you have said."

Jesus reached out and laid his hands on the old man's eyes. When he lifted his hands, the old man's eyes were bright and clear, and he looked around as though seeing the world for the first time. The young man on the hillside began to run, and came shouting for the old man to see him, and the old man did see him.

"Who are you?" asked the old man.

"Do you not know my voice?" asked the boy, and he embraced his grandfather. "Let us go and give thanks to God, for you can see me."

"Wait," said the old man, and he called for Jesus. "In what way should we give thanks to God for this work that you have done? For no doctor could heal my eyes. We are poor, but we will do as you say and bring gifts to the Lord."

Jesus placed his hand on the old man's shoulder, and he spoke to him, saying, "Go and see the things that God would have you see. Your eyes are open, may your heart remain open as well."

With that word, the old man and the young one turned and began to walk away from the house of Jesus and the crowd of disciples who were watching.

"Lord, when will we have power to do such things?" asked the one called Peter.

"The power of God works among you when it is needed," said Jesus. "A season and a time for all things."

When it was known that Jesus was at home, the children began to come. They would come by ones and by twos, and they would look into his windows or look into his doorway, and when Jesus would see them he would laugh and would go to a wooden box in his house and find a toy that he had made and give it to them. The children would embrace him and thank him and, taking the toy, they would run back home to play.

One day Peter and Andrew took out a toy and began to marvel at it. Then James the brother of Jesus turned to him and said, "Will you overthrow Rome with men who play with toys?"

And Peter was angry, but Jesus held up his hands and bade them stop.

"I have come to build the kingdom of God, not to tear down the walls of Rome. Those who would seek the kingdom of God will find it, and those who seek to destroy Rome will themselves be destroyed by it.

"Rome is like a great tree that grew in the land, and all manner of creatures came to live in it. And those creatures already dwelling in the land found themselves in the shade of the great tree. And the tree said, I am great, and there is none in the land to compare to me, and all who live in my branches and under my shade must worship me, for I have made the shade and the air and the land beneath me and the sunlight that falls through my leaves.

"But then came men from another land, and they saw the tree. And they took axes and cut the tree down, and with part of it they built their houses, and with part of it they made their boats, and part of it they placed upon the fire to burn. Soon all that remained of the great tree was a memory of how tall were the branches of it and how great the fall, but the land and the sun and the wind did not change. So it is with the kingdoms of men and the kingdom of God. The kingdoms of men will grow and fall, but the kingdom of God does not change."

Jesus had four brothers, James and Joseph and Simon and Judas, and their father was Joseph. Sometimes one or more of the brothers of Jesus walked with me as I rode the donkey that Jesus had given to me, and we went to visit Jesus or came back to our home. They talked with their sisters, Martha and Salome, of all that they had seen Jesus do and say. And my children marveled in their hearts at their brother, and they would ask again what things the men of the east had said when they had come to bring him gifts as a child. And I would tell them the stories once again, and I pondered all these things in my heart.

At the Passover, the brothers of Jesus wished to go up to Jerusalem, for James had been to see Jesus and learned that he himself was going up to Jerusalem. And so only Judas remained with me and his sisters, and James and Joseph and Simon went up to Jerusalem to see their brother and to observe the Passover.

When they arrived in Jerusalem, they found a great uproar at the temple, for Jesus had himself been there ahead of them. James asked of those who were there what had taken place, and they began to tell him, for they did not know that he was the brother of Jesus.

And so they told the brothers of Jesus of how he had come into the temple and stood peacefully it seemed for a time, and few had taken notice of him. Then he had taken a rope from a stall, though it was not his rope or his stall, and with it he had begun to drive the cattle and the sheep from the temple. Then he threw over the tables of the moneychangers and began to speak in a loud voice, so that all in the courtyard of the temple could hear him, and he told the animal merchants and the money changers that they had no place in his father's house.

The men turned to James, not knowing who he was, and they said, "He said that the temple was his father's house." And they asked the brothers of Jesus, "Could the man be slow of mind, or have a demon, that he believes this to be his father's house?"

James and the others said nothing, but they left the temple and went to where Jesus had told James that they would be staying. But they remembered that I had told them about the angel who had appeared to me before Jesus came, and that Joseph the father of them had not been the father of Jesus, but that Jesus had no father upon this earth. And they wondered how such things might be and what Jesus had meant when he called the temple the house of his father.

Some days later James and Joseph his brother came and told me that they had followed Jesus from Jerusalem into the countryside of Judea and to the Jordan river near Bethany. There the people had come walking many miles to hear Jesus teach them, for they had seen the miracles that he did in Jerusalem and in the other places where he had been, and they believed that he was a prophet of God. They came and were baptized in the River Jordan. I asked my sons whether Jesus also baptized people, as did John the son of Elizabeth and Zechariah. They told me that Jesus did not baptize, but that his disciples baptized a great many people.

And I sent James and Joseph to John, their cousin, the son of Elizabeth, and I told them to speak to him and to ask him to come and to share a meal with us. John did come, though he did not bring any of his disciples, but he himself came alone to dine with us. He was a man like an animal, wild in his appearance, with long hair and rough clothing, and he did not drink wine for he was a nazirite. And I asked him about Jesus because we had heard that he was baptizing people as well, though James said that only the disciples of Jesus were baptizing while John himself held the people in the water.

John said that it was true, that he had seen and known that people were also going to Jesus to be baptized.

"And what does it matter?" he told me. "Some are baptized by Jesus, and some by me, but it matters only that they come and are baptized, remembering the Lord their God."

Then John went on speaking, and he said, "Your son is great and must become great, for the people have awaited their messiah, but I have served my purpose. Soon my time here will end."

And I was amazed at his words, and alarmed, and I asked him how it was that his time would end.

"It is no matter how my time will end," he said. "I have served God, and I serve God, and I will serve God. Our lives here are like the water that falls upon those who come to be baptized. It shines but for a moment and then it is poured out."

And John left us, and he returned to the Jordan where he preached to the people and baptized them. And I sent James back to his brother Jesus to tell him that we had heard of the baptizing done by his disciples, and that the people had said that Jesus baptized more than John. The Pharisees also heard, and they spoke and whispered among themselves. And so I sent James to tell Jesus and to warn him, because I was afraid of the Pharisees. They believed that their view was right and true in the sight of God, and so I feared them, for there are evil ones and there are those who do not love their neighbor, but none is more dangerous than one who believes that he is right and true in the sight of God.

And James returned and told me that Jesus had heard him and heard of the fear in my heart, and he had taken his disciples and gone away to Galilee once more, far from Jerusalem, and my heart was less troubled. Still, I was worried for him and for those who followed him. Only God is more patient than evil, and evil never leaves. Evil always sits waiting at the door.

At the market a woman came and spoke to me, and I was amazed for this woman was a Samaritan woman.

Other women at the market did not speak to her, but she came and spoke to me, saying, "Is Jesus of Capernaum your son?"

And I answered her and spoke to her, even in the marketplace, and I told her that I had a son named Jesus who dwelled in Capernaum, but that I did not know whether he was the one about whom she spoke. She said that this Jesus had come and lived with them in their city for two days, and that he had sat in their temple and taught them about God and mercy, and that he had healed many among them of their sickness. And I knew in my heart that this Jesus was indeed my son.

"This man is my son," I said. Some of those in the marketplace, hearing me say that this man who had dwelt with the Samaritans for two days was my son, withdrew from us and shook their heads at us.

The woman looked at me and she knelt in the street in front of me, and she spoke, saying, "Truly you are blessed among women, and blessed is the one who came from your womb."

And I took her by the hand and lifted her up, and I took her to our home so that she sat and talked to me until the sun was low in the sky. We made room for her and prepared food for her, and she stayed that night with us, telling the brothers and sisters of Jesus and me about his words. She said that Jesus did not speak slowly or with fear as did their teachers, but with power and with life, and that many gave thanks to God for the works that he had done among them.

The next morning I sent James and Joseph his brother to walk with the Samaritan woman back to her home of Sychar in Samaria.

"And will we enter the city of the Samaritans?" asked Joseph. I looked at him, but James spoke first, saying, "Yes, brother, we will enter the land and the city of the Samaritans. If your brother and mine will go and dwell among them and work the work of the Lord among them, then we shall also walk among them to see that no harm comes to this woman, for she has walked far and alone to bring us thanks and news."

But the woman shook her head, and she said that no one needed to walk with her. I placed my hand upon her shoulder and I kissed her, and told her that the brothers of Jesus would walk with her, to keep her safe.

And she was thankful, and spoke to us all, saying, "No, you need not enter the city, for I know that Jews do not wish to enter the city of the Samaritans. Walk with me only to the well of Jacob, our father and your father, for there I can see the gates of my city and there I met your son and brother."

And they left walking to Samaria, a basket of food to share among themselves on the way. I stood at my window and watched them leaving, a Samaritan woman walking with two of my sons, and I wondered what God might do among the Jews and the Samaritans, whether we might not find one another again as brothers and sisters in the worship of God.

My cousin in Cana, whose wedding we had attended and where Jesus had made wine from the water, sent word and asked that I come back to visit with them. And her husband sent word also, saying that it would be good if Jesus could return, for in their amazement they had never thanked him for the wine. And I sent James again to his brother, to say that we were to go to Cana.

James returned, and I asked whether Jesus had come with him, and he said that Jesus had given him to say, "What is Cana to me?" And I knew that he would come.

When we arrived in Cana, we saw Jesus and his followers walking in the road. When Jesus arrived he kissed me and sat beside me at the home of my cousin, and we had food and more wine that had not been drunk at the wedding. Then there came a man in rich clothing, and he came into the house of my cousin seeking Jesus.

The man told Jesus that he must come, that his son was close to death, and that the doctors could do nothing.

"You want only miracles," Jesus said to him. "You have no faith."

"I do not know about such things," said the man. "But I know that my son is dying, and I know that you can save him."

Jesus looked at him for a long time, and no one spoke, and the man knelt and wept in the courtyard. Jesus got up and took the man by the hands, and he lifted him from the ground and said to him, "Go, your son lives."

The man only looked at Jesus, and he bowed his head, believing the words that Jesus spoke to him. He left, hurrying back to his home, and Jesus stood marveling.

"Truly, I tell you all, this man has faith. Many would not believe unless I went and touched the child, and lifted him from his bed to show him that he was well, but this man has believed the words that were spoken to him. Truly, this was a man of faith."

Another day James the brother of John came and told us that Jesus was teaching on the other side of the Sea of Galilee. And so I called James the brother of Jesus and his other brothers, along with his sister Martha, and we entered the boat with James and crossed the sea. Already there were a great many people, and we saw Jesus moving among them. Those who were sick were brought to him, and he healed them. This he did in the light of the sun on the side of the mountain, for all to see, and many were amazed to see the sick healed. And we did not know how it was done except by the power of God.

Then Jesus sat on a rock nearer the water, and he held out his arms and the people sat and were quiet and his voice could be heard by all of them.

"You have heard it said that Rome is our master. You have also heard it said that we should fight against them. I say to you that the Lord is our God, and there is only one God."

When we heard these words we were alarmed, for many there were in the countryside who would take his words back to the Romans. And there was much murmuring in the crowd.

"I also say to you that God has said, Vengeance is mine. Therefore put your trust in God.

"Blessed are those who make peace, for you will have peace. Blessed are those of you who are poor, for you already dwell in the kingdom of heaven. Blessed are those whose hearts are pure, for you will have that which is pure. Blessed are you when men despise you for your faith. Blessed are you when men curse you and speak evil of you because of your faith, for God whom you cannot see will bless you in ways that they cannot see. For to you the kingdom of God belongs, and you belong to the kingdom of God. And blessed are you when you mourn, for the Spirit of God shall comfort you.

"Do not place your faith in that which you see, for you do not see the things that last. Only that which you cannot see will last into eternity, and only that which you cannot touch will last into eternity.

"Fear not those who can harm the body, which you can both see and touch. The body is dust, but the spirit is eternal. The words that I speak to you are words of the spirit.

"I have not come to destroy, but to build. I have not come to end the law and the prophets, but to fulfill them. You have heard it said, 'An eye for an eye and a tooth for a tooth.' Such was the mercy of the prophets who came before you, to place a limit and a wall around your anger to do no more harm to others than was done to you.

"But I say to you, love your enemies. If one takes from you your eye, do not seek to take his eye. If one should take from you your tooth, do not seek to take a tooth. If one takes from you that which is in your right hand, offer that which is in your left. Show mercy and forgiveness, as your God in heaven shows you mercy and forgiveness. Even if the evil ones should come to take you, to despise you and to hang your body upon a tree, do not let your heart be given to hatred and to revenge. Forgive and have pity upon them, for they cannot take your spirit, which is eternal, and they do not understand what they do.

"They hate and they kill what they do not understand. Perhaps it may be that they will look upon that which they have broken, and their hearts will be changed and their eyes will be opened, and they will turn to seek the kingdom of heaven. And you will already be there waiting for them as for your brother or your sister who was lost.

"They do not yet understand, but you do understand, and so you must love your neighbors and pray for them and seek the good. And when you pray, do not pray to be heard by the people, nor even by those you love. Rather go and pray in secret, that God alone may hear your prayer, so that you may know that you pray to God and not for the benefit of being heard by others. And when you pray, remember that God in heaven already knows that which you need, and do not ask for that which you do not need. Do not think that God will hear you because of your clever words, for so pray the pagans thinking to impress the gods they have made with the words they have spoken. Rather, this is how you should pray:

"Our God in heaven,
Blessed be the name that is yours,
May the kingdom come that is yours,
May the will be done that is yours,
Here on earth as also it is in heaven.
Give to us the bread of our need.
Forgive us our failings,
As we forgive those who fail us.
And lead us not into temptations,
But keep us from the evil one.

"So should you pray, and forgive, and be thankful for that which God in heaven gives you. Be thankful to have neither too much, that you might forget the Lord your God, nor too little, that you might be tempted to sin against the Lord your God and against your brothers and your sisters.

"Do not worry about your life on this earth, that you have too little of the goods of this world. Why do you worry about your food, or your clothes, or your houses? See the birds of the air that neither plant nor gather, but God blesses them with food. See the fish that give no thought to building houses, but God gives them the sea for their home. Even the grasses and the flowers of the field are clothed with beautiful clothing, and tomorrow they will be gone. How much more will God give you the means to provide for your needs and for the needs of your children? So do not let your hearts be filled with worries, but rejoice, for you are already entering into the kingdom of God.

"Not all who call out and say pious words know of the kingdom, but only those who walk in mercy and peace in the Spirit of God. Many will come and tell you that they bring the word of the Lord, and many will come and prophesy to you and tell you that the great and terrible day of judgment is coming, and many will claim to do miracles in the name of God, but they are liars and evildoers, whitewashed tombs full of death and ashes. Do not listen to them, neither let them make fools of you. For I will tell them plainly in that day that they have never known God nor have they ever walked in the Spirit of God. Better it would be to have a mountain tied around your neck and to be thrown into this sea than to lead the children of God astray.

"For those who build upon these things that I tell you will have built their homes upon the rock, and the storms may come and the winds may blow, but that rock shall not be moved. And those who build upon the words of men are like those who build their homes upon the sand, and the storms will come and the winds will blow, and all will fall, and even the sand will be washed away into the sea."

And we were amazed at his words and at the authority of them, and I remembered in my heart the words of the angel that had appeared to me when I was but a girl. The angel had told me that this, my son, would be called the son of the living God, and blessed among men, and I began to think again on those words and what they could mean. For I had not known the father of Jesus, and I was afraid as I watched him and heard his words. For who was my son that he could do such things and speak such words?

And I sent Simon and Martha to look in the boat in which we had traveled to hear Jesus, for we had brought a basket with some food for our meal. As I waited I looked around me, and the crowd was large, some thousands of people along the shore and upon the mountainside, and the place was remote. A few of them had brought food, but it seemed to me that many of them had heard that Jesus was there and had begun walking to find him, and they had nothing in their hands. Simon and Martha brought back the basket, with some fish and some bread that we had brought. I called to James, the brother of Jesus, and told him to go and to tell Jesus that the people were hungry but that we had a little food that they might share.

James stood, looking toward the hillside where Jesus was standing, and he said to me, "Mother, there is no need, for see, he already knows." He pointed, and we rose and saw Jesus standing and looking around at all of the people. A boy was standing beside him with a small basket.

Jesus raised his hands and the people were quiet once more and sat upon the ground to hear what he would say. He took a loaf of bread from the basket, and he held it up to heaven and gave thanks, and he began to break portions of the bread and of fish that were brought to him and to place them in baskets. And the disciples of Jesus found and brought more baskets, and they took the portions of the fish and of the bread and they walked with the baskets among the people, giving a little to each person.

We also gave of our food to those around us, as did all who had bread, so that all of them had something to eat. After we had eaten, Jesus sent his followers to collect that which was left over, and there were baskets full of bread remaining from the little that was in the beginning. And all of us were amazed to have eaten and to see even more food remaining.

We took our leave of Jesus, and I and his brothers and his sister returned across the sea in the boat that James the brother of John had used. Another boat remained for Jesus and those followers who would cross back to Capernaum with him. We took also a cloak that belonged to James the brother of John, to keep it safe for him, for we could not find him in the crowd but knew that we would see him on the other shore.

The next day James the brother of John came, and John with him, and they were strange, and we knew that something had happened to them. And they sat, and James stared at me. John his brother reached out and touched him upon the arm, and James moved like a man who had been sleeping.

"It is because of what we saw in the night," said John. "We have come to wonder what manner of man is Jesus, and whether he is a man at all, but we know that you gave birth to him."

There had been a storm in the night, and we had worried about Jesus and those with him, whether they had crossed safely or were still on the other side of the Sea of Galilee. John and James told us that Jesus had indeed sent them away in the boat to cross to this side, but that he himself had remained behind on the shore, and he had gone up onto the mountain alone to pray. During the night, the winds had grown and the storm had come upon them when they were still on the open water, and they were afraid. And by the light of the lightning in the storm, they had seen a man walking as it seemed upon the water, with no boat or any way that could be seen. And John had seen him and had known that it was Jesus, and had called out his name. All of them in the boat had looked and had seen that it was Jesus coming toward them upon the water as though walking upon the land. And they were terrified.

They did not remember all of what had taken place, but Peter had leapt from the boat and called out to Jesus, saying, "Lord, save us!" And they had seen Jesus take him by the arm and bring him back to the boat, both of them standing as though upon the shore. And they heard Jesus speak and say words into the storm, and suddenly they were at the shore, though they had been in the middle of the sea, and the storm had passed, and the wind and the clouds had passed. Only they and Jesus had remained in the night, and by the moonlight they had seen his face and known that it was indeed Jesus, though they did not understand how he could have crossed to them from the far shore, nor did they understand how he had stood upon the waters of the sea, nor did they understand how they came to be at the shore when they had thought themselves out upon the sea.

James, the brother of John, bowed his head and said, "Jesus is no man, not a man like we are men. You may have given him birth, but truly this man is of God, for even the sea obeys him and bears him up."

And the two men John and James stayed with us a day and told us many more things that Jesus had said and many miracles they had seen that Jesus had done. And the brothers and sisters of Jesus began truly to believe in their hearts that Jesus was sent of God.

John took his brother James and they returned to the house of Jesus to join him and the other followers. As we sat to eat our meal that evening, the brothers of Jesus told me that they wished to go to Jerusalem for the festival of Tabernacles. They said also that they would go to find Jesus and bring him with them to Jerusalem, for they said that he should be known there and teach there. I was anxious, for Jesus might speak the words in Jerusalem that he spoke on the mountainside, and I feared for him and for what the Romans might do to him.

We had heard also that John who had baptized many in the Jordan in the wilderness near Pella had been arrested and taken away, and his followers were scattered and afraid. Some had gone to their homes, and some had gone to the Essenes in the hillsides, and some remained in the wilderness near Pella. Some also came to hear Jesus, and of these some remained to follow him.

James and Joseph and Judas and Simon, the brothers of Jesus, arose in the morning and went to the house of Jesus where they found him with his followers. There were many of them, people who came from all regions to hear Jesus teach and to bring the sick to be healed, and there were some who stayed with Jesus continually like Peter and James and John and other men and women besides. They were fed in part by the money that Jesus had laid aside and in part by the gifts of food and of money that people would bring to them. Even now some gold remained of the gifts of the men who came from the east when Jesus was a child.

Judas and Simon returned, saying that they had left Jesus sitting in the synagogue in Capernaum. He had said that he would not go up to Jerusalem with them but would stay in Capernaum. I was glad when I heard it, but they said that there also were some even there who questioned Jesus and who shook their heads at the things he had said.

"He has said to them that they must drink his blood," Judas told us. "They did not understand, and some were offended. We also questioned what could be meant by this word, for it was a strange saying.

"Then he spoke again to them, and he told them that his words were not of the flesh of his body or of the blood of his body, but that the words were of the Spirit of God, and that they should eat his words and drink their meaning, for then they would have food indeed and drink indeed."

Many of those hearing him had taken offense. Even some of those who followed him had walked away from him, and there were not so many followers left around

Capernaum as there had been, but Jesus was still permitted to teach in the synagogue.

James and Joseph went ahead to Jerusalem for the festival to make provision for us, but their brothers and their families stayed with their sisters and with me until we should go also. And there came to us friends who had heard Jesus teaching in the synagogue, and who had heard the words that he had told them of his flesh and of his blood.

"These are hard words. Who can understand them?" they said. "Jesus is not like your other sons, nor is he like the other teachers who sit and read to us. Their words are dull and old, so that we might sleep to hear them, but he speaks with power so that many days later we are still thinking upon his words." And I thought about these things and also about those disciples who had walked away and no longer followed him.

And the next day we took two donkeys and we went up to Jerusalem. Judas and Simon led the donkeys. I rode upon one and our food and clothing was on the other, and Martha and Salome walked beside me with the wives of James and of Joseph. There were many on the journey to Jerusalem for the festival.

On the third day there came running to us Judas and Simon, and they said that Jesus had come and was teaching in the courtyard of the temple. And we rose and went up to see, and he was there with a great crowd. We also stood among the people and listened to all that was said, but they did not know that I was the mother of Jesus or that these were his brothers and sisters, for they turned to us and spoke to us, saying, "Hear his words, and see the signs that he does. Can this be the messiah?" For it was said that there were many who had been blind or sick, and that Jesus had healed them.

Then guards came from the temple, and they would have arrested Jesus, but they could not for fear of the crowds. And more people came each day thereafter to hear him speak, and no one did harm to him for fear of the people. There were many questions among them, and they asked one another whether Jesus was a prophet, and some asked whether he was the messiah, and I heard all of these things with fear.

That evening Jesus came to our rooms, and he shared his evening meal with us. And I asked Jesus why he had been teaching in the courtyard of the temple. And he looked at me and said, "Woman, do you not yet know that I must be in my father's house and about my father's work?" And I said nothing else, but wondered at his words. And I looked, and it seemed to me that I could see standing in the room the angel that had appeared to me so many years before, or one like to it, but no one else looked at it or saw it, and so I said nothing, but kept this also in my heart.

And on the last day of the festival, when we had gone to the temple to see whether Jesus would come again, we saw him come through the crowds and take a place where he could be seen. And he looked around at the crowd and they grew still, waiting to hear his words.

And Jesus said in a loud voice, "Come, all who are thirsty, and all who are hungry, come to the waters of God. For here is wine and milk, without price and without cost. Listen to my words, and let them fill you and flow through you, for my words are food indeed, and my words are water indeed. Whoever believes these words that I say to you shall have rivers of living water flowing through them, and never will they thirst again."

And the guards of the temple were standing some distance away, unable to come closer for the crowd drew together and pressed one against another as stones press upon stones in a wall. Jesus looked upon them and upon the leaders of the temple also who stood a distance apart. Then he looked upon the crowd, and he said, "I am with you but a little while longer, and then I return to where I came. You will come, and you will seek me, but you will not find me."

And the people murmured, and some were saying, "Where does this man mean to go then? Will he go among the Greeks?"

And Martha his sister turned to me and said, "See, mother, he returns to Capernaum." But I knew in my heart that he did not speak of his home on this earth, and it seemed to me that there were few days left upon this earth for my son, for I saw fear and the hatred in the eyes of the temple leaders, and I saw the Roman soldiers looking down upon us all from the walls and from their towers.

Again Jesus spoke to the people, and he said, "I am the light of the world. I have come from God and was sent by God, and I have come to make you free."

The people murmured, thinking that he meant freedom from the Romans.

"You know nothing," shouted the priests, for they were afraid. "You are from Galilee, but we serve in the temple of God."

"If you served God, you would welcome me, for God has sent me," said Jesus. "We each serve our fathers. I serve mine and you serve yours. God sends me, but you have been sent by the evil one. He is your father, and the father of lies and of darkness. I am of Abraham, but you are of the evil one."

The Pharisees among them said, "Abraham is our father. Who do you claim to be?"

And Jesus said, "Truly, truly, I tell you, before Abraham walked from the east, I was here."

And the leaders began to search for stones to throw at Jesus, but Jesus turned and walked into the crowd. The people made a way for him, and he could not be found. We also followed him, for his brothers said to me, "See, he is out of his mind, for the things that he is saying. Let us find him and take him home, or they will kill him."

And we followed where he had gone, for we knew the place. And we found that there were gathered around him those who were called his disciples and many others besides. And we sent word to Jesus through the crowd, to say that we were there and asking for him. Jesus came to a window in the room where he was and looked out upon us and upon the crowd. He lifted his arms and pointed to all of the people gathered there.

"Behold, these are my brothers and my sisters. All who hear and know the word of God are my brothers and my sisters." But then he came down to where we were, and he kissed me and brought us inside to where his disciples were gathered.

And James my son began to speak to Jesus and to upbraid him. "Do you not know that you are saying things that may be said by God alone? You must stop saying these things and come home with us until you have received your mind again, for if you continue they will kill you."

"No man takes my life from me," said Jesus. "I am like the good shepherd, who comes and cares for the sheep. I know my sheep, and they know me, just as God knows me, and I know God. Only the hired hand runs before the wolf. I am the good shepherd, and I will not suffer the wolf to harm my sheep. Though I lay down my life for my flock, I also have the power to take it up again, for such has been given me by my father."

Then Jesus looked at me, and I knew that he was not of this world, not as his brothers and sisters were of this world. For Joseph was their father, but of Jesus I knew not, unless the thing be of God as the angel had told me. And it seemed to me again that I could see something of the angel, or another like it, near to Jesus and to his disciple John, brother of James, sitting by the feet of Jesus with Mary of Magdala, who sat also with John at the feet of Jesus. And it seemed to me that Mary also could see something of the angel.

Then Jesus turned and said, "Come, let us go out. It is time to leave the city." And he rose and walked to the window where he had looked out upon us, and he looked out upon the city streets. Again he spoke, and we did not know whether he spoke to us, saying, "Jerusalem, Jerusalem, yet shall I return, and I shall gather you to me, but the time is not yet."

I looked again where the disciples John and Mary were sitting, but I could not see the angel. We rose and we went out, and Mary of Magdala came, and she kissed me and said, "Blessed are you among women, that you gave birth to him. But before the end you shall know great pain, as also will I."

And I took her by the arm and spoke to her, but quietly so that the others could not hear, saying, "I know that you love him."

"Yes," said the other Mary. "But he is greater than I, and I must follow him until I cannot follow."

Just then we heard voices in the street, and quickly we went out to where Jesus and the others had gone. In the street were more of the Pharisees who had been at the temple and who had heard the things that Jesus had said.

"If you are the messiah, tell us plainly," they said.

"My sheep know my voice," Jesus said. "I know them, and they know me and follow me. They will not be taken from me. My father is greater than all, and no one can take anything from my father's hand."

"Then you claim that you have been sent by God?" they demanded.

"I have told you and you do not believe. The words that I have given you are life, and the works that I have done testify that I have come from God, but you do not believe because you do not come from God."

"You have a demon," they said.

"I do not have a demon, but you serve the darkness that is your father. You turn away from the light, because you prefer the darkness. I have come from that which is above. You have chosen your father who is below."

"Abraham is our father," they said. "You are conceived in sin. We have asked and know that you have come out of Nazareth. Does any good thing come out of Nazareth?"

"God has sent me into the world to save the world, not to condemn it, but you have condemned yourselves, for the light has come and you prefer the darkness. Those who serve God come to the light, that their deeds may be seen in the light. But no one can receive anything except that which is given by God. As the pharaoh's heart was hardened, so are your eyes closed and so also your ears cannot hear. For the words that I speak are given to me by the father."

"Then you do claim to be sent by God," they said.

"Even as you are one with your father, I and my father are one," said Jesus.

And the Pharisees tore their robes and cried out, "Blasphemy! He makes himself one with God!" And they began to pull stones from the street that they might stone him. But Jesus turned away and walked into the crowd once again, and in a moment he could not be seen.

Mary touched my arm, knowing the fear in my heart. "Do not worry," she said. "He has told us that men will try to kill him, but that no one can take his life before his time has come." John the son of Zebedee the fisherman was with her.

"What does this word mean? In what time does his death come? Does he plan then to die at their hands?" I asked her, for I did not know what it meant that his time would come. But she did not answer me.

"We go back across the Jordan," she said. "In a few days you may find him there, in the place where John stayed."

And the crowd departed, each going his own way. The Pharisees remained standing in the street with the stones in their hands, but they could find nowhere to throw them.

James brought me and his brothers and sisters, and we left Jerusalem and returned to our home.

But I was not content as we waited for word of Jesus, and so I took Simon and Salome and we journeyed down along the Jordan River to the wilderness where John had dwelled with his disciples. And there we found a great number of people, coming and going, all of them seeking Jesus to hear his teaching or to seek his help. And we stayed there in the wilderness some days with him and with his disciples.

And there came word from Bethany that the man Lazarus was sick. His family was known to us, for they were friends of John the baptizer and of his mother and father before us. His sisters sent a message to Jesus, asking him to come. And Jesus sent the messenger back to tell the sisters of Lazarus that he would come to them. He did not follow after him, but instead stayed that night where we were. The next day he sat once again and taught the people.

"The kingdom of God is like a light set upon a hill, so that all may see it and come," said Jesus. "I am the light of the world. Whoever follows me will not stumble in the darkness but will have the light of life. Behold, the light is with you but a short time longer. Come to the light while it may be found."

Taking a loaf of bread in his hands, he lifted it to heaven and then began to break it as he walked, passing the pieces of bread to this one and to that one as he walked among the people. "I am the bread of life," he called out. "Your fathers ate manna in the wilderness, bread that fell from the sky and kept them alive as they wandered in the desert lands. I am the bread that has come down from heaven. Whosoever eats this body shall never hunger again, for the food that I give is food indeed, and my words are life and light."

And he walked to the river and out into the water where his disciples were baptizing those who came, pouring water over the heads of some and holding some under the water, as they were able. Jesus took water in his hands and held it up so that the drops of water were seen falling from his hands. "Behold, my words are the water of life. Whosoever drinks of me and my words shall never thirst but shall have life everlasting pouring out from within him. Come, take of the bread and of the water while you may. Come in the day, for night is coming like a thief, and they will seek to take away the bread that you would eat and to pour out the words that you would hear, and they will seek to put out the light, for it is the darkness that they love."

"As long as I am in the world, I am the light of the world," said Jesus, still standing in the waters of the Jordan. Then something as a voice or as thunder came, and the people heard it. And they were divided, wondering whether it may have been a sign. Some said that an angel had spoken to him, but the voice was not like that of the angel that appeared to me many years ago.

"Now is the great day of the Lord at hand. Now shall the power of God be seen, and the evil of this world shall be driven out. And I, when I am lifted upon the tree, shall draw all men to me."

And my heart was afraid within me when I heard these words. I looked and near me I saw the man John who followed Jesus, and I called him over with my hand, and I said, "What does this mean, to be lifted up onto a tree?"

And John looked into my eyes and away at Jesus, and he answered me, saying, "I do not know, but I fear what is to come. Still, I have come to know in my heart that this man is from God, and God will not abandon him."

Jesus climbed upon a rock, and stood looking down at the crowd who were still and quiet, listening to his words. John and I walked nearer to where Jesus stood.

"The light is with you only a little longer," he said. "Walk in the light while the light may be seen, that you may not fall in the darkness. If you walk in the darkness, you will not know where you tread. Walk in the light, and have faith in the light, that you may also become children of the light, children not of Abraham only but children of the living God."

"If you believe in me, you believe also in the one who sent me. If you see me, you have seen also the one who sent me. If you hear me, you hear also the voice of the one who sent me. I have not come to judge, but I have come to save. The words I speak are the words that God has given me. Hear them and believe."

Many in the crowd were glad of his words, and some would have come then and made him king, but there were still others who held back, weighing what they had heard.

And Jesus turned then and walked away, back into the wadi, the stream that fed the Jordan, and into the hills so that we could no longer see him. John moved to go also, saying that he must follow his master. And I remembered about Lazarus and the word that had come, saying that he was sick. John told me that Jesus had said that he would go to them, but he had not said when he would go or by what means, though the distance from the Jordan to Bethany was not great.

I considered these things, and I rose to go to Bethany myself along with Salome, while Simon remained longer with his brother and the believers gathering at the wadi beyond the Jordan. Jesus had sent word that he was coming, and so I knew that I would see him there, and the sisters of Lazarus could use more hands to do the work of their home while their brother was ill. When I reached the house I found Martha and Mary, the sisters of Lazarus, but Lazarus himself was already dead, being dead from the day that the messenger had found Jesus beyond the Jordan. The sisters of Lazarus had placed him in his tomb that very day.

And we rose and went to the market, Salome and I, to buy food for the household. For we had brought food and coins with us, but there were many who came and who went away from the home of Mary and Martha, so that they were worn out with their coming and going. There in the marketplace we saw men whom we had also seen coming from the temple, for they were servants of the high priest. They did not see us, nor did they know our faces, for we were women and nothing to these men.

And we were surprised to see such men in this market, for did not Jerusalem have everything? And so we asked of the women there in the booths, and they shook their heads and said that such men had come also to find John the baptizer in the days before he had been arrested.

"What do you mean?" asked Salome of them, for she was less wise in the ways of men. "Did these men come all the way from the temple to be disciples of John?"

And the women shook their heads again and laughed to hear it, and they said that such men did not seek John to be his disciple, but to bring him to the prison. For word had come from Jerusalem in those days that John the baptizer was dead at the hand of Herod.

"Why then have they come?" asked Salome. And the women told us that these men had come to find Jesus and to report to the high priest all that happened, so far as they could learn of the teachings and whereabouts of Jesus and his followers. They feared Jesus, for some said that there would be a rebellion. And Salome would have said more, that she was the sister of Jesus and that I was his mother, but I held her hand and we said no more, but we went about buying the food for the household, for when Jesus came there would be many to feed. And we said nothing more to anyone there, for again I was afraid in my heart of what might happen to Jesus.

In two days time we heard that Jesus was coming and many of his followers with him. And Martha rose and went out to meet him and Salome also. For Martha was angry that Jesus had not come sooner, supposing as she did that had Jesus been present then her brother would not have died but would still be alive. Soon Salome returned and said that Jesus had come. He and Martha waited at the place where they had met for Mary to come to them, that they may talk more quietly than in the house, for there were still a great number of mourners and others idly waiting in the house and watching.

So Mary rose, and I with her, and we went out to meet him. And Mary's heart was heavy within her, and she was crying in her grief, thinking also of how her brother had died and that Jesus had not been there to save him. I walked with her and felt her grief, and we found Jesus sitting by the road with Martha. And some came following us and were also crying and weeping, as though we had just placed Lazarus in the tomb. Jesus rose and looked into the faces of the people and of Mary. Then last of all he saw me and he saw the tears upon my face, and Jesus also then began to weep.

And Mary knelt by him and said, "Lord, we sent word, but you did not come. If you had come, we would not have placed him in the tomb."

Jesus lifted her to her feet and asked where they had laid him. Martha and Mary said, "Come and see." And we all walked, a great crowd gathering now, to the tomb of Lazarus. It was not far from the place where we were, Bethany not being a great city.

At the tomb Jesus stood in front of the stone and wept, and we all wept. Then he stepped away from the tomb and said, "Take away the stone."

And Martha and Mary, the sisters of Lazarus, said to Jesus, "We cannot, for there will be a stench. Did you not hear us say to you that he has been in the tomb four days?"

And Jesus said, "I have told you that in these days you would see the glory of God, and that you would know that the God of Jacob was with you. Take away the stone from this tomb."

The sisters of Lazarus looked at his face, and they turned and nodded to some who were standing there. Some of the men stepped out of the crowd, and they pushed away the stone from the opening of the tomb, and it was dark, and there was the smell of death. But Jesus raised his arms and looked up to heaven, and he began to pray aloud, saying, "Lord, I thank you that you hear us. I know that always you hear my words, as I hear your words, but I say these things that these gathered here may know your power."

And Jesus stepped closer to the tomb, and he cried out in a loud voice, "Lazarus, come out!"

The place was silent. All of the people were hushed and watching. Then from within the tomb we heard a sound, and Lazarus himself came walking out of the darkness of the tomb, his burial clothing wrapped around him. He stood in the light of the sun, and we were amazed. Mary and Martha rushed forward to their brother and helped him, and he began to walk with us back to their home.

Just then I turned and looked back through the crowd, and I saw the men from the high priest, the ones who had been also in the marketplace. They were watching in amazement, and then they turned and began to walk quickly back toward Jerusalem. All of the people gathered there were also amazed, and many believed then that Jesus had come from God. I could hear some saying that he was the messiah who had come to deliver us, and I was afraid.

At the home of Lazarus, the sisters removed his clothing and helped him to bathe and to dress himself, and then he sat and he ate, and still we were amazed for we had never seen this, a man who had been dead for four days but who lived. Jesus took Lazarus apart, and they sat together in the garden near the house, and they talked, and no one heard the words that he spoke but Lazarus. And the crowd who had seen Lazarus come from the tomb were continually there at the house and around it, amazed and talking of what Jesus had done, and they wondered aloud what miracle he might perform next.

In the night Jesus and Mary Magdalene and the followers of Jesus went out to the wilderness, for many were coming and his fame had spread among the people. Word had reached Jesus that the priests and the Romans hated him, and so he began to stay out of the sight of them. They traveled north toward Ephraim and east across the Jordan, but Salome and I stayed with Mary and Martha and Lazarus, for the Passover was near and we would be near to Jerusalem.

Lazarus was quiet. We would ask him to tell us what it was like to die and to return to life, but he would not tell us, saying only, "Pray it does not happen to you as to me." Once even we sought him, for he had gone out of the house and we did not know where he was. Finally he was found, sitting in the empty tomb that was left open. When they asked him why he would go to sit in such a place, he would say nothing. And Mary and Martha made him eat each day and bathe and to put on fresh clothes, and they kept a watch on him from that day so that he did not slip away from them again.

Some days later Jesus returned to Bethany and to the house of Lazarus. They rejoiced to see him, and I also, and we prepared food for him and for his followers. On the next evening there came one from the town, a man named Simon, and invited all of us to his home where he had prepared a dinner for Jesus. Simon was afflicted with a disease of the skin, and some of the people said that it was leprosy. And Peter, seeing the man, said to Jesus that it would be better if they did not go, for they may catch the disease, and Passover was close at hand.

And Jesus turned to Peter and said, "Have you been with me this long, and yet you do not believe? Truly I have said to all of you, though the dead should be raised to life again, still there would be among you those who do not believe in the power of God." And Jesus touched the man and told him to go and to bathe, and that his skin would be made whole. And the man Simon went out to do as Jesus had commanded him.

When we arrived at the house of Simon, he stood in the doorway to greet us. He was wearing new robes, and when he stepped into the courtyard he kissed Jesus and knelt at his feet. And all of us could see that his skin was clean and new. Peter also stepped forward and stared at the man's skin, and Peter said to Jesus, "Truly you are the messiah, the one sent by God."

And Jesus said, "Many such signs have you seen, Simon Peter, and greater signs than these will you see. Remember them, for truly I say to you that the days will come when you will seek me that you may walk beside me, and you will not find me. But truly also, I tell you, I will always be with you."

And we went into the house, as many of us as there was room for, and more remained in the courtyard at tables that had been set up, and Simon and his wife themselves served us. Martha and Mary also helped them, and Mary Magdalene and Salome my daughter. As we sat dining, Mary the sister of Lazarus rose and went out, and we did not know where she had gone. Soon she returned, and she held a jar of alabaster. She approached Jesus as he sat, and kneeling behind him she began to pour out the oil of nard upon his head and to wipe the remainder with her hair. And Mary Magdalene saw what she was doing and went to Mary and kissed her and held the jar so that she could anoint also his feet. And the smell of the nard filled the house.

Judas the follower of Jesus then pointed to the jar and said, "My Lord, is this a thing to be poured out?" For he was a thief and thought only of his own gain. John had told me of gifts brought to Jesus, and that the gifts had disappeared, but that Judas would say only that they had been given to the poor.

Jesus said, "She has done a beautiful thing, for now I am anointed for the day of my burial. There are other things you may give to the poor, but I am always with them."

And Peter said, "What is this thing you have said, Lord? For surely you will not die!"

But Jesus turned to him and said, "Unless a seed falls into the earth, it cannot grow. If you would hold to your life most of all, it will flee from you. If you love me more than your own life, then you will have eternal life. Where I go, my servants must go also. Whoever would serve me, the Father will keep, and they shall know and dwell within the Spirit of God."

The next day there were crowds of people gathering in the street, for they had heard of the raising of Lazarus and they wished to see Jesus and Lazarus. Jesus wished to go up to Jerusalem to the great festival, but when I saw the crowd, I remembered the faces of the servants of the priests. And I told my son Jesus that he should remain in Bethany, or go back to his home in Capernaum, or else go out into the wilderness, but that he should not go up to Jerusalem. He kissed me and said, "Woman, for this I came into the world."

And I found Mary Magdalene and Salome, for they were in the garden of the house of Lazarus, and I told them of my fears. And Mary embraced me, and there were tears in her eyes.

"I also am afraid, for I have seen the faces of those men as well. But he will not step aside from this way. We must follow him to Jerusalem," she said.

And Jesus sent Peter and another of his followers, and they brought two donkeys. And we all set out for Jerusalem, but Lazarus and his sisters remained at home. Jesus went ahead on the road, and some of the crowds had run ahead of him to tell of his coming. When we looked, we saw that the way was lined with people, and they were putting their cloaks and the leaves of the trees on the road. Jesus rode on a donkey, and Peter and the others followed near to him. The rest of us followed as well, and Salome guided my donkey for we thought that it would be afraid of the people and the noise, but it did not stumble on the way or turn back.

And the face of Jesus was set for Jerusalem, and the people shouted that it was the coming of the king, and no one could turn aside his coming into the great city. There were shouts of hosanna and of messiah, and no one stepped out into the street to stop Jesus.

When he had reached the walls of the temple, he dismounted his donkey. We also reached the place where he was, and he stood staring up at the temple. We saw the temple guards on the walls and the steps, but they did not move against us or against the crowd, for there were too many.

And Jesus shouted out to the people, "Do you believe in the son of man?" And the people cried aloud, "Messiah." Jesus looked at them and held out his arms, so that the crowd grew quiet, a great multitude of them. "If you believe in me, believe also in the one who sent me. I have come as a light into the world. Walk in the light that you also might become children of the light."

Saying this, he stopped and the crowd began to shout and to acclaim him as messiah and as king. But Jesus turned and moved away through the crowd, and he disappeared from their sight.

We went then to the place where we would stay for the days of Passover, the house that had been of the family of Zechariah, the father of John the baptizer. Jesus was already there ahead of us, having gone up to the upper room, and he stood watching from a window. I together with some of the women began to prepare the evening meal. When the followers of Jesus came and began to enter the large room where Jesus stood, they found that he had filled a basin with water, and for each man and woman who entered, Jesus knelt and washed their feet, and no one said anything, for they did not know what to say. They had just heard the crowds calling out that Jesus was to be their king and their messiah, and now they found him with a towel. And seeing Jesus kneeling before them and washing their feet, Judas son of Simon rose and went out.

We did not know that he rose to go out to the priests that he might sell Jesus to them for money. Though he was a thief, we did not think that he would do such a thing.

We thought only that perhaps Jesus had sent him to obtain some provision, for Jesus alone was not astonished that Judas went out just as we were about to begin the meal.

Jesus rose and putting on his robes once again he sat at the table. And he began to speak and to tell us many things. "Now my heart is heavy within me," he said. "Now has the time come when I go where you cannot follow. As I told the people so now I also tell you that where I go you cannot follow. But for this purpose I have come into the world."

These words were like wounds to my heart. Looking around at the others I saw that tears were in the eyes of Mary of Magdala, for she also understood what he had told us. Peter said, "Lord, surely we can also follow where you are going. Have we not followed you all these days, through the wilderness and even up to Jerusalem? We will follow you now."

Jesus said, "Where I go you cannot go, but in time you shall go also. Do not be afraid, and do not be troubled, for if I go to the Father, I send the Spirit of God among you, and as I dwell in the Father so also shall the Spirit of God dwell within you, and I shall truly know you and you shall truly know me, for we shall be one. If you love me, love also one another, and even as you love one another and as I love you, so also does the Father love you and will keep you. We shall be one."

He lifted a cup and filled it with wine. "I am the vine, the true vine, and you are the branches. The Spirit of God flows within me and within you as the life flows in the vine. This is my life that is pressed out for you. Take now this cup and share of it, that you may know that you also share of me."

And he passed the cup, and it passed from one to another that all in the room might drink, men and women alike, and our tears mixed with the wine though many still did not understand the sorrow within them or what Jesus meant when he said that he was going.

Then Jesus took also a piece of bread and tore it and passed the pieces, and he said, "As I tear this bread that you might eat it, so also I give myself to be torn for you. Whatsoever you shall see and do in the days to come, do not fear the one who can destroy the body, but fear only the one who can destroy both body and soul, for that power is of God alone. I have the power to lay down my life and to take it up again, for such is given me by the Father, and I and the Father are one. As bread gives no strength unless it be taken and torn and eaten, so also I shall be taken and torn and given for you, and not only for you but also for those who shall come after you, for they also are one with you and I with them. They are already your brothers and sisters, yet you do not know them, even as you do not yet know me."

Again Peter spoke, not understanding, and he said, "Lord, how is it you say that we do not know you? You are Jesus, the messiah, the one who comes into the world from God, and we have known you all of these many days."

And Jesus said, "This knowledge has come to you from God, Simon Peter, and in days to come you shall be a rock of strength for these who are gathered here. Before the sun rises you shall all be scattered, and you shall not know me, for such is the path that I must walk. But the morning comes when I shall rise, and you shall know me once more, and you shall know and understand who I am and from where I came and where I am going, and the Spirit of God shall lead you, and you shall have need of no man to follow for you indeed shall be followers and children of God in the highest."

After the supper Jesus rose and kissed me and he went out, and many of the others followed him though they did not know where they were going in the darkness. I remained in the upper room of the house with Salome. When they had been gone for some time in the night, there came running my son Simon and also a few others, and they were terrified.

"They have taken him," said Simon. Salome did not understand at first, but I had known in my heart that it would happen. And Simon and the others began to tell us of how they had gone to a garden where Jesus prayed, as he often prayed outside in the wilderness. There had come a group of soldiers with Judas, son of Simon, and they had thrown Judas to his knees and beaten him and asked which of the others was Jesus. And Jesus himself had stepped forward so that the soldiers fell back in fear, and Jesus had kissed Judas and told him not to be afraid.

"You seek Jesus, and he has found you," Jesus told them. They stepped forward to arrest Jesus, but Peter became enraged and ran against the men, and he took one of them by the ear with one hand and began to beat him with the other so that the man cried out. But Jesus reached out and touched Peter's arm and said, "It is enough. For this have I come, and this is the path I must walk." Then they took

Jesus and arrested him and bound him, and they took him to the high priest, and the followers of Jesus fled.

To my son Simon I said, "Go and find your brothers, and tell them what has happened." And so Simon went out at that hour to return to our home, for his brothers had not come to Jerusalem.

"Let us go to him, to see what they will do to him," I said to Salome, though in my heart I already knew what would be. And we rose and went out into the night, Salome and myself. We went to the house of the high priest, for it was large and known to us, and there at the courtyard of the house we found John the son of Zebedee and also Peter and Mary of Magdala. There were tears on the face of Mary and of John, for they knew already what would take place. And John spoke to the woman who was watching the gate, and she let us enter the courtyard, for she knew him.

After some time had passed, we heard a noise of the guards and of other men, and we saw them taking Jesus out of the house and along the street toward the praetorium of Pilate. We followed them, and they took Jesus inside the praetorium where we could not see him, and so we waited to see what would become of him. There came the sound of more men, and the high priest and others of the temple came and stood outside waiting for Pilate. Soon there began to be a crowd, for in some way word had spread of what was happening, and many whom we did not know were gathering outside the praetorium.

Pilate himself came out to speak with the priests, who would not enter the ground of the Romans at the time of Passover. Pilate was angry at the noise and at the hour, for it was very early, and he demanded of them to know what was meant by the noise and the disturbance.

"We bring you a criminal," said the high priest, but Pilate told him they should have dealt with the matter themselves, for their laws were nothing to him.

"This man makes himself a king," he told Pilate. "We know no king but Caesar, but it may be that you recognize other kings." When Pilate heard these words he was angry, but he could say nothing against the high priest for praising Caesar. And I had not known until that moment how much the high priest feared my son and the power that he had.

Peter looked at the faces of the people who were gathering outside the gates of the praetorium, and he said to us, "These have been gathered by the priests, for they have never followed us. I do not know them." But John stood quietly watching through the gates to see what would happen. He said nothing, but he took his cloak and placed it around my shoulders and Salome that we would be warm and safer from the crowd.

After a time, the doors inside the courtyard opened and they brought Jesus out. He was wearing a purple robe, and there was a rough crown on his head. The high priest and his guards began to shout, "Crucify him!" The people gathered in the street, many sent by the high priest, also began to shout. And Peter said, "They will kill him."

Pilate raised his arms for silence, and the crowd became quiet. "I find no wrong in this man. He has been beaten for his insolence. Take him yourselves and deal with him according to your laws."

And the high priest said, "By our law this man must die, for he has blasphemed against heaven and made himself to be God."

At this we saw that Pilate was afraid, for the Romans also believe in gods. He walked down the steps and approached Jesus in the courtyard. They struck him so that he knelt on the stones before Pilate, and Pilate spoke to Jesus. I could not tell what the words were, but John heard them.

Jesus lifted his face then and looked out of the courtyard to where we stood, and he looked up to Pilate and said, "Those who brought me to you have the greater sin, for it is to them that I came."

Then the high priest said in a loud voice, "This man would rule over Israel. We will have no Caesar but Caesar." This he said knowing that he had trapped Pilate into killing Jesus. And as at a sign the crowd around us began to shout, "Crucify him!"

Pilate then gave Jesus over to his guards to be crucified. And they took the purple robe from him and they whipped him, and the high priest and his men watched. The Romans brought out a cross beam and placed it on the back of Jesus, and they took him out of the city to a hill where criminals were crucified. We followed through the streets, and others began to come out and to see, for it was now the middle part of the day and word had spread of these things among many of those who had welcomed Jesus. And they were standing along the street, and some followed us out of the city gates. Some of them went ahead of us and placed the palm branches in the street as they had done when Jesus came to Jerusalem, and the Romans did not stop them for they themselves were afraid when they saw how the people loved Jesus.

Upon the hillside they stopped, and a great many were coming from the city to see what would happen. And we stood watching, Peter and John with me and Salome and Mary. They held Jesus and took his clothes, leaving the crown of sticks upon his head. They laid him down upon the cross beam, and they nailed his hands to the wood so that Jesus cried out in a loud voice. Then taking ropes they lifted him up on the pole that stood there, and they drove nails through his feet into the pole, and it was done.

We stood there then, as close as the Roman soldiers would permit, and we wept. After a time, Jesus lifted his head and looked at us. When he saw me, he said, "Woman, behold your son." Seeing John standing beside me, he said, "Son, behold your mother."

Then he gazed across the crowd and at the others who had been crucified nearby.

"I am thirsty," we heard him say after the space of an hour. One of the Romans took a sponge from a jar of wine and placed it on a stick and held it to the mouth of Jesus.

Soon afterward Jesus looked at us once more, and he said, "It is finished." And when he had said these words, he was gone. I knelt on the ground and wept, and those with us also wept. And we went nowhere, for we had no place to go, and we waited for the body of Jesus to be let down from the cross.

There came more soldiers then, making their way across the hillside, seeing whether those who were crucified were dead, and they broke the legs of some and did other things to them that their deaths might be more terrible. When they came to Jesus, the guards standing there said, "This man is already dead." And one of them stabbed Jesus in the side with a spear to see that it was so, and they passed on.

Then we looked and saw that Nicodemus had come, and with him a man named Joseph of Arimathea, and they had brought a donkey like the one that had carried Jesus into the city. And Joseph gave to the soldiers a note, for he had heard what had happened to Jesus and had gone to Pilate to plead that Jesus might be taken down from the cross and be allowed to live as was the case when the Romans showed mercy. Pilate had refused, but he had given permission to take down the body and to bury it according to our custom once Jesus was dead. And so the soldiers took Jesus down from the cross, not having seen such permission brought to them before, even with the seal of Pilate upon it, and they took the nails from his hands and his feet.

Peter and the men took Jesus and laid him upon the donkey, and we wept and walked with his body to a garden where the man Joseph had a tomb. There we placed Jesus and cleaned his body as well as we could, for the day was nearly ended, and they placed him upon a ledge in the tomb with some spices that had been brought. Mary Magdalene kissed Jesus then, and I also kissed him, and we went out. The stone was placed against the opening of the tomb for it was nearly dark, and we wept, for Jesus my son was dead.

Having no other way to follow, we returned to the house where Jesus had chosen to observe the Passover feast, and we gathered in the upper room. We supposed when the days for the Passover were finished that we would return to our homes. Only Mary of Magdala said that we should return to the tomb, for we had hastily buried Jesus, and that we should place more spices upon his body, for there were those among us and also Joseph and Nicodemus who knew where such things could be obtained in the city.

Very early in the morning on the day following the Sabbath, Mary rose and awakened me. And so we went, Mary, Salome and myself, to the tomb, and we carried among us the spices that were brought to us. We wondered how we might remove the stone from the tomb, but Mary of Magdala said, "If one man may move it, three women may surely move it." And we wondered about the time that had passed, whether there would already be a smell, but we knew that the spices we carried would cover the odor.

When we reached the tomb it was still early and the sun had just risen. The light of it shone upon the entrance of the tomb, so that we could see it very well. The stone of the tomb was already rolled away, and the tomb stood open. We ran then to the tomb, and a young man came out. He was dressed in white robes, and the sunlight shone upon him.

"Do not be afraid," he told us. "You have come to find Jesus. He has awakened, and he is not here."

We stood still, for we did not know what to do or how to understand his words, neither did we know him.

And he spoke to us again, saying, "Look and see the place where you laid him. He is gone."

And Mary of Magdala went forward, and I also went forward to the tomb with Salome, and we saw that it was truly empty. All that remained was the linen cloth in which we had covered him.

"Go and tell the others," said the young man. "He is alive, and he goes ahead of you out of Jerusalem. He has returned to Galilee, and there you will see him." And turning from us he walked away from the opening of the tomb. We stood looking at the place where Jesus had lain, and when we came out of the tomb the young man in white was gone, and we were left alone. We were ecstatic, and we wondered whether it could be that Jesus was alive.

And so we returned to the house where we were staying and found John the son of Zebedee and Peter and others of the followers of Jesus. We told them that we had been to the tomb, but that it was open and empty, and we told them also of the strange words of the young man who told us that Jesus had awakened. Immediately John and Peter ran from the house, going as we supposed to see the tomb for themselves. Mary then also rose, and she left to return to the tomb for some other sign of Jesus, saying, "Perhaps he has lingered, after all."

After a time John and Peter returned, and they also were amazed, for they saw the empty tomb for themselves, but they did not know what it could mean. Then John came holding the burial cloth and sat near to me, and reminded me of the words that Jesus had spoken on the cross.

"In days to come, you shall be as my own mother, and I shall be as your son," he said, for his own mother had been dead for many years. And it would come to pass in the years yet to come that I would go to dwell with John the son of Zebedee the fisherman, for there were too many who came to find the mother of Jesus and to ask for signs and miracles. I had no sign to give them except the son whom I had borne to them.

On that same day as we were still gathered in that upper room, Mary Magdalene came running back to us. She had been at the tomb, and she told us that she had seen Jesus, and we wondered at her words. She had not recognized him, she said, for he had shaved away his beard and his hair to cleanse himself from the tomb, and he would not let her touch him for he said that he had been laid in the tomb.

"He said that he goes ahead of us to Galilee, for his work here in Jerusalem is done," she told us. And we rose and departed from that place, and we returned to Nazareth and to Galilee and to those places in which we had dwelled in former times. But I went to dwell in the house of Jesus in Capernaum, for it seemed good to me to do so, and in my heart I hoped that I would again see Jesus there. And the followers of Jesus came also, though many returned to their homes and their work.

It came to pass in a few days that Peter said to the other disciples that he was going to fish, for we needed more food in the house. And he and the others who were there rose and went out to the Sea of Galilee where Peter still had his boat. When they returned, they were amazed and their eyes were wide with their astonishment, for they said that they had seen the Lord on the shore.

That night as we were gathered for the evening meal, Jesus came and he stood among us. He showed us his body, his hands and his side, and we saw the wounds from the cross. And he again took bread and broke it and passed it among us saying, "Take this and eat, that you remember me and all that you have heard and seen." Then he took also the wine and poured it into a cup and he passed it among us saying, "This you drink now in remembrance of my blood which was shed in your sight, but I will not drink of wine again until the kingdom of God is accomplished." And by this saying we understood why he had shaved his hair when he left the tomb, for he was holy unto God as John the baptizer had been holy and a nazirite.

And when he had said these things, he stood and he said, "You have the holy Spirit of God within you. Wherever you shall go from this day, you shall know that God is with you and within you. And they shall know in all the world that you are mine and that I am in you by the love that is in you."

The following day we rose from that place and went out once again to the wilderness beyond the Jordan where the people would not see that he had returned to his home. There Jesus stayed with us and told us many things that he had not said to us, and he performed signs that we had not seen, for he told us that we could not have understood them.

Jesus walked with me and with the other Mary, and we sat in the wilderness at the wadi. And I began to weep, for I remembered seeing him upon that cross.

"Woman, do not weep," he told me. "See, I am alive." And he began to talk with us and to tell us that it was needful that they should have killed him. "Unless men killed the God whom men had made, they would not know the God who has made them. For this I came into the world, that men might learn to walk in the light."

Then after those days Jesus arose and went up the mountainside, and we began to follow him. But he raised his hands and said to us that the time had come for him to leave and for us to return.

"Peace be with you," he said. "My peace is with you. As you have walked with me, so now the Spirit of God walks with you." And saying these words he went up the mountainside, and I saw him no more.